THE
VOID
PROTOCOL

F. PAUL WILSON

A TOM DOHERTY ASSOCIATES BOOK • NEW YORK

This is a work of fiction. All of the characters, organizations, and events portrayed in this novel are either products of the author's imagination or are used fictitiously.

THE VOID PROTOCOL

A Forge Book
Published by Tom Doherty Associates
120 Broadway
New York, NY 10271

www.tor-forge.com

Forge® is a registered trademark of Macmillan Publishing Group, LLC.

ISBN 978-1-250-17733-9

Our books may be purchased in bulk for promotional, educational, or business use. Please contact your local bookseller or the Macmillan Corporate and Premium Sales Department at 1-800-221-7945, extension 5442, or by email at MacmillanSpecialMarkets@macmillan.com.

First Edition: January 2019
First Mass Market Edition: February 2020

Printed in the United States of America

0 9 8 7 6 5 4 3 2 1

BY F. PAUL WILSON

THE ICE TRILOGY*
Panacea / The God Gene / The Void Protocol

REPAIRMAN JACK NOVELS*
The Tomb / Legacies / Conspiracies / All the Rage / Hosts / The Haunted Air / Gateways / Crisscross / Infernal / Harbingers / Bloodline / By the Sword / Ground Zero / Fatal Error / The Dark at the End / Nightworld / Quick Fixes—Tales of Repairman Jack

THE TEEN TRILOGY*
Jack: Secret Histories / Jack: Secret Circles / Jack: Secret Vengeance

THE EARLY YEARS TRILOGY*
Cold City / Dark City / Fear City

THE ADVERSARY CYCLE*
The Keep / The Tomb / The Touch / Reborn / Reprisal / Nightworld

OMNIBUS EDITIONS
The Complete LaNague / Calling Dr. Death (3 medical thrillers) / *Ephemerata*

EDITOR
Freak Show / Diagnosis: Terminal / The Hogben Chronicles (with Pierce Watters)

THE LANAGUE FEDERATION
Healer / Wheels Within Wheels / An Enemy of the State / Dydeetown World / The Tery

OTHER NOVELS
Black Wind / Sibs* / The Select / Virgin / Implant / Deep as the Marrow / Mirage* (with Matthew J. Costello) / *Nightkill* (with Steven Spruill) / *Masque* (with Matthew J. Costello) / *Sims / The Fifth Harmonic / Midnight Mass / The Proteus Curse* (with Tracy L. Carbone) / *A Necessary End* (with Sarah Pinborough) /

THE NOCTURNA CHRONICLES (WITH THOMAS F. MONTELEONE)
Definitely Not Kansas / Family Secrets / The Silent Ones

SHORT FICTION
Soft and Others / The Barrens and Others / The Christmas Thingy / Aftershock & Others* / The Peabody-Ozymandias Traveling Circus & Oddity Emporium* / Quick Fixes—Tales of Repairman Jack* / Sex Slaves of the Dragon Tong*

* See "The Secret History of the World" (page 451).

ACKNOWLEDGMENTS

The usual suspects: my wife, Mary; Jennifer Gunnels and Becky Maines at the publisher; Steven Spruill, Elizabeth Monteleone, Dannielle Romeo, Ann Voss Peterson, Alfred Caplin, and my agent, Albert Zuckerman. Thanks for your efforts.

THE
VOID
PROTOCOL

THEN

Maureen LaVelle had spent forty minutes cooling her heels in the stuffy waiting room in a rear corner of the USAMRMC offices. The mystery man who'd summoned her, whoever he was, wasn't just wasting her time—she had work to do, dammit—he was wasting the government's money as well, because she was on the clock. If she'd known about the delay, she'd have come prepared, brought journals, or a novel. Everyone on base was reading *Pet Sematary* so she'd picked up a copy. She hadn't figured it for her kind of book but she was getting into it.

An MP suddenly appeared and ushered her into a tiny office.

About time.

A thin, pale man she'd never seen before sat behind a general-issue desk. Without looking up he indicated the lone chair as he told the MP to leave and close the door behind him. The desktop lay bare except for a personnel folder and a small metal canister emblazoned with the international biohazard symbol.

He opened the folder, saying, "Doctor Maureen LaVelle," in a flat, dry tone. "Your Ph.D. is in molecular biophysics, is that correct?"

He wore a gray suit, white shirt, and navy blue tie.
He hadn't looked at her yet.

"That is correct. And you are . . . ?"

Now he looked up—puffy face with gray eyes behind rimless glasses. Add a little mustache and he
could go trick-or-treating as Himmler.

"Benjamin Greve, at your service."

"Are you new here? I haven't—"

"—seen me before? That's because I'm not here."
A twist of his thin lips that maybe passed for a smile.
"Not officially. I came up from D.C. this morning and
will be heading back tonight. To Anacostia, to be pre-
cise."

Anacostia . . . she sensed he'd dropped that for a
specific purpose, and then remembered the Defense
Intelligence Agency was headquartered at Anacostia-
Bolling. Shit. A DIA spook. What did he think she'd
done?

Greve was looking at her file again. "Born in Pikes-
ville twenty-seven years ago, blasted through under-
grad in three years, then on to your doctorate. Both
at UMD, I see. Don't like to stray far from the nest,
is that it?"

Maureen's mouth felt a little dry. She cleared her
throat. "I have family in the area and I did some research here on my thesis."

"And you stayed on."

"They made me a nice offer as a civilian employee."

Government benefits—hard to beat in the current
job market.

"How do you like the work?" he said, still flipping
pages. This couldn't be the first time he'd seen her file.
"Challenging?"

"It's holding my interest."

Truth was, everything got routine after a while. Her work centered on defense against biological weapons—early detection and treatment—and as a result she got to work with some deadly organisms and impressive toxins. But she'd never broken security. Why was DIA here?

Finally he looked up again. "How would you like a *real* challenge?"

She felt her shoulders relax. So that was it: a problem that needed solving. She was sure she could handle whatever they threw at her. Well, pretty sure.

"I'm all ears."

He tapped the metal biohazard cylinder to his right, about the height and width of a half gallon of orange juice.

"We want you to identify what's in here."

"What is it?"

An impatient scowl. "If I knew that, I wouldn't be here asking you to identify it, would I?" He shook his head. "Damn! They told me you were smart, the best they had. Am I going to regret choosing you for this?"

...the best they had? She wondered who'd said that. USAMRMC wasn't quick with the compliments.

But she was not about to apologize. "The question isn't as dumb as it sounds, Mister Greve. I'm curious as to whether it's animal, vegetable, or mineral. Because if it's mineral—"

"We don't know what the hell it is, Doctor LaVelle," he said in a testy tone. "That's the problem."

"Where did you get it?"

"That I can't tell you."

"Can I ask you why Fort Detrick?"

"Because you have a level-four biosafety lab."

"So it's toxic?"

A dramatic sigh. "We don't know for sure. So far there's no indication that it is, but it might be. We expect you to tell us if it is and, if so, exactly *how* toxic."

"Fair enough. But why me?"

"Besides coming highly recommended as a researcher, another of the reasons you were chosen is because, in a very short time, you have built a reputation for taking anti-contamination and security protocols very seriously."

"That's simple common sense."

"Which many people lack. Also you appear devoted to your work. I can tell by your frumpy clothes and lack of makeup that you're not on the hunt for a husband."

Maureen couldn't help bristling, but she refused to acknowledge his words' sting.

"I call them 'comfortable' clothes, and makeup bores me."

She might have added that her hair was short and simply styled because she couldn't be bothered fussing with it. Her mother had forced her to wear it long during high school and it had annoyed her to no end. And as for a man . . . true, she wasn't on the hunt, but if the right one came along—and he'd have to be *very* right—she'd be game.

He tapped the container again. "I cannot impress upon you strongly enough how highly classified this substance is."

Okay, now she was *really* interested.

"Does it have a name?"

"It's been designated 'Substance A.'"

A? she thought. As in the letter *A*?

"Does that mean there are substances B and C and so on after it?"

"'Substance A' is all you need to know."

"Well, can you tell me if it's liquid, gaseous, or solid?"

"Semi-solid. It pours."

Good. Now we're getting somewhere.

"Synthetic or natural or—?"

He held up a hand. "It *is*. That's all I can say. You will gain firsthand knowledge while you are investigating its properties."

"When do I get started?"

"In a few moments." He lifted a briefcase onto the desk and removed a sheaf of documents. "But first, some NDAs for you to sign."

She'd signed a ream of nondisclosure agreements when she'd done her thesis research here, and even more when she'd hired on.

"They're already on file."

That non-smile again. "Not these. These are ad hoc documents."

"The first thing I want you to do is weigh it," Greve said. "Then I'll leave you to your investigations."

Well, that was a relief. He'd followed her to the BSL-4 lab and she'd been afraid he'd be keeping watch over her shoulder for as long as this took—which might stretch to days or weeks. He gave her the creeps.

The sealed specimen cylinder sat on the other side of the glass. Maureen slipped her hands into the gloved sleeves that stretched into the containment area and placed a 600-milliliter glass beaker on a scale. After zeroing it out, she unscrewed the cylinder top and gently tilted it over the beaker.

A glistening, viscous substance, reddish-purplish-blackish—the color of a bad bruise—began to ooze out. When it reached the 400-milliliter mark on the beaker it stopped. Maureen examined the inside of the cylinder and saw no trace of residue.

She checked the scale. The LED display read zero. She tapped it. Still zero. She pressed gently on the top of the beaker and the numbers climbed, but when she removed her hand, back to zero.

"That can't be."

"At this point, that's the only thing we know about it," Greve said, literally hanging over her shoulder.

"But that's impossible. It has mass, it pours, it obeys the pull of gravity, so it can't weigh nothing."

"You checked your scale. It's working."

"But if it were weightless, it wouldn't pour, it would . . . float."

"So one would think." He bent and lifted his brief-case. "I leave you to your work, Doctor LaVelle. My secure fax number is on my card. I expect a report every evening by five P.M."

Maureen nodded, his words barely registering. She couldn't take her eyes off the bruise-colored mass in the beaker.

Where on Earth do you find weightless slime? Or maybe not on Earth.

She shook off the discomfort and reached for the radio. She liked music while she worked. A top-forty DJ announced the number-one song in America, and "Ghostbusters" began to thump through the tiny speaker.

The line about "something weird" that "don't look good" struck her.

How appropriate, she thought. Almost prescient.

And who y'gonna call?

Moe LaVelle, of course.

"Okay, you slimy mess. Let's see what other spookiness you're hiding."

NOW

Tuesday

1

BROOKLYN, NEW YORK

Rick Hayden clung to an overhead grab handle as the Volvo sedan raced along Eastern Parkway.

"Can you elaborate on what we're up to?" he said. "Just a little, okay? Like where we're headed, for starters? And are we going to arrive alive?"

Luis Montero had the wheel. A full-blooded Cuban, light brown skin, stocky build, dark eyes, black hair gelled into some weird and glossy configuration. Rick knew all about him. He'd backgrounded the guy before Stahlman hired him. Age thirty-two, the son of Castro refugees, Ph.D. in neurobiology, supposedly brilliant. His résumé claimed he'd published a bunch of papers. Rick couldn't understand their titles, let alone what they were about, but he'd checked the journals to make sure the articles had appeared. They had. Montero could have nabbed just about any academic position he wanted, yet he was working for Clayton Stahlman. Rick didn't have to ask why. He'd seen all the zeros on the deal memo.

"Didn't Stahlman tell you?" Montero said, looking at Rick.

He was one of those guys who had to look at you when he spoke to you, even when he was driving.

"Told me you were picking up a specimen in Brooklyn and might need a little help."

Montero laughed. "'Specimen'? He really said that?"

"Could you watch the road, please? Yeah. 'Specimen.'" Typical Stahlman, he'd hung up before Rick could extract any details. "Which is about as specific as 'Brooklyn.'"

"Okay. The specimen is a human being named Ellis Reise who's in trouble with one of the local families over gambling debts."

"'Families' as in folks with vowels on the end of their names?"

"Right. Some Gambino-Mangano offshoot—I didn't bother unraveling the relationships. All I know is it's run by a guy named Vincent Donato."

Rick grunted. "Vinny Donuts."

"You've heard of him then?" Looking at him again. "Not many civilians have. He keeps a low profile."

"I'm not your average civilian."

Rick's security work for Stahlman's varied projects and operations involved backgrounding everyone he hired. Ties to organized crime were a major no-no. Vincent "the Donut" Donato, aka Vinny Donuts, had his pudgy fingers deep into gaming, ponies, numbers, and loan sharking.

"You—" he began as Montero made a screeching Ralph onto Utica Avenue, swerving across the lane into oncoming traffic. "Jesus! What the hell?"

"Sorry," he said as he pulled back into his lane and headed south. "The turn snuck up on me."

"Yeah, 'cause you're looking at me instead of the road. Talk to the windshield. I have good ears. I'll still hear you."

"Yeah. Sure. Sorry."

"Where's the next turn?"

"Remsen. Still a ways."

"You keep your eyes straight, I'll keep mine peeled. Anyway, as I was about to say before you almost killed us: You qualify as an average civilian. How come you know about Donato?"

"Only through researching Ellis and his gambling."

Strange way for a neurobiologist to occupy his time.

"So how much is this Ellis in to Vinny Donuts?"

"Well, that's where it gets tricky. Donato's operation owes Ellis over four hundred grand."

"What? How'd *that* happen?"

"Totally killed them in roulette—and they don't want to pay."

"Can't blame them, but welching's bad for business."

Mob-run games would fleece a tourist up the wazoo, but tended to play it straight with their regulars, paying out whatever the winnings. Otherwise high rollers would stay away.

"They say he cheats. They're going to make an example of him."

"Why is this our business?"

"Because Ellis is a valuable, um, specimen."

"Just what does that mean?"

Montero glanced at him. "If Stahlman hasn't told you, I probably should wait until he does."

Rick felt a little miffed at that. He knew pretty much everything about Stahlman's operations except . . .

"This have anything to do with the Long Island City warehouse?"

Montero nodded. "You've been there?"

"Back in the spring."

"He was just setting it up then."

"Yeah, well, I was talking to Stahlman when I saw something through one of the doors . . . or thought I did."

Montero was smiling. "Oh, like what?"

"Like a guy floating above the floor."

Montero laughed. "Leo! Always showing off!"

"You mean he really was—?"

"I'll defer to the boss on that, if you don't mind." He leaned forward, squinting through the windshield. "Is that Remsen ahead?"

"Yep. I was just about to—" The light went amber but Montero didn't slow. "Aw, you're not gonna—"

Yep. It turned red and he kept going, skidding into the turn as he ran through it.

"We in a hurry?" Rick said.

"Kinda. I'd like to get to Ellis while he's still alive."

"Stahlman sends a Ph.D. to deal with the mob?"

"I sort of have to go because I'm the only one who knows about Ellis. He sent you along to do the dealing. That is, should any dealing be needed." He glanced at Rick. "And I can see why."

"What?"

"I mean, look at you. If I saw you coming I'd get out of the way."

"Hey, I know I'm not a small guy, but I'm not *that* big."

"It's not size, it's—I don't know. You're like a coiled spring. You look like you could be a nice guy or very dangerous—either way, depending on the situation."

Not the first time Rick had heard that.

"Whatever. So anyway, Donato's people are right?"

"About Ellis cheating?" Montero paused, looking like he had to think about that. "Yes and no."

"Gotta be one or the other. Either he's cheating or he isn't."

"Oh, he's definitely cheating, but he doesn't know it. He just thinks he's lucky."

"Winning over four hundred K in roulette? That's *very* lucky."

"Especially when you consider he started with a ten-dollar chip and only played three spins."

Rick tried to do the math. "Had to be letting it ride each time."

"Exactly. He won on his first number which, at thirty-five to one, netted him three-fifty for his ten bucks. They allowed him to let his winnings ride on another number, which he also won. At another thirty-five to one, the house now owed him over twelve grand."

"And they let him ride again? No table limits?"

"I'm sure somebody's in big trouble for suspending the limit, but you can see why they'd take the risk to get back their twelve grand. I mean, the chance of hitting a number on the nose is about two-point-five percent. The chance of hitting your number three times in a row is still two-point-five percent, but the house figured no way that could happen."

Montero managed to take the right fork off Remsen onto Ralph without incident or drama.

"Obviously it did. So how do they plan to make an example of him?"

"Disappear him. Crush him inside one of Vinny's scrap cars and dump him in the Atlantic along with—"

"Truck-truck-truck!" Rick shouted, pointing.

Montero had been looking at him and didn't see the big box truck backing out of a driveway. He slammed on the brakes and the Volvo screeched and fishtailed to a stop. The driver looked at them with a WDF look, as in *what da fuck?*

"Get out!" Rick said.

"What?"

"Get out. I'm gonna drive."

"No-no-no. It's okay. I promise. Not far now."

Rick paused, then relented. He pointed at the receding truck. "Stay behind him." After a few hundred yards, he said, "What did you say about dumping him in the Atlantic?"

"Vinny owns a scrap yard and a trawler, in case you didn't know."

"Didn't. And you know about this how?"

"We've had Ellis's phone hacked for a while, and added Vinny's capo's just recently."

"How'd you manage that? Oh, Kevin Hudson, right?"

Stahlman liked to hire ex-hackers for his IT matters. He'd had a fellow named Russ Tuit for a while, but he'd left to work for the NRO, of all places. Before leaving he'd recommended Kevin. Rick had checked him out and he passed muster, so now he was Stahlman's go-to guy for IT.

"Right. Kevin's amazing. Anyway, Donato and his crew are talking about having the croupier and the guy who suspended the table limit keep Ellis company so he doesn't get lonely while he sleeps with the fishes. Ellis thinks he's meeting them at the scrap yard for his payout."

"He as dumb as he sounds?"

Montero smiled. "Don't be too hard on him. He's an astounding pool player but has a weakness for cards. He's played Donato's games before—poker and blackjack usually—and he's won and lost with never a problem collecting when he won. Last night was the first time he'd ever tried roulette and he thinks he was astoundingly lucky."

"But you say he cheated. How?"

Montero chewed his lip. "I guess I can tell you what we *think*. We still need to prove it."

All this beating around the bush.

"For Chrissake, spill, will you?"

"All right, all right. We think he's telekinetic."

That took a bit of digesting. "You mean he moves things with his mind?"

"Or brain."

"Same difference."

"Not even close. But yes, he can move things without touching them. That's how he can run a pool table every time he picks up a cue."

"And can hit a roulette number three times in a row."

"Exactly. I'm thinking he visualizes a pool ball dropping into a certain pocket or a roulette ball dropping into a certain slot, and it just . . . does."

"And now he's visualizing this middle-level mob boss just handing over four hundred K?"

"Yeah. I was hoping we could head him off at the pass but he got a head start."

The neighborhood around Ralph Avenue had deteriorated from redbrick residential to car-parts-and-repairs commercial.

"What's he driving?"

"A red Kia Forte." He pointed to a train trestle over the road. "Okay, once we pass that we're officially in Canarsie. Look for Preston Court."

Rick spotted it two blocks in. Montero hung a right onto an even crummier street with rusting warehouses, scrap yards, and bumpy, crumbling pavement that showed more dirt than asphalt. He pointed to a scrap yard on the left as they passed.

"That's Donato's."

Rick saw *Preston Salvage* on a canted sign slung

over a gap in the corrugated steel wall that served as an entrance.

"Not 'Vinnie's Vehicles' or 'Donato's Discards'?"

"Told you: He's low profile. Doesn't want his name out there. He came up during the days of the Dapper Don; he saw how Gotti became a lightning rod for the feds."

"Think he's there now?"

"Doubt it. If his guys are going to disappear Ellis, he'll want to be visible elsewhere—like having dinner at Peter Luger or the like."

"All right. Turn around. I'll go in and see what's happening."

"What about me?"

"Park across the entrance so nobody gets in or out, and be ready to drive."

"What are you planning?"

Rick had no idea.

"Gotta play it by ear. What's this Ellis look like?"

"A weasel. Sort of Anthony Weinerish."

"Got it."

Montero stopped the car.

"You carrying?" he said as Rick got out.

Rick grinned. "You just said 'carrying.' Don't say 'carrying.'"

"Why not?"

"Just don't."

"Okay, are you armed?"

"Sort of."

"With what?"

"Guns, knives, bludgeons, chainsaws. The usual. Why're you asking?"

"I just don't want to have to call 911 for you."

"I appreciate the thought."

Rick stepped over the chain strung low across the entrance. Straight ahead sat a two-story clapboard structure—looked like a garage on the ground floor with outside stairs leading up to an office on the second level. Two cars parked in front, neither a red Kia. Maybe in back . . .

He walked around to the left and saw piles of flattened junkers clustered around a crusher behind the building. In front of the crusher a guy was siphoning gas from the tank of a red Kia into an even redder gas can. That gave Rick a second's pause; then he realized if they were planning to crush Ellis in his Kia, a full gas tank could be dangerous.

The garage had double overhead doors, one of which was up. A quick glance revealed three men of various sizes, all duct-taped, hand, foot, and mouth. One of them, a guy with hair so gelled it probably reflected X-rays, had a definite Weineroid look.

Let me guess: Ellis Reise plus the croupier and the reckless pit boss.

Rick pulled a knife from his front pocket but kept it hidden in his fist with the four-inch blade folded. All it would take to free it was a flick of his thumb.

He poked his head inside for a quick look around. No one else besides the three bound men.

Nice. Maybe this would work out with no hassles. Spirit Reise away with no one the wiser until later.

"Who the fuck are you?" said a voice behind him.

Shit.

Rick turned to see the guy from outside, standing there with a plastic gas can in each hand.

"Hey, I just stopped by to see about getting a little cash for my old junker but I see you're in the middle of something so I'll just—"

"You'll just nothin', asshole." He dropped the cans and grabbed a tire iron. "Sit down over there with the others."

"Now wait a minute," Rick said, slipping the knife into a back pocket. He was going to need both hands. "I didn't see nothin' so I'm just gonna ease on down the road and—"

He'd started moving toward the door as he spoke, but the gas guy had a different idea. He swung the tire iron at Rick's head. Rick ducked, came up as it whistled by above him, grabbed the arm with the iron and yanked it down while bringing up his knee. Arm and knee connected at the elbow, which bent backward, a direction not allowed in its design, and broke with a grisly snap.

The gas man turned dead white, his tire iron hit the floor, followed immediately by his knees. Clutching his elbow he bent over as if praying toward Mecca and blew dinner chunks all over the floor.

Yeah, that had to hurt.

Rick flipped open his knife and cut the duct tape on Ellis Reise's wrists and ankles.

Reise ripped the tape off his mouth. "I don't know who you are," he said in a voice that could have passed for Joe Pesci's, "but am I glad you came along. Just watch out for Joey."

"Joey?" Rick looked around. He'd expected at least two, considering the two cars out front. "Where would he be?"

"He went upstairs to the office."

Sure enough, footsteps started pounding down the outside stairway. Rick motioned for Reise to be quiet, then picked up the tire iron and stood by the doorway. Now, if Joey could just pass the windows on the side of the garage without looking in . . .

"Tone?" The cry was tinged with alarm. "Tony!"

Joey had looked, damn him. Rick bent into a crouch and readied the tire iron in a two-handed grip.

When Joey entered, pistol in hand, Rick swung for the fences, catching a knee in mid-stride. As Joey's eyes bulged with pain, Rick struck again, this time at the gun arm. The radius gave off a loud *crack*. Joey and his semi-auto clattered to the floor. Rick booted the pistol out the door.

Reise's eyes were bulging almost as much as Joey's. "Who *are* you, man?"

Rick didn't know how to answer that so he didn't.

Reise continued to stare. "You are fucking scary, you know that, right?"

Rick shrugged. Probably seemed that way as far as the average person was concerned. He'd been trained to put the hurt on without hesitation when necessary, and not to apply more than necessary. Even though people didn't consciously perceive the lack of hesitation, they sensed it, and that was what scared them.

"Get their phones," he told Reise. "And if Tony there has a gun, get that too."

Tony had a revolver and an iPhone, but was still in too much agony to offer resistance or even speak.

Not so Joey. As he was relieved of his phone, he managed, "You're a dead man, Reise. Dead man walking."

"Not so tough now, are you?" Reise said, standing over him. "'Reise's pieces'? 'Reise is gonna be in pieces'? Where are the wisecracks now, asshole?"

He kicked Joey in the ribs.

None too gently, Rick grabbed Ellis's arm and yanked him away. "Don't do that. Don't ever do that."

"What?"

"Beat on a guy who's out of the fight."

"He was mouthing off."

"Do *not* do that. It's low rent."

He spotted Joey giving him a strange look.

Reise turned back to the mobsters and yelled, "Where's my money? You owe me 428,750 dollars and I want every fucking penny!"

That did it. Wishing he'd left the tape over Reise's mouth, Rick threw the phones and revolver out the door. How stupid was this guy?

"You kidding me?" he said, this time grabbing Reise by his scrawny neck and propelling him out into the night. "Forget about your money. You won't be seeing a penny of it. You're lucky you're alive."

"Hey! Where we going?"

He steered him toward the entrance where Montero's Volvo idled. "Somebody wants to talk to you."

"Who?"

"A guy who knows more about you than you know about yourself."

"What?" He started struggling. "I ain't getting in no car with somebody I don't know!"

Rick towered over Reise who weighed next to nothing. Tightening his grip on his neck, he lifted the scrawny man off his feet and carried him kicking and twisting to the Volvo where he threw him into the front seat.

"This man is going to drive you someplace safe and you'll listen to what he has to say along the way."

"No fucking way!"

"There's still a whole roll of duct tape back there," Rick said. "Only take me a few seconds to go get it. Your choice. Because one way or another you're going with him. We clear?"

That took some of the starch out of Reise. "My car," he whined.

Damn.

"I'll bring it. You sit and listen." Rick leaned over and looked at Montero. "The warehouse?"

Montero nodded. "Yep."

"Meet you there."

He watched the Volvo zoom off, wondering if Ellis would survive the drive to Long Island City, then headed back to refill the Kia's tank. As he retrieved the gas cans, he found the garage pretty much as he'd left it. Tony was now lying on his side next to his vomit, still clutching his elbow. Joey had risen to a sitting position and, with his good arm, was half crawling toward his gun and phone outside.

Ignoring Joey's howls of pain, Rick dragged him back to Tony and zip-tied their good arms together.

"You seem like a stand-up guy," Joey said. "How come you're involved with that little shit?"

"I'm not. Guy I work for is."

"We're gonna have to come after you, y'know."

"Not necessarily. Tell Mister Donato that Reise's debt is settled. He doesn't owe him anything."

"But me and Tony owe you," Joey said. "Look at his elbow. And you broke my arm. We owe you big time."

"I didn't come here for a fight," Rick said. "If your pal hadn't started swinging a tire iron and you hadn't been pointing a gun, things'd be different right now."

"Still . . ."

Rick moved closer and stood over him, giving him a hard look. "Hey, you're not going to become a problem now, are you? I've learned the hard way that unsolved problems have a habit of biting you in the ass when you least expect it, so I don't like to leave them lying around. Get what I'm saying? Now, are you going to be a problem?"

Joey looked away. "Guess not."

"Good."

Rick took a quick look around. The two other guys were still bound and gagged. He considered cutting them free, then decided against it. They might try to take him down to get back in good with their boss.

What we have here, he thought, is what you might call a family matter. Best not to interfere.

He shook his head. The things Stahlman asked him to do at times . . .

Good thing he paid well.

As he replaced the Kia's gas, he thought about Ellis Reise and his supposed ability to move things with his mind. He'd leave it a *supposed* ability until he'd seen it up close and personal. If true, it would give him a great excuse to call Laura and get her involved.

Not so long ago he'd figured he wouldn't ever again need an excuse to call her, but things between them hadn't gone the way he'd hoped. Not even close.

2

QUEENS, NEW YORK

Rick remembered the address of Stahlman's warehouse—a quarter mil square feet spread over two floors in one of the older buildings squatting in the industrial zone between Queens Boulevard and the LIE. Traffic was light and he made good time. Some guy on the radio was talking about how we'd just passed the autumnal equinox, that day every September when the nights started running longer than the days. It meant summer was over and fall was taking charge.

He parked the Kia at the end of the block and walked to a steel door under a heavy-duty roll-up security shutter that served as the entrance.

He liked how the ground-floor windows were set high, a good ten feet off the pavement. Made it easier to keep out the rats—human and otherwise. He knocked, waved at the security camera, and was buzzed in. Adão Guerra loomed behind a desk that looked too small for him. Rick had backgrounded him for a security position earlier in the year.

"Hey, Mister Hayden," he said, extending his hand. "The doc said you'd be coming soon."

"The boss here?"

Guerra nodded and pointed. "With the doc and the new guy right through there."

Another buzz and the door to Rick's right unlatched, allowing him into a huge rectangular space running four hundred feet on its long side, with fifteen-foot ceilings. The floor had been divided into curtained areas of varying sizes. Dead ahead, Stahlman, Montero, and Reise stood staring at a flatscreen TV mounted on the wall.

"You mean you've been *spying* on me?" Reise was saying as Rick approached.

Clayton Stahlman spotted him and motioned him aside.

"Mister Hayden," he said, offering his hand. "I hardly see you anymore. I miss our talks."

Always *Mister Hayden*, never *Rick*. And because they'd had little face-to-face contact since Stahlman's

cure, Rick still experienced a pop of surprise at his
healthy appearance. The man who'd hired him years
ago had been a frail, feeble, moon-faced ghost, sucking oxygen twenty-four/seven as he dwindled away in
his wheelchair. Although his barrel chest remained as
a reminder of the pulmonary fibrosis that had almost
laid him low, he now looked younger than his late
sixties, a picture of senior citizen health.

"So do I," Rick lied. He liked Stahlman, but wasn't
looking to be buddies. He gestured toward Reise.
"This on the up-and-up?"

"His telekinesis? I believe so. Come over here and
listen in on Doctor Montero explaining it to him."

". . . and I'm betting you could run any table any
time you want," Montero was saying.

Reise gave a self-satisfied shrug. "Yeah, I suppose."
He spotted Rick. "You!" He jabbed an index finger
toward Montero. "You put me in a car with a fucking
maniac!"

"Well . . ."

"I almost got killed."

"Better than definitely killed if you'd stayed at the
scrap yard."

Reise didn't seem to have a response to that.

"Let's stay on topic, shall we?" Montero said. "You
could run a pool table every time, but you don't. Why
not?"

Reise gave him a *dumb question* look. "I'd never
get anyone to bet against me if I didn't miss once in
a while!"

Stahlman leaned close to Rick and spoke in a low
voice. "We were tipped to Ellis, so—"

"Tipped how?"

"It's complicated. You'll meet her soon."

Everything was complicated. And who was "her"?

"Anyway," Stahlman went on, "over the summer we set up a camera above his favorite pool table, supposedly as a promotion for the camera-and-playback system. At the end of a game, players could replay their best shots on the connected TV. The owner was cool with the free installation and the players loved the overhead shots. They felt like they were in a televised match."

Montero said to Reise, "But your pool hustles were just to finance your poker, right?"

A smile. "Cards are where it's at."

"But while you were hustling your fellow players and having fun taking their money," Montero said, "we had a computer analyzing all the shots on the table, and that's how we found you."

The smile faded. "What's that mean? 'Found' me?"

"Very simple," Montero said. "Your strokes tend to break the laws of physics." He worked the remote in his hand. "Easier if I show you."

An overhead shot of a pool table filled the TV screen on the wall. A stick struck the white cue ball, which then struck the red three ball, sending it flying toward a corner pocket. The screen froze after the red had traveled two feet. A dotted line appeared, connecting the ball to the cushion just to the left of a corner pocket.

"Here's a stroke by one of your opponents," Montero said. "Computer analysis of the speed, direction, and rotation of the ball predicts that this shot will miss."

The screen came to life again and, sure enough, the ball bounced off the cushion exactly where predicted.

Another stick appeared, struck the cue ball, which in turn struck the striped twelve ball. Again action was stopped and another dotted line appeared, showing this shot would miss too.

"This is your shot, Ellis. The computer says you're going to narrowly miss too, but watch what happens."

The ball began rolling again, following the projected path for another foot or so, and then deviating just enough to land in the pocket.

"Proves nothing," Reise said. "Except maybe your software needs fixing."

Montero sighed. "I understand how you're in denial. But I can stand here all night and show you example after example of how your opponents' shots follow the predicted path to the millimeter and yours do not. You're unconsciously influencing the path of the balls, Ellis."

"Come on," he said with a tremulous attempt at a smile. "That's Harry Potter stuff."

"How are you at cards, Ellis?"

A shrug. "Pretty good. Better than average."

"How come you've never played roulette before?"

"It's a sucker's game."

"And yet you won four hundred grand your first try."

"Four hundred twenty-eight-plus."

"So, you're unbeatable in pool and you broke the bank your first time out in roulette. What do those two games have in common?"

Reise averted his gaze. "Balls."

Rick was convinced, and he could see Reise's resistance crumbling.

"Right. Moving objects that can be influenced by someone with telekinesis."

Reise shook his head, his voice barely a whisper. "Jesus."

Stahlman slapped Rick's shoulder. "Let's repair to my office, shall we?"

The office turned out to be a windowless box with bare walls, a scarred desk, and two chairs. Rick didn't know Clayton Stahlman's exact net worth, but if it didn't sport nine zeroes, it didn't miss by much. At the end of the nineties he'd cashed out of the dot-com revolution before it imploded and invested elsewhere. He'd told Rick once that, no matter how he tried, he couldn't spend even the interest on his holdings, let alone dent the principal, and so his net worth kept growing.

What Rick liked was how unimpressed Stahlman was with his wealth. This office was a perfect example. Function took precedence over form. No bells and whistles, just a private place to set his ass down and open his laptop and make calls on his cell.

"Was I right sending you along with the doc?" he said, indicating the office's second chair. "Did you need to intervene?"

"A little. Nothing that won't heal."

"Good." He pulled a bottle of booze and a couple of glasses from one of his desk drawers. "That calls for a celebration."

"What are we celebrating?"

Stahlman poured two fingers of amber fluid into each glass. "Locating another nadaný."

"Reise?" Rick said, accepting the glass. "I'd say he's more of a ninny. What's a nadaný?"

"A Slovak word I picked up from my grandmother. It means 'gifted.'" He reached his glass toward Rick. "Cheers."

They clinked, Rick sipped, and flavors exploded in his mouth.

"Holy crap, what is this? I mean, I know it's Scotch, but . . . wow."

"It's from the Isle of Arran, finished in a wine cask—Amarone, to be specific."

Rick sipped again. Man, he could get used to this stuff. He leaned back and stared at Stahlman.

"So what's the deal here? You said 'another na-daný.' You've got more people who can make pool balls roll the wrong way?"

Stahlman smiled. "As a matter of fact, yes. One other telekinetic. I've also found a guy who can levi-tate, one who can make things disappear, another who can generate heat with his hands, a—"

Rick had to laugh. "So what do we call you now? Professor X?"

Stahlman's lips gave a wry twist. "If only!"

"What other . . . gifts?"

"The most impressive is a gal who can teleport."

Rick straightened in his chair. "Bullshit."

Stahlman raised a hand. "I swear."

"But that's . . . that's amazing." He pushed his empty glass across the desktop. "So amazing I think it calls for more celebrating."

Stahlman grinned and added a generous pour to both glasses.

"I'll drink to that. But this teleporter . . . she hates her gift. Convincing her to use it is like pulling teeth."

"It's painful?"

"No. Let's just say she's a teenager and she has is-sues and leave it at that for the moment."

"Okay, but . . ." Rick spread his hands. "What's the point?"

Stahlman smiled. "You mean, what's in it for me?"

"Well, commercial applications are your thing. Where's the profit?"

"I don't know yet. Probably none. Be nice to learn if these gifts can be taught. Wouldn't that be some-thing? But in the end I expect this will turn out to be just a fascinating way to waste my excess cash."

"You can always throw some my way. Less complicated."

Stahlman leaned forward. "Are you short? Just say the word and—"

Rick waved him off. Stahlman paid him plenty. "Just kidding. Really."

"Okay. But any time . . ."

"Thank you."

"Anyway, right now we're at the basic research stage. I'm paying the nadaný—even housing some of them in apartments I built on the second floor. In return they allow Doctor Montero to test the limits of each gift and see if there's some way they can enhance it. And as I said, hopefully find a way it can be learned by others."

Rick had known Clayton Stahlman long enough to sense something else at work here.

"There's more, isn't there?"

Stahlman nodded. "For me, the real question isn't the nature of their gifts, but how they obtained them. I mean, why them and not you or me? Is there a common thread that connects them?"

Rick figured he'd like to know that too. For his own reasons.

"Well, if Montero comes up empty, you can always fall back on alien abductions."

Stahlman laughed. "If anyone else said that, I'd be sure he was joking. But with you . . ."

Rick spread his hands. "Hey, you know I'm not into aliens. ICE, on the other hand . . ."

"Ah, yes. Your Intrusive Cosmic Entities."

"Yep. And they've earned the *I* in Intrusive."

"Well, I suppose bestowing these gifts on random people would certainly qualify as intrusive."

Rick was still having trouble wrapping his mind around the nadaný. Really, a girl who could teleport?

"So these gifts are for real?"

Stahlman held up a hand, oath-taking style. "For real."

"And it involves their brains?"

A nod. "Most certainly. Doctor Montero says their abilities are associated with some sort of brain-wave activity that I don't pretend to understand."

"You've got to let Laura get involved," Rick said.

"Doctor Fanning? I'd love to see her again. If she's interested, she's welcome, of course, but . . ." He smiled. "These folks aren't dead yet."

"She's quitting the ME's office and applying for a neurology residency. This would be right up her alley."

Stahlman spread his hands. "I owe her my health . . . my life. She can be in as deep and for as long as she wants to be. Are you seeing her tonight?"

"Um, no."

"Talking to her?"

"Hadn't planned on it, but I guess—"

"I thought you two had a thing going," he said with a frown.

Was it that obvious the "thing" had died?

"We've kind of drifted apart." Rick didn't want to talk about it. "But I'll call her on this. Call her tonight."

"Just make sure she knows this whole project is sub rosa."

"Will do."

But first she had to take his call. Sometimes she did, sometimes she didn't.

3

SHIRLEY, NEW YORK

Laura checked the caller ID.

Rick.

His first call in a while. And that made sense. They'd run out of things to say. Not his fault. She'd been the one to pull back, not him.

The Düsseldorf atrocity . . . those children. Her mind understood, sympathized, even agreed to some extent, but her heart, the emotional side of her, couldn't tuck it away and keep it out of sight. It kept slithering free.

Would he ever do something like that again? She couldn't imagine him or anyone else being faced with a choice like that twice. But just knowing what he'd been capable of in the past had tainted her feelings and their relationship.

Oh, hell.

She hit *TALK.*

"Rick?"

"Hey, Laura."

"Hey, Rick."

"What's up?"

Awkward, awkward, awkward.

"Not much. Oh, as of yesterday I'm officially in the residency matching program."

When she'd decided to change the focus of her career from dead people to the living, this year's residency match had been over and done. She'd have to wait for the match for next year.

All medical school seniors—and doctors already in practice, like her—looking for post-graduate residencies in specialty training had to go through the National Resident Matching Program. She'd had to wait till now to enter her name for a neurology residency. Rick had called it the "residency Sorting Hat," and in a way that was true. Now that she was in, she could set up interviews with the neurology departments of area medical centers like Columbia, Mount Sinai, Stony Brook, and NYU/North Shore. She needed a place within an easy commute.

"Great. Still neurology?"

"Of course."

"Good. 'Cause that's why I'm calling."

"About my residency?"

"No, about neurology. Stahlman's into something very strange that might interest you. In fact I know it will interest you."

"Stahlman?"

"Look, I know you've got issues with him, but he's a stand-up guy and this is right up your alley."

Clayton Stahlman . . . yes, Laura had issues with him. She'd found the cure for his terminal illness—all illnesses, for that matter—and in return he'd made her rich enough to quit the Suffolk County Medical Examiner's office and retrain for another field. But he'd played fast and loose with her during her travels for him, withholding critical information. In the end his tactic had wound up saving his own life as well as her daughter Marissa's, so she couldn't hold it against him. But the matter of trust remained.

"I don't know . . ."

"Hear me out. This is confidential, so you've gotta keep it to yourself, okay?"

Easy enough, since she couldn't imagine talking about Clayton Stahlman to anyone.

"He's got these people with . . . powers."

Uh-oh. "Powers?"

He laughed. God, she missed that laugh.

"Hey, I know that tone. And I know it sounds whacked out, but I met this guy tonight who can change the course of a pool ball just by wishing it into the pocket."

"'Wishing'?"

"I should have said 'guiding.' He guides it into the pocket with his mind."

"You're talking telekinesis."

"Yeah. I am. Exactly."

She felt disappointed. Rick was not the gullible type.

"It's a trick, Rick."

"No, Stahlman has computer analysis and—"

"A trick. There's no such thing as telekinesis."

"He's got this neuroscience guy working for him and he sure seems convinced."

"Every field has its share of kooks."

"I checked him out for Stahlman and Doc Montero is legit."

"He might look good on the surface but—wait. Did you say Montero?"

"Yeah. Luis Montero. He's got a Ph.D. in—"

"Neurobiology. Right-right-right. I've read some of his papers. And you're telling me Stahlman has got Luis Montero on retainer?"

"No retainer. Full-time."

Well, this was interesting.

Rick added, *"The doc thinks these powers are related to some sort of brain waves and—"*

"Okay. I'll check it out."

"You will? Great. When's good for you?"

"Tomorrow morning. Marissa will be in school and—"

"How's she doing?"

"Great. I just put her to bed."

She misses you terribly bubbled to her lips. A sad truth, but no way could she say it.

Rick had hit it off with her nine-year-old Mets fanatic who insisted on using their proper name, the New York Metropolitans. Not a baseball fan—Rick claimed it put him to sleep—he'd nevertheless studied up on the team and had been able to trade stats with Marissa like a *SportsCenter* groupie.

"Her Metropolitans have a chance for a wild-card slot again."

"So I've been told—endlessly."

"Hey, any chance I can drop in sometime and catch a game with her?"

Marissa would love that.

"Well, she's pretty busy, what with the new school year and all."

A pause, then, *"Yeah, I can see that. Some other time."*

"Yeah. That would be great."

"Want me to pick you up tomorrow?"

Alone in a car together with nothing to talk about but *us?*

"Better if I drive."

A quick, soft sigh. *"Okay. It's in Long-I City. I'll text you the address and the time when it's set up."*

"Great."

"See you tomorrow."

She thumbed *OFF* and somehow managed to keep from throwing the phone across the room.

What's the matter with me? Selfish bitch! Marissa would have loved to watch a game with Rick, but no, *I'd* be uncomfortable, and we couldn't have *that,* could we?

Get over yourself, dammit!

She laid the phone—gently—on the counter and stalked to the sliding glass doors leading to the rear deck. With her arms folded across her chest she stared out at the backyard and saw nothing.

She and Rick had been thrown together by Stahlman and started out with a tense, almost adversarial relationship. They'd journeyed through nine or ten countries on five continents, witnessed destruction and death, nearly died themselves a couple of times. They'd bonded, become friends—close friends—before they became lovers. The sex had been good—no, great—but then, as the two of them were sailing across the Mozambique Channel, he'd felt he had to come clean before they committed.

Düsseldorf. Goddamn Düsseldorf.

That had been the start of their unraveling. The affair carried on awhile longer, but then what he'd told her started to creep into bed with them, and soon she was finding excuses to put off seeing him, and eventually they stopped getting together at all.

They'd been friends before they'd become intimate. Could they ever be just friends again after sharing each other like that?

She was friends with Steven these days. Her ex had betrayed her numerous times during their marriage, leaving her no choice but to call it quits. But now they shared Marissa without rancor or bitterness. Actually got along better than during the marriage.

Rick had been totally honest and up front with her from the get-go and . . . she'd called it quits.

What the hell's the matter with me? Is anyone going to work out? What am I, some starry-eyed teen who thinks she's going to find the perfect man? There *is* no perfect man. Not at my age. Not at *any* age!

She felt her throat tighten and took a deep breath to ward off the threat of tears.

Okay. She'd put on her big-girl panties and go to Stahlman's place tomorrow. No more of this avoidance bullshit. Rick was a brave, tough, decent man. They'd walked through fires together. They'd been friends before. That bond hadn't dissolved. No reason they couldn't be friends again.

Right?

Right?

THEN

"I must say, Doctor LaVelle, I am impressed."

Benjamin Greve of the DIA had called her lab and told her to meet him in the same back corner of the USAMRMC offices as before. And as before, he sat behind the rickety desk, looking as pale and thin as ever, with the same embalmed expression. But no waiting this time.

"Impressed by what?"

"By the amazing amount of data you've compiled in seven weeks."

"Not so amazing. You're impressed only because you underestimated me."

Everybody underestimated her. She was used to it.

That smilelike grimace appeared. "Are you always this blunt?"

"I simply did what was asked of me."

"Yes, you did, but . . . let me tell you something. You were one of four researchers at four different facilities given a sample of Substance A to investigate. Not one of them has compiled anywhere near the data you have."

"Melis proved something of a challenge."

Probably the understatement of the year, she thought.

"'Melis' . . . ah, yes. Your term for Substance A. Where did you come up with that, may I ask? I'm guessing it's an acronym of a list of its properties."

Greve watched her with an expectant expression, as if waiting for a nugget of brilliance.

"It's an anagram for 'slime.' 'Substance A' is pretty lame."

She watched his look of expectation fade. Sorry. You guessed wrong. You lose.

"An anagram for slime . . . how . . . interesting. Well, be that as it may, if I had shown up on a Saturday at any of those other facilities, I am quite sure I would not have found the designated researcher in his lab."

Okay, she admitted it . . . well, to herself, at least: She'd become fixated on melis. Obsessed was probably more like it. Since that first instant when it had weighed in at zero, she hadn't been able to get it out of her mind. It had taken over her brain.

She'd subjected it to thousands of degrees of heat, but it didn't boil, desiccate, or harden. She'd cooled it to near absolute zero, but it remained pliant and pourable. She'd electrocuted it and dropped it into caustic acids. She'd put it into a blender and emulsified it in various fluids, but when the mix dried out it returned to its original state.

After exposing mice and rats to melis with no ill effects, she tried feeding it to them, but they weren't interested. So she emulsified it in normal saline and administered it via intraperitoneal injection, again with no ill effects. She determined it was not toxic. The damn stuff was too inert to be toxic.

"Your most recent fax stated that you had some

unexpected results from the rodent studies, but you didn't mention what they were."

"I wanted to confirm the preliminary reports. The rodents injected with the melis-saline emulsion appeared unaffected, so I sent them off to be studied for changes in motor function. They were run through standard mazes and performed no better or worse than their unexposed brethren."

Greve looked bored. "How, pray tell, was that unexpected?"

"It wasn't. But some of the rats happened to be pregnant at the time of the injection."

"Oh?" He straightened in his chair. "You have my interest. Mutagenic effects?"

"If you call improved maze performance a mutation, then yes."

"Improved how?"

"The animal behavior people called me all excited, wanting to know what I'd done to the rats."

Greve leaned forward. "I trust you didn't—"

"Of course not." She remembered the stringent terms of the NDA she'd signed. "I said it was classified."

"And why were they excited?"

"The melis offspring were absolute star performers in the mazes. But I didn't want to report that unless I was sure they could replicate the results."

"And?"

"And that's where I was when you called—watching maze-naïve baby rats zoom this way and that toward the cheese."

"Let me get this straight: The melis-treated rats showed no effects one way or the other, but their offspring demonstrated increased intelligence?"

"I didn't say that. No one's ready to say any more

than the offspring demonstrated improved maze performance. Assessing actual intelligence will take more refined testing."

He waved her off. "Spoken like a true scientific tight-ass. We'll arrange for it."

She groaned. "That'll mean applying for grants and—"

"Grants? Wherever did you get that idea? Did you know that there are one thousand three hundred thirty-seven words in the Declaration of Independence, and twenty-six thousand nine hundred eleven words in federal laws regulating the sale of cabbages? We do *not* want bureaucratic oversight."

Great. She hated applying for grants.

"I'll need more melis."

"No problem. We have plenty of it."

"Can I ask where—?"

"No, you may not."

Maureen vented a blast of frustration. "After all the work I've done? I probably know more about this damn stuff than anyone on Earth, but I'm not cleared to know where it came from?"

"Maybe someday."

"Because it's not *from* Earth, is it?"

Greve's expression froze. "Why do you say that?"

"Because it behaves like nothing on Earth. Our spectrometers here are capable of analyzing the molecular structure of anything, but they can't analyze melis because they don't recognize its existence. We enter a sample for analysis and the machine tells us it's waiting for a sample. Under an electron microscope it looks like a glob—no resolution. Melis is like nothing on Earth, so it has to be from someplace *other* than Earth."

Greve shot to his feet behind the desk. "You will

keep your unfounded opinions to yourself, Doctor LaVelle! Your duty here is to provide us with facts, not wild speculation."

He was right, of course, but *damn,* she wanted to know where this stuff came from.

He added, "You are, however, correct about one thing."

"Oh?"

"You are indeed the world authority on what you call melis. And as such you will be involved in every phase of the investigation."

Yes! If she stayed with this wonderfully mysterious goop, she was confident she'd learn where it came from. *Unfounded opinion* it might be, but she was positive melis was not of Earthly origin.

"I won't let you down."

"To that end, we will begin primate trials immediately and you will oversee them."

"I'm a molecular biologist. I don't do animal studies."

"You just did—the mazes, remember?"

"That was an ad-hoc thing, and only rodents."

She considered melis *hers*—her baby. She didn't want anyone else taking over. But primates? Too much like humans.

"They're just dumb animals," Greve said.

"I don't do primates."

"You do now."

NOW

Wednesday

1

QUEENS, NEW YORK

Laura inspected the newspaper clipping framed on the wall of Stahlman's office.

> ***Do you have a special talent?***
> ***One you keep to yourself?***
> ***You know what we mean.***
> ***Let us help you develop it.***

"That's the personals ad I placed to start things rolling," Stahlman said.

"But why? What inspired you to place it?"

She'd arrived on time but couldn't find a parking spot. As usual, Rick had anticipated that, waiting out front to direct her to the garage built into the rear of the building.

The sight of him had stirred such an odd mix of emotions, most of them good, except for regret that they'd drifted apart. And that was all on her. Tall, dark-haired, broad-shouldered—the classic hunk. Seeing him made her realize how much she missed him.

After a brief awkward hug—yeah, after all their intimacies, they'd regressed to the brief-awkward-hug stage—he'd led her inside to where Stahlman waited. He started with the "Doctor Fanning" stuff but she put the kibosh on that, insisting on "Laura."

Stahlman said, "One of my janitors in the main office, a young fellow named Cyrus, was the kick-off. I was working late and he was emptying the wastebaskets. As he was leaving I pointed out a scrap of paper he'd left on the floor. I happened to glance his way as he bent and picked it up. He didn't realize I was watching when he closed it in his fist. As he straightened up, he opened his hand and I saw it was empty."

"Sleight of hand," Laura said.

"Exactly what I thought. And that's exactly what he told me when I called him on it and asked him to do it again. I gave him a small stone I use as a paperweight." He pointed to a beige-brown rock on his desk. "Pretty much exactly like this one. He took it, closed it in his fist, and when he opened up again—nothing."

"There must be a zillion amateur magicians who can do that," she said.

"As a matter of fact, he works as a magician—small-time stuff, kids' parties and the like. But here's the thing: When I asked him for the stone back, he couldn't give it to me. I demanded it back because, like this one, it was one of a number of souvenir rocks I brought back from a trip to the cave in Bronson Canyon."

"Souvenir *rocks*?" Laura said.

"Yeah-yeah. Out near Hollywood. But that's not important. The point is, he said he was sorry but it was gone for good. Cyrus was my first nadaný."

He'd already explained the term to her, but Laura found herself far from convinced about this supposed gift.

"You believed him? You truly believed it had vanished?"

Stahlman spread his hands. "I know it sounds incredibly gullible, but—here, see for yourself." He indicated the door. "Rick, would you be so kind as to ask Cyrus to come in?"

Rick had kept his distance since their hello hug. She was glad for that, and then again she wasn't. Not like she was contagious or anything.

Rick stepped outside and returned with a chubby twenty-something black man. Stahlman introduced him, then faced him toward Laura.

"Doctor Fanning here doesn't believe in your gift, Cyrus. Care to convince her?" He held up a half-foot length of quarter-inch wood doweling. "Try this."

Laura could see she was going to have to take control here. She waited until Cyrus reached out with his right hand.

"If I may," she said, taking the doweling from Stahlman and approaching Cyrus. "Would you please roll up your left shirtsleeve?"

"Sure." Cyrus smiled as he pulled it above his elbow.

Laura had him stretch his arm out, left palm up. She checked between all his fingers, then placed the doweling on his palm.

"Okay. Make it disappear." As he started to close his fingers—"Uh-uh. Leave them open."

"I can't do it unless I close my fist." His accent was Deep South, thick as molasses.

"How convenient. Go ahead then."

He closed his fingers around the doweling, leaving the ends exposed. Those ends abruptly fell to the floor, and when he spread his fingers his palm was empty.

"Impressive," Laura said, checking his hand. No sign of anything amiss. "Very impressive. Where is it?"

He shrugged. "I don't know. It just goes away."

"Can you bring it back?"

"Nope."

"What kind of a magician are you?"

"It's really gone," Stahlman said.

She looked at him. "And your souvenir rock?"

He shook his head. "Gone for good."

She turned back to Cyrus. "Let me get this straight: You hold something and it vanishes to who-knows-where and you can't bring it back?"

"Yeah. But it goes away only if I want it to."

"You *wish* it away?"

A shrug. "Yeah, I guess. But only little things that can fit in my hand—like candy wrappers and bugs and stuff." A shy smile. "I'm kind of a garbage disposal."

"Except for something like this," Stahlman said, holding up a length of solid steel curtain rod.

Cyrus took it, squeezed, but it remained whole.

"Density of the material seems to be a factor." Stahlman grinned at Laura. "I know you're a skeptic, and I took some convincing myself. But the clincher was this." He held up a blue plastic disk the size of a quarter. "It's a tracker. You attach it to your key chain or wallet, anything you might misplace or might get stolen."

He placed the disk on Cyrus's palm and handed Laura his iPhone. The screen showed a blue dot blinking on a map of Long Island City at the address of the warehouse.

"Okay, Cy," Stahlman said. "Do it."

He made a fist around the tracker and the blue dot winked out on the phone. He opened his hand again. The tracker was gone.

Laura felt her stomach ripple. Okay. This was a little scary. This kind of thing wasn't supposed to be possible.

"Convinced?" Stahlman said.

"I think so. Maybe. You could be pranking me."

Stahlman smiled. "Of course I could. I've got nothing better to do than hoodwink the woman who saved my life."

Laura raised her hands, surrendering. "Okay. Touché."

"After finding the panacea, I'm surprised you're such a hard sell."

"Old habits die hard, I guess."

He sent Cyrus off with a thank-you, then pointed again to the framed clipping.

"Cyrus's gift prompted me to look for someone else who could do the same. But I didn't feel I could be too specific, so I advertised for 'special talents.'"

Rick laughed. "Bet you wound up with a parade of stupid human tricks."

"You wouldn't believe. But I found Leo in the crowd. And then Ruth. Knowing Laura, I think I'd rather show you than tell you."

"Fair enough." She turned to Rick. "How long have you known about this?"

"Since last night. I'm learning right along with you."

"It was Rick's idea to bring you on board. He said you were heading for a neurology residency, and since these gifts seem to be brain wave–based, I—"

A zap of excitement hit her.

"Brain waves? Really? How do you know?"

"Because that's what Doctor Montero tells me, and if he says so, I believe."

"Is he here? I'd like to meet him."

"He's here and you'll meet him in a moment. But first . . ." He tapped out a message into his cell phone. A text? "There's someone else I'd like you to meet first."

A young woman entered—white, maybe late twenties, with short dark hair. Stahlman introduced her as Marie Novotna.

"Marie is absolutely critical to this project. She answered the ad and said, 'I know what you are looking for. I can find them for you.' And she's done just that."

"How?" Laura said.

She shrugged. "My gift is knowing when someone has a gift," she said with a slight Eastern European accent.

Laura had to ask. "Do I?"

Marie shook her head. "I am the only nadaný in the room."

Laura wasn't sure if she felt disappointed or relieved.

"Marie found Ellis for us. She was walking by a pool hall and sensed a nadaný inside. She can point and say 'a nadaný is over there.'"

"But I can't say how far over there."

"How many are we talking about, say, here in New York?" Rick said, speaking for the first time in a while.

"Maybe twenty-five."

"Just in New York?" Laura didn't know whether to consider that a lot or a little, but her thoughts were veering in an epidemiological direction. "What about the country?"

A shrug. "Hundreds. Not thousands, but hundreds."

"Maybe there's a connection between these . . . *nadaný*." There. She'd used the word.

"We've been looking into that," Stahlman said. "So far, no correlations. Now, do you want to meet our neurobiologist?"

"Most certainly."

As Stahlman led her out to the vast expanse of the warehouse's first floor, she noticed Rick hanging back. She paused.

"You're awfully quiet this morning."

He shrugged. "I had last night and earlier this morning to get ahead of you on the learning curve, so I'm staying out of the way."

Far out of the way. Even now he was keeping his distance.

I don't have cooties.

And then the thought struck her: *Maybe he thinks I believe* he *has cooties—moral cooties.*

Not even close.

She stepped up to Rick, took his arm, and towed him toward the door.

"Come on. We'll learn together."

Ellis

They found Dr. Montero standing by a pool table, watching his iPad as a whippet-thin young man wearing strange headgear worked a cue.

"I'll hang back on this one," Rick said. "I've already had the pleasure of meeting Mister Reise."

Something about the way he said that . . .

After an introduction to Dr. Montero and some

small talk, during which she revealed her intended career switch to neurology, Montero explained that the fellow playing pool, Ellis Reise, was able to move small objects simply by thinking about it.

"He's wearing an ambulatory EEG headset," Montero said. "His gift is telekinesis. And, just like every other nadaný I've tested, use of his gift causes zeta waves to appear on his EEG."

"Zeta waves?" Laura had been boning up on neurology during her unaccustomed free time. She ran through the five types of brain waves: gamma, beta, alpha, theta, and delta. "I'm not familiar with—"

"It's a rare slow delta-wave variation, sometimes seen with structural lesions in the brain. So far all the brain MRIs on our nadaný show no abnormalities, so it's something else. A clue to their gifts." He turned to the young man at the table. "Ellis, give our guests a demonstration, if you will?"

He scowled. "What am I? A trained seal?"

Nice attitude, Laura thought. Now she understood Rick's tone when he mentioned *Mister Reise*.

"Never mind," Montero said. "I'll get someone else."

"Nah. Forget it. I'll play. Just remember to throw me a fish when I'm done."

Laura figured a gummy fish would be emotional age–appropriate.

"They're gifted," Montero said under his breath, "but not always with a pleasant personality." Then louder as he held out his iPad: "Watch the screen here. No zeta waves."

"I'll have to take your word for it," Laura said, eying the confusing array of squiggles trailing across the screen. "What do they look like?"

"Trust me, you'll know when they appear."

Laura positioned herself so she could see both the tablet and the pool table. She watched Ellis hit one of the balls, sending it toward the far left corner pocket. Halfway there it veered sharply to the right.

The move took her by surprise. Yes, she'd been told he could move an object by thinking about it, but she hadn't quite accepted it. She was so taken she almost forgot about the EEG. The tablet screen now showed a large, slow, saw-toothed waveform joining the others. When the ball dropped into the far right pocket, the wave stopped.

Laura blinked at the table. Had she really seen that?

"Thank you, Ellis," Montero said.

Laura decided it wouldn't hurt to echo him. "Yes, thank you. Very impressive."

He bowed. "I'm here all week."

That young man had just moved an object with his mind—just by thinking about it. How could brain waves—weak electrical impulses generated by neuronal activity—impact a physical object? She didn't care what kind of waves, gamma, or zeta or whatever, how could they do that?

"I don't know what to say," she told Montero. "You see this stuff in movies, but . . ."

"I know." Montero's eyes sparkled. "Isn't it wonderful?"

She sensed him imagining the papers he was going to write.

"Are you going to be able to publish?"

He nodded. "Eventually. We're just gathering data for now. But this is going to blow the doors off, well, everything. Not just the biosciences, but physics and chemistry as well."

"I can see that."

Great vistas were opening before her.

He took her arm and led her toward one of the curtained-off areas. "But you ain't seen nothin' yet!"

She motioned for Rick to follow and he quickly caught up.

"Where're we going?" he said.

Montero said, "To visit a fellow who's the complete opposite of Ellis."

From behind, Stahlman called to them. "Marie and I will be in the office. Stop back when you're done."

Leo

Montero pulled aside the curtain and Laura gasped.

Beside her, Rick said, "Hey, that's the guy I saw last spring!"

A slim Hispanic man in his early twenties sat—so to speak—in a cross-legged position as he hovered above a brown leather hassock. He too wore ambulatory EEG headgear and was doing something with a yardstick behind his back but Laura wasn't sure exactly what.

"Leo?" Montero said. "I'd like you to meet—"

"Up to twenty-two inches!" he said, grinning.

"Great," Montero said, moving ahead of them.

He introduced him as Leonardo Flores. He took the yardstick from Leo and swung it back and forth below the young man's suspended butt—to show nothing was holding him up, she supposed.

"As you can see, Leo levitates."

Yes, she could see. Very clearly.

Leo pointed to the EEG display on the television screen. "This technique seems to be working."

Laura noticed the distinct pattern of zeta waves among the others.

"I'm experimenting with feedback training," Montero said. "Leo doesn't simply float. He has to *will* himself to float—i.e., create zeta waves to . . ." Montero frowned. "Did I just say 'i.e.'?"

"You did indeed," Laura said.

"Sorry. Rick, if I do that again, please shoot me."

Rick deadpanned, "With pleasure."

"Not fatally, of course."

"Of course. What about 'e.g.'?"

"That would deserve two wounds."

"Got it."

Laura looked between the two of them. "Have you two known each other long?"

"This is maybe the third time we've met," Rick said. "But multiple near-death-by-auto experiences with Doctor Earnhardt Junior here tend to accelerate the bonding process."

"I drive just fine," Montero said. "Anyway, I set up the EEG display so that Leo can watch his zeta waves while he levitates. The idea is to increase their amplitude. He could levitate only sixteen inches tops when he arrived. Now he's up to—"

Leo grinned. "Twenty-two!"

That's it? Laura thought. Just twenty-two inches?

Wait. What am I *thinking*? Even an inch is amazing.

"So maybe that means it's a learnable skill?" Rick said.

Montero nodded enthusiastically. "Exactly what I'm hoping." He patted Leo on the back. "Keep working on it."

"Can I ask you something, Leo?" Rick said. "This is an incredible talent, gift, whatever. And I do mean 'incredible' because I'm seeing it and still not believing it. Why aren't you world-famous?"

"I don't want to be," Leo said. "I want to keep this to myself."

"You mean, nobody knows about this?"

"My parents do. My mother caught me one day in high school when she came home from work early."

Rick grinned. "Most teenage boys get caught doing something else."

"This is almost as much fun!" Leo said through a laugh. "She caught me a couple of times and wanted me to do it for our neighbors, but I never would. She'd call them in but I'd pretend I didn't know what she was talking about. You know, like that singing-dancing frog in the cartoon?"

"*One Froggy Evening*, sure."

Leo's eyes widened. "You know the *title*?"

"It's sort of his thing," Laura said. She looked at Montero. "What next?"

"We have only one other nadaný here this morning, but Ruth is truly amazing. She teleports."

Laura stopped in midstride. "You're serious?"

"Very. But she's . . . difficult."

Rick said, "Stahlman mentioned her last night. Said she hates her gift and doesn't want to use it."

"Well, I wouldn't say she 'hates' it, exactly, but she's less than enthusiastic about using it." He lowered his voice. "Add to that her noncompliant personality and her general downer mood—"

"Downer?"

"Sort of makes Sylvia Plath look like Miley Cyrus."

"Okaaaaay."

"One thing all the nadaný have in common is a deep inhibition about going public with their gift. They want to keep it to themselves."

"Leo doesn't look too shy," Rick said.

"Here they let loose. They're among others with gifts, so they relax. Except Ruthie."

"Doesn't she like the way it feels?" Laura said.

"It's not that. She says there's no pain, no vertigo, not even a sense of movement."

"But she can really do it? Disappear here and appear there?"

"Only if 'there' is a place she's been before."

"Then what's the problem?"

"She can only teleport herself."

"So?"

"All clothing and jewelry she's wearing gets left behind. Which means she arrives nude as a jaybird. And since she's only nineteen, with body issues, and more than a little shy . . . well, you get the picture."

"Oh, my."

"Right. Oh, my."

Ruth

Montero stopped outside a curtained area. "Ruthie?" he called. "Coming in with company."

"Reeeally?"

Laura could almost hear an eye roll.

Montero parted the curtain to reveal two young women, one a chunky African American, one a slim Hispanic, both in gray sweat suits. The latter was seated, eating pink cotton candy—which Laura had never liked because it looked like attic insulation on a stick—while the former stood behind her, braiding her hair into two long pigtails.

"Iggy," Montero said to the Hispanic girl. "I wasn't expecting you here."

"Just hanging out. I spent the night." Slim and kind of pretty, she'd bleached her hair to a bright orange.

He introduced the braider as Ruth Jones and the braidee as Igdalia Ortiz, whom everyone called Iggy.

"I've brought Doctor Fanning so you can show her your gift."

"Ain't in the mood."

"One of those days?" Laura said, trying to sound understanding. "I get them too. More than usual lately."

Now why had she said that, true though it might be?

Ruth looked at Laura. "Where you get those eyes?"

Laura was used to the question. Her pale blue eyes didn't go with her dark skin and black hair. They seemed to pop right out of her face.

"My dad helped."

"But you're like, what—Mexican?"

"Mayan. Well, half."

Ruth's dark eyes widened. "You mean like those people with the calendar that was supposed to end the world?"

"We did the Long Count calendar, yes." A nice, noncommittal response. She wasn't going to get into that end-of-the-world nonsense. "We were there before it was Mexico."

"And you a doctor too?" she said, as if the two were mutually exclusive.

Laura nodded. "For some time now."

"What kind? You a real doctor, like an M.D., or a phud like him?" She jerked her head toward Montero.

Laura said, "I'm a medical examiner." Wrong! She hadn't meant to say that, it just slipped out.

Ruth made a face. "You mean you cut up dead people? You think I'm gonna die or something?"

Everybody's going to die sooner or later sprang to her lips but she bit it back.

"No-no-no. I'm quitting that and I'm going to be studying the human brain."

"Yeah? You think you can tell me why my brain does crazy stuff? Because *he* can't." Another head jerk.

Apparently she had issues with Dr. Montero.

"Show me this crazy stuff," Laura said. "Please?"

"Told you already. Ain't in the mood."

Laura tried another tack. "Okay. Fair enough. How about you tell me when you discovered your gift? Can you do that?"

"Why you wanna know?"

"Well, if I can figure out how you do it, maybe I can learn how to do it myself. I'd love to be able to leave one place and instantly wind up in another."

"Don't be so sure," she said, shaking her head. "Not when you always wind up in your birthday suit."

Iggy apparently thought this was funny. She laughed and slapped Ruth on the leg.

Laura smiled. "Yeah, I can see how that would be a drawback. But when did you first do it?"

"About three years ago. I was a soph and this senior guy asked me if I wanted to go see the new *Star Wars* and I said sure." She plucked at her sweat suit. "I wasn't a tub of lard back then. I was hot, know what I mean? So anyway, after the movie we stop at this party at his friend's house and they all drinking and smoking and suddenly he and his friend pull me into this bedroom and they're both all over me and I can't get away and they start pulling off my clothes and I scream and nobody hears me and I'm looking for some way to get outta there when alla sudden I'm back in my bedroom. I ain't got a stitch of clothes on, but I'm safe in my bedroom."

Stress trigger, Laura thought.

"So after that, you found out you could do it whenever you wanted?"

"Yeah. I checked it out from the girls' locker room at school and the dressing room at the Y pool. I had to pick places where a pile of clothes wasn't gonna freak nobody out."

"Clever girl," Laura said, meaning it. "And I'm guessing you always headed back to your bedroom?"

Her eyes widened. "I wasn't gonna show up nowheres else buck naked!"

Iggy laughed again and Laura joined her.

"Won't you show me? Just once?"

Ruth rolled her eyes. "Oh, okay. Just once."

"Ooh, yes!" Iggy said, bouncing up and down and clapping her hands like a little kid. "But put on the makeup!"

"No."

"Y'gotta put on the makeup! I love when you have makeup!"

What was this all about?

Another eye roll. "A'ight."

Iggy pulled some blush from a bag on the floor and brushed a thick coat onto Ruth's cheeks and forehead. It looked hideous.

Weirder and weirder.

"Where are you going?" Montero said.

"My place."

"Ruth lives in one of the upstairs apartments," Montero explained.

Ruth looked at Laura. "Ready?"

Iggy was bouncing and clapping again. "Oh, this is so cool!"

And then with a *shoop* of air rushing into a vacuum, Ruth was gone, leaving a mist of blush swirling in the air where her face had been, as her empty sweat suit, bra, and panties dropped onto her equally empty sneakers.

"Holy crap!" Rick said.

Laura gaped at the pile of clothing. My sentiments exactly.

"Isn't that cool?" Iggy was grinning and pointing to the settling mist of blush. "Look at the makeup! I love how she leaves the makeup!"

Laura said, "That. Is. Amazing. She's upstairs now?"

Montero nodded. "She should be down in a minute after she gets dressed."

Laura stared again at the pile of clothing, trying to process it all. Apparently Ruth had gained considerable weight since the first time. A defense against predatory boys? Or maybe an attempt to weigh too much to teleport—if that were even possible.

"She prefers to live here?"

Montero said, "Issues with her stepdad, I think."

"Yeah, he's a beast," Iggy said as she started bundling up Ruth's fallen clothes.

Rick said, "What's your gift, Iggy?"

Iggy shrugged her slim shoulders. "Ain't got one."

"Not that you know of," Montero said. "Marie says you're a nadaný and she hasn't been wrong yet." He turned to Laura. "Iggy's EEG shows steady, low-amplitude zeta waves. *Something* is going on in there, we just don't know what."

Iggy smiled. "When you find out, you let me know, okay?"

Ruth reappeared, this time in a black sweat suit. She looked around with a sour smile. "Happy?"

"Impressed as all hell," Rick said.

"Absolutely amazed," Laura said. "You can do that any time you want?"

She nodded. "Uh-huh. Although I usually *don't* want. I mean, think about it: How many times a day you wanna get dressed? And I especially don't wanna when I'm on the rag."

Behind her, Rick made a little choking noise.

Laura said, "What's different then?"

"Embarrassing enough I gotta leave all my clothes behind, but a bloody tampon too? Uh-uh!"

"TMI," Rick muttered. "TMI."

Ruth must have heard him because she burst out laughing. "I like this guy! You two got a thing goin'?"

"Used to."

"What happened?"

She glanced at Rick, who looked acutely uncomfortable. "I guess you could say we drifted apart."

"But you still like him though, right?"

"Like him? I love him."

Silence as the words hung in the air.

Why did I say that?

No, *why* wasn't the right question. *How?* How had that come out? She'd intended to say, *Like him? Of course I like him.* And that would have been true. But not the whole truth.

Rick's expression showed shock and disbelief, like he didn't believe what he'd heard.

"You mean that?"

She realized she did. She hadn't truly known how she'd felt—or maybe hadn't admitted it to herself—until she'd blurted it out.

"Of course I mean it. That doesn't mean I can live with you."

He frowned. "Well, there's that."

"Maybe we should continue this another time?"

"Yes," Montero said with a bemused expression. "Let's head back to the office."

"Great idea," Laura said.

She led the way, feeling as if everyone's eyes were on her. And maybe they were.

2

"How many nadaný have you found?" Laura said.

She'd regained her composure during the brief walk back to the office. She remained flummoxed at the way her mouth had run off on its own, but she'd managed to put all that aside until later. She needed to stay in the moment here.

Someone had brought in extra chairs while she and Rick were taking the tour, so now Rick, Montero, and Marie sat before Stahlman's rickety desk, with the boss himself behind it.

"Ellis makes ten," Stahlman said. "Ten so far."

"They all seem so young," Rick said. "Is anyone over thirty?"

Marie raised her hand. "I am thirty-one."

"Marie is our oldest," Montero said. "We had a sixteen-year-old turn up with her mother. She can 'read' things."

"Meaning?" Rick said.

"You can hand her a shoe or an earring or a pen and she can tell you where it's been for the past day or two and even a vague idea of who it belongs to. She can tell things about people too."

"Wow." Rick's tone dripped sarcasm.

"I can see a definite forensic use for that," Laura said.

She wished he'd stop staring at her.

"I suppose so," he said with a shrug, then turned to Stahlman. "But somehow I don't see a mutant crime-fighting team in your future, Professor X."

Stahlman made a sour face. "More like Professor Z. And you know damn well I'm not that civic-minded. Besides, we have NYPD to fight crime around here."

"Granted. But I hope you and Luis here won't get offended when I say that, except for Ruth, if there's one thing these nadaný have in common it's how *puny* their gifts are."

"Oh, I wouldn't say that," Montero said.

"Come on, let's face it. They look more like magic tricks than mutant powers. I mean, Leo can levitate, but only twenty inches. Ellis can manipulate pool and roulette balls and not much else. What about that kid you told me about—the one who can generate heat from his hands?"

"Sam, yeah."

"Let me guess: not exactly the Human Torch, right?"

Stahlman gave a chagrined sigh. "He can brown toast."

"I rest my case."

"You're missing the point," Laura said. "It's not the *extent* of their powers, it's the *existence* of those powers. And judging from what Doctor Montero showed me—"

"Luis, please."

"Okay. Based on what you showed me, their gifts are definitely linked to the brain. And that means I want in." She tapped the desktop with each word. "I. Want. In."

Stahlman raised a victory fist. "Great. I was hoping you'd come on board. You're my good luck charm."

"Let's not get carried away."

"You know what I mean."

Laura did: The *ikhar* she'd tracked down had given him back his health and his life. He was lucky she'd found it. *She* was even luckier she'd found it.

"Be that as it may, can someone get me up to speed? Can someone tell me what your nadaný have in common, besides zeta waves?"

"I can," Montero said, tapping on his tablet. "The nadaný we know fall within a fifteen-year age range, from sixteen to thirty-one. MR brain scans on the eight we've done show no abnormalities. We've sequenced the genomes of three so far and found no matching anomalies."

"Why only three?" Rick said.

"In-depth sequencing takes time, especially when you don't know what you're looking for. The analyses you get through Ancestry-dot-com and the like are superficial. These were very detailed, then we compared them for matching anomalies. The result: *nada*. Which was pretty much as I expected, so I called off further DNA testing."

Laura didn't follow. "What made you think—?"

Montero shrugged. "Just a hunch. None of them discovered their gifts until they hit puberty. Which hints that they're developmental."

"All ten?"

"Well, Ellis is twenty-six and he didn't realize he was telekinetic until yesterday."

They seemed to be striking out everywhere.

"What about geography? Are all ten New Yorkers?"

He shook his head. "Only four. And born in different hospitals. Marie was born in Coney Island, Ellis in Maimonides, and Ruthie and our mysterious Iggy in Kings County."

"All Brooklyn," Rick said.

Luis was nodding. "You might be tempted to make a case for Brooklyn until you look at the other six. They were born all over the country: one each in Atlanta, Compton, New Orleans, and Chicago, and two in St. Louis."

"All urban," Rick said, frowning. "No suburban nadaný? Marie? You grew up in Coney Island?"

"Brighton Beach. My parents moved there from Bushwick shortly before I was born."

Luis said, "So far the nadaný are mostly nonwhite—three blacks, five Hispanics, with Marie and Ellis as the only two Caucasians."

"It looks totally random," Rick said. A smile played around his lips as he turned his gaze on Laura and adopted a portentous tone. "Which leaves us . . ."

Stahlman laughed and finished for him. "ICE?"

She had to smile. Rick's Intrusive Cosmic Entities.

"Somehow I knew you'd bring us there eventually."

Montero and Marie looked totally confused, and rightfully so.

"I'm missing something here," Montero said.

"Later," Rick told him.

Laura added, "Much later. But in the meantime, I want to check on prenatal care. We know the birth hospitals were different, but maybe we can find some sort of overlap in their obstetrical care."

"I'm thinking the key to all this is neuroelectrical," Montero said.

"I'm not disagreeing. The key to the mechanism of the gifts is definitely neuroelectrical. But the consistency of those zeta waves from nadaný to nadaný hints at a common origin. Finding that could answer a ton of crucial questions."

"Put her to work, Luis," Rick said. "She's a forensics whiz."

"Okay. I can go with that. You take the epidemiological end and I'll stick with their brains. If we ever figure this out, we'll publish together. Deal?"

Laura nodded. "Deal."

Yes, deal! Her name on a paper like this would open countless doors in the worlds of clinical and academic neurology.

But publication or no, these nadaný had piqued her interest. Piqued, hell—they fascinated her to no end. They'd started her forensics juices flowing full force. They were all linked, these nadaný, and she was going to find out how.

3

As the impromptu meeting ended, Marie leaned over the desk, talking to Stahlman while Laura and Montero had their heads together by the door. Rick didn't want to interrupt, so he hung back. But he had to talk to her.

Like him? I love him . . .

His head spun. She'd admitted she loved him, right in front of everyone. That wasn't at all like her. Not the kind to say that even in private. Back when they'd been close—okay, intimate—they'd agreed they weren't ready for the L word, even though he'd known he was already there.

"Mister Hayden?" Stahlman said. "I wonder if I might prevail upon you to accompany Miss Novotna to a mattress shop on Queens Boulevard."

Most bosses would say do this and do that, but Stahlman was always wondering if he could prevail or if he might ask. "If" left the door open for a refusal, but nobody walked through that door. Well, Rick hadn't. Not yet, at least, although he was tempted to this time. He needed to talk to Laura. Like now.

"What's up?"

"I live in Sunnyside," she said. "The last two nights now I have walked by the mattress store on Queens Boulevard and sensed a nadaný inside."

Stahlman said, "Why don't you take her over there and see what's what?"

Sunnyside sat directly east of Long Island City. They could probably walk there, but he wasn't about to try that.

Rick spotted Laura heading back onto the main floor with Montero. He'd have to catch her later.

"Sure." He jerked his head toward the door. "Let's go grab some wheels."

On the way to the garage, he saw Laura talking to Cyrus and jotting on a notepad. He found Reise in the garage, getting into his red Kia.

"Where you headed?" Rick said.

"Back to my place. Stahlman said I could stay here, and I tried it last night, but I'd rather be home."

"What about a certain guy who likes donuts."

"Not a problem. They don't know where I live."

"Don't count on it." Rick thought a second. "Do yourself a favor and cab it over."

"I need my car."

"They *know* your car. Before you get out, have the

cab cruise the street to see if anyone's watching your place."

"Whatta you care?"

"Saving your ass last night made me a few enemies. I don't need enemies. And I especially don't need them following you back here—assuming they don't finish you off on the spot."

Rick left him chewing his upper lip.

Once Rick and Marie were belted into a pickup and rolling, he said, "So, you live in Sunnyside?"

"I rent part of a three-family home there. I work at the Boston Market down the street from Slumber Party."

"No kidding? Slumber Party? That's what it calls itself?"

"That is what the sign says. I walk past on my way home. Today is my day off."

"You have a bit of an accent," Rick said. "Ukraine?"

She laughed. "Yes! Very good. How did you guess?"

"Just lucky."

Not really. When he was assigned to Europe, the Company had trained him to differentiate the nuances of accented English. He hadn't been all that good at it, but Marie's mention of growing up in Brighton Beach—known as "Little Odessa"—had provided an excellent clue.

"I was born here a year and a half after my parents arrived, so I grew up bilingual."

He turned onto Queens Boulevard and cruised beside the elevated subway tracks, passing the usual assortment of New York stores: a pawnshop, Starbucks, Duane Reade, Pearle Vision, GameStop. Finally *Slumber Party* in big red letters at the end of a strip mall. A sign said parking in the rear so he pulled around.

"You sense anyone now?" Rick said as he eased into a spot.

She shook her head. "No. He's somewhere to the west."

"'He'? You can tell the sex?"

"No. Just a generic 'he.' Could be a woman. By the way, did I mention that both times I passed, the store was closed?"

"No, you didn't."

"Sorry."

"Not a problem, but it does change our approach."

Rick sat a moment, working through various ways to handle this. The place was too small to rate a night watchman. Someone working late, maybe? Finally . . .

"Okay, let's not mention that we know someone was in there after hours. My business card says 'security,' so we'll let the manager or whoever think I'm looking to sell him a system."

"Do you?"

"What? Sell security systems? No. No systems, just security." He turned off the truck. "I'll do most of the talking, but when I ask you for input, you ask about a night watchman."

Slumber Party had a rear entrance and they used that. The door gave off a high-pitched *ding!* when opened. A slim young man in a white half-sleeve shirt immediately approached them.

"Can I help you? You're just in time for our fall sale."

"Looking for the manager or the owner, actually," Rick said. "That be you?"

"I'm the only one here at the moment, so I guess I'll have to do. What can I do for you?"

Rick had his card ready and handed it over. "Wondering how you're fixed for security here. I can put you online with a new system or upgrade the one you have to state of the art, all at a very reasonable price."

"I'm in sales," he said, "so that's not a decision I can make. But we've got door and window alarms, and cameras too."

"CCTV?" Rick said, stepping into the center of the showroom.

He spotted a camera at each end of the rectangular space. He looked for wires leading from the cameras but didn't see any. He stepped to the front door and pushed it open. Same *ding!* as the rear.

"Wi-fi cameras, I take it?" he said when he returned to the salesman.

The salesman shrugged. "I guess so. Like I said, I'm in sales."

Wi-fi CCTV was good news—a point of entry.

Rick turned to Marie. "Anything I miss?"

She showed the salesman a bright smile. "We can provide a night watchman if desired."

"Night watchman?" He almost laughed. "Oh, I hardly think so."

Rick expected her to stop there, but she pressed on. "Do you have anyone stay after hours? An accountant, perhaps, you know, doing the books? Or maybe a cleaning service?"

He frowned now. "Hey, what is this? You two sound like you're casing the joint."

In a sense that was exactly what they were doing, but Marie had gone a tad too far and set off an alarm bell in the salesman. Rick needed to shut it off. He forced a laugh.

"My assistant is just thinking about motion detectors. After-hours help tends to present problems for

them. We don't see any installed and we usually in-
clude them in a proposal."

"Whoa-whoa-whoa!" the salesman said. "Let's
not get ahead of ourselves here. The owner will be in
later. I'll give him your card."

"Good man. Tell him to give me a call. I'll make it
worth his while."

"Yeah, I'll be sure to do that."

Outside, Marie said, "Do you think he'll call?"

"Not in a million years."

"Did I say too much?"

She had, but she was new at this.

"You did just fine. But it points up a puzzling question: What's our mystery nadaný doing in there after
the place is closed?"

"Sleeping?" Marie said with a smile.

Rick laughed. "Sounds logical, but it's gotta be
something more than that."

4

Laura spotted Rick and Marie heading across the
floor toward Stahlman's office. She wanted to talk to
Marie but still felt embarrassed about her bald-faced
declaration of love for Rick. She didn't understand
how it happened, but what was done was done, and
she'd just have to deal with it.

And deep in her heart she was glad for her blurt.
She'd have kept silent if she'd had time to think.

Rick spotted her and stopped and waited while
Marie went on ahead.

"We need to talk," he said.

"We do indeed. Maybe we can find a coffee shop."

"Great. Marie and I have got to update Stahlman first."

"So do I. Let's go together."

Just then Ellis stepped out of the office.

"Good call on that cab," he told Rick. "I did the cruise-by and recognized a guy in a car across the street from my place. That's the second time you've saved my ass."

"So, you're gonna move in here?"

"Don't see as I have much choice. I still need to fig-ure a way to get some things from my pad, though." His eyes lit as Iggy walked by with a smile and a wave. "Then again, when someone hands you a lemon . . ."

He strolled off after Iggy.

"I sense trouble brewing," Laura said.

Rick gave a little laugh. "On the plus side, I don't think he's Iggy's type, and even if he was, nobody likes him much."

Laura counted herself among that number.

As they entered the office, Stahlman said, "Marie has already briefed me on the mattress store. Where do we go from here?"

Laura wasn't sure exactly what they were talking about, but she made quick inferences from the con-versation.

"She's sensed the nadaný there after hours only," Rick said. "They've got two security cameras on a wi-fi system, probably backed up to the cloud. Kevin shouldn't have a big problem hacking into their sys-tem and—"

"Who's Kevin?" Laura said.

"Kevin Hudson," Stahlman said. "He sets up and maintains all my computers."

"Used to be a hacker," Rick said. "Got arrested

once but slipped through on a technicality. After that he decided to go straight." He smiled and glanced at Stahlman. "But he still gets off on hacking a system once in a while. The wi-fi should make this hack easy peasy. If we can get copies of the security feeds from last night and the night before, we should be able to identify our nadaný."

Stahlman made a show of rubbing his hands together. "Covert action. Espionage. I love it. And the best part is finding out what kind of gift he has, because you never know. I'll get Kevin right on it."

Rick said, "Tell him he can park behind the store and nose up to the rear wall. Should be no problem tapping into the wi-fi from there."

As Stahlman reached for his iPhone, Laura said, "Wait a sec. Just want to let you know I'm getting a line on prenatal care for the nadaný. I'm not going to even bother contacting the hospitals about who their mothers used for OBs. HIPAA laws keep all records zipped unless there's written consent, and even then the turnaround time can be next to forever. So I'm going straight to the mothers."

"Good luck with Iggy. Both her folks are dead. She lives with an aunt and uncle who have five kids. That's why she's here all the time."

"Are she and Ruthie a couple?"

Stahlman shrugged. "I don't know. Does it matter?"

"I don't care if they're straight or gay," Laura said, "but Ruth is prickly and if I can avoid stepping on her toes in any way . . ."

"Ruth has mama's-boyfriend issues—seems he's a bit too touchy-feely. So I offered her one of the upstairs apartments."

Laura checked her notes. "Ruthie knows where she was born but nothing about her mama's prenatal care. Same with Leo, Cyrus, and Ellis. They're calling home now."

Leo had been raised in Compton, L.A., and born in Martin Luther King Hospital there. Cyrus grew up in NOLA's Ninth Ward and was born in LSU's medical center. Ellis was a local—Maimonides.

"Marie?" Laura said. "Could you call your mom and ask her where she received her prenatal care? Somewhere in the Coney Island–Brighton Beach area, I imagine."

She shook her head. "I don't know where, but it had to be in Bushwick. My folks moved to Brighton Beach just weeks before I was born. I'll ask her."

"Great." Laura checked off Marie's name. "I've got a good sample now. If I don't find any correlation between these five, most likely there isn't one to be found."

"Keep me posted," Stahlman said, tapping his phone.

Laura glanced at Rick, who pantomimed drinking from a coffee cup. She nodded.

"Rick and I are going out for a bit. Be back later."

Phone to his ear, Stahlman waved them off.

They wove their way among the curtained-off areas, waving to Luis as they passed.

"I spotted a Starbucks up on Queens Boulevard a little while ago," Rick said as they reached the pickup truck he was using.

Laura had been drinking coffee all morning, leaving her stomach a little sour.

"I think I'm coffeed out. How about we just drive? You can pick up a coffee along the way if you like."

"Nah. I'm good."

Out on the street, traffic was stop-and-go, but they had no destination.

"Thanks for asking me aboard," she said, wanting to put off the Inevitable Topic for a while. "This is going to be totally fascinating."

"Working with living people . . . good warmup for your residency." He cleared his throat and Laura thought, *Okay, here it comes,* but instead he said, "Did you ever consider that moving to living patients is moving toward chaos?"

"What are you talking about?"

"You've spent your career with dead people. Dead people are linear equations. Whatever butterfly effects they've experienced in their lives are done, finished, because they're static. Living folks, on the other hand, are nonlinear equations. They're prime targets for chaos effects because they're enormously complex systems that are sensitive and extremely dependent on initial conditions."

She had to admit she missed Rick's out-of-left-field observations, and she could see immediately how right this one was.

"As a matter of fact, I recently autopsied an example of just that: a young man with Marfan syndrome."

"The tall, skinny folks?"

"Exactly. A perfect example of the butterfly effect—what did you just say it was?"

"Sensitive dependence on initial conditions."

"That's what happens in genetics, because so many of our twenty-thousand-plus genes are interdependent, and the wrong amino acid in the wrong place in a single gene can have huge effects down the line. Marfan folks have a single out-of-place amino acid within the FBN1 gene on chromosome fifteen, affecting production of one of the body's elastic fibers.

They often show no signs at birth, but as that body grows, all sorts of changes become evident."

Rick said, "For want of a nail, a shoe was lost . . . for want of a shoe . . ."

"They call it 'chaos,' but as far as I can see, it's deterministic as all get-out."

"You got it. The ICE method, that's their MO."

She groaned. "Back to them again?"

"They fit right in. Chaos works best on complex systems because they're very sensitive to initial conditions, very dependent on them. And what's more complex—and nonlinear, to boot—than a civilization? So ICE test the butterfly effect of a panacea like the ikhar on human civilization."

"How's the ikhar have a butterfly effect?"

"Think about it. How can a panacea *not* have one? Here you've got this developing human civilization, merrily going its own way, and along comes an ICE and, just for kicks, changes just one thing: It gives these folks the ability to cure any illness and watches to see what effects that will have down the line in this huge complex system called human civilization. The result will be a civilization totally different from what we see today."

Laura couldn't help a chagrined smile. "Not much call for doctors."

"Not to worry. They'd still need medical examiners. But then, when all that's established, another ICE—maybe one with a mean streak—decides just for the pure hell of it to pull the rug out and make the panacea stop working. Diseases now go unchecked and everything falls into ruin because the panacea has left everyone unprepared to deal with disease."

"Pretty malicious."

"Don't forget: To them we might be fascinating little sapient bugs, but we're still bugs. I can see the same butterfly scenario with that creativity gene the dapis were carrying."

"Hsa-mir-3998." Laura surprised and pleased herself at being able to remember.

"I'll have to take your word on that. It deserted my brain months ago. But anyway, an ICE gets the idea of adding a creativity gene like hsa-whatever to a hominid species to see what will develop." He pounded his chest, gorilla style. "*We* happened."

"You really think the nadaný might be an ICE scheme?"

"For me? Yes—until proven otherwise. And I say that because they shouldn't be able to do what they do. In other words, they shouldn't *be*. Just like the ikhar shouldn't be, and the dapi shouldn't be."

They'd passed through the warehouse warren, then continued along 48th Avenue past the upscale high-rise apartments until they came to a small park that overlooked the East River. Midtown Manhattan rose on the other side, with the UN Secretariat building dominating the view. Rick ad-libbed a parking space that faced the view and turned off the engine.

"Isn't that huge Pepsi-Cola sign somewhere around here?" Laura asked.

"Off to the right. Wanna see it? Doesn't look like much from the back end."

"No. This is fine."

Rick twisted in his seat to face her. "Sooo," he said, drawing out the word. "Shall we discuss the elephant in the room?"

Here we go.

"Whatever do you mean? Certainly not my professing my undying love for you in front of strangers?"

"Don't remember the 'undying' part, but you came pretty close to knocking me off my feet. I mean, I thought we were kaput. What on Earth—?"

"—possessed me to say it? I have absolutely no idea. When Ruth asked me if I still liked you, I intended to say something like, 'Absolutely. He's a great guy who'll never let you down.' But something else came out."

"Right. You said, 'Like him? I love him.' Or something like that."

She laughed. "*Exactly* like that. What'd you do, memorize it?"

"Didn't have to. It's etched on my brain. Is it true?"

Laura leaned back against the headrest and sighed. "Yeah, I suppose it is."

"Then why—?"

"—are we apart instead of together? Me. All me. And please don't ask for an explanation, because I don't have one."

"I do. Düsseldorf."

"Yeah, okay, Düsseldorf."

"Pardon the cliché, but I can't change the past, Laura."

"I know that. And it might not have become an issue if we'd been able to stay together in Mozambique and right after."

But she'd had to return home to Marissa while Rick was mired in dealing with the suspicious circumstances of his brother's death, and then shipping the body back to Long Island once it was released. He'd been tied up for weeks in Africa while she'd been home safe and sound. That time alone had played a big part in the unraveling of their relationship.

"While we were apart," she said, "the Düsseldorf thing kept expanding like some toxic cloud, poisoning everything. You weren't there to counteract it and it just sort of took over."

"But you just said . . ."

"Don't ask me for a logical, sensible explanation, Rick, because I don't have one."

"Okay. You 'suppose' you love me. I know I love you, and I can't undo Düsseldorf. Where do we go from here?"

"Nowhere."

He blinked. "I don't get it."

"Just because I have deep feelings for you doesn't mean it will work. It doesn't mean I can live with you. You've done things that I'm not sure I can get over. I need *normal* inside my house, Rick. Marissa needs—"

"Marissa? We get along great."

"I know you do. But she needs to grow up with normal concerns—her friends, her school, the Mets— not worrying about whatever's Out There."

"Why would she?"

"Because she adores you, and you . . . you view the world differently from other people, and I don't see how she can avoid picking up on that."

"So . . . I'm gonna *infect* her?"

"Don't put it like that. It's just that you . . . you bring the Outside inside."

"And you don't? Has Clotilde sent you your next dose of ikhar?"

"Yes, but what's that got to do—?"

"And where are you keeping it?"

"Hidden in a cabinet, but that's not—"

"Not the same? The ikhar is from Outside—you know that as well as I do—and you've brought it inside."

"But it'll be gone soon."

"You mean, as soon as you effect another miracle cure."

"Right. But that will happen *out of the house*."

"But not out of your head. And what we learned on that island off Madagascar . . . is that out of your head? By now you know as well as I do that the world is not what we think it is, that all sorts of things nobody has a clue about are playing out behind the scenes. Face it, Laura: As far as your house is concerned, as long as you're there, the Outside is already inside."

Was he right?

The pickup's cab suddenly seemed very stuffy. She rolled down her window.

"You okay?" Rick said.

Her mind whirled. She felt bad for him. She felt bad for herself. She felt bad for *them*.

"I need to get back."

He was silent a moment, then he started the truck.

"Okay," he said softly.

5

Heart heavy, Rick watched Laura drive off.

After cruising the crowded streets in silence, he'd brought her to her car so she could get home in time for Marissa's return from school.

He thought about how things would be so different now if he hadn't come straight with her about Düsseldorf. But how could he not? He'd lived lies for years. He was through with that.

As he crossed the floor he spotted Kevin fiddling by the flat-screen TV on the wall outside Stahlman's office.

"Heading over to the mattress place?" Rick said as he approached.

Kevin looked up and smiled. "Hey, Rick. Been there and back."

"Already?"

"Never had it so easy. Guess the Slumber Party's wi-fi password."

Rick hated guessing games, but . . . "Okay. You're gonna tell me it's 'password,' right?"

"Even worse. Ever see *Spaceballs*?"

On a different day, Rick might have laughed. "One-two-three-four-five? No way."

"Yes way."

"You get the camera feeds?"

"Yep. Cloud storage, twelve-hour files, midnight to noon, and noon to midnight, archived for two weeks, then dumped. So I copied the two days you wanted, and this morning as well."

"Excellent."

"Um, what exactly are you looking for?"

"Not sure." Something in Kevin's tone . . . "You see something?"

He shrugged. "I was fast-forwarding through to check on the quality and thought I saw weirdness."

Weirdness . . . his life was weirdness.

"Like what?"

"I'll let you see for yourself. Stahlman wanted a look too."

He stepped over to the office door and stuck his head inside. Seconds later the boss man emerged with Marie. Kevin had his laptop hooked up to the monitor and a tiny remote in his hand.

"Okay. This is the morning feed two days ago from the camera on the eastern wall. I'm going to run it fast."

A dim image of the mattress showroom appeared,

a digital time counter running in the lower right corner. Everything looked exactly as Rick remembered except—

"Wait-wait-wait," he said. "Can you stop it?" When Kevin did, Rick stepped closer to the screen. "Is there someone in that bed?"

The queen bed at the lower end of the frame didn't look right. An oblong, human-size lump huddled under the covers; the covers were pulled up high, leaving only a shock of dark hair visible on the pillow.

Stahlman and Marie came up beside him.

"Damned if there isn't," Stahlman said.

Rick said to Marie, "That's the night you sensed a nadaný in there, right?"

"Yes."

Kevin laughed. "As the infomercials say, 'But wait, there's more.'"

The digital clock started racing again. The store brightened as light from the rising sun leaked through the big front windows.

As the clock neared seven A.M., Kevin said, "If I remember, it happened around now."

The clock slowed. Rick stared at the bed and saw the hair disappear. Then the covers flew back to reveal an empty bed. After a few seconds, the bed started to make itself.

"Holy crap!" Rick said.

Stahlman started laughing. "Well, well, well! Our mystery nadaný is an invisible man! I want him!"

"But why does he sleep in a mattress store?" Marie said.

Rick could think of only one reason. "I'm guessing he's homeless."

"Perfect!" Stahlman said. "We'll offer him a generous stipend and a place to live. How can he refuse?" He pointed to Rick and Marie. "I'm putting you two in charge of bringing him in."

Rick hid his dismay. He'd hoped, after Laura's earlier declaration, that he'd be hanging at the Fanning house tonight. Yeah, right.

"Sure, why not?" Nothing better to do. "We'll apprehend him on sight."

Stahlman blinked, then laughed again. "Very good, Mister Hayden! Excellent, in fact. Do your very best."

6

Rick checked the dashboard clock. "Fifteen minutes to closing."

He'd nosed the truck into a parking space in the lot under the subway trestle that ran down the center of Queens Boulevard. The space sat directly across the street from Slumber Party's front door. He'd checked the store hours on their earlier visit. Tuesday through Saturday they closed at eight P.M.

"Are you all right?" Marie said.

"Yeah. Fine. Why?"

"You seem down. You never seem down."

Was it noticeable? Couldn't have that. He was security. Had to be a rock.

"I'm okay. Is he coming?"

"He's close," Marie said.

Rick made a show of peering through the window. "Funny, I don't see him."

She laughed. "I've been thinking. He can't enter visible and then turn invisible. After his second or third time they'd recognize him and wonder what he's up to."

Rick had been thinking the same thing. "Right. He's got to be invisible from the get-go. The doors chime when they open, so he has to sneak in and out with somebody else, then wait around for the last employee to lock up."

Marie said something but was drowned out by the horrendous rattle of the 7 train on the tracks above.

"Sorry. Come again?"

She said, "I'm pretty sure he's in there now, but he could be standing by the front door."

"We'll just wait."

At eight sharp, a middle-aged man locked the front door and headed toward the rear. The overheads in the showroom went out, leaving a night-light at the end of the hallway by the rear entrance as the only illumination. Rick waited an extra five minutes to give the employee time to drive or walk away.

"Okay, Marie. Walk over there and stare through the window for a few minutes."

"Why?"

"I want him to get a good look at you. Because when we do catch up to him—and I'm pretty sure we will—I want him to know your face before you start persuading him to join your nadaný gang."

Marie shrugged. "I'll give it a try."

He watched her cross the boulevard and approach one of the front windows. As she stared into the dark showroom she folded her arms behind her back and gave him a thumbs-up.

Good. The nadaný was in there. They'd be back at opening time tomorrow to see—well, probably not see. They'd find a way to follow him from here.

Rick dropped Marie off at her place, then headed back to the warehouse. As he was pulling in, he saw Ellis Reise pulling out. Rick started to wave but Ellis was looking elsewhere. Deliberately, he thought.

Inside he ran into Iggy and Ruth.

"You gals know where Ellis went?"

Iggy nodded. "Back to his old place to get some things."

Uh-oh.

"You suddenly got a worried look," Ruth said.

"Might run into trouble over there."

Iggy grinned. "He knows, but he say he can handle it. He been studying."

"Studying what?"

"The body. He got a book."

"Anatomy," Ruth said, nodding. "He know all about the neck now."

Shit.

Rick hurried toward Stahlman's office to find Ellis's address. He still had time to stave off disaster.

7

Ellis cruised his block and spotted one of Vinny Donuts's guys parked with a view of his building's front steps. Not the same guy as earlier, but he'd seen this one around. Vinny didn't have a real big crew but Ellis had watched this guy playing pit boss on gambling night. Not that he'd expected Tony or Joey to be waiting, what with the way Rick had busted them up. He wished one of them had come along as backup, though. Didn't matter which—Joey with his wiseass cracks about Ellis's name and his Kia—"we're gonna make kimchi outta your car"—or Tony who'd taped him up and emptied the gas out of his car. The two of them had been all psyched up to stick Ellis and his Kia into the crusher.

Well, Ellis Reise wasn't the same guy as then. Ellis Reise had learned a few things about himself in the meantime. Not looking for more trouble than he already had, but he wasn't about to run from it either. Not anymore.

He'd considered sneaking in through a back window he knew how to open. But it was tricky and dirty and, seeing as it was just this one guy, he decided to go in the front. Tell the truth, he was just a little ticked they'd sent only one guy. Donato owed him over 400 Gs. Wasn't that worth at least two?

Whatever. Maybe Vinny couldn't spare two guys to sit and wait for someone who might never show up.

Well, here I am, baby. Ellis Reise, in the flesh and in your face.

As usual, no parking spots on his street this time of night. Never were. No matter. He wouldn't be long. He parked in front of a fire hydrant, checked to make sure Vinny's guy saw him, then bounced down the front steps to his basement efficiency apartment. Inside, he pulled the shades and flipped on the lights.

He didn't own a suitcase so he grabbed an old duffel and started stuffing it with clothes and underwear and sneakers and such. He didn't have much so it didn't take long. He was just about finished when he heard the door open and close behind him. He turned to find Donato's guy standing there, twirling a nasty looking knife in his hand. Six-inch blade, easy.

Despite all his preparations, Ellis felt his mouth go dry. This had better work.

"Reise," the guy said with a nasty grin. "I thought Vinny was wasting my time out there. Never dreamed you was stupid enough to come back." The grin widened. "But here you are, right in my lap."

Ellis put on his best game face.

"What's your name?" Ellis said.

"Whatta you care, fuckwad? You ain't gonna need to know where you're goin'."

"I just want to give you a chance, okay? You can turn and go and no hard feelings."

"Really? Ain't that, whatchacall, gratuitous of you."

Ellis didn't think that was the word he meant, but at the moment he couldn't come up with the right one.

With all the confidence in the world, the guy said, "Let's get this over with," and jumped forward.

Then Ellis struck. He'd been checking out the human neck, wondering how he might be able to choke someone without touching him. Easiest would be to crush the windpipe. Karate guys could do that with a punch, but Ellis didn't think his gift was strong enough to crunch all that cartilage.

But the anatomy book had showed him two arteries in the neck—the carotids—like small hoses. If he could squeeze those—press them flat, really—he could cut off the blood supply to someone's brain. Do it long enough and that someone dies.

Ellis did that now. He visualized the arteries running up the inside of the neck and pressed. The guy's face got this sudden funny look, like he knew something was wrong but didn't know what. He stutter-stepped yet kept coming, but slower. Another step and he put his free hand to his throat. He must have felt the pressure there, but on the inside rather than outside, and he knew Ellis wasn't touching him, so he had to be asking himself, *What the fuck, man? What the fuck?*

Ellis backed away but not too far. His gift had a range, and got weaker with distance, and he wanted to keep those carotids as flat as could be.

And now the guy's face was turning white.

That's right, pal. I just shut off the blood flow to your whole head.

His eyes bulged as he realized something was wrong, really seriously *wrong*. He stopped coming for Ellis and dropped the knife so he could use both hands to claw at his throat. Very soon his knees gave out and he landed hard. Ellis swore he heard a knee-cap crack but the guy was too panicked and his brain too blood-starved to notice.

Still pulling at his neck, he fell onto his side, where he lay kicking and squirming, and then just squirming, and then nothing.

Ellis pulled out his phone and checked the time. He hung over the guy and kept up the pressure another full minute before stepping back and dropping onto his ratty sofa. That had taken more out of him than he'd expected.

He stared at the guy who in turn stared at the dirty throw rug. No sign of breathing, not even a muscle twitch.

"I did it!" he whispered to no one. "I fucking did it!"

The door flew open.

Aw, fuck, did Donato send a second guy? No, wait . . .

"Rick?"

Rick spotted the body, froze for a second, then closed the door.

"You didn't!" he said as he squatted beside the guy and checked for a pulse. "Shit, you did!" He shot to his feet, towering over Ellis. "Where are your brains?"

"Fucker tried to kill me! Look—his knife's right there!"

"You could've just knocked him out. You didn't have to kill him."

"Why the hell not?"

"Because he's a made guy who works for Vinny Donuts, you jerk! So now not only does Donato think you cheated him, you went and offed one of his guys! He'll turn this city upside down looking for you!"

"So fucking what? He's already out for my head. What's he gonna do? Kill me twice? And besides, no one can say I killed him."

"And why not?"

"Because there ain't a mark on him. I never touched him. For all anybody knows he had a stroke or a heart attack."

"You think that matters to Donato? His kind aren't exactly into the finer points of forensics. And speaking of forensics, you've now got a dead body in your apartment, which means the cops will be looking for you too. What an idiot!"

"Don't talk to me like that! Nobody talks to me like—"

"Well, what else am I gonna call you? How about a *fucking* idiot?"

That did it. This asshole had no idea who he was dealing with.

Ellis stood. "You think you're so goddamn tough. But you know what? You're the *Titanic* and I'm the fucking iceberg. You're going down, man. *Down!*"

With that he jammed down hard on Rick's carotid arteries. Rick's eyes widened for an instant, then he stepped in and smashed a fist into Ellis's face.

Lights flashed, his ears rang. Ellis tried to reorient himself and apply the pressure again, even harder this time, but his knees were wobbly and his brain felt too scrambled to focus his gift.

Rick's voice seemed to come from far away. "Don't try to pull that shit on me!"

Laura slouched on the couch next to Marissa, pre-tending to watch the Mets game with her, but aware of virtually nothing transpiring on the big LED screen.

Am I doing the right thing? she wondered. Can it be the right when it seems so wrong?

I need normal inside my house . . .

Who am I kidding?

And that stuff I said about bringing the Outside inside—how stupid was that? I've seen things very few people have seen and been places virtually no one else has been. The Outside has taken up residence in-side my head.

"Did you see that, Mom?" Marissa cried. "Every-body shifted right and he pulled that double to left field!"

"Hmmm? What?" Laura had no idea what she was talking about.

"You weren't watching," she said, getting a bit pouty. "I wish Rick was here."

"I do too, honeybunch." Rick had proved far better at feigning interest in the games.

"How come I never see him anymore? He used to come a lot. Is he mad?"

"Oh, no. Anything but. We know he loved the Mets—"

"Metropolitans, Mom," she said with infinite pa-tience.

"Sorry. The Metropolitans." Not. "I know he really wants to be here." True. "It's just . . . it's just that he's awfully busy with his work."

She frowned. "Is it because he's depressed?"

"Depressed?" Where'd she hear about depression? She'd turned nine over the summer, but still . . . "I don't think so. What makes you think he's depressed?"

"I don't know. He just is." Marissa's smile broke through. "But I make him happy. I can tell."

Laura couldn't reply right away . . . couldn't squeeze words past the lump that had formed in her throat.

Yes, you do, she thought. You make him happy. And I'm keeping you two apart.

Marissa filled the silence. "So, next time you see him you tell him I said he should come over for a game. The season will be over soon."

After what she'd said today, Laura didn't know if she could promise that. "I know he wants to, hon." No lie there.

"I miss him, Mom. When he's around I feel . . ."

"Feel what?"

She shrugged. "Like . . . I don't know. Like everything's all right."

What was she trying to say?

"You mean 'safe'?"

Another shrug. "Yeah. I guess."

She stared at her daughter. Well, that said a lot, didn't it. That said pretty damn much everything.

My little work in progress . . . my little state of becoming . . . leukemia knocked the world out from under your feet, and that CMV infection almost delivered the knockout punch. No wonder you don't feel safe, even in your own home—that's where you got sick.

Rick had that power when he was on the scene to make you feel things were under control. Even a nine-year-old could feel it.

Damn me.

"You know what?" She put her arm around Marissa and hugged her near. "You're going to call Rick right now and tell him that he needs to catch a game with his old pal, Marissa."

Marissa's face lit up like a Broadway marquee. "Tonight?"

"No, silly. The game's almost over. He'll never make it in time. But ASAP, okay?"

Marissa hugged her. "Yay!"

9

One hell of a day.

Rick popped the cork on a bottle of Krug and poured half a dozen ounces into a tumbler. Flutes were supposed to be better for Champagne but they didn't hold enough. He'd always been a beer drinker. Never dreamed he'd turn into a bubbly fan, but ya likes whats ya likes. Besides, he could afford it. No one else to spend it on.

Yep, one hell of a day.

First, Laura tells him they've no future. Then the discovery of an invisible man. Then Ellis goes and strangles one of Donato's thugs with his talent. And if that's not enough, he tries the same thing on Rick.

Well, Rick put the kibosh on that, but it revealed something about Ellis—guy was a straight-up psychopath. Not the least bit fazed by killing someone, even if in self-defense. At the very least, the first time left you shaken, changed you, no matter how justified you might think you were. It meant you'd crossed a line, one you could never cross back. You'd taken away someone's tomorrows—all of them.

Hadn't bothered Ellis a bit. Was ready to do it again, to someone he knew, just for calling him out on how stupid he'd been.

Gonna have to watch that guy.

Things had gone a bit smoother after he'd straightened Ellis out on what he could and couldn't get away with, at least with Rick. The two of them had stowed Donato's boy's body in the trunk of his own car and left it parked along the curb. Soon enough the city would tow and impound it. Eventually someone at the lot would notice an odor emanating from the trunk of the unclaimed vehicle.

He'd followed Ellis back to the warehouse, then headed home.

He took a gulp of Champagne, savored the bubbles fizzing down his throat. Yeah, you were supposed to sip and savor the good stuff. Well, to each his own. *My bottle, my Big Gulp.*

The good news was, the nadaný would keep him in contact with Laura. Who knew? Maybe his irresistible charm would break her down.

Then again . . .

He looked around his empty apartment. He was used to empty, used to alone. Good thing, he guessed. Looked like he was going to get more practice. Maybe he should decorate the place a little. The bare walls, the spare furniture . . . serial-killer décor.

His phone rang. The ID said Laura. That couldn't be good. He was pretty sure their I-called-just-to-see-how-you're-doing days were over, so this had to be serious.

"*Hi, Rick!*" Marissa's voice.

Cautious warmth seeped into him. "Hi, Marissa. Everything okay?"

"Yeah! I'm inviting you over to see a Metropolitans game!"

"Hey, that would be—" Be careful here. "Does your mother know you're calling?"

"Yeah, she's right here. Wanna talk to her?"

"Maybe I'd better."

Laura came on. *"Did we interrupt anything?"*

"Not particularly. Thinking of sorting through my thimble collection."

"You don't have a thimble collection."

"It's imaginary. I've always wanted one. Actually I'm sorting through my confusion. Marissa just asked me to—"

"Come over to watch a Mets—"

"Metropolitans!" Marissa cried in the background.

"A Metropolitans game at your earliest convenience. I put her up to it."

Rick was dumbstruck.

"Rick?"

"Sorry, I—did I hear right?"

"You did. And I'm as confused as you are. I was thinking about what you said earlier and you make a good case, so . . . let's see when we can work this out. That is if you can fit a game into your schedule."

"I'll make room."

She spoke away from the phone. *"Honeybunch, you're on."*

A *"Yay!"* from Marissa.

Rick's throat constricted. He loved that kid. Too bad he couldn't work a similar bond with her mother.

"We'll talk tomorrow," Laura said.

"You bet we will."

They ended the call. Rick couldn't help a smile. A little of the hell had just gone out of his day.

THEN

"The Pentagon is extremely impressed with your primate trials, Doctor LaVelle," said Benjamin Greve from his usual position behind the desk in the back office.

Maureen sat stiffly in her chair. After dozens of meetings with the man over the past two-plus years she remained uncomfortable in his cold, serpentine presence.

"The Pentagon? The whole Pentagon? I thought this was hush-hush."

Greve's laugh sounded more like a cough. "Of course not the whole Pentagon. Only a handful of higher-ups are even aware of the existence of melis; even fewer know what it can do."

Well, she was a long way from knowing *all* it could do, but Maureen had proven beyond a doubt that it increased the intelligence of the offspring of melis-treated squirrel monkeys and macaques. Thirty percent increase in the former, and a good fifty percent in the latter.

"We've still got a ways to go."

She'd spent over two years now working with melis and monkeys. Their gestation and developmental periods were so much longer than rats and mice and she found that frustrating. Too much waiting around before the monks were ready for testing.

"A ways to go till when?" Greve said.

"Well, I assume human trials are dancing in someone's head down there in Arlington."

"Like visions of sugarplums."

Knew it. She'd suspected all along where melis was headed and wasn't sure she wanted to be a part of it. Making monkeys smarter, fine. Making children smarter, fine, but not without knowing the mechanism of how their intelligence increased. They'd done all sorts of scans, and even sacrificed a number of the melis offspring without finding any discernible changes.

"Well," she said, "they'll all just have to wait until we do chimp studies, and we haven't even started those."

Greve tapped the desk. "We're bypassing chimps and going straight to humans."

Maureen stiffened in her chair. "You can't do that! It's too soon."

"The higher-ups are impatient. We're all primates and since there's been not a single complication with the monkeys—"

"Moneys and humans occupy two entirely separate branches of evolution. You can't extrapolate."

"Well, it's not your decision. A small trial has been set in motion. We will be using federal prisoners."

"You mean *pregnant* federal prisoners." Maureen felt queasy.

"Of course. That's the whole point."

"How are you going to get them to agree? Shorten their sentences?"

His eyes widened behind his wire-rimmed glasses.

"Agree? Only a handful of people will know about this, certainly not the prisoners."

Maureen couldn't believe this. "They won't know they're being dosed?"

Greve gave her an are-you-crazy? look. "Tell them we're going to try to change the brains of their unborn babies? Of course not. Some of them wouldn't care, but none of them can be trusted to keep their mouths shut."

"But what if something goes wrong?"

"Nothing will go wrong."

"But what if it *does*?"

A wry twist to his lips. "Well, it's hardly a big loss, if you know what I'm saying."

Maureen shot from her seat. "I know exactly what you're saying, and I'm out of here."

"That's not an option," Greve said as she marched toward the door.

"Watch me." She pulled it open and found the hulking, ever-lurking MP blocking her way. "Let me by!"

Behind her, Greve said, "You can't opt out, Doctor LaVelle. You're in too deep. You may be an independent civilian contractor, but that doesn't mean DoD can't ruin your life. You have no idea how miserable your future can be."

She kept her back to him. "I'll deal with it."

"Come, come. I don't like to use threats. I much prefer the carrot to the stick."

"You haven't got a carrot for this."

"How about the origin of Substance A . . . your melis?"

She turned to face him. "Don't try lying to me. You said I wasn't cleared."

"You weren't, but I anticipated resistance on your

part, so I finagled a clearance for you. I told the powers that be that you already knew more about the substance than anyone on the planet and so it was only right you be apprised of its origin."

She wanted so much to know. However . . .

"That's all well and good, but it won't make a difference."

"Ah, but it will. Once you know, you'll change your mind."

Maureen very much doubted that. Even if melis came from Mars or the Moon, she wasn't going to test it on unborn children.

She folded her arms across her chest. "Okay. Tell me."

"Oh, I can't tell you. Words are completely inadequate where Substance A is concerned. I'll have to show you."

"And when will that be?"

He rose behind his desk and gathered his papers. "Today. Right now, in fact. I have a car ready."

Nonplussed, Maureen took a step back. "Wait . . . what . . . now?"

"Yes. I'm not letting you out of my sight until you've seen the source. After that, you'll be on board."

Don't count on it, buster. She'd play along, see the source, and then it would be sayonara, Fort Detrick and USAMRMC.

Greve did indeed have a car ready—a big black Suburban with tinted windows. The driver held the door for her; Greve let himself in on the passenger side. When the doors were closed, the dark tint reduced the bright daylight outside to a moonlit night. A similarly tinted privacy glass had been raised between the front and rear seats.

"Where are we going?" she said as they started rolling. "The Pentagon?"

"I can't tell you," Greve said and handed her something. "Put this on."

"A mask? No way."

"Cooperate and graduate, Maureen."

He'd never used her first name before. It put her off balance. And on edge. Her few friends called her Moe. *No one* called her Maureen.

"You have such a way with words, *Agent* Greve." She hit the designation extra hard.

"I'm not playing games here. You're cleared to see the source but not to know where we keep it."

She wondered what he'd do if she tossed it back at him and told him to shove it. But she'd never been the rebellious type. And she wanted to see the source of melis—*needed* to know its origin.

"Oh, all right."

She slipped the padded sleep mask over her head and adjusted it. Not so bad.

"Lean back, relax," he said. "Catch some shut-eye if you want. We've got three hours to kill."

She was too wired to sleep.

Three hours from Frederick, Maryland . . . that covered a lot of ground, especially if she couldn't tell which direction they were headed. Pittsburgh, Philadelphia, Richmond, West Virginia, Ohio—could be anywhere.

"I'm too wound up to sleep."

"All right, then. I'll use the time to tell you what we're planning—what we started planning as soon as we heard about your results with the maze rats. I'm talking about big, intricate plans, and the need to keep everything secret—funding, personnel, locations— only complicates the process."

Secret . . . in her years at Detrick she'd heard whispers of rogue operations financed by so-called black funds. This was probably one of those, or maybe a mix of black and legit. How could it be anything *but* rogue if they were messing with the brains of unborn babies?

"The operation has been dubbed 'Synapse,'" Greve said.

"Synapse—as in the connection between neurons?"

"Exactly."

It made a weird sort of sense, especially since melis had improved rat brains, and what were brains but networks of synapses? But that made it a lousy name for a covert operation.

"'Synapse' gives away the farm, don't you think? Anyone who hears it is immediately going to think *nervous system* or *brain*."

"You and I think alike, LaVelle."

Well, at least he wasn't using her first name. She did *not* want to be on a first-name basis with this man. And, truth be told, she wanted even less to think like him.

"Oh?"

"I had the same objection, but those above me are locked into the name. Apparently the more dramatic the name, the easier the funding."

"'Operation Synapse'" she said, not holding back on the sarcasm. "Someone's been reading too many spy novels."

"So it would seem. The project, along with most of its funding and personnel, is buried within another bigger, older project. But nothing is untraceable. With

ARPANET and DDN growing by leaps and bounds, the name can't help but get out there. If the wrong somebody gets wind of 'Synapse' and decides to investigate, some sensitive information might come to light."

"Like this mysterious source I'm going to see?"

"Exactly."

What the hell was the source? The anticipation was killing her.

"Plus other experiments down the road," he added.

"Like what?"

"We're taking it all step by step. But I came up with a solution."

Something that felt like a business card was shoved into her hand.

"What's this?"

"Lift the lower edge of your mask and take a brief look."

Maureen did as she was bid and saw . . .

"I get it," she said, readjusting the mask into place. "A graphic for a synapse."

"Precisely. But would you have guessed 'synapse' had we not been discussing the term?"

"Doubt it." It looked like a spoon.

"Neither would anyone else. After talking myself blue in the face, I managed to convince the higher-ups to limit all communications about Synapse to paper—absolutely no Internet—and even on paper to use only the symbol, never the word. Therefore, in the future, when you receive a file or any sort of communication marked with that symbol, you'll know what it references."

These spooks . . . they loved their games.

"No worry," she told him. "I'm not going to be involved in Synapse."

They fell into silence and time dragged. Maureen tried to figure if they were heading north, south, east, or west, but the car had made too many turns. Then she had an idea.

"If I can't watch the scenery, can we at least have some music?"

"No."

"Hey, I'm the one in the mask."

"First, I've experienced your top-forty taste on visits to your lab and don't share it. Second, the call letters of the stations will let you know our route."

Damn. Greve was no dummy.

The trip seemed to last a lot longer than three hours in subjective time. But finally the car stopped and the engine turned off.

"Not yet," Greve said as she reached for the mask.

She was helped from the car—by the driver, she assumed—and told to walk ten feet straight ahead and stop. She felt a breeze and heard rustling tree branches all around. She smelled pines. She was in the woods somewhere. Not a terribly specific locator, but something. After the ten steps she heard doors latch closed behind her.

Greve said, "Okay, you can remove the mask."

Even though the overhead fluorescents weren't all that bright, she blinked in the unaccustomed light. She found herself in some sort of Quonset hut, maybe twenty by forty. Greve, the driver, and two burly men in grease-stained coveralls stood watching her. The new guys were trying to look like mechanics but had *security* written all over them. A huge cabinet labeled *PARTS* dominated the center of the hut that was otherwise littered with fenders, engines, transmissions, and such.

Was Greve going to tell her they'd found melis in a Ford crankcase?

"This is it?" she said.

"Hardly."

Greve signaled to one of the security men, who pulled opened the doors on the cabinet to reveal another set of doors. He pushed a button and they slid back to reveal . . .

"An elevator?"

Greve motioned her forward and followed her inside. The control panel had two unlabeled buttons. He hit the lower one. The doors closed and they began to descend.

"Can I at least know what state I'm going to be under?"

"No."

"Okay, how about *how far* under?"

"Fifty feet."

The elevator cab stopped and they stepped out into a damp concrete corridor that seemed to go on a long, long way. A single row of solitary incandescent bulbs, one hung every twenty feet or so, trailed along the ceiling into the distance. The tunnel had an old feel, like it had been built during the Cold War or before. The ceiling was only eight feet high, lending it a cramped feel despite its length.

Greve indicated one of the four golf carts parked to the side. They got in and he drove them a good half mile to a set of doors where more carts were parked.

"Another elevator?"

"No. This is the bunker for a project you will learn about on a need-to-know basis. Right now you don't need to know."

He tapped a five-digit code into a keypad and the doors slid open with a low rumble. He ushered her through, then, after another tapped code to close the doors, he led the way down a well-lit, low-ceilinged hallway lined with rows of doors standing open on empty rooms.

"This used to be quite a bustling project but much of the original research here ground to a halt when . . ." His voice trailed off.

"When what?"

"Since they discovered the source of your melis . . . Substance A."

At the far end of the hall they stopped before a heavy steel door with a small window of very thick glass. Black and yellow chevrons surrounded an ominous sign:

WARNING
RESTRICTED AREA
NO ADMITTANCE

Maureen couldn't help a sense of foreboding. She pointed to the door. "And the source is in there?"

"Yes. Prepare yourself. Whatever you're expecting, you're wrong."

Now her gut was crawling. "It's something horrible?"

"Depends on your frame of mind. It's simply . . . different."

He pushed open the door and led her into a large rectangular space with a higher ceiling—fifteen feet at least. On her right, a bank of ancient, inert electronic equipment jutted into the room. Were those really vacuum tubes? The walls straight ahead and to her right were lined with banks of more modern equipment blinking various colors.

Greve led her around the bank of antique electronics and pointed to a square, floor-to-ceiling, glass-walled chamber, maybe ten feet on a side. And within . . .

Maureen didn't know what she'd been expecting. Melis was the most confounding substance on this and perhaps any other world. She'd been expecting the unexpected and the inexplicable, but she hadn't foreseen this. She'd thought she was prepared for just about anything, but she couldn't help the scream that escaped her.

NOW

Thursday

1

QUEENS

Rick had picked up Marie at her place, part of a multifamily row house faced with Hudson brick. All the houses in the neighborhood had pretty much the same design.

Laura had dominated his thoughts on the drive down from Westchester. She'd all but slammed the door on him yesterday afternoon and then reopened it last night. At least he wasn't the only bewildered party. She'd admitted to her own confusion.

Time to put all that aside and focus on the mission with Marie—who, by the way, looked . . . different. Rick realized she'd added eye shadow and mascara. Her jeans were tighter than yesterday and the scoop neck of her jersey dipped lower.

Not for me, I hope.

Rick had dressed down, wearing worn jeans and a long-sleeved collared shirt open over a Taggart Railroad T. They drove the easily walkable distance back to their previous parking spot under the trestle. The dashboard clock read 9:42 when he turned off the engine. The store opened at ten.

"My shift at Boston Market starts at two," she said, "so we have until then."

"Isn't Stahlman paying you?"

She nodded. "He's very generous."

Rick hadn't discussed the boss's arrangements with the nadaný.

"Can I ask how much?"

"Two thousand a week—one hundred thousand for a year."

Rick gave an appreciative whistle. "Just for letting Montero test you. Nice. So why are you bothering with Boston Market?"

"Work is a good thing. I'm late-shift manager and I like the job. It's not demanding—except when workers don't show up—but it has paid my bills and gives structure to my days."

Rick hadn't had any feelings one way or another about Marie before, but found himself warming to her now. Not in a man-woman sense, more in a person-person way. She had a work ethic—probably absorbed from her immigrant parents—and he liked that. Didn't see enough of it these days.

"Anyway," she said, "I've been thinking about how to handle this. On the camera, the invisible nadaný got up early and made his bed. But he can't leave without setting off an alarm. So he either has to slip out the back past whoever opens up, or go out as the first customer comes in."

Rick nodded. She'd pretty much nailed it. "Which do you think—front or rear?"

"Rear, as the first employee comes in. Otherwise he has to wait for a customer, and that might take hours. I know just the spot where I can watch."

"You?" He wasn't sure he liked that. They knew nothing about this nadaný. The guy could be dangerous. "I'm not sure—"

"It has to be me. I'm the only one who can tell you

if he's left the store and which way he's going. You can do the following. After all, he's seen me. If he recognizes me, he may run or hop a train."

As if on cue, the 7 train rattled by overhead.

"Fair enough," he said after it had passed. "You've got my number. Call me when he's out and moving."

They both hopped out. Rick leaned against the front grill of the truck and admired her slim figure as she dashed across Queens Boulevard and disappeared around the end of Slumber Party's strip mall. An attractive young woman. But he wasn't on the hunt.

He watched the dash clock advance toward ten. At five to ten his phone rang.

"The same salesman as yesterday just went in," Marie said, *"and I'd swear I saw the door make a second move on its own before it closed. Okay, yeah, he's out and moving away behind the stores. He should be appearing at the corner to your left."*

"Appearing?"

"Sorry. He's staying invisible."

Keeping the phone against his ear, Rick started moving. He hurried across the street and timed his arrival at the west end of the strip mall to coincide with the estimated pace of the nadaný.

"He's still moving west."

Rick crossed to the next block and kept an even pace along the sidewalk, watching ahead, searching for some ripple in the air, some odd refraction of the sunlight that would tip off the invisible man's location, even a hint that one of his fellow pedestrians had bumped into something they hadn't seen. Nothing. Not a clue, until . . .

Just ahead, the door to the Starbucks opened—seemingly by itself, because no one entered or exited.

Gotcha.

Wait. This didn't make any sense. How was an invisible man going to buy coffee?

Rick stepped inside and looked around. The morning rush-hour crush was over and the laptop crowd had commandeered the tables. Rick pretended to study the coffee presses. Was the nadaný using the men's room? If so, why here? Slumber Party had to have an employee bathroom.

"Damn!"

A laptopper had splashed some coffee on his table. Rick watched him cross the shop to grab some extra napkins. When he returned he stopped dead and stared at his table.

"My coffee! Who took my stuff?"

He looked at Rick who shrugged and held out the flaps of his shirt.

To his right, the door opened by itself.

Rick stepped out onto the sidewalk and looked both ways. The victim joined him. No likely suspects in sight.

"You see anything?"

Rick shrugged. "To tell you the truth, I wasn't watching."

"This ain't the first time this has happened. But nobody sees anything. Shit!"

"Could be an invisible man," Rick said.

The laptopper didn't seem to think this was funny. His tone dripped acid. "Well, then we'd see the cup and the sandwich floating out the door, wouldn't we."

Grumbling, he went back inside just as Marie showed up.

"We're practically on top of him," she said. "Where—?"

Just then a somewhat disheveled young woman with wild hair and very dark skin stepped out of the

Chase ATM recess carrying an egg sandwich and a Starbucks cup.

"Wait," Rick said, stepping close to block her view of Marie as she passed. "Gotta be our nadaný."

Marie kept her face averted until it was safe to look.

"You mean we've got an invisible *woman*?"

"Sure looks that way. Let's see where she goes."

She crossed westbound Queens Boulevard, cut under the tracks, then across the eastbound lanes to a tiny park where she settled herself on a bench. With her back to them, she chowed down on her purloined goodies.

"Perfect time for you to approach her," Rick said.

"But what do I say?"

"Maybe start off with, 'Hi, remember me?' as an icebreaker. That was why I had you stand outside the window last night. Talk, tell her she's not alone, not the only one. She can join others like herself, hang out, have a place to live, and just be herself without any worries."

"What if she vanishes and takes off?"

"Maybe tell her early on that you can 'see' her. Convince her woman to woman she's got nothing to lose and lots to gain. You can do it. I'll stay back here."

"Okay," she said slowly. She didn't sound too confident. "I'll give it my best shot."

"Go for it."

He watched her cross the park, seat herself on the end of the bench, and start talking.

2

Laura found Ruthie and Iggy hanging out at the pool table, watching Ellis and a slim, Afroed young black woman Laura hadn't seen before play pool—or try to. Ellis would hit the cue ball and send it rolling off at an impossible angle and then circle around to race toward another ball only to veer off in another direction. All four of the nadaný were laughing.

After the cue ball finally ended up in a pocket, Laura stuck her hand out to the new girl. "Laura Fanning. We haven't met."

"Tanisha Little," she said, taking Laura's hand. "I heard you'd joined the team."

Laura nodded. "Helping Doctor Montero. I'm assuming you're another telekinetic?"

"Yeah. I've never played with anyone else like me. It's kind of a riot."

"Is one of you stronger than the other?"

"That would be me," Ellis said from the other side of the table.

Laura noticed a swollen bruise on his left cheek but didn't say anything.

Tanisha rolled her eyes. "We're pretty evenly matched."

Laura turned to Ellis. "Did you find out what I asked you?"

Ellis frowned. "You mean my mom's OB doc? Completely slipped my mind."

"Too busy running into a door," Iggy said. Ruthie laughed.

Ellis gave them a brief glare as he pulled out his phone. "I'll call her now."

Ruthie said, "My moms went to some free clinic in

Bed-Stuy but she don't remember the name. Mother-hood something."

Laura made a note of that.

"My mom did too," Iggy said. "At least that's what my aunt says. But she couldn't remember the name."

"Also in Bed-Stuy?"

She nodded. "Uh-huh."

Both were born in Kings County Hospital, so a good possibility their mothers attended the same clinic. Way too early to read much into that.

Marie was out with Rick, chasing their invisible man, so Laura would have to wait until they got back to gather her info.

And then she'd have to talk to Rick too, explain her change of heart. But how was she going to do that when she couldn't explain it to herself?

She wandered over to Leo's area and found him with both feet on the ground watching *Law & Order* on the same monitor that had run his EEG yesterday.

"Hey, Leo. Got that info for me?"

"Yes, ma'am. The Modern Motherhood Clinic."

Motherhood again. Laura kept the brakes on any hope of a possible connection. Motherhood would hardly be an unusual part of a name for a prenatal clinic.

"Here in the city—in Bed-Stuy?"

He made a face. "What? Told you I was born in Compton."

"And that's where this clinic was?"

"Well, ye-ah," he said in a *du-uh!* tone.

She found Cyrus with Luis, working on increasing the size of the objects he could make disappear.

His response caused a definite tingle that she couldn't suppress.

"The Modern Motherhood Clinic."

"Really? And that would be in . . . ?"

"N'awlins. Ninth Ward."

He said "Ninth Ward" like it had some significance. If so, it went right past Laura. She knew nothing about New Orleans. She put two hash marks next to the *Modern Motherhood* entry. Odd to have two clinics with exactly the same name a thousand-plus miles apart. Connection?

Ellis called from across the floor. "She's says Modern Motherhood Clinic in Bed-Stuy."

Whoa. She added a third hash mark, then a fourth. Ruthie's Bed-Stuy "Motherhood" clinic was almost certainly the same as Ellis's.

She spotted Luis's iPad on a nearby table.

"Hey, Luis, can I borrow your tablet?" She could have used her phone but wanted a bigger screen.

"Sure." He grabbed it, tapped in his entry code, and handed it to her. "All yours."

Laura Googled "Modern Motherhood Clinic" and was immediately rewarded with a Wikipedia entry. But before she could read it, Rick's voice echoed through the warehouse.

"Attention, everyone. Please welcome the newest member of the clan: Anulka M'Bala!"

He and Marie flanked a very dark-skinned young woman in a worn sweatshirt and ankle-length skirt that had seen better days.

Laura and those present singsonged, "Hiiiii, Anulkaaaa!"

Laura saw Leo come out from behind his curtain and stare.

"Care to show them your gift, Anulka?"

The young woman looked embarrassed for a second, then . . . disappeared.

"Holy shit!" Luis said, and then clapped along

with Leo and everyone else when she reappeared and curtsied. Her smile was dazzling.

Rick stared at Laura and raised his eyebrows. She gave him a quick salute.

"I'm gonna introduce her to the boss," he said and led Anulka toward Stahlman's office.

Marie hung back, so Laura took the opportunity to approach her.

"Did you get a chance to ask your mother about—?"

"Oh, yes. She said the Modern Motherhood Clinic in Bedford-Stuyvesant."

Oh, God.

"But you were born in Coney Island. That's quite a haul—"

"Remember, my parents lived in Bushwick during her pregnancy."

Right next to Bed-Stuy . . .

"Got it!" Laura said, pumping her fist.

Luis was approaching. "Got what?"

"The common denominator for the nadaný. Doesn't matter whether they were born in New York or L.A. or New Orleans, their mothers received prenatal care at something called the Modern Motherhood Clinic."

Laura opened the Wikipedia piece and began reading.

3

Rick leaned against the office wall as Stahlman and Anulka seated themselves facing across the desk. Marie came in and closed the door behind her, then stood at Anulka's side.

"If you're sleeping in a mattress store," Stahlman

said in a gentle voice, "is it fair to assume you're homeless?"

Rick saw Anulka's throat wobble as she nodded in reply.

"You're so young," Stahlman said. "How did that happen?"

"Long story."

When Anulka offered no more, Stahlman shrugged. "We don't need to know. But those days are over if you want them to be. We have apartments of a sort upstairs where you can stay. A few are already occupied, but we still have room."

Anulka looked ready to cry.

"We're gathering a family here," Marie said.

"A family of what?"

"Of people with . . . talents."

Stahlman said, "I will pay you two thousand dollars a week to let us study your talent. You can walk away at any time."

"Two thousand a week?" Tears began to run as Anulka's hands fluttered to her mouth. "I've been folding laundry for minimum wage."

"For the time being, those days are over—if you want them to be."

Rick noticed how Stahlman kept emphasizing the voluntary nature of the arrangement—how Anulka would stay in control.

"How did you find out you could turn invisible?" Rick asked.

She leaned back in her chair and composed herself. "I was thirteen and home sick from school. My mother had to do food shopping but I didn't feel like going out, so she let me stay home. She told me if anyone came to the door, don't say anything and whatever I did, don't open the door."

"Not the best advice," Rick said.

Marie frowned at him. "Why not?"

"Because if someone's checking to see if the house is empty . . ."

"Exactly what happened," Anulka said. "Someone knocked and knocked but I ignored them. Then I heard the door open. I was reading in my parents' bedroom so I panicked and hid in my mother's closet. Worst place to go. That was like the first place the thief looked. I was crouched on the floor with all her shoes, trying to make myself as small as possible, when the closet doors opened. The light wavered and then dimmed, like I was going to pass out. I was too terrified to scream. Good thing, too, because he ignored me and started going through the boxes on the top shelf—stood right over me, but didn't tell me to keep quiet or anything. Finally he moved on. But he left the doors open. Right across from the closet was my mother's full-length mirror. I could see her black high heels to my right, and her beige flats to my left, *but I couldn't see me.*"

"Wow," Stahlman said, grinning. "That must have been a mind-blowing moment."

"I almost screamed then. I sat there frozen until he left the room, then I crawled out and got to the bedroom phone. I managed to press 911 and whisper 'Help.' I left it off the hook and crawled under the bed until the cops arrived and caught him."

"Were you visible again by then?"

Anulka nodded. "Yeah. I didn't know how I'd become invisible and didn't know how I'd reversed it. And no matter how I tried, I couldn't do it again—not for years."

"But eventually you got the hang of it," Rick said.

She smiled. "Obviously. But—"

4

Laura burst into the office without knocking. Bad manners, yeah, but wait till they heard this.

"Sorry, sorry, sorry!" she said. "But this can't wait."

Rick, Stahlman, Marie, and the new girl stared at her.

Stahlman leaned back in his chair. "I defer to your sense of urgency, doctor."

"I've tracked down the link between all the nadaný—at least I'm ninety-nine percent sure." She consulted Luis's tablet. "The nadaný who were able to find out where their mothers received prenatal care, no matter where they were born, all said the same place: a Modern Motherhood Clinic. There were ten of them. In 1991, something called the Horace B. Gilmartin Foundation opened ten free inner-city prenatal clinics around the country. One in Bed-Stuy, right here in Brooklyn, also in New Orleans, Atlanta, Anacostia in D.C., Compton in L.A., Indianapolis, Chicago, St. Louis, Little Rock, and Jackson, Mississippi."

"All inner cities?" Rick said.

"Yep. The mission statement was to bring quality prenatal care to the poorest populations to offset the high infant mortality rate plaguing inner cities."

"Never heard of them," Stahlman said.

Laura couldn't help smiling. "You weren't exactly a member of the target population."

"No, I guess not. They still around? We should—"

"They all closed up in 2006. Pretty much without warning from what I've gathered. The doctor who oversaw the operation, an Emily Jacobi, left that year and wasn't replaced. The ten clinics shut their doors and never opened again."

"Well, then, we'll get ahold of this Doctor Jacobi and—"

"She died of a brain tumor in 2007—probably why she left."

Stahlman gave a frustrated sigh. "All right, then, what about this foundation?"

"Another dead end. It's no longer operative. In fact, it seems to have disappeared—no listing anywhere, no website, and only a brief, cryptic Wikipedia entry in connection with the Modern Motherhood Clinics."

"I have a foundation of my own," Stahlman said, "so I know something about them. If it closed down it had to file articles of dissolution."

"I didn't delve that deep," Laura said. "Frankly, I wouldn't know where to begin. But I know a forensic accountant who's pure bulldog."

Rick grinned. "Hari Tate."

"Well," Stahlman said, "we'll call him in if it comes to that. But first—"

"*Her*," Laura said. "Hari's a woman."

"Whatever. These clinics started in 1991, you say? Dinkins was mayor then and I was just starting my first tech fund. I hobnobbed with some of the politicos back in the day—Giuliani's people as well, later on. Let me check and see if any of the Dinkins folks I knew are still around. But in the meantime, good work, Doctor."

"*Laura*, remember?"

"Right. Laura."

Marie was staring at her, looking distraught. "You are saying these clinics did something to us before we were born?"

Laura realized she probably should have waited until she'd had Stahlman, Luis, and Rick alone.

"I can't say that. No one can say that. We have

what we call a 'correlation,' a common factor—a *connection*. That's not the same as cause and effect."

Marie didn't look comforted, and Laura couldn't blame her. The correlation was *very* high.

"Look," she added, "if it turns out there is a cause-effect relationship, some innocent vitamin or supplement or combination they were using could be the link. We don't have to make a big dark conspiracy out of it."

She glanced at Rick and could tell by his expression that his conspiracy meter was redlining. He lived for this stuff.

Anulka looked as uneasy as Marie. "I thought I was alone, an accident. Now I—"

A knock on the door stopped her.

"Come in," Stahlman said.

The door opened and a pretty woman with skin almost as dark as Anulka's stuck her head into the room. "Am I interrupting?"

Stahlman rose from his seat. "Not at all, Mrs. Joyner. Come in."

She guided a slim, shy teenage girl, just as pretty, ahead of her. The girl wore leather gloves

"And Sela!" Stahlman said. "So glad you could come." He turned to Laura and the rest. "Sela's talent is she can *read* objects."

"Sela . . ." Laura said. "Pretty name."

"From the Bible," her mother said quickly, as if to assure all present that she hadn't named her daughter after an actress.

"Just for the record, Mrs. Joyner," she said, "did you receive your maternity care at a Modern Motherhood Clinic?"

"Why, yes," she said. "In Bed-Stuy. How did you know?"

Laura suppressed a fist pump. *Yes!*

"I can explain later. But for now, how does Sela 'read objects'? What does that mean?"

Sela looked up at her mother for help, but Stahlman answered. "Hand her an object and she can tell you things about it—where it's been, who owned it."

The medical-examiner lobe of Laura's brain immediately flashed on what a forensic treasure this girl could be—if what Stahlman said was true.

"Here." He picked up a rock off a stack of papers on his desk and handed it to her. "Do your thing."

She removed her gloves and handed them to her mother, then took the sand-colored rock and turned it over and over in her hands without the slightest bit of theatrics beyond closing her eyes.

She opened them. "California?"

"Are you asking or telling?" Stahlman said with a smile.

She smiled back, revealing bright white teeth. "Telling."

"Right. It's one of the rocks I brought back from Bronson Canyon in Hollywood."

She started to hand it back, then pulled it close again, her expression puzzled. She cocked her head, then shook it and handed the rock to Stahlman.

"You were going to say something?"

A sheepish look. "Yeah, but it's silly."

"Let me decide what's silly. Shoot."

"I kept seeing this weird Batmobile, not the one in the movies."

Stahlman's eyes widened. "Holy shi—sugar! That's incredible!"

"What's incredible?" Laura said.

"The rock's from the cave in Bronson Canyon that served as the Bat Cave in the *Batman* TV series back

in the sixties. I was a big fan of the show. They'd raise
a door and the Batmobile would roar out."

Laura turned to Sela. "You got that just from
touching a rock?"

The girl shrugged, saying nothing. A real shy one.

"Everything has a story," her mother said. "That's
why she wears gloves when she's out. She can also
read people."

Sela stiffened and grabbed her mother's arm.
"Mom! I don't like that. You know I don't like that."

"Why not?" Laura said, although she thought she
had the answer.

Mrs. Joyner answered for her. "Some people are
hiding things. But Sela sees them, and sometimes
it's . . . not nice."

The forensic possibilities blossomed in Laura's
head. To have someone like Sela present at a post
mortem . . . she could touch the cadaver and see . . .
what? Cause of death? The perp? Or touch a suspect
and determine guilt or innocence on the spot? Detec-
tives would know immediately whether to pursue a
case against him or look elsewhere.

"I get a look at . . . like . . . I don't know . . . something that's important to them, to their life."

"Important how?" Laura said.

Sela shrugged. "I don't know how to say it. When I
touch my mother, I get me."

Her mother beamed. "Aw, honey."

"When I touch my father—on my weekends with
him—I get *his* father."

"That makes sense," Mrs. Joyner said, "because
your daddy's father beat him terribly as a child."

"So . . ." Laura said, "something important to your
life, something that shaped it."

"I guess so."

Stahlman held out his hand. "Try me."

Sela hesitated until her mother nudged her forward. She took Stahlman's hand, then made a face.

"*Ikhar?* What's that?"

Stahlman nodded. "Something very important to me." He glanced at Laura. "I wouldn't be here today without it. How about you, Laura?"

Laura hesitated, then held out her hand. "Sure. Why not?"

Sela's grip was loose at first then tightened.

After a few heartbeats, she said, "Someone named Marissa."

Laura didn't know why she felt relief. No other answer could fit.

"My daughter."

Mrs. Joyner beamed again. "We mothers love our children."

Of course she loved Marissa. But more than that, her little girl's leukemia, all the failed therapies and then the successful stem-cell transplant, had defined Laura's life for years.

She noticed Rick had retreated to the far wall and stood stony-faced with his hands behind his back. Like a soldier at parade rest.

Laura understood, or at least thought she did.

Marie stepped forward and extended her hand. "I have no children. Try me."

Now this could be interesting, Laura thought.

They shook hands, Sela frowned and said, "Osterhagen . . . Maximilian Osterhagen."

Marie's expression morphed from anticipation to confusion. "What did you say?"

Sela repeated the name.

Marie shook her head. "I have never heard that name in my life." She thrust her other hand at Sela. "Again."

And again, Sela said, "Maximilian Osterhagen."

Still no sign of recognition as Marie shook her head in bafflement.

Laura felt a chill of premonition as Anulka rose and extended her hand. "My turn."

Sela took her hand, and now Sela looked confused.

Her mother stepped closer. "What is it, honey?"

Sela shook her head and dropped Anulka's hand. "Maximilian Osterhagen."

Laura had been half expecting that but still her stomach fluttered as she began tapping the name into Luis's tablet. Had Sela just given them a window into the nadaný origin?

"Who the hell is Maximilian Osterhagen?" Anulka said, staring around.

Stahlman looked baffled. "I've no idea, but we're going to find out. Laura?"

"I'm on it. Searching."

"Good." He pointed to the door. "In the meantime, Rick, would you be so good as to check out there and have the nearest nadaný join us?"

Rick ducked out, then reappeared with Tanisha Little, the telekinetic. Stahlman asked her to shake hands with Sela and the result was the same: Maximilian Osterhagen.

"Find anything?" Stahlman said, turning to Laura.

Laura sighed. "Yeah . . . thirty-three thousand hits."

"Put it in quotes," Rick said. "Otherwise you'll get a hit for every Maximilian and every Osterhagen on the net."

Laura did. "Okay, that's better. Down to a hundred and twelve, and only one with a Wikipedia entry." She did a quick read of the scanty entry and summarized. "Born April 29, 1910, died December 6, 1995, was a German physicist who worked with Werner von Braun in Germany's rocket development program. He helped design and develop the V-2 rocket at Peenemünde during World War II. Brought to the U.S. after the war where he worked on the space program, including development of the Saturn V rocket, until his retirement. He died at his home in Toms River, New Jersey, of complications of lung cancer."

Rick grunted. "Toms River? A Nazi rocket scientist living at the Jersey Shore? I'll be damned."

"Nothing here says he was a Nazi."

Stahlman said, "I don't think you could work on government projects if you weren't a party member. But what's a German rocket scientist got to do with the nadaný?"

"I'm not liking this," Tanisha said, rubbing her hands together as if to warm them. "Nazis doing things to us."

"Wait-wait-wait," Laura said. "Let's just take a step back. He was a physicist and his expertise was in rockets and he died years before you were even conceived."

"Then why is he inside of us?" she said, her lips quivering. "Why does his name come out when Sela holds our hands?"

Lurid scenarios of Osterhagen secretly being Hitler and the nadaný being his clones played through Laura's head—the kind of tale Rick would concoct, just for fun. Or maybe not for fun. She glanced at him and saw his eyes boring into her. What *was* he thinking?

"I don't know, Tanisha," she said. "None of us do. But he's not the only Maximilian Osterhagen that popped up."

"But the only one in Wikipedia."

Yeah, there was that.

"That's it?" Rick said. "Kind of thin. What else you got?"

She scrolled through the list of hits. "Mostly Facebook pages and blogs."

"We'll give them careful study," Stahlman said. "Maybe there's a connection between him and these maternity clinics. Right now, let's get Anulka settled in her new digs." He touched Mrs. Joyner on the arm. "I'll be back in a minute and we'll discuss where we go next with Sela."

Despite the lack of logic, Laura sensed a connection. A German rocket scientist and maternity clinics . . . it seemed so unlikely. A connection, any sort of connection, might not provide a lot of answers itself, but at least it would give her some direction.

As Stahlman was leading Anulka, Marie, and Tanisha out, Mrs. Joyner looked at Rick.

"Do you want Sela to read you?"

Rick shook his head and kept his hands behind his back. "I don't think that would be a good idea."

"You look like a nice man," Sela said. "You're the only one—"

"Let's drop it," Rick said.

"Done with my tablet?" Luis said, appearing at her shoulder.

"Yeah. I'll bring my own next time. Listen, we've discovered a few things."

She started giving him a quick rundown and had just reached the Osterhagen connection when a high-pitched scream split the air.

Sela slammed against her mother and wrapped her arms around her waist.

"My gloves! Gimme my gloves! I wanna go!" She had her face buried against her mother and was pushing her through the doorway. "I wanna go! I wanna go! I wanna *go!*"

Rick stood frozen and silent, staring after her with a stricken look on his face. "She grabbed my hand. I told her not to but she grabbed it anyway."

Laura understood exactly what had happened. Rick's life, the one he was living today, had been shaped by the horrors in Düsseldorf, and Sela had tapped into them.

He looked so lost. She gripped his upper arm. "It's okay, Rick. It's okay."

5

LANGE-TÜR BUNKER

Urgent. Imperative we meet at the bunker. We have trouble. Be prepared to stay for a while.

Maureen LaVelle hadn't seen Benjamin Greve in years, but she doubted he'd changed. His cryptic message indicated he was still indulging his flair for drama. Normally she would have called him and said she didn't have time for clandestine, subterranean meetings, and let's get this over with now. But just above his signature on the email he'd inserted a symbol she hadn't seen in over a decade.

Synapse . . . speak the word only when absolutely necessary. Nothing relating to Synapse could be recorded anywhere now, on any medium—all the old papers had been burned. All Synapse matters had to be discussed face-to-face.

He'd even sent a car to Frederick for her—a Lincoln Continental that had seen better days. Older, low-value cars had long been the rule around the bunker entrance. No shiny black Escalades allowed. She'd used the ride time for some leisure reading. Or in this case, rereading: *Ghost Story* by Peter Straub. She'd always been intrigued by its first line, its signature question: *What was the worst thing you've ever done?*

She knew her answer: allowing herself to become involved in testing melis on pregnant women. Nothing bad had happened, no one had suffered because of it, but only through sheer dumb luck. Things could so easily have gone so wrong.

Shadows had lengthened by the time the car pulled off the road and into the junkyard lot. It stopped by the *We Buy Scrap Metal—All Kinds* sign to the left of the battered Quonset hut that comprised one of the property's two structures. The last rays of the late September sun filtered through the pines as she stepped out.

The driver pulled her carry-on from the trunk and extended the handle for her. She glanced up at the security camera atop the curved edge of the roof, and at the others in the trees, to make sure they got a good look at her. Then she waited until a middle-aged man in grease-stained coveralls stepped out of the hut.

"Can I help you, ma'am?"

With his scruffy beard he didn't look like the typical DIA type who had manned the entrance back in the day when the bunker was the center of her universe. They were usually younger too.

He and the other agent inside had seen her car on the security cameras, no doubt already scanned the license plate, and knew exactly who she was.

"I'll show you my ID inside."

He held the door for her and she signaled her driver that he was free to return the car to wherever it had originated. Then she rolled her carry-on toward the hut.

Be prepared to stay for a while.

She'd come prepared, but had no intention of staying here. Her back had been giving her problems and the bunker's mattresses hadn't been replaced in decades. No, she'd grab a room at one of the boardwalk hotels in Seaside. The season was over. She could have her pick.

A similarly garbed and equally scruffy agent sat at a desk inside and gave her an appraising up-and-down. Maureen kept herself in shape and watched her weight, but for Christ sake she was old enough to be his mother.

She didn't recognize either of them, but anyone working the entrance back in the day would have either moved up or been shipped out by now. She opened her ID folder. The man at the desk scanned it and handed it back.

"Agent Greve is expecting you," said the first. "I'll take you down."

"No need," she said. "I used to work here."

This earned her a pair of strange looks: *Work here? Nobody worked here.* Not unexpected. They weren't cleared to know what lay beyond the barrier at the far end of the bunker below.

The first agent opened the doors to the elevator and she took it from there. As she descended the five stories to the corridor, she couldn't help remembering her first trip here back in '86. Blindfolded until she was enclosed in the Quonset hut, she'd had no idea she was in New Jersey. The cart ride down the corridor had seemed so long at the time, and then her introduction to the source of melis.

Greve had been right. She wouldn't have believed him if he'd simply told her. He had to *show* her. As he'd said, seeing proved believing; seeing was a game changer. Suddenly all her determination to walk away from the human trials had melted away like Icarus's wings. Her high-and-mighty resolve had vanished and she'd plummeted back to Earth, to the new, mind-boggling reality that had been presented to her. No way was she going to miss out on being a part of that.

The elevator stopped, the doors slid back, and a familiar musty smell of old concrete mixed with mold assailed her. She unplugged the charging cord on one of the golf carts and started rolling the half mile to the bunker-*cum*-laboratory hiding unsuspected fifty feet below a pine forest. The eight-foot ceiling seemed even lower than she remembered.

She parked her cart outside the wall that marked the end of the corridor. Greve had given her a code for the keypad. She noticed the old one had been replaced and the new model had a slot to accommodate a swipe card as well. Just for the hell of it she tried her old code but the indicator light remained red. The new code turned it green, however, and she waited for the doors to rumble aside as the lock buzzed.

She entered the bunker and spotted Greve waiting for her at the far end of the central hallway. She doubted he'd been there long. The agents up top had surely given him a heads-up that she'd arrived and was on her way.

"Welcome back," he said with the grimace that passed for his smile.

Still thin and pale, though he'd developed a stoop and a paunch. His hair had grayed and thinned, his face grown lined, but his rimless glasses remained the same. She was surprised he hadn't retired—he had to be flirting with seventy or beyond by now. But maybe she shouldn't be surprised; he didn't seem the type to retire.

She'd passed sixty herself and suspected that for him, like her, work offered a reason to get out of bed in the morning. Neither of them had married. She'd had off-and-on affairs through the years, but nothing serious. She didn't know about Greve. Certainly he'd shown no interest in her, for which she would be eternally grateful. A man was supposed to warm your bed, not chill it.

She was aware that some acquaintances and family members had remarked ad nauseam about how much she'd sacrificed in the pursuit of knowledge, so she'd quietly accepted the mantle of martyr to science or some other such bullcrap. But she knew the truth: She hadn't sacrificed anything that mattered, at least not to her. Mainly because she'd never met anyone she deemed worthy of an extended outlay of her time. She knew how arrogant that sounded, but should the day come when she met someone whose presence was preferable to being alone, she might change her mind. With the passing years the probability of that day arriving had diminished toward null. So she'd have to be content with her own company. Which was fine. Other people were, for the most part . . . interruptions.

As for Greve, she knew nothing of his private life. He seemed asexual. For all she knew, he longed for companionship, but that wasn't going to happen. The man was a control freak and just plain toxic. Maureen was alone by her own choice. Greve, she was sure, was alone because of everyone else's choice. And so he kept working. Besides, he probably knew too much about too many people for anyone to dare tell him he *had* to retire.

Or maybe he kept working in the hope that he'd come across a project that would make up for the dismal failure of Synapse. All the time and resources, black and white, that had been squandered on the Modern Motherhood Clinics with nothing—absolutely nothing to show for it.

Greve had tried to hide it when the clinics were shut down, but she knew he'd been bitterly disappointed. And she knew what a blow it had dealt his career. The people behind Synapse at the Pentagon and DIA had had such high expectations. They were going to be the ones to transform all the U.S. pawns into queens and take over the world's intellectual and technological chessboard. So what if they'd bent the rules a little? Look what they'd accomplished.

But when the pawns remained pawns, they'd slunk away, leaving Benjamin Greve twisting in the wind. Overnight he'd gone from fair-haired boy to schmuck.

Welcome back, schmuck, she thought as she marched past the empty rooms that lined the hallway.

For the first twenty or so years of the bunker's existence, the twenty rooms had all been occupied as the place hummed with activity, with technicians actually living down here. Then the activity and population tapered off, only to resurge in the nineties.

"Miss the place?" he said as she neared.

Something different about him. He seemed wound up, almost excited. Greve rarely got excited about anything. What had happened to his post–Modern Motherhood bitterness?

"Not really." Seriously, who could feel nostalgia for the Lange-Tür bunker? "Where is everybody?"

"We've been in a low-level holding pattern with a skeleton crew since you returned to Detrick."

"Low-level is right. Even your DIA people up top—"

"Oh, they're not DIA. They're outside contractors."

That surprised her but it didn't really matter. The reason for his summons, however . . .

"I hope this is important."

"Oh, it is. Trust me."

That was just it—she didn't trust him. Greve always seemed to have a private agenda.

"Fine, but we could have met in the middle. Baltimore's a lot closer for both of us."

That pseudo-smile again, but close up now she could see it looked a bit twitchy. He looked wired. "In a few moments you'll understand why the bunker is much more appropriate."

Okay, he had her interest.

He turned and led her toward the heavy steel door at the end of the hall with the small window made of very thick glass. The door to the rear chamber.

"Not there," she said.

"Don't you want to see it? Been a long time."

"I'll pass. I can't concentrate in there."

She didn't know how anyone could concentrate in there.

But the truth was, she found the rear-section situation too frustrating. Possibly the greatest discovery in human history and they couldn't tell anybody about it. Even after all these years—strict silence.

Of course, the number of suicides of current and past employees helped keep the secret.

"No worry," he said. "Oddly enough, the conference room is free."

Was he attempting sarcasm? With a skeleton crew manning the bunker, what else could it be?

In the conference room they seated themselves on opposite sides of the long oval table where she'd suffered through many a boring meeting during her years here. The wastebaskets overflowed with sandwich and candy bar wrappers. A refrigerator hummed in a corner; a microwave oven sat on a cabinet next to it. The conference room had always doubled as a break room for the staff.

"I'll get right to it," Greve said. "I got a call from NSA: One of the search strings I submitted for monitoring after we closed down MM has had some hits. ECHELON has registered a sudden uptick in phone calls mentioning Modern Motherhood Clinics, also web searches for MM, all coming from New York."

Maureen couldn't believe this. Her fists tightened. "You've got to be kidding! I made a three-hour drive from Frederick for that? You could have told me on the phone."

His face remained impassive. "Also online searches for Doctor Osterhagen from the same IP address as the Modern Motherhood searches."

Maureen's spine went rigid. Okay. That was different. That was . . . bizarre and unsettling.

"How is that possible? They have no connection."

"Of course they do," he said, his tone bordering on contempt. "How can you say that?"

"*You* know they do," she said, "and *I* know they do, and maybe half a dozen people in DoD know they do, but there's no real-world connection. And besides, I thought you scrubbed the net of any mention of him."

"I did, except for what we want people to think. Like that Wikipedia entry."

She'd helped him write that fiction. They'd left it out there and tagged it to send out an alert should anyone access it.

"This is the first time someone has searched Wikipedia for Maximilian Osterhagen?"

"The very first. Which would be of only minor concern by itself. But when the query comes from the same address searching for Modern Motherhood Clinics, it's potentially catastrophic."

Somehow someone had made the connection.

"But how?"

"Exactly what I wanted to know. And the answer is . . ." That excited look again. "The answer is *astounding*."

"Well, are you going to tell me or are we playing twenty questions?"

"When I learned of the searches I had the code heads at DIA look into it. The queries originated from a company called H-N Research owned by a Clayton Stahlman. I had them crack their servers."

"And?"

Come *on!*

"This Stahlman fellow is gathering a group of melis children."

It took Maureen a second or two to process that.

"Wait, what? That's impossible. No one knows about melis but us."

"We didn't follow the children long enough, Doctor LaVelle."

"Stop playing games. What on Earth are you talking about?"

"If what this Stahlman and his team are documenting on their servers is true and not deluded ravings, the melis kids have developed what would be described in the popular press as 'paranormal powers.' I know you don't believe in the paranormal, and neither do I, but how would you categorize telekinesis, levitation, and even teleportation?"

A tingle of excitement gathered in the pit of Maureen's belly and seeped outward, a wave of needles and pins. She fought it. She couldn't allow herself to buy into this.

But melis was involved, and melis was like nothing else in the world.

"I would normally categorize it as *Bullshit* with a capital B, but . . . you say these are all melis kids? You're sure?"

"Absolutely. I cross-checked with our own records. Stahlman and his people don't know about melis, but they somehow discovered the kids and, like any good researchers, they looked for a common denominator. Naturally they found the MM clinics."

Maureen was having difficulty wrapping her mind around all this. Telekinesis? *Teleportation*, for Christ sake?

"But they never showed—"

"Exactly. Because it appears their odd talents never manifested until they hit puberty."

"Then I guess you're right," she said. "We didn't follow them long enough."

Greve shrugged. "It might not have made a difference if we had. We were following their grades, not their personal lives. And none of them has made a show of these talents. But we're going to change all that. We'll show the powers that be that all the time and money devoted to Synapse was not wasted. Synapse was not a wild-goose chase. We are going to present them with a whole gaggle of uniquely talented geese. This is our vindication, Maureen."

Your vindication, you mean.

She'd always felt more of a need for redemption than vindication.

But she wasn't so sure she liked the sound of this. "How do we do that?"

"We bring them here. *We* investigate and delineate their powers, not some strangers."

"How do we convince them to—?"

"Convince? We don't need to convince anyone. It's already in the works. There'll be no refusal."

"What?"

"They're our *children*, Maureen. We're their *parents*. They'll do what we want them to do."

She stared at him. It had finally happened. Benjamin Greve had gone totally around the bend.

6

QUEENS

Laura and Rick finally found a moment to themselves in a corner of the warehouse.

"So, about that Mets game," he said. "Is that for real?"

"It is. But if things go like last night, it might not be such a cheery occasion."

"Oh?"

"Well, as you may or may not know, the beloved Metropolitans are scratching and clawing their way to a wild card spot in the playoffs."

"So I've heard. I also heard that they lost by a single run last night."

"Yes, further diminishing Marissa's postseason hopes. She was close to tears when she went to bed."

"Those Mets . . . still breaking little hearts."

He seemed distracted. Laura had caught him with a thousand-mile stare now and then during the day. She thought she knew why.

"Still rattled by Sela?"

He sighed. "Who wouldn't be? She grabbed my hand and screamed and ran to her mother. Am I that black inside?"

"She wasn't sensing *you*. She touched me and said 'Marissa.' She sensed the ikhar for Stahlman. It's not who you are, it's what *makes* you who you are, what shaped you."

"And she sensed Düsseldorf."

"Of course she did. You're still traumatized by it. It changed your worldview, your whole *life*. It's why you're no longer in the CIA."

"Still . . ."

"'Still' nothing. It shaped the present-day you, sure, but it's not who you are."

Finally he looked at her. "You sound so sure. How can you be so sure when I can terrify a teenage girl with a simple touch."

"You don't frighten Marissa."

"She's not nadaný."

"But she's a great judge of character and she adores you."

At last a smile. "Well, there's that. And it's mutual."

"She's with her dad this weekend but the Mets play the Phillies Sunday night. You on?"

"You bet."

She debated asking him to Sunday dinner but decided against. Keep It Simple, Stupid.

"Busy day tomorrow," she said. "Luis and I are going to be working with our invisible girl to see how she does it, and then Tanisha told me her mother remained friends with one of the nurses at the Bed-Stuy clinic. She's arranging a little tête-à-tête with her tomorrow afternoon."

"And I've got a date with the CIA—I hope."

Laura hadn't expected to hear that. "I thought they were denying your existence."

"They are. But you remember Nelson Fife, right?"

"How can I forget?"

He'd tried to kill them. She still remembered the hatred in his eyes when he'd looked at her.

"Called his superior in the Company—well, former superior. Guy named Arnold Pickens."

"You can't think the CIA has anything to do with the Modern Motherhood Clinics?"

"The Company has its tentacles everywhere, but

no, I don't. I asked him for a simple favor: everything
he can find out about Maximilian Osterhagen."

"Ah, now I see."

He was nodding. "Osterhagen's name popped up
three for three with the nadaný, and yet there's virtually nothing about him on the net. We have his birth
and death dates and a story about postwar work with
von Braun and other scavenged German scientists,
but when I looked up specific projects—supposedly
he worked on the Saturn V—there's no mention of
him. Not a freaking word."

"Which means he might have been working on
something else."

"'Zackly. Something someone wants to keep under
wraps."

She frowned. A rocket scientist and prenatal clinics . . . how could they possibly be connected? And
then she had a thought.

"Wait . . . you just asked this Pickens and he
agreed?"

Rick gave her a crooked smile. "Made him an offer
he couldn't refuse."

"You threatened him?"

"Not physically. I met Pickens years ago; he's
known as a guy who never sticks his neck out, and
the Fife fiasco has put him in a precarious position.
He wants it all to blow over. I offered to make some
noise if he didn't listen to me. He put on a bluster
show, but I'm not asking for much. With his clearance level, all he's got to do is spell the name right
when he enters the search string. Got a promise to
meet late afternoon."

"So maybe by this time tomorrow, we'll have some
answers."

THEN

The house smelled of death.

Or so Benjamin Greve thought as he stepped through the front door. Maybe not death. Maybe simply old-man, never-open-the-windows staleness. But he sensed death lurking in the corners, readying to make its move.

Well, no secret that Maximilian Osterhagen was dying. His doctors said he didn't have long—six, eight weeks at most—and mentioned transferring him to hospice care soon. Benjamin needed to talk to the good doctor before then.

"Doctor Max?" he called. "It's me, Agent Greve."

"I'm over here," came the hoarse reply.

Greve looked around. Where was "over here"? The living room walls were planked with tongue-and-groove knotty pine and hung with nondescript seashore paintings—by marginally talented local artists from the look of them. Double French doors on the far side of the room stood open. He followed the light to a jalousied porch that overlooked a gravel backyard abutting a bulkheaded lagoon that opened onto Barnegat Bay. Max had bought the two-bedroom ranch back in the fifties, probably for a song. Worth a tidy sum right now, what with waterfront property at a premium.

The man himself sat in a wicker chair, basking in the autumn sun. His denuded scalp gleamed. The unruly, rarely combed thatch of white hair had fallen victim to the radiation treatments and multiple bouts of chemotherapy in the war against his widely metastatic lung cancer. Even his eyebrows were gone. Greve doubted a hair remained on the man's body. Clear plastic tubing trailed from his nostrils to a small oxygen tank beside him.

"Agent Greve," Max said, his German accent still thick. "You've never visited before."

My, how he'd wasted away. The once full cheeks had hollowed, the bull neck withered to a wattle. His cancer was quite literally devouring him.

"Well, it's not a social call."

Max smiled. "I had no such illusions."

Greve indicated the matching wicker chair next to him. "May I?"

"Of course. To what do I owe the honor?"

Greve slid the chair closer. Once seated, he leaned in toward the dying man. The houses here along the lagoon sat cheek-by-jowl, and the porch jalousies, though closed, offered scant privacy.

"I'll get right to the point."

"Excellent. I haven't a lot of time left."

"I know."

Greve was a bit surprised by the man's blithe acceptance of his impending demise.

"Which provides a perfect lead-in to the reason for my visit. As you know, the Lange-Tür Project has been a huge disappointment."

Max's eyes widened. "It produced the Anomaly."

"Which has proven next to useless. All the physicists and engineers on the project agree that they have run into a wall that appears insurmountable."

"I'm so sorry to hear this. I had hoped that my years of effort, if not successful in my lifetime, would at least lay a foundation for future success."

Greve nodded. "The government had the same hope. Yet all the millions invested have yielded nothing of strategic value."

The Department of Defense would have pulled the plug years ago if not for the Anomaly. Nobody knew what to do with the fucking Anomaly.

"My theories are valid," he said. "I'm sure of it."

"Others agree with you, but I'm told we are missing a vital piece, an equation that might trigger a breakthrough."

Max shook his cue ball head. "Obviously we are missing *something*."

And now Greve came to the meat of the matter. "Doctor Osterhagen, is it possible you've held something back?"

He stiffened in his chair. "What? Absolutely not. The Lange-Tür was to be my legacy, my guarantee of a place in history. Why would I hold anything back?"

"Well, you *were* a member of the Nazi Party back in the day."

"Bah!" His hand gave a dismissive backhand wave. "I had no choice! If you didn't join the party, you had zero chance of funding. You could propose the most brilliant innovations and all would be for naught if you weren't a member. The funds you sought would go to a party hack instead."

"So you're telling me you were a Nazi in name only?"

"Of course! That master race nonsense—ridiculous!"

"You wouldn't happen to be holding back on the

future possibility of a Fourth Reich, now, would you?"

He stared at Greve. "Are you insane? Of course not!"

"Then what are you hiding in your safe deposit box?"

"My what?" He looked genuinely puzzled. "I have no such thing."

"Ah, but you do. In Provident Bank. You've had it for over thirty years."

"That's a lie!"

"Really? In 1961 you traveled to your parents' home in Düsseldorf after the death of your mother. You returned with personal belongings, some of which you immediately placed in a safe deposit box."

Whatever he'd hidden away had remained hidden for more than thirty years. The DIA could have used legal or extralegal means to get into the box, but wanted very much to avoid attracting any attention to Maximilian Osterhagen. If his Nazi Party affiliation ever came to light . . .

Max's jaw dropped as he gazed at the ceiling. "*Gott im Himmel!* I'd forgotten! You are right!" He looked at Greve and grabbed his hand. "My memory—it's not so good these days. I must go there and empty it before I die. You will help me?"

Greve stared, nonplussed for a heartbeat, then nodded vigorously. "Yes. Yes, of course."

He'd expected denials and resistance and had come prepared to counter both. But apparently the initial denial had been genuine—old Max's age-and-chemo-fogged mind truly had forgotten the safe deposit box. And now that he remembered, he wanted to empty it. Which told Greve that it most likely held nothing of strategic value.

Still, he'd been assigned to get into that box, so . . .

There followed a two-hour ordeal of transporting a frail, cancer-ridden, oxygen-dependent octogenarian to and from a local bank branch where he emptied his safe deposit box. The contents consisted of one large, square object wrapped in brown paper and tied with string, which Max held crushed against his chest all the way back home.

If that's a photo album, Greve thought when he first saw it, I will strangle him.

When Greve finally deposited Max, panting and pale, in a fireside easy chair in his living room, the man looked all in.

"Could you start the fire?" he said. "It's gas so it's no work. I'm freezing."

Greve felt uncomfortably warm in the closed-up house, but guessed the doctor's wasted flesh offered little insulation. He found the on/off dial down by the grate and turned it to max. With a soft *pop,* bluish natural gas flames started licking the artificial logs.

Without asking, he tugged the package from Max's spotted hands.

"No!" Max said, reaching for it, but Greve ignored him.

"Heavier than it looks," he said, heading for the kitchen. He used a steak knife to cut the strings and let the brown paper fall away. "All right, now let's see what you've been hiding all these years."

A book—thick, with heavy black leather covers, maybe twelve by sixteen inches, bound by three iron hasps.

"What the—?"

This was no photo album. Too damn old. He opened it and flipped a few of the heavy pages. The

typesetter had used some fancy, serif-loaded font that
made no sense. Then he realized—

"Oh, hell, it's in German."

"Do you speak German?" Max said softly.

"Not a word. What is this thing?"

"An old book that I gather has been in my family
for generations."

"You 'gather'?"

"I found it among my mother's things when I
was clearing out her house—our neighborhood escaped the Allied bombing raids. My maternal great-
grandfather's name is written inside the front cover."

Greve checked that and saw the date. "Eighteen
thirty-nine?"

"It's a very old book."

"What's it about?"

"Unsavory things. I think the author was a mad-
man. I read only a few pages here and there and that
was quite enough. I didn't want to expose the family
to it so I brought it back and put it away until I could
decide what to do with it." He reached out his trembling hands. "May I? It's been a long time."

Greve hesitated. He didn't know whether to believe him. Not knowing a lick of German put him at
a disadvantage here.

"How do I know this wasn't the inspiration for
Lange-Tür?"

"From 1839? You are silly." He wiggled his fingers.
"Gib es hier."

Max laid it unopened in his lap and rested his
hands on the cover.

"Would you be so kind as to pour me a glass of
schnapps? I could use a pick-me-up, as you Ameri-
cans say. Please join me."

"Not a bad idea," Greve said. "Where—?"

"I keep a bottle of kirschwasser in the refrigerator."

Greve found the bottle and poured two generous servings of the clear liquid. He'd heard of kirsch—cherry flavored, wasn't it?—but had never tried it. He hoped for something palatable, but if things held to their current course, he figured he should be prepared for something that tasted like crap. This trip had proved a complete waste of time.

He handed Max a glass and held up his own, saying, "What's a German toast?"

"We say *Prost!*"

Max knocked back the whole glass in one long gulp. Greve wasn't about to try that. He was raising his for a sip when he noticed Max's empty lap.

"Where's the book?"

Max stared at his glass. "Where it belongs."

Greve looked past him at the fireplace where the flames were licking at the black book. He dropped his glass and grabbed the tongs.

"No!" cried Max, clutching his arm. "Leave it!"

"Like hell!"

"Let it burn!"

Greve managed to maneuver it out of the flames and onto the hearth where it lay smoking but not burning. It hadn't been in long enough to catch fire.

He turned on Max. "What the hell are you up to?"

"It's a vile book! Evil! It should never have been written!"

"Bullshit! You're hiding something, and I'll find out what."

"No, please, Agent Greve. Put it back in the fire. Nothing good can come of it."

"We'll see about that."

He hadn't been all that interested in the book before, but that had changed. Something lay hidden in those pages, something relating to Lange-Tür. He was sure of it. The first thing to do was have it translated . . .

NOW

Friday

1

MANHATTAN

"We could have taken my car," Laura said as the chauffeured stretch limo inched along East 60th Street.

Stahlman laughed. "No-no-no. This is the only way to arrive at the Regency."

He'd called her at the crack of dawn and asked if she could get to the warehouse a little earlier than planned and to "dress up a little." When she'd asked how much was "a little," he'd said, "Appropriate for a power breakfast."

Whatever that meant.

She'd found the gleaming limo waiting, liveried chauffeur and all. Stahlman wore gray slacks, a blue blazer, and an open-collared dress shirt. So easy for men to "dress up a little."

"We're meeting Willard Beasley," he said as they lounged in the spacious rear compartment. "He was a big shot in the Koch and Dinkins administrations, and then out of the limelight when Giuliani took over, but that doesn't mean he's out of politics. He's still got some suck in the New York Democratic Party."

"What's that got to do with us?"

"I called him yesterday and asked him about the Modern Motherhood Clinic in Bed-Stuy. He vaguely remembered it from his Dinkins days. Told me if I'd spring for breakfast, he'd refresh his memory and tell me all he knows."

Okay. Breakfast for info—not a bad deal. But . . .

"We need a limo to have breakfast with this guy?"

"Beasley wanted breakfast at the Regency Bar and Grill. It's the New York Power Breakfast. All the city's movers and shakers show up to be seen and make deals—politicos, Wall Street honchos, publishing and theater people, Hollywood folks in town for whatever reason. Beasley's getting old. With all his cronies retiring, his power base is slipping away. Probably hasn't been seen in the Regency in a while."

"And we couldn't arrive in my minivan?"

Another laugh. "No. And I didn't want to bother driving myself in the Maybach. Anyway, renting this limo for the day will probably cost less than breakfast for the three of us."

Laura filed that away as hyperbole. At least she hoped so.

"Isn't he curious as to why you're interested?"

"First thing he asked. I told him this was research. I said I'm looking for charitable ways to spend some money and free prenatal care in poor areas looks like a good path. I'm wondering if the Modern Motherhood model is still viable." He cleared his throat. "I can't very well tell him the real reason, can I."

Laura nodded. "He'd think you're crazy."

She stared out at the traffic. They'd come over the 59th Street Bridge—now the Ed Koch Bridge—from Long Island City, a total of maybe three miles that was taking forever.

"If you think the traffic's bad now," Stahlman said, "wait till this afternoon when the president visits."

"That's today?" She'd known he was coming to town but thought he arrived tomorrow.

"Noonish. A quick trip to the UN and then he's settling in for the weekend. A super gridlock alert."

"Worse than this?"

"You have no idea. Luckily, we'll be out of here before it gets started."

Still staring out the window, she noticed something.

"We're heading west on Sixtieth. I thought the rule was 'evens run east.'"

"Every rule has exceptions."

The driver took them across Park Avenue, up Madison, then back onto Park—beautiful this time of year with the planters in its central divide still awash with color. They had to wait in line while the limos ahead of them disgorged their well-heeled passengers in front of the Loews Regency New York Hotel.

Laura said, "Every time I see 'Loews' I expect a movie theater."

"It's a beautiful old-style hotel. The Tisch family runs it."

The limo passed the hotel entrance and pulled to the curb before a blue awning emblazoned with *The Regency Bar & Grill*. Laura automatically reached for the door handle but Stahlman tapped her shoulder.

"Uh-uh. Let the driver do his job."

So she waited until he hurried around and opened the door. As he took her hand to help her out, she thought, *I could get used to this.*

No, not really. She wasn't comfortable with people fussing over her. It seemed like giving up control and she liked control. She was damn well capable of opening a car door and stepping out herself.

Laura found the crowded interior of the Regency Bar & Grill about as impressive as the exterior, which was not all that much: chrome lighting fixtures, beige upholstery on the padded chairs, and a very busy carpet. But the atmosphere was redolent of ambition and acquisitiveness.

"During the mid-seventies," Stahlman said, once they were seated, "when New York was on the edge of collapse and default, the money men and power brokers met here to figure ways to save the city. Those were the original power breakfasts."

Laura was only half listening. She was staring at a man with a salt-and-pepper beard two tables away in earnest conversation with a younger man with long sideburns.

"Is that . . . ?"

Stahlman craned his neck. "Looks like Steven Spielberg and Colin Farrell. And I believe that's Glenn Close back by the wall."

"Okay," she said. "I'm officially impressed. But where's our guest?"

"He'll arrive in about a minute. My guess is he's been here, watching for our arrival, waiting for us to be seated before making his entrance. Speak of the devil, here he is now."

The first thing Laura noticed about the man in the gray suit was his belly, preceding him into the room like a spinnaker. He had a shock of white hair combed straight back until it curled up at his collar. He grinned as he paused at this table and that to shake hands with this one or pat that one on the shoulder.

"The grand entrance," Stahlman whispered out of the side of his mouth as he rose. "Willard! Been a long time!"

They shook hands, Laura was introduced, coffee was poured, small talk was generated while menus were perused. Laura suppressed a gasp as she saw the prices. She ordered some berries and kept drinking coffee, while Stahlman ordered a three-egg omelet and Beasley had eggs Benedict with all the trimmings.

Finally Stahlman broached the subject that had brought them all together.

"Ah, yes," Beasley said in a deep voice. "The Modern Motherhood Clinics. I keep a journal and it took only a brief look to bring it all back. In March of 1990 the city was approached by an obstetrician named Emily Jacobi. Dr. Jacobi's credentials were impeccable: Harvard Medical School, Brigham and Women's Hospital in Boston, glowing recommendations, and a string of articles in peer-reviewed obstetrical journals. She was representing the Horace B. Gilmartin Foundation to set up inner-city prenatal clinics around the country. With no cost to the city—the foundation would foot the entire bill—how could I say no? We settled on Bed-Stuy as the site and I ushered it through."

"So the city had nothing to do with running the clinics?" Laura said.

"Oh, well, the Department of Health folks had their noses a bit out of joint since Doctor Jacobi would be calling the shots and not them, but they did their due diligence and begrudgingly admitted how impressed they were with her dedication. She oversaw ten clinics around the country and made regular stops here until she quit."

"Quit?" Laura said. "Any reason why?"

Beasley waved his hands. "That happened during the Bloomberg years, long after my time. I understand she died of a brain tumor shortly after, so I assume the discovery of her condition precipitated her departure."

Laura could understand that. But what she didn't understand . . .

"Was there anything unusual about Doctor Jacobi's approach to prenatal care, anything to set Modern Motherhood apart from other prenatal care clinics? Any special medications or the like?"

Beasley shoved in a huge, Hollandaise-coated forkful of eggs Benedict and chewed awhile before answering.

"Not really," he said after a convulsive swallow. "The vitamin shots were a sticking point at first, but that got sorted out."

Laura straightened in her chair. *Injections?*

"What kind of vitamins?"

He shrugged. "B-complex and such, I imagine. Doctor Jacobi had wanted to make them mandatory but our health department honchos said pills would do the same. Jacobi said pills allowed her no control over whether the vitamins would be getting into the mothers in the proper amounts, whereas with the shots she could be sure. They finally agreed on making the shots optional."

She glanced at Stahlman and found him looking back. They both knew their next avenue of investigation: What was in those injections? Anything besides vitamins?

Stahlman said, "We couldn't learn a whole lot about the operations of the clinics, but apparently they closed up after Doctor Jacobi's departure. What happened?"

"Again, none of this happened on my watch, but I keep my ear to the ground and as I recall, everyone received pink slips one day and the places closed a week later. All ten of them around the country. With-out any warning, the foundation pulled the financial rug out from under the whole operation."

A foundation that no longer seemed to exist. Stahlman had called Hari Tate yesterday and she was already on it.

"A shame too," Beasley added. "The MM Clinics showed a lower infant mortality rate than our city clinics or even private care."

Now *that* was interesting. The injections?

"Say, Clay," Beasley said, "if you decide to go ahead with your own prenatal plans, I'm doing some consulting in the private sector now. I'll be glad to help you set things up—you know, grease the chute on permits and such."

"That's good to know, Willard. Never hurts to have an insider in your corner."

As Beasley ordered a brioche to finish off break-fast, Laura's phone vibrated in her pocket. Sneaking a look she saw Hari Tate's name and excused herself.

"Hari," Laura said, stepping out onto Park Avenue. "I was just thinking about you."

"*Good thoughts, of course,*" she said.

"Of course. I suppose you've dismantled the finan-cial workings of the Horace B. Gilmartin Foundation already."

"*All done.*"

Laura had been kidding. "What? You're amazing."

"*I am. I'm even more amazing when there's noth-ing to dismantle.*"

Laura's nape tightened. "What do you mean?"

"*I'll explain in person. When and where?*"

"You can't tell me over the phone?"

"*Oh, no, my dear. Because there's so much more—and less—to this than you can imagine.*"

2

LANGE-TÜR BUNKER

Maureen LaVelle yawned. She'd been up very late reading Luis Montero's research data on his crew of nadaný. She'd started out thinking of them as melis kids but had found a certain elegance in the nadaný appellation. After a few hours of sleep in one of the dorm rooms, she'd returned to her computer terminal to pore over the data.

Greve sat across the conference table from her now. He'd been up and down and in and out all night, mostly on the phone, haranguing this department and that department at the DIA to be ready to move at a moment's notice.

"You know," she said, "this Montero fellow is doing excellent work. I think it might be smart for us to—"

"—leave him alone and let him do the work for us?"

Apparently they were thinking along similar lines, which Maureen found disturbing. She did *not* want to think like Benjamin Greve.

"Yes. Exactly. The guy's brilliant. We wait until he's exhausted his resources or hits a wall with the nadaný, then we sweep in and take it from there. It's much safer than what you're planning and, though not exactly legal, a lot less *il* legal."

"First off, I don't approve of using this foreign word to refer to our children."

"I really don't give a damn," she said. She was too tired to argue.

He blinked. "Well, then . . ."

"And they're *not* our children. They have their own mothers and fathers."

"But they'd be just ordinary humans without us. We made them what they are—special."

"Yes, we mutated them." Saying those words aloud turned her stomach, but that was exactly what they had done. "I don't know what kind of crime that is, but there's got to be a law against it somewhere. And now you want to compound the situation by opening us to kidnapping and false imprisonment and who knows what other federal charges."

That excuse for a smile. "In for a dime, in for a dollar, Doctor LaVelle. Besides, I *am* the federal government."

Mad-mad-mad . . . truly mad.

"How did you find DIA agents willing to abduct these people without warrants?"

"As I believe I told you yesterday, they're outside contractors."

"You mean, like Blackwater?"

"Quite a bit *un*like Blackwater. Blackwater is a PMC. This group—Septimus Security—is much smaller."

"No one from the old crew is left?"

"Well, Stonington is still here."

Stonington had been the chief technician forever.

"Couldn't get along without him, I suppose. You still have your office here?"

Back in the day, he used to stay here for weeks straight. He'd commandeered one of the rooms as a remote office, a satellite of his official space down in Anacostia.

"Of course. I need it now more than ever since I'm in charge now. In fact, I handpicked everyone else who works here."

"How'd you manage that?"

"After we closed the clinics, DoD lost interest in Lange-Tür. For obvious reasons, they can't shut it down, but they didn't want to devote any more personnel. I volunteered to stay on and suggested a skeleton crew manned by Septimus Security. So Synapse—via one of DIA's shells—hired them."

"How many bones in this skeleton?"

"Only eight at the moment: two topside, two down here, and four off."

"And they're okay with abducting the nadaný?"

"They do whatever I tell them. But that will be another crew with a better skill set than these men. And by the way, I prefer the term 'apprehending.'"

"Really, Greve?" This scared her. "Seriously?"

"Here's the thing, Maureen," he said, getting all sincere. "This is the chance to justify all that money we spent. We wanted to make them smarter, we wanted to give them higher intelligence. Instead we gave them more. We gave them super powers."

She couldn't help a sharp, bitter laugh. "Hardly 'super.'"

"Not now, not yet. But with our help, who knows? Look how this Montero fellow has increased some of their powers just by creating feedback loops."

"Which is why we should let him go on increasing their powers."

"He's not moving fast enough."

"You're forgetting that Montero has their cooperation. We won't. Right now they want to see how far they can push their powers and they've devoted themselves to it. We lock them up here and the only thing they'll be devoted to is getting the hell out."

"Ah, but we have something Montero doesn't have. We have melis. What will fresh doses of melis do to their powers, ay? A potentiating effect, maybe? Ever think of that?"

Well, no, she hadn't. But it wasn't a very good thought. Melis had wrought changes in the developing fetuses, but it had never shown any effect whatsoever in a fully formed mammal. However, she saw no reason not to try it on the nadaný.

What interested Maureen more—much more—was the genetic aspect. Montero had sequenced the DNA of a few nadaný and found no changes. But that didn't mean changes didn't exist. And if they did exist, were they germline changes that could be passed on to offspring? And if so, what if two telekinetics like, say, Ellis and Tanisha, were to mate? Would their children be able to move mountains?

Listen to me . . . I sound like a bloody Nazi . . . planning a master race.

Maureen sighed. This wasn't who she'd wanted to be, thought she'd ever be. The transformation had been slow, but she knew the exact moment it had begun: when she'd seen what lay behind those locked doors at the back end of the bunker.

Even so, Greve's plan sickened a deep part of her, but she saw no way to stop it.

He said, "I want to go over some priorities with you."

"Like what?"

"More like *who*. The warehouse Stahlman is using is too secure. Short of a full-frontal assault—which is not feasible—we're going to have to depend on opportunity outside the warehouse. We won't be able to corral all of them, so which ones do we designate as high value?"

Maureen mentally reviewed the list. "Ruth Jones, the teleporter, would seem to have the highest value, followed by the invisible woman, Anulka. In fact, I'd rank them both at the top. Even if those are the only two we bring in, it's still a win. They have the most extraordinary powers."

Greve nodded as he scribbled on a yellow pad. "Agreed. But there's one with even greater value."

Maureen frowned, then realized who he meant. Of course.

"Marie Novotna."

"Exactly. With her we can track down and build our own inventory—as many as we want."

He talked about the nadaný as if they were widgets.

She said, "We'll want one of the telekinetics."

"Absolutely. We'll skip that teen, Sela. She has potential but I don't want to have to deal with Amber Alerts and all that nonsense if we grab her. And I see no use in wasting our time with this Igdalia girl. No one knows her talent or even if she has one."

"Apparently Marie Novotna says she does."

"Fine. Let Montero keep her and find out what she can do, if anything."

"The levitator?"

"We definitely want him."

She shook her head. What were they going to do with all these nadaný?

"Marie should not be a problem. But how are you going to keep Ruth Jones from teleporting herself to safety any time she wishes?"

"It's all been worked out. I came up with an ingenious solution."

She couldn't help smiling at his unabashed ego. "'Ingenious' . . . really."

"Yes, really. You'll agree when you see."

She could wait. "When do these abductions begin?"

"*Apprehensions*. And they start today—as soon as the teams are in place."

"Why the big rush?"

"Because last night someone from the CIA accessed Max Osterhagen's file in the Operation Paperclip archive."

Maureen straightened in her seat. "The CIA? Why on Earth—?"

"I have no idea. This Clayton Stahlman has no known connection to the agency nor to the individual who did the search."

"High level or low?"

"Mid. The deputy director of the Office of Transnational Issues in the Manhattan office."

"Manhattan again."

"Yes. It can't be a coincidence. That's why I'm pushing up the timetable. I want our kids out of circulation and safely ensconced here as quickly as possible. The sooner we have them, the sooner we can pursue our own agenda with them."

"You mean *your* agenda."

He shrugged. "No difference. Like it or not, we're in this together. You're in too deep to back out."

She knew that. She also knew that, much to her dismay, she wouldn't back out now even if she could.

She thought about the *Ghost Story* question and how her answer hadn't changed because of this new info. In fact it had only further solidified.

"Tell me, Greve. What is the worst thing you've ever done?"

He blinked. Obviously he hadn't expected the question. Who would?

"Let me think about that. It's hard to remember anything I'm sufficiently ashamed of to classify as 'worst.'"

Typical . . . soooooo typical.

"Oh, wait. This is ugly, but . . . when I was a kid, I was playing with my pet cat when it bit me. In a fit of rage I broke its neck."

"Your own cat?"

"I'm not proud of it."

Pretty awful but she'd expected worse from him.

3

QUEENS

Rick had been waiting for Laura to return from her power breakfast to fill him in on what she'd learned about Modern Motherhood, but before she could start, Luis burst into Stahlman's office and couldn't contain himself.

"Annie!" he said, grabbing Stahlman's arm. "She—"

"Who?"

He started talking at warp speed. "Anulka—she wants to be called Annie. I've been working with her all morning and her invisibility is the most amazing process. It's mediated by her Z-waves, just like the rest, but she achieves it by bending light."

Stahlman gave him a dubious look. "Bending light? I've heard of galaxies doing that, but—"

"She bends it around her, letting just enough through so she can see, otherwise it never touches her, and if it can't touch her it can't bounce off her, and if it's not being reflected then she can't be seen. It's amazing, simply amazing. I've only tried visible light, but I'm going to try ultraviolet and infrared and maybe even microwaves. She might be able to bend the entire electromagnetic spectrum. Can you imagine what that means?"

Finally he took a breath.

Rick put on his driest tone. "So, I gather you're kind of excited about this."

"Excited? I'm . . . I'm . . ." And then he got it. "I'm rattling on, aren't I."

"Try Ricochet Rabbit on meth."

"Okay, but think about it: a human being bending light with her brain. It's astonishing."

Rick made a face. "More than teleporting?"

"Okay, no. But teleportation is like fantasy to me—magic. I've witnessed it but I have no sense of the process. With Annie I can understand the process of her invisibility even if I don't know how she's achieving it."

Just then Adão Guerra, the big guy on the front entrance, stepped inside and handed Rick an envelope.

"Somebody dropped this off for you, Mister Hayden."

Rick tore it open. A note from Pickens, Nelson Fife's superior from the CIA. He handed it to Stahlman.

"Got a meeting in Midtown. Five o'clock."

"We just came from Midtown."

"I'm sure you were in a nicer place."

Stahlman said, "Important?"

"The dope on this Osterhagen character."

Stahlman's eyes widened. "So soon? Fast work. Fill me in as soon as—"

Adão reappeared. "A Ms. Tate is calling. Says you're expecting her."

"Tate?" Stahlman said.

Laura said, "The forensic accountant we hired to look into that foundation."

"Oh, right-right. She's going to be late?"

"She says she's here but she's lost."

"Let me take that," Rick said.

"Where the hell is this warehouse?" she said without preamble.

"Closer than you think, I'm sure," he said. He sympathized. The street numbers were insane here.

"I had Lyft pick me up and all we did was sit in traffic. The East Side is a parking lot. Finally I hopped on a subway. But now that I'm here . . ."

"Can you get back to the subway station?"

"Pretty sure."

"Okay. Do that and I'll meet you there."

He handed the phone back to Adão. "I'll go get her."

He decided to walk and found Hari pacing beneath the elevated platform—a short, thick, bustling Indian woman wearing a dark blue pantsuit and carrying an attaché case

"Hello, Hari," Rick said as approached. He gestured to the suit. "I was sort of hoping for . . ."

"A sari?" She offered a tolerant smile. "That's strategic wear, dearie. For people like your mother. This is report-the-findings wear."

"Got it. How was the ride?"

"Sartre was right."

"Oh?"

"Hell definitely is other people."

"Crowded?"

"Beavis and Buttheadville. Jammed with mouth-breathers, guys reeking of crotch sweat with chin hairs and backward caps and their pants rolled up to their knees, interlaced with pierced-naveled Kardashian wannabes wearing too much perfume and chewing cuds of gum with their mouths open. Did I mention the yuppies with the baby strollers? And the screaming kids who didn't want to be in them? I did mention jammed, right? Really jammed. But did that stop the manspreading?" She shook her head. "Noooo. Where's your car?"

"I walked. Just a couple blocks."

"There a coffee shop along the way?"

"Why? Low on caffeine?"

"Not critical yet."

Rick liked Hari but knew how she got when not properly caffeinated. He pointed across the street to a storefront labeled *L. I. City Roasters*.

"Ask and you shall receive."

Once inside, Hari grabbed a sixteen-ounce cup and stepped up to the carafes.

"This Cuban blend says 'bold.' Bold is good."

But the well proved dry.

"Hey," she called, "your Cuban roast is dead— dead as Che and Fidel."

The guy behind the urns, a twenty-something sporting hairnets over his bushy head and even bushier beard, gave her a blank look. "Whuh?"

"Never mind."

"Actually Che was Argentinian," said a tweedy guy to her left, pouring hazelnut.

"I knew that!" she snapped, then turned to Rick. "Do you believe this? Caught between Grizzly Adams and Sheldon Cooper."

Grizzly replaced the empty urn with a full one and soon they were back on the sidewalk heading for the warehouse.

"Yuck!" she said after a sip. "My mother made coffee like this. My father died young. 'Cuban blend'? Tastes like Castro's socks."

She tossed the cup in a trash receptacle.

"Speaking of Castro," she said, "I hate to sound like an old fart complaining about the younger generation, because I'm not old. I'm forty-two. But don't these kids know anything? How can you draw a blank on Fidel Castro? I mean the guy was dictator of Cuba forever."

"Perhaps I shouldn't show you my favorite T-shirt."

"Why not?"

"It's got that iconic portrait of Che with a caption that goes *I have no idea who this is*."

She laughed. "That's smart and ironic. But what I'm bitching about has nothing to do with intelligence. I've got very intelligent people working for me, and yet when I walked into a meeting yesterday hauling two big briefcases and said, 'I feel like Willie freakin' Loman,' you know what kind of response I got?"

"Crickets?" Rick said.

"Not even. Willie Loman is not an obscure reference. *Death of a Salesman* has won every award except the Nobel Peace Prize. Yet these kids had no idea."

"Maybe they're developing their own culture."

"What? Miley Cyrus and the Kardashians? Spare me."

Rick put on a hoarse codger voice. "Damn young'uns! They're draggin' the country to hell, Hari. Straight to hell at a hunnert an' two miles an hour."

"Oh, shut up."

4

Laura wasn't sure why, but she gave Hari a hug. She liked her attitude and sometimes wished she could be as upfront with her opinions. *Sometimes.* Rick then introduced her to Stahlman.

"Helluva place you've got here," Hari said, shaking his hand.

"You like it?"

"Not at all. And it's pure hell to get here. What sadist came up with this insane way of numbering buildings? I aged twenty years trying to find this place. Finally had to give up."

"The system has its own logic," Stahlman began. "You see—"

Hari held up a hand. "I'm sure it's fascinating, but since I'm never coming back here, do I care? No. And anyway, what I have for you trumps any numbering system in the fascinating department."

Stahlman looked at Rick. "Is she having a bad day?"

Rick grinned. "No. This is Hari." He nodded toward her. "The floor is yours."

"Okay. Let's do this." She pulled yellow legal sheets from her attaché case. "You asked me to look into the Horace B. Gilmartin Foundation, and I did. Unless it's something hinky like the Clinton Foundation, poking through the innards of a foundation is about as exciting as watching a bunch of grapes turning to raisins. In Pasadena. On a Tuesday. Expect my bill to reflect that."

"Duly noted," Stahlman said. "What did you find?"

"Nothing."

Stahlman straightened in his chair. "It doesn't exist?"

"Presently it exists on paper only. Same with its founder, by the way: Horace B. Gilmartin exists only on paper as well. As for his foundation, hold it up to your ear and you'll hear the ocean roar."

Stahlman looked baffled but Rick got it. "You're saying it's an empty shell."

"Bingo. It hasn't got a penny and was only a shell to begin with, a conduit for funds to Modern Motherhood, which it fully funded until it pulled the plug. It never did anything before and has done nothing since."

Laura said, "Is that as weird as it sounds?"

"Weirder. There's no record of who was supplying the funds."

"They had to come from somewhere," Stahlman said. "Contributors to a U.S. foundation have to identify themselves. No anonymous donations allowed."

"Right. Its one and only donor was a Canadian foundation called the Foundation for Reproductive Progress."

Rick shook his head. "What does that even *mean*?"

"Your guess is as good as mine, dearie, but it's in the same shape as the Gilmartin Foundation: an empty shell. And, as you may or may not know, Canadian foundations *can* accept anonymous donations. Whatever came in was funneled straight to the Gilmartin account as a donation."

Laura said, "Wouldn't somebody somewhere notice that? I mean, wouldn't that raise a red flag and trigger an audit or investigation or something?"

"Not if the Canadian contributor wanted to remain anonymous and never filed for a charitable deduction. And here's something else: You know the doctor who ran those clinics, Emily Jacobi? She's a fiction."

Shocked, Laura looked around for a place to sit but found nothing. "How can she be a fiction?" She looked at Stahlman. "Just this morning we spoke to a man who met her."

"He may have met someone, but he didn't meet Emily Jacobi, M.D. When the foundation proved bogus, I decided to do a little checking on her. And guess what? I couldn't find any record of an Emily Jacobi at Harvard or Brigham and Women's Hospital, or anywhere else."

"How is that possible?" Stahlman said. "She was involved with ten city governments. Somebody must have checked on her."

"I'm sure many somebodies did. And I'll bet her legend held up under the closest scrutiny."

"'Legend'?" Laura was beginning to feel like she'd fallen down the rabbit hole. "What's that supposed to mean?"

"I'm sure Rick can give you a much more detailed explanation. But in a nutshell, it's what they call a fake background. But that was back in 1990 when most records were kept on paper. Everything's been computerized over and over since then. She's been dead for more than a decade. With nobody updating her legend, it fell apart."

"She's a fiction?"

"Total fiction—and an expertly crafted one, I'd say. Whoever invented her really knew what they were doing."

Laura looked at Rick and saw his eyes going flat and his lips tightening into a thin line. That couldn't be good.

She shook her head. "I can't believe this." And yet she did.

"Believe it, dearie. And believe something else:

Emily Jacobi wasn't fashioned by amateurs. Whoever created her got her name added to research papers, to hospital staff lists, the whole deal. The clandestine services are experts at fashioning legends with this level of sophistication. It's the kind of thing they do really well."

"Clandestine services?" She looked at Rick. "Really?"

His expression was grim as he said, "CIA, KGB, those sorts of folks."

Hari put her hands on her hips and made a slow half turn. "What have you folks got yourself into?"

5

MANHATTAN

The 7 train stopped a few blocks from the warehouse and also at Times Square. Rick hated Times Square, though he rather liked the painted desnudas who were still out in force with the continuing warm weather, and didn't mind the costumed panhandlers hustling for photo ops.

The crowds . . . the crowds got to him.

And Fridays at five P.M. were the worst. The usual crush of people released from their jobs for the weekend was augmented by the international tourist horde, the weekend bridge-and-tunnel rats, and the theatergoers in for drinks and an early dinner before the eight o'clock curtain on Broadway. A madhouse.

None of them seemed to know how to navigate urban sidewalks, especially the out-of-towners. They walked four across and stopped without warning smack dab in the middle of the pavement to stare up

at a sign or a building and take photos, blocking anyone else who had someplace to go.

The address Pickens had sent him led to an underground parking garage in the theater district—West
46th Street. He'd included a parking ticket in the envelope. A note below the address had said, *Wear a
hat and keep your head down.*

Rick had picked up an *I ♥ NY* cap on his way
through Times Square. When he reached the address,
he pulled the brim low. He strolled down the ramp,
passed under a sign that read *PULL ALL THE WAY
UP TO THE STOP SIGN*, and headed for a tall fellow with very dark skin and linebacker shoulders. He
wore overalls and smiled as Rick approached.

"Do you have a ticket, sir?"

"I do."

He handed it over, wondering what happened next.
One quick look and the smile disappeared.

"Follow me."

The fellow led him to a shadowed corner where a
middle-aged white man waited in the rear compartment of a big black Jimmy SUV with tinted side
windows.

Arnold Pickens.

Rick entered the other side of the rear compartment.

"You're calling yourself Hayden now?" Pickens
said without preamble.

A fat, florid, balding guy in a suit, typical Company desk jockey. Rick doubted he'd ever been called
"Slim."

"That's my name."

"Wasn't always."

His tone annoyed Rick. "And this is what? A point
of information? As if I don't know?"

"Just sayin'. And I'm telling you this meeting is a one-time thing. You will not ever contact me again."

Rick didn't bother with a reply. He wondered if Pickens felt guilty about Nelson Fife. If not guilty, at least uneasy. As deputy director of the Office of Transnational Issues in Manhattan, he'd been Fife's immediate superior during Rick and Laura's hunt for the ikhar. Scotland had to be upset—understandably—about those Hellfire missiles detonating in the Orkneys. He was probably portraying Fife as a rogue agent who went off the reservation without Pickens's knowledge or authorization. Probably felt lucky to still have a job, but that could change.

Pickens no doubt wanted to see all this simmer down and go away. And it might very well be in the process of doing just that.

But Pickens had known damn well that Rick and Laura were the intended Hellfire targets. He'd pretended not to know who Rick was when Rick called yesterday, but that bullshit hadn't lasted long. No way Fife wouldn't have told him an ex–field agent had been involved. Rick wanted nothing more to do with the Company, and had kept quiet . . . so far. That gave him some leverage with Pickens. If he started making waves—say, emails to certain people up the Company chain of command or to agitated politicos in Edinburgh—the Orkney mess could all come to a boil again.

Rick made a show of looking around the garage. "Company own this place?"

"Not your concern."

Which Rick translated as *Yes*. Pickens didn't want to be seen with Rick and this was the best way to eliminate unforeseen variables—like showing up together on some tourist's YouTube video. Rick had hidden his face from the security cameras on the ramp, and this car was no doubt parked in a blind spot.

He handed Rick a thumb drive. "It's all on here."

"How do I know that?"

"You'll have to trust me."

"What a concept. Interesting stuff?"

"Fascinating."

Rick detected no sarcasm.

"You read it then?"

"Couldn't stop. How'd you hear about this guy?"

"It's complicated. What say you give me a quick rundown—an abridged version? I'm a good listener."

"What am I? Your fucking tutor?"

Rick had expected that sort of response and had asked simply to annoy Pickens. But now he detected something unexpected. He sensed that Pickens, despite the snarling bluster, was dying to talk about Maximilian Osterhagen. Something in the scientist's story had wormed under his skin.

"You can give me a rundown or I can pull out the trusty old tablet I carry everywhere, plug in this nifty thumb drive you gave me, and read it here. You know, just in case I have questions."

He had no such tablet, but it sounded good.

Pickens growled. "All right, all right. Anything to see your back. You know anything about World War II? The V-2 rockets?"

"Some. I know they were blowing the hell out of London."

"The V-2 factories were hidden inside a hill in the center of Germany called the Kohnstein. All the rocketeers like von Braun had labs there. Maximilian

Osterhagen had one too, but he wasn't a rocketeer. He was a physicist and his project was called *Lange-Tür*, which translates as Long Door."

"'Long Door'? What—?"

"Don't ask what it was about because I don't know and I couldn't find anyone who does—or would admit it. Anyway, the Allies learn about the Kohnstein and start bombing the hell out of it, stalling a lot of the research. As soon as the war ends we start a program called Operation Paperclip to round up all the rocket scientists. Because he was in the Kohnstein, Maximilian Osterhagen gets rounded up along with the rest. But when the U.S. learned he wasn't a rocketeer, they quickly lost interest in him. They were readying to cut him loose when this army major in the Jet Propulsion Section interviews him about what he was working on under the Kohnstein, if not rockets. Whatever Osterhagen told him about his Lange-Tür Project must have impressed the hell out of the major and those above him because he was immediately moved to Fort Dix."

"New Jersey."

Rick remembered his obit saying he died in Toms River.

"Right. Here's where it gets really interesting." Rick could see Pickens warming to his tale now. "All the rocketeers were shipped out to Fort Bliss in Texas, the White Sands proving grounds, those sorts of places. But not Osterhagen. The army kept him here in the East, right on the edge of the Jersey Pine Barrens. Dug him a huge lab-slash-bunker fifty feet under Lakehurst Naval Air Station."

6

QUEENS

"Don't care what you say," Ruthie said, "you got the best power. Girl, I can't tell you how many times I just want to disappear."

Shadows were lengthening as she walked along with the new girl who could turn invisible. Her name was Anulka but she told Ruth to call her Annie. Ellis—the white pool-ball guy nobody liked—was walking about twenty feet ahead with Iggy. The four of them had gone over to Van Dam to this food cart with the most dee-damn-licious gyros on this Earth. Ruth made the trip whenever she could. Didn't know for sure what was in them, but as usual she was re-tasting that cucumber yogurt sauce again and again as they were walking back. Which wasn't a bad thing, since she liked the flavor.

"Hey, you know you got your own way to disappear," Annie said. "Any time you want."

"Yeah. And wind up somewhere else totally naked."

"Yeah, well, I can see how that's a problem. How far can you go?"

"Don't know. Don't do it much because of the naked thing."

"Well, you could flash to the middle of a desert. No one there to see you. Then you could jump right back. Man, I'd love to be able to do that."

"The naked part don't bother you?"

Annie shrugged. "A little maybe."

That's 'cause she got a nice bod, Ruth thought.

Who knows? Maybe she liked to show it off. I'm two of her and built like a Gummi Bear.

"Well, I ain't never been to a desert. And I can only jump someplace I already been, someplace I can picture in my head before I jump. No, girl, I much rather be invisible and sit in a room and listen to what people say about me."

Annie laughed. "What if they ain't talking about you at all?"

"Well, they'll be talking about *somebody*. Everybody always talking about somebody."

"How long you been with these people?" Annie said.

"'Bout six weeks."

"And they're straight? I mean, I been here one night and it seems too good to be true, you know?"

Ruth nodded. "I know. But Mister Stahlman's an all-right guy. He do everything he say he will. He opened a bank account for me with two thousand, got me a debit card, and every week there's another two thousand added."

"How you know it's added?"

"I just go to an ATM and I check the line that say *Current Balance*. And every week I got another two thou. First time in my life I got money, and it's all *mine*."

Annie was shaking her head. "Like I said: too good to be true."

"Believe it, girl." Ruth glanced up ahead at Ellis and Iggy, yakking away as they walked. "Why don't you turn invisible and see what they talking about? Bet it's about me."

"Why you?" Annie said.

"I think that ugly white boy's making a play for my pretty girl."

Annie's eyebrows shot up. "Your—you and her a thing?"

"Yeah, well, sorta." Not like it was any secret or nothing.

Iggy been staying over her place. Only one bed, so they been sleeping together.

Up ahead—behind Iggy and Ugly—two men got out of a van and started taping a paper with cut-out letters against the sliding door. They put on those little white masks like doctors wear in surgery and pulled out cans of spray paint.

"What they up to?" Annie said.

"Looks like they gonna paint a sign on the side. Let's see what it say."

She and Annie had just stopped to watch when the two guys spun and sprayed them in the face with their paint cans. Only it wasn't paint and it smelled funny and suddenly everything was blurry and Ruth panicked and tried to picture her room back at the warehouse but instead of jumping she was falling . . .

7

MANHATTAN

"Lakehurst?" Rick said. "They weren't keeping the bunker much of a secret then, were they?"

Pickens frowned. "What do you mean?"

"I mean, I've been there. Wanted to see where the *Hindenburg* blew up." He didn't mention that he'd also visited Hangar One where they'd laid out all the burnt bodies from the crash. Supposedly haunted. "Lots of people work on that base and lots more live around it—I mean tons. Burying a bunker fifty feet down must have attracted a helluva lot of attention."

"Not back in 1946 when they broke ground. Dug up the woods at the northern corner of the base and finished in less than a year. You say you visited? Well, then you probably drove along a nice two-lane blacktop called 571. The files on your little drive there have aerial pictures of the excavation and you'll see that no one but an occasional Piney lived out there in '46. And Route 571 was an unpaved county road that hadn't even been assigned a number yet."

"Still, had to take a lot of workers to make it happen."

"Of course. Most of whom are either dead or doddering now. We're talking more than seventy years ago."

Rick supposed he had a point. The people currently working at the base—they now called it Joint Base McGuire-Dix-Lakehurst, or something equally unwieldy—liked to talk about the weird sounds and lights people witnessed in and around the supposedly haunted Hangar One, but not a peep about the deserted bunker somewhere below their feet. They didn't seem to have any idea it existed.

Pickens said, "The blueprints show it had only one way in through a junkyard elevator, and two ways out—the junkyard and an emergency stairway straight up from the bunker to a camouflaged trapdoor in the woods. Apparently DoD wanted to keep the Lange-Tür Project *very* secret."

"But you've no idea what they were researching?"

He shook his head. "Not a clue. Classified up the ass."

Rick was thinking they hadn't been testing rocket

engines—you don't burn rocket fuel underground. The only kind of research you bury fifty feet down is something potentially dangerous or, at the very least, risky. They'd buried it on an air base in the Jersey sticks—well, what was considered the sticks back when they buried it. Lange-Tür . . . Long Door . . . what the hell did that mean?

"If I had to draw conclusions," Pickens was saying, "I'd guess that whatever they were looking for or whatever was supposed to happen . . . didn't. At least not for a decade. But in 1957, ten years after it started, Lange-Tür received a big bump in funding that lasted into the late eighties and then tapered off as the money was diverted to something called Project Synapse."

"'Synapse'? That's a brain thing, isn't it?"

Rick immediately flashed on the odd pattern Montero had found in the nadaný brain waves.

"DoD project names are deliberately misleading. You know what they called their secret bombing runs into Cambodia during Nam? 'Operation Menu.' Go figure. One thing I did learn was that your boy Osterhagen remained attached to Fort Dix and Lakehurst in one vague capacity or another until he died of lung cancer in '95. What was he doing from '57 to '95? No record. But he was being paid by Synapse."

"So what's Project Synapse?"

"Don't know and happy to leave it at that. Did a few probes, ran into locked doors, and backed off. It reeks of black funding and I don't want the Pentagon sending the DIA my way. Especially after reading that paper on the suicides."

"What suicides?"

"People who transferred out of Lange-Tür after '57."

Rick's years with the Company had taught him never to take the suicide of a government employee at face value.

"Real suicides, or the arranged kind?"

"Apparently real. The study was commissioned by DoD itself. Seems there was genuine alarm over the number of former Lange-Tür folks offing themselves—genuinely offing themselves. The study never came up with a reason, although the notes they left behind often mentioned a void in their lives and indicated severe depression."

Rick held up the thumb drive. "That's on here too?"

"Yeah. Classified like everything else there." Pickens's sudden smile had a nasty twist to it. "I also included something that might be of personal interest to you."

"Oh?"

"A link to something called 'the Düsseldorf massacre.'"

Rick froze. "What?"

"Yeah. Would have loved to read it but the link goes nowhere except a 404 page."

"But how—?" Rick began but Pickens cut him off.

"That's your abridged version. The rest is on the drive—including the Düsseldorf link. See for yourself. Good day, Mister Hayden."

Feeling blindsided, Rick exited the car and started back up the ramp toward the pre-theater horde.

Düsseldorf?

8

QUEENS

Iggy . . . Ellis had always thought of it as a guy's name. This Russian kid in his old neighborhood had been named Ignat. Everyone called him Iggy. But this Iggy walking next to him now was no guy. Not with that bod. She had a sweet bubble butt—not J-Lo class, but a nice one. He'd always had a weakness for spic chics.

Had to be careful about that spic thing. What did they like to be called now? Hispanics? Latinas? He knew what he called Iggy: hot. Even if she was supposedly a lez.

Ellis wasn't so sure about that. Yeah, she was rooming with fat Ruthie, but Iggy didn't seem all that much into her. Despite what anyone said—like they're born that way and all that—he couldn't get over the feeling that a lezzie just hadn't met the right man yet.

But he was taking it slow with Iggy, just strolling along, yakking about small stuff, nothing heavy. Let her get comfortable with him before he moved in on her. And truth was, he kind of liked her—really liked her. Even if she turned out to be total lez, he wouldn't mind hanging with her.

"So, like you really don't know if you've got a talent like the rest of us?" he said.

She shrugged. "If I do, I haven't found it yet. I'm thinking Marie might have made a mistake. They say she hasn't been wrong yet but . . ."

"But there's always a first time, right?"

"Right."

He was running out of small talk. They'd talked about the gyros and fast food in general, about the weather and . . . what else was there? Usually he had good patter, ran his mouth at the card table. But now the silence was lengthening and . . .

I'm tapped out, empty.

"You're so quiet," Iggy said. "What you thinking?"

"I'm wondering if you're a lezzie or not."

She laughed. "You're *what*?"

Shit! Why the fuck had he said that?

"Hey, I didn't mean—I mean, you and Ruthie—"

"Hey, I am what I am and Ruthie—" She glanced back. "Hey! Where'd they go?"

Ellis stopped and looked. The sidewalk behind them was empty except for these two guys in painter's masks spraying a panel truck.

"They playing games with us?" he said.

Iggy started walking back. "There's no place for them to hide."

He followed her. "Those two don't need no place to hide. Annie coulda turned invisible and Ruthie coulda done her teleport thing. Unless they ducked into a doorway."

When they came abreast of the truck he stopped by the painters.

"'Scuse me, guys. Did you see—?"

The nearer guy whirled and sprayed something in his face while the second spun toward Iggy and sprayed her as well.

The world got foggy around the edges. He was dimly aware of the side panel sliding open to reveal Ruthie and Annie asleep on the floor. Then the fog closed in . . .

9

THE BRONX

"Doctor Jacobi was absolutely wonderful," said Fabricia Alvarado.

Tanisha had arranged for Laura to meet her in her Bronx apartment where she babysat her grandson. Laura had introduced herself as a doctor and stayed with Stahlman's line about plans to open clinics similar to Modern Motherhood's.

"How long were you with her?" Laura said.

They sat in her kitchen while her grandson napped in a Pack 'n Play in the front room. The kitchen was bedizened with incomprehensible drawings—little more than scribbles, really—as if they were Picassos. Crayons littered the floor. Laura remembered that stage with Marissa.

"From the day the clinic opened till the day it closed." She shook her head. "That was a sad day, let me tell you."

"I'm sure it was. I understand it happened very suddenly."

Fabricia snapped her fingers. "Like that. Tuesday I had a job, Wednesday I was unemployed."

"And no explanation?"

"It was that foundation—I forget its name."

"The Horace B. Gilmartin Foundation," Laura said.

A sham foundation fronting a sham director.

"That's the one. Pulled the plug on us without so much as a by-your-leave. But they gave us each a month's severance."

"I understand you had a lower than average infant

mortality rate," Laura said, zeroing in on the real reason for her visit.

A proud smile. "Yes, we did."

"Do you think it was the vitamin injections?"

"Could be. Doctor Jacobi was very insistent that every mother get one on every visit."

"Any idea what was in them?"

Fabricia shrugged. "Just B-complex and C, that's all."

Laura doubted very much that was all.

"Do you remember the label? We might be interested in following Doctor Jacobi's lead in this if those injections lowered the mortality rate."

"The label?" she said, reaching across the table and grabbing a crayon box. "See for yourself."

Laura took the box and quickly realized it was a compartmentalized ampoule container, with thirty-six chambers inside arranged like a honeycomb.

"I used to bring them home for my daughter's pens and pencils. Now the next generation gets them."

Laura could barely make out the worn label on the side.

Complete Organic

Multivitamin Injection

There followed what looked like a typical multivitamin list. The print was rubbed and faded. She thought she could make out "D.C." but couldn't be sure. Laura pulled out her phone and took a photo. Maybe someone back at the warehouse could work some magic and make it more legible.

"Did you use any other brand of vitamins?"

"Oh, no," Fabricia said with an emphatic shake of her head. "We administered one ampoule per mother per month, and only the Complete Organic brand. Doctor Jacobi was very specific about that."

I'll bet she was, Laura thought.

10

QUEENS

The sun was sinking behind the Manhattan skyline as Rick stepped off the 7 train at the Rawson Street stop. He speed-dialed Laura's number as he trotted down the steps to Queens Boulevard. He hadn't wanted to discuss anything from the Pickens meeting while within earshot of his fellow passengers on the train.

"I'm ba-ack," he said when she answered. "Where are you?"

"In my car on my way back from the Bronx."

"The Bronx?"

"Remember? To talk to that former nurse at the Bed-Stuy clinic. Tell me you've solved our mystery so I don't have to track down Doctor Jacobi's 'vitamin' injections."

"Oh, right. Sorry, no solution, I'm afraid. Not even close, in fact. Just more puzzle pieces with no idea where they fit."

And now Düsseldorf was in the mix. But he wasn't

going to get into that with her yet—not until he'd opened the thumb drive and investigated the link himself.

"*Damn.*"

"But I do have an avenue of pursuit. Osterhagen was connected to something called Project Synapse or something like that."

"'*Something like that*'?"

"I know 'Synapse' is part of the name."

"*Well, synapse goes with brains, and the nadaný have altered brains. How do we learn more?*"

"That will prove a challenge, I'm afraid. My contact thinks Pentagon black funding was involved. If we can connect Synapse to the foundation that funded the clinics, we'll have a start."

"*Maybe Hari—?*"

"We've probably said too much on the phone already, even though it's beginning to sound like fiction. I'm talking a mysterious German scientist and an underground bunker and major weirdness. It's all on a thumb drive we can open and discuss with Stahlman when you get back."

"*Deal. Beat you there.*"

"Never happen."

As he clicked off the call he spotted a familiar figure strolling under the trestle.

"Marie?" She turned and smiled when she recognized him. He remembered she lived nearby in Sunnyside. "Heading home?"

She shrugged. "Not much for me to do at the warehouse lately, and I work tonight."

"You usually walk?"

"When the weather's nice, otherwise I Uber it."

"So that's a verb now?"

Another smile. "I guess so."

He was about to say goodbye—the warehouse was the other way—when he saw a guy and a gal in their thirties trying to push a stalled panel truck over a low curb into one of the under-trestle parking areas. They weren't getting far.

"Need a hand?" Rick said.

The gal looked relieved. "I was just about to ask. Thanks."

Marie followed along.

"I got this," he said.

She put on a thick Ukrainian accent and said, "You think I am veak but I am strrrong *divchyna*."

With the four of them pushing, they rolled it over the curb and into the deeper shadows of the lot with ease. As Rick stepped back, brushing off his hands, the truck's rear doors swung open revealing two surgery-masked men with aerosol cans. The spray caught Rick square in the face. Half-blinded and feeling an immediate buzz, he turned away, bumping into the second man as he shoved his aerosol into Marie's face. Before he could spray, Rick hammered a fist into the guy's face, slamming him back into one of the truck's rear doors.

Then he shoved Marie toward the street. "Run! Get help!"

As she ran, screaming for help, the guy they'd foolishly helped started after her. Shaking off the buzz as best he could, Rick reached for him and got a fistful of his T-shirt. It ripped and he caught a glimpse of an intricate scar on his back.

Rick's balance had gone wonky and he stumbled, giving the first guy a chance to spray him again. The buzz increased. Again he tried to shake it off but a third faceful turned his knees to putty. Color drained from the world around him as multiple pairs of hands grabbed him and hauled him into the rear of the truck. And then everything became very, very dark.

11

When Laura returned she found the warehouse in chaos.

It took her a while to sort through the hysteria, but it seemed someone—more than one someone, it appeared—had tried to kidnap Marie and Rick. Rick had managed to save Marie but he'd been gassed somehow and dragged into a panel truck. While Marie had been screaming for help and dialing 911, the truck had raced off.

Suddenly Laura found herself on a chair, breathing hard.

Rick? Abducted?

Why would anyone want Rick? Unless it had something to do with meeting that CIA guy? But according to Marie, they'd tried to grab her too.

Marie had managed to get the license plate number and given it to the police when they finally arrived.

And then people realized that Ruth, Iggy, Anulka, and Ellis were missing. They'd all gone out for lunch together and never returned. Frantic calls had been placed but not one of the four was answering.

Marie said she'd been traveling her usual route to work. Was it possible they'd been waiting for her?

And had Rick blundered into the middle of their plans and wound up being taken instead?

The air in the warehouse was spiked with tension, edging toward panic.

She saw Stahlman waving at her from his office door. She hurried over.

"Any news?"

He shook his head. "Just got off the phone with the cops. They found the van. It was stolen yesterday. No sign of Rick. And no sign of the other four either."

"The fact that they're not answering their phones can only mean—"

"I know." His expression was bleak. "Someone's grabbing the nadaný."

The inescapable conclusion.

"But who knows about them?"

"Nobody. At least no one we know of. I'm having Kevin check the servers to see if we've been hacked."

Laura didn't get it. "But why would anyone hack us?"

Stahlman shrugged. "Who knows? Maybe asking questions about the wrong things set off alarms."

"Like Modern Motherhood?"

"Or Maximilian Osterhagen."

The office became claustrophobic.

"What do you think they want with them?"

Stahlman gave another shrug. "The same thing we do, I guess. Find out what makes them tick. I mean, these could be the same people who made them this way."

The people behind Modern Motherhood.

"But they've got Rick."

Stahlman showed a wry smile. "Yeah, they've got Rick."

"Why do you say it like that?"

"You remember the story of Troy, don't you? Whoever they are don't know it, but they've wheeled the Trojan horse into their city."

SATURDAY

1

LANGE-TÜR BUNKER

Midnight had come and gone when Greve appeared in the doorway to the conference room, holding an iPad or some similar tablet.

"Ready to meet our guests?"

Maureen sighed. "I suppose."

"You might try to sound a tad more enthusiastic."

"I'm not comfortable with this whole situation."

"After what you've already done to them, aren't you being just a wee bit hypocritical, Doctor LaVelle?"

After what you've already done to them . . .

Greve had an undeniable point there.

After her first visit here, after seeing the source of melis, Maureen had fallen under the spell of the project. Though she'd sworn she wouldn't do human studies, she became a believer and a willing participant in anything related to melis.

When the prisoners' children showed no ill effects, the higher-ups decided to go wide—set up free OB clinics to serve the lower end of the socioeconomic spectrum. Increasing the intelligence of these children would allow them not only to pull themselves out of the economic slums, but perhaps give the U.S.

an intellectual edge on the international stage. Who knew? Melis might produce the next Einstein.

They created a legend for Maureen: Emily Jacobi, M.D. In 1991 Project Synapse, under her guidance and behind the front of a bogus charitable foundation, opened ten Modern Motherhood free obstetrical clinics around the country. High-quality prenatal care was rendered along with vitamin injections. The techs administering those injections were not aware they contained melis.

Greve, with the help of unwitting staff, tracked the school progress of all the kids of melis-treated mothers until 2006. When they proved no brighter than their peers—no evidence of an iota of increased intelligence—Project Synapse was abandoned as a failure.

Now it had come to light that, although Synapse failed to achieve its intended effect, it had resulted in startling unintended consequences.

"Bring your equipment and let's get started," Greve said.

Pushing a converted hospital crash cart, Maureen followed him into the hall. She'd stayed in the conference room while the nadaný were wheeled in and set up in different dorm rooms.

"Who's first?" she said.

"I thought we'd start with our invisible girl, unless you have a preference."

Maureen didn't, and said so.

"As you can imagine," he said as they walked, "we are dealing with a far less than ideal setup here. Far less than even *adequate*, I might say."

"It's certainly secure enough."

"Yes, I'll give it that, but I would dearly love CCTV cameras in every room and a monitoring station where we could keep tabs on them. But we had no time."

"Even if you had time, this whole place is ferroconcrete. Retrofitting it would be—"

"Wireless surveillance has been around for quite some time, Doctor," he said in a testy tone.

Oh? Well, what did she know about security?

"A bit tense, are we?"

"Not in the least. I simply like to do things right. Until today, the only surveillance we've needed is at the entrance. And the rear chamber, of course, which is simply a video recorder running twenty-four/seven. But within seventy-two hours we will have a wireless closed-circuit system up and running."

"Well, that's a relief." She doubted he'd catch the sarcasm, and he didn't.

He shook his head. "Every advantage the bunker offers is counterbalanced by a hindrance. But I'm dealing. I'm dealing."

Not terribly well, she thought.

They entered room eighteen, a small drab space. Profoundly drab. Poured concrete floor, walls, and ceiling, all steel reinforced. All exactly like the room Maureen had used during the heyday of melis research, even sleeping here on occasion when the work ran late. She'd always thought of it as living inside the Berlin Wall. But hardly anyone remembered the Berlin Wall these days. She was sure mentioning it to Anulka would earn only a questioning stare.

Furnishings consisted of a bed, a TV, a dresser, and a wardrobe; a door led to a small bathroom with a stall shower. Exactly like the room where she'd grabbed some shut-eye a while ago. Her plans of a beachfront hotel had been put on hold.

Unlike Maureen's borrowed room, a gurney had

been added to this one. And on that gurney lay a twenty-something African-American girl with very dark skin. Electrodes had been attached to two small shaven areas of her scalp with wires running to a thick metal collar around her neck.

Maureen pointed to the collar. "What—?"

"Something Stoney put together—to my specs, of course. An example of my genius, if I may say."

"But what does it *do*?"

"You'll see soon enough, I'm sure. Get your samples, then wake her up."

Maureen took an oral swab for DNA—they planned to do deep sequencing on all of them. Next she took three vials of blood. She'd become pretty handy with a butterfly needle during the primate and human trials. She left it in the vein and injected a cc of the antidote to the knockout spray. She'd asked about that spray but Greve told her she wasn't cleared to know anything about it. Same with the antidote. She'd gathered it was some sort of selective neuromuscular blocker.

By the time Maureen had put a Band-Aid on the puncture, Anulka's eyelids were fluttering. She came to quickly.

"Where—?"

"You're safe," Maureen said. "Really."

Anulka looked around and freaked.

"What?" she cried. "No! Where am I? What's going on?"

Knowing she was a cause of the panic in the poor girl's eyes sickened Maureen.

"We can't tell you where," Greve said, "but I'm sure you know why."

Her expression said she did.

"It's all right, Anulka," Maureen said, gently patting her arm. "It's all right."

"Yes," Greve said. "No one's going to hurt you. This is a government facility and you've been brought here so that we can investigate your powers."

"But Mister Stahlman—"

"—was not sanctioned to investigate anything. I am. This is an operation of the U.S. government and your powers are a matter of national security. We will under no circumstances harm you, but you will cooperate."

"I don't think so," she said, and began to fade from sight.

BZZZZT!

The sound burst from her collar. She squealed in pain and came back to full view.

Another fade, another *BZZZZT!* followed by another squeal and a return to full visibility.

She tugged at the collar. "What *is* this?"

Maureen said, turning to Greve. "Exactly what *I'd* like to know."

"It's a modified shock collar—you know, the kind they use to train dogs? Only we've swapped the standard equipment with stun-gun contacts and set it to be triggered by a spike in zeta waves, monitored through those scalp electrodes." He showed Maureen his tablet and pointed to a spiky surge in the pattern on the screen. "Montero discovered the pattern; we're putting it to good use. Ingenious, no?"

"I'm thinking more along the lines of sadistic," Maureen said, appalled. "That's ghastly."

"A matter of perspective, my dear."

"Don't 'my dear' me."

"Whatever. The fact remains that we can't have

these . . . nadaný running around using their powers
willy-nilly. We need structure. Organization. Disci-
pline." He turned to Anulka. "We're going to find out
how you vanish from sight."

"Doctor Montero says I bend light. Okay? Happy?
Can I go now?"

"I've read his notes. We didn't bring you all the
way to Fort Knox to rely on his notes. We're going to
do our own investigations. The question I want answered is *how* you bend light. As you can imagine,
the strategic uses are, well, legion."

They'd agreed beforehand to drop hints that would
lead the nadaný into believing they were in Kentucky.

Anulka had been feeling around her scalp and was
working her thumbnail under one of the electrodes.

"You know, maybe I'll just yank off this little
motherfucker and—"

"I advise against that," Greve said softly.

The collar went *BZZZZT!* as the contact peeled
from her scalp and Anulka jumped. It went *BZZZZT!*
repeatedly, shocking her until she'd replaced the electrode.

Greve said, "Told you not to do that. I was about
to say that the collar is also triggered when the flow
of brain waves stops. It will keep on zapping you until it starts perceiving brain waves again." He turned
to Maureen. "You see? I've thought of everything."

Anulka began to sob and the sound tore at Maureen.

"We'll leave you for now," Greve said. "Get some
sleep. We'll be starting early tomorrow."

Maureen hated leaving Anulka like this, but Greve
was hustling her toward the door. Back in the hallway, he locked the door and showed her an old-
fashioned lever-lock key.

"These doors used to lock from the inside. A simple matter to have the locks reversed."

He returned the key to the lock and they moved next door to room seventeen. Greve opened it but didn't enter. A rather large man lay unconscious within. His feet extended beyond the end of the gurney. One of his wrists was manacled to a side rail.

"He's an accident, I gather?" Maureen said.

"Why do you say that?"

"He's too old to be nadaný."

"You're right about that. His name is Rick Hayden and he works for Stahlman in a security capacity."

"Then why is he here?"

"He interfered with the apprehension of Marie Novotna."

Maureen couldn't help being concerned about Mr. Hayden's future.

"Can't blame him for doing his job."

"But we can blame him for other things," Greve said. "Because of him, Marie Novotna escaped; because she escaped, she was able to raise an alarm; because of her alarm, all the other nadaný are on alert and have gone to ground. I'd hoped to round up six or seven. Instead I have only four, one of which is useless."

"What do we do with him?"

"I'm keeping him heavily sedated. One of the Septimus operatives has EMT training. He's keeping an eye on him, making sure his sedation doesn't get too light."

"And then what?"

He gave her a sidelong look with the grimace that passed for a smile. "You're thinking I might have something terminal in mind?"

"Well . . ."

"Not that I'd lack for volunteers for the deed from

our Septimus operatives. He sent one of them to the hospital with a dislocated jaw—and he did that *after* he'd been sprayed. They tell me it took three sprays of the gas to bring him down."

He closed the door and turned the key. She sensed evasion in Greve's tone . . . He was hiding something.

"What aren't you telling me?" she said as they moved down the hall.

He hesitated, then shrugged. "Mister Hayden and I have a history."

"He knows you?"

"Not exactly. But he will. We have a matter to discuss."

"And after that?"

"Don't worry. We'll sedate him again and drop him somewhere—the hills of West Virginia, maybe. I want him to wake up far from Lakehurst."

They entered the room across the hall where a chubby girl snored on a gurney.

"Allow me to present Ruth Jones," Greve said. "Our teleporter."

Maureen had read all of Montero's notes on Ruth but still couldn't accept the ability to disappear from one spot and instantaneously appear in another. It smacked of bad science fiction. Or fantasy. Even *Star Trek* had fabricated complex machinery to accomplish it. But to have the ability merely to think about going to another place and suddenly be there . . .

It bent her mind.

She took the oral and blood samples, then injected the reversing agent.

"Is your collar going to work on her?" Maureen said as Ruth's eyelids started to flutter.

"I don't see why not. As soon as it detects her zeta waves, it will shock her, which will disrupt those zeta waves, just like with Anulka. Where do you see a problem?"

"The latency between the zeta waves and the shock."

"It's almost instantaneous."

"Yes, but the 'almost' might prove a problem."

Ruth blinked her eyes open, looked around, and said, "What the fuck?"

"Nothing to be alarmed about—" Greve began.

Perspiration broke out on Ruth's dark brown skin as a look of pure terror contorted her features. Then she disappeared with a *shoop*, leaving her clothes and the collar along with its attached electrodes on the gurney, the empty collar going *BZZZZT! . . . BZZZZT! . . . BZZZZT! . . .*

Maureen could only gape at the empty gurney. The girl had done it . . . really done it . . . popped out of existence here and wound up . . . where? Ruth Jones could teleport. The rules of physics, as Maureen knew them, had just been turned inside out and upside down.

And deep inside she was glad she'd escaped.

Greve muttered a hoarse "Fuck."

Maureen couldn't resist: "I don't know about you, but I'm thinking 'almost instantaneous' didn't cut it."

2

QUEENS

Ruth arrived stark naked in her place in the warehouse. She pulled on a sweatshirt and sweatpants and blasted out the door. As she ran down the stairs to the ground floor, the first person she saw was that woman doctor, Laura, who spotted her at the same time.

"Ruthie!" she cried. "You got away!"

She was so glad to see a friendly face. Before she knew what she was doing, she'd wrapped her arms around Laura and begun to sob.

"Me and Annie! They sprayed us with something and shoved us into this van!"

"You're okay now," Laura said, hugging her and rubbing her back. "You're safe here." After a moment, she pushed her back to arm's length. "Who did this? Who were they?"

"I don't know."

Over Laura's shoulder she could see Marie and Luis and Mr. Stahlman hurrying their way.

"Where'd they take you?"

"I don't know! I woke up on some kind of bed and there was this old guy and old woman looking at me. I got scared and left."

"But you don't know where you were?"

She shook her head. "Some room. Stone walls, I think. I didn't see any windows. I just wanted to get outta there, you know?"

"I can imagine."

Mr. Stahlman arrived first. "Where are the others?"

"I don't know." Wait. "Others?"

"They took Annie and Ellis and Iggy too."

Ruth's hand shot to her mouth. "Iggy? Oh, no!"

"And Rick too," Marie said.

"But who are they? What do they want?"

"They want you," Luis said. "Nadaný."

"But Rick's not—"

Laura said, "Rick kept them from grabbing Marie, and they took him instead."

"They took four nadaný," Mr. Stahlman said. "Now they've got only three. Question is: Where?"

Ruth looked at Marie. "You're the finder. Don't you know?"

She shook her head, looking miserable. "I've been trying like crazy, but all I can say is they're somewhere south of here."

"How far south?"

"I don't know. I can't tell. It could be Staten Island or it could be Florida. I don't *know*."

"Then what good are you?" Ruthie shouted.

"Dial it back, Ruthie," Luis said.

She felt panic swelling within. Would they hurt Iggy because she didn't have a gift?

"You've got to find them! Bring them back!"

"We're trying," Laura said, "but they seem to have fallen off the Earth."

"What about their phones? On TV they can always find people through their phones."

Mr. Stahlman was shaking his head. "They found a stolen van with your phone, Iggy's, Ellis's, Annie's, and Rick's in the back. Whoever they are, they're smart."

Laura said, "Sounds like they might have done this before."

"Pros?" Luis said.

Mr. Stahlman nodded. "That's what I'm thinking." He turned to Ruth. "Marie said they sprayed Rick with something and tried to spray her. Is that what happened to you?"

"Damn right! I thought they was spray-painting but it wasn't paint. Went right up my nose. Burned like fire and then my muscles sort of went all gushy."

"Up the nose," Laura said, nodding. "Quickest route to the brain."

Luis said, "You told me once you've been someplace you can go back to it, right?"

He wasn't her favorite person, not by a long shot. Always poking and prodding and never forgetting a thing she said.

"Yeah. I mean, I guess so."

"Can you go back there—to the room where you woke up?"

"I don't know." He couldn't really want her to go back, could he? "I don't know where it is."

"But you don't have to know exactly where it is, right? You just have to have been there. Isn't that what you told me?"

"I guess so."

"Well, then, you can go back and find out where it is."

"How can I do that? It's just a room with no windows. It could be anywhere!"

"If you can't find out, you just jump back to your place upstairs. What's the problem?"

What's the problem? he says? No problem for fucking Luis. He ain't gonna show up all naked and not knowing who'll be there. And for what? To look at some bare walls? That room could be in Canada for all she knew—for all she'd *ever* know!

"Let's not rush into this," Laura said.

Thank you, Laura!

"We don't know how much time we have," Luis said. "They might move them now that Ruthie's escaped."

Fuck you, Luis.

Laura laid a comforting hand on her arm. "Right, but let's think this through. If Ruth is going to go back, we want to make the most of her trip." She patted Ruth's arm. "Why don't you get some rest while we figure this out, okay?"

That sounded great to Ruth.

"Yeah. Yeah, good idea."

She hurried back up to her place—not to rest, just to get away from everybody looking at her like she was the answer to the problem. But she wasn't. They'd have to find some other answer.

At the top of the steps she stopped and listened.

She heard Laura say, "You were a little rough on her, don't you think?"

Luis said, "Not rough enough, apparently."

"She's scared half to death."

"At least she's free. Think how scared the other three feel right now. Getting any cooperation from Ruthie's always been like pulling teeth. But it's not about her now. Her friends are in trouble and it's time for her to step up and help out."

Fuck you, Luis, she thought, sobbing as she hurried to her place. *Fuck you!*

3

LANGE-TÜR BUNKER

"Wake up, Mister Reise," Greve said. "Rise and shine."

Maureen watched Greve out of the corner of her eye as she labeled her samples. Initially he'd seemed taken aback by the teleporter's escape, but now he appeared unfazed.

Maureen felt . . . was there such a word as "fazed"? If so, she was fazed. Quite fazed. Teleportation . . . it broke all the rules. And yet she'd witnessed it.

Okay. Focus on the here and now. You're in room sixteen, administering the antidote to counter the neuro blocker that's paralyzing the . . . telekinetic.

Jesus.

She swallowed. "You don't think Ruth poses a threat?"

"The teleporter?" Greve shook his head. "I don't see how. She can't tell anyone where we are because she doesn't know. She certainly can't lead them here. So I'm not worried. She was a long shot anyway."

"How do you mean?"

"How were we going to test her? Even if the collar did work, we couldn't test her while it was operating. And as soon as we turned it off . . ."

"She'd be gone."

"Exactly. But we both witnessed her disappearance, which means it's a genuine talent. And that means there's probably more like her among the melis kids. All we have to do is find another one—one who's willing to cooperate."

"Do you think she'll be back? According to Montero's notes she can jump to any place she's already been."

Greve offered his pseudo-smile. "Did you see that look on her face? She's probably home hiding under her bed."

Ellis Reise stirred and opened his eyes. A yellowing bruise marred his left cheek. She wondered how he'd got it.

Greve positioned his tablet before him and said, "Hello, Mister Reise. Welcome to your new home."

Ellis sat up and looked around the room, then directly at them.

"Who the fuck are you?"

Greve made a *tsk*ing noise. "Such language. You are now a guest of the United States government and we—that is, the good doctor here and I—are in charge of delineating your telekinetic abilities."

"You had me knocked out and brought here? Fuck that!"

"We expect you to cooperate, Mister Reise. It will make things easier all around."

"Cooperate? I'll show you cooperate."

Maureen felt an instant of pressure on her throat before the collar did its *BZZZZT!* thing. The pressure released as Ellis jumped with the shock.

"What the fuck?"

"Language, Mister Reise. Please."

Again the brief pressure on her throat before the collar shocked him.

"Get this offa me!" he shouted and started tugging at the collar, which only caused it to shock him again.

He stopped struggling and glared at them.

"Let me explain how this is going to work," Greve said. "You are now an asset of the United States Department of Defense. You have been drafted, so to speak. This is your boot camp. Cooperate with us and you'll receive an honorable discharge. Refuse to cooperate and you succeed only in prolonging your time here."

Ellis lunged off the gurney and came at them with outstretched arms, his fingers curled into claws. Greve appeared to have been expecting that. He tapped the tablet and the collar buzzed.

Ellis's charge faltered, then he lunged again. This time the *BZZZZT!* was louder. His knees buckled but he didn't fall.

"God *damn* you!" he gasped.

"I can up the voltage to Taser levels if you wish, Mister Reise."

"Do your fucking worst!" he screamed and lunged again.

The shock this time drove him to his knees and

then to the floor where he lay twitching and howling in frustration. Maureen felt her stomach churn as she spied blisters under the collar.

"Are you familiar with the phrase 'Resistance is futile,' Mister Reise?" Greve said in that infuriatingly bland tone. "Well, it applies here. You are in a bunker fifty feet below Fort Knox Army Base. Yes, the same Fort Knox where the country's gold reserves are stored. You're not leaving until we say so. But we don't need an adversarial relationship. Mister Stahlman was offering you a weekly stipend equivalent to one hundred thousand a year. We will double that."

Ellis groaned. "Chump change compared to what I can take from the casinos on a single night."

"Not after we circulate your name, face, vital statistics, and particulars of your unique ability to every gaming company in the world."

This earned a baleful glare from Ellis but no further verbal response.

"Give that careful thought as we leave you to contemplate your options. Good day, sir."

When they reached the hallway, Maureen said, "Was all that really necessary?"

Greve locked Ellis's door and turned to her. "It's called establishing the pecking order. Doctor Montero's notes indicate that he believes Reise suffers from a personality disorder. And after that display in there, I tend to agree."

He's defiant, she'd give him that. And certainly violent.

"Did you feel a pressure on your throat?"

Greve nodded. "Trying to choke us, I imagine. Be thankful for those shocks. I also felt my tablet try to jump from my hands."

"Iggy next?" Maureen said.

"Our ungifted nadaný?" Greve sighed. "I suppose so. I've been debating whether to keep her sedated along with Hayden, and dump them both in a field somewhere."

"Marie Novotna says she's a nadaný and Montero's notes say she's got low-level zeta waves running twenty-four/seven. That's got to mean something."

"Montero couldn't find anything."

"Maybe we'll have better luck."

"All right," Greve said. "Let's get it over with."

4

QUEENS

"I've got an idea," Laura said.

She and Montero were sitting in Stahlman's office. Marie had retired to one of the second-floor efficiencies. Stahlman had convinced her to stay in the warehouse overnight. She'd been feeling beat and so she'd said her good-nights.

Laura had called Steven's place earlier to check on Marissa. He'd taken her out to dinner and the new Pixar movie and they'd had a great time. Her ex doted on his daughter and worked hard to nurture their relationship.

If only he'd been that devoted to ours . . .

"We're all ears," Stahlman said from his usual spot behind the desk.

"Remember the tracker you had Cyrus make disappear?"

Only three days ago but it seemed like forever.

Stahlman was nodding. "Sure."

"Why don't we give one to Ruthie and let her take it back to wherever they had her? It'll tell us where she ends up and that's where the others will be."

"First off," Montero said, "there's the matter of sending her back into the lion's den. Do we want to do that? *Should* we do that?"

Laura held up a hand. "Is this the same guy who said it's not about her now and she needs to step up for her friends?"

"Guilty," Luis said with a sheepish look. "But I'm thinking she's just a kid and we shouldn't browbeat her into it."

And I'm thinking Rick's with them and where did they take him, dammit?

Yeah, he was tough and resourceful, but Laura didn't share Stahlman's blithe Trojan horse assessment. He'd been gassed unconscious, which meant he was totally defenseless. The abductors were obviously after nadaný, which meant Rick was of no use to them. Best case: They'd toss him back unharmed, like an inedible fish snagged in the net. Worst case: They'd consider him a liability and make sure he never interfered again. The latter possibility made her sick.

Shouldn't browbeat Ruthie? I'll browbeat the hell out of her.

She shook her head. *Listen to me. I never thought I could be like this. But I am. Right now I sure as hell am. And no apologies. To anyone.*

"She can hop to a safe spot any time just by wishing it," she said. "You said 'first off.' What's second?"

"Her inability to take anything along with her—even makeup."

"Oh, right." Laura remembered the cloud of blush

Ruth had left behind during her demonstration. "Maybe she could swallow it?"

"Even if that worked, those trackers have limits. She could have been taken anywhere. She hasn't been exactly cooperative in the testing, you know, and because of that we haven't been able to determine the extent of her ability. So far she doesn't seem to have a distance limit. She could have been loaded on a plane and delivered someplace a thousand miles away. A tracker small enough to swallow would have a very limited range."

"Okay," Laura said through a sigh. "Scratch that idea."

Kevin stuck his head in the doorway. "As suspected, we were hacked. I found how they got in and sealed it off, but we have to figure they've already taken everything they wanted."

"Too little, too late," Stahlman said.

Seeing Kevin reminded Laura of her visit to the Bronx earlier, and Fabricia Alvarado's repurposed ampoule box.

"How are you with photo enhancement, Kevin?" she said, pulling out her phone.

He shrugged. "I know my way around Photoshop but I'm no way an expert."

She found her photo of the ampoule box on her phone and showed him. "I need to make that label legible. What do you think?"

He started tapping on the screen. "Lemme email it to myself and see."

She followed him to his computer station and watched as he opened the photo on his widescreen monitor. As before, she had no problem reading the logo.

Complete Organic

Multivitamin Injection

He clicked here and there, slid brightness and con-
trast gauges back and forth, and slowly, surely, she
began to make out the smaller letters.

The vitamins listed were the standard B-complex
components with hefty doses of folate that were standard with prenatal preparations. But she was more
interested in the address.

3919 S Capitol St SE
Ste 103-#164
Washington, D.C. 20032

"D.C.?" she said. "Not exactly a manufacturing
hub."

"Sounds like a mail drop," Kevin said. "Let me
stick that into my map program."

A map popped up on the screen with a marker on
Capitol Street.

"Anacostia," Kevin said. He shifted to street view
and they found themselves looking at a UPS Store
in a strip mall that had seen better days. "Told you.
Mail drop."

Laura made a note to call the place, but first . . .

"Can you go back to the street map?"

"Sure."

From overhead she could see a large area behind

the strip mall labeled *Joint Base Anacostia-Bolling*. She tapped it on the screen.

"What's that? An Army base?"

"'Joint Base' usually means more than one service involved. Easy enough to find out."

He typed and clicked and eventually a list filled the screen.

"Wow. Everybody's here: Marines, Navy, Air Force, Coast Guard, National Guard, DIA—"

"What's DIA?"

"Defense Intelligence Agency. Sort of like the Pentagon's CIA. Says they're headquartered there in Anacostia."

Pentagon . . . Rick had mentioned Pentagon black funding for something called Operation Synapse. And now, according to the label, the vitamin injection Jacobi had insisted on using was connected to a mail drop right next door to the headquarters of the Pentagon's CIA.

"Let me see that label again." Something about it . . .

Complete Organic

Multivitamin Injection

Complete Organic . . . she'd have to learn if they were still in business or, like Emily Jacobi, if they'd ever existed at all. She'd—

"Holy crap!"

"What?" Kevin said.

"Look at that logo. What's it look like to you?"

He shrugged. "I dunno. A stylized *C* around a spoon."

"Yeah, maybe. But . . ."

"But what? What's it look like to you?"

"A synapse. A goddamn synapse."

"Really?"

Yeah, really. Staring her right in the face. Here was the connection: According to Sela's gift, Maximilian Osterhagen was somehow crucial to the nadaný. Rick's contact had connected Osterhagen to something called Operation Synapse. If Laura was right about this label, Operation Synapse was connected to the injections administered to the mothers of the nadaný.

Tenuous . . . very tenuous . . .

But then add to that how Operation Synapse was connected to the Pentagon, and the mail drop for Dr. Jacobi's vitamin injections was a stone's throw from the Defense Intelligence Agency's HQ. And then what had Hari said?

Emily Jacobi wasn't fashioned by amateurs. The clandestine services are experts at fashioning legends with this level of sophistication. It's the kind of thing they do really well.

Clandestine services like CIA and KGB, Rick had said.

And DIA as well?

"Hey, Kevin, search 'Complete Organic' for me, will you?"

"Sure." He typed. "Yow! A quarter million hits! Let me quote it." He put the name inside quotation marks and tried again. "Big whoop. Still like fifty thousand."

Further searches revealed nothing. The company had no website. In fact, the completeorganic.com domain was for sale if they wanted it.

A front, a *legend* . . . just like Dr. Jacobi. The interconnections had become more likely.

But really . . . where did that leave her? She still had no idea where they'd taken Rick and the nadaný.

Somehow—Laura had yet to figure out exactly how—Ruthie was the key. If a location tracker wasn't practical . . .

"Say, Kevin. Is there such a thing as a location recorder?"

"Sure. GPS recorders . . . lots of companies use them to track their cars and trucks."

"You mean like LoJack?"

"LoJack simply broadcasts its position. But you can buy a gizmo that doesn't broadcast but simply records a series of GPS locations and stores them. The employer downloads the data later on to see where his vehicle's been. You know, to check out if the driver's making any unauthorized side trips."

"Do you think . . . ?"

He turned back to his computer and started working the keyboard. "They're making them smaller and smaller. Maybe . . ."

5

LANGE-TÜR BUNKER

In room five they went through the wake-up routine with Iggy. Her bleached hair and twin pigtails gave her a childlike look.

As they waited for her to open her eyes, Greve

said, "We had to adjust the sensitivity on this one's collar."

"Why's that?"

"Constant low-level zeta activity. If she spikes for some reason, she'll receive a shock, but if we kept the sensitivity at the same level as the others, she'd be getting shocked all the time."

Maureen considered that. "Montero had her MRI results in his notes and she's got no underlying structural lesion in the brain, so the zeta activity confirms she's a nadaný."

"But not a very useful one. Still, I'm going to keep her EEG under constant monitoring. If she ever spikes, I want to know the circumstances."

Iggy opened her eyes and, after the initial confusion and panicky questions about who, what, where, and why, settled down surprisingly quickly.

After going through his "guest of the government" spiel, Greve said, "Has Doctor Montero made any recent progress on identifying your gift?"

She shrugged. "If he has, he ain't told me."

"Too bad. It would save us time and most likely wasted effort. But we're going to keep at it and do whatever it takes to find out."

Maureen thought she seemed terribly calm. Maybe she wasn't the kind to show her emotions. Maybe she didn't have any.

Iggy said, "Doctor Laura thinks we all got some connection to some Modern Motherhood Clinics. I know I do."

"Doctor Laura . . ." Greve said, checking his notes on the table. "Oh, yes. Laura Fanning. The new addition. A medical examiner." He glanced at Maureen. "An odd choice, don't you think?" Back to Iggy: "Is she the one who's been poking her nose into the clinics?"

"I guess. Is she right? About the connection, I mean?"

"Yes," Maureen said.

"Were you involved?"

"Intimately."

Why had she used that word? Accurate, for sure, but . . . why had she answered at all?

"What did you do to us?"

Maureen said, "Your mothers were given monthly doses of melis while they were pregnant."

Iggy frowned. "Melis? What's that?"

"A long story. It began—"

Greve grabbed her arm and pulled her away. "Since when did you become so gabby?" he said in a low voice.

Maureen shrugged, unsure. Laying it all out had seemed like the thing to do.

"I don't see the harm."

"What next? A tour of the rear chamber?"

"Don't be ridiculous."

Greve returned to Iggy. "We want to find out all about you and your fellow nadaný. Are you going to cooperate?"

"Mister Stahlman was paying me."

She's *negotiating*, Maureen thought. This is one cool customer.

"We'll pay you even more—double."

She smiled and looked even more like a child. "Well, then, sure."

"Excellent! At least one of you is showing some sense."

"Make yourself at home," Maureen said, indicating

the bed against the wall. "That will be more comfort-able, though not much."

When they'd returned to the hall, Greve grumbled, "Just our luck."

"What?"

"The only one who's willing to cooperate has no talent. Like trying to assemble a choir and the only volunteer is tone deaf."

My, my, my. A metaphor? From Greve? Or was that a simile?

She was pretty sure she'd once known the differ-ence but had misplaced it in the mists of the past. The artsy-fartsy fluff had never been her strong suit, anyway. She lived for the hard stuff.

Greve crossed the hall and peeked in room seven-teen where the big guy still lay shackled to his gurney. He stirred, raising his hand, then letting it fall.

"He's getting light," Greve said. "I'll go order him a booster dose." As he walked off, he said, "Get some sleep. We start at 0700."

Sleep? She couldn't imagine sleep. The nap had helped, but even without it, for Christ sake she'd just seen a young woman vanish—right in front of her. Where to? Who knew? Someplace more welcoming than this bunker. Still hard to buy into. One second there, the next second nothing but air rushing in to fill the space she'd vacated.

And Anulka, fading from sight—the gurney she sat on becoming visible through her body until the shock brought her back.

Ellis . . . had that been his mind exerting pressure on her throat?

Oh, yeah. Ellis. She grimaced at the memory of those blisters on his neck. She headed for her nap room where she'd stashed her carry-on.

She rummaged around in her travel kit and found the small tube of bacitracin ointment she kept on hand for cuts and scrapes. Just in case. She admitted to being a just-in-case person, packing things that she never needed. Like this ointment. Probably out of date. Still, the greasy vehicle would help by itself.

6

Goddammit, now what? Ellis thought as he heard the key turn in the door lock.

He lay on his back on the gurney. They'd left him chained to it but he'd wheeled it around the room, exploring. He'd tried the locked door about a hundred times, drank some crummy tasting water from the sink in the bathroom, surfed the TV but couldn't find anything worth his attention. He'd checked the dresser drawers and found them packed with camo fatigues. As if he was gonna wear that shit. So finally he wound up back on the gurney, bored as all fuck.

And now someone at the door. Should he stay down or sit up? Staying down won, but the door didn't open. So he sat up.

Now the door opened.

The woman stepped in—the doctor type who'd had the rolling cart stacked with test tubes and shit. The Band-Aid on his arm told him someone had taken blood while he was out. He assumed she'd done it.

"Back for more fun?" he said.

Shit. That sounded like fronting.

"Not at all," she said, approaching.

She looked sixtyish. Gray hair, a bit thick in the waist, horn-rimmed glasses like the hipster jerks sport but these looked like she'd had them since they were new. Loose shirt over baggy jeans. Not bad looking for an old lady, if he was into granny groping, which he wasn't.

He looked past her. "Where's your Nazi pal?"

That other guy scared him. Ellis felt like he'd been locked up in Arkham Asylum with the Joker running the place. And here was his faithful assistant, Harley Quinn.

"Busy elsewhere," she said.

She came alone?

He studied the open door. No sign of anyone outside. He could make a grab for her, strangle her. So easy. Wouldn't have to worry about getting shocked if he used his hands. Maybe she had some keys to unlock the cuff and the collar. Take her down, search her pockets . . .

He was readying to spring when she stopped before him and handed him a small tube.

"Here."

He stared at it. "Toothpaste?"

"Ointment."

He took it and turned it over in his hands. "What, baci . . . baci . . . ?"

"Bacitracin. It's an antibiotic. For your neck."

"My neck?"

"The burns. It'll help them heal and keep them from getting infected."

He stared at the tube, baffled. "Why would you . . . ?"

"I don't want to hurt anybody. That's not what I'm about."

"Coulda fooled *me*, bitch."

She sighed. "I cannot offer explanations. I'll simply say that I am not in charge here and there are many aspects of this operation I do not control."

"Did you really come here alone? Or you got a Navy SEAL or somebody like that waiting outside the door just in case I get it into my head to start kicking the shit out of you?"

Which I still might do, he thought.

He'd expected some kind of reaction—like scared or something—but she just kept looking at him, cool as can be.

"No backup. I just figured you needed that ointment."

The ointment . . . yeah. What's up with that?

After what had gone down earlier, he hadn't expected anything like this. He didn't get it.

"Why?" His voice sounded a little thick . . . like his throat.

"Because I feel responsible."

"For what?"

"You."

"I don't get it."

"Long story." She walked back and turned in the doorway, her expression grim. "You'll learn eventually. And who knows? Maybe then you *will* kick the shit out of me."

What the fuck did *that* mean?

She closed the door and he heard the key turn in the lock.

No question: Arkham Asylum, or someplace a lot like it. Was he really fifty feet below Fort Knox? The underground part he could buy—no windows of any sort, no hint of outside noise, and that damp feeling that wormed into your bones. And maybe Fort Knox made sense if this bunker was like an ultra-secret installation.

But why did this granny feel responsible? Was she connected to those Motherhood clinics people were talking about back at the warehouse? He wished he'd paid more attention to all the chatter but he'd had too much of his own shit to deal with.

He squeezed some out of the ointment and rubbed it on the blisters under the collar. Felt good. For some reason she'd done him a solid. Hadn't expected anything like that. Not here.

Still trying to figure out what to make of it all, he lay back and tried to grab some shut-eye.

7

Rick had been conscious for a while.

First the disorientation, accompanied by instinctive vertiginous thrashing leading to the realization that his right arm was restrained. That in turn set off a gallop toward panic, which he managed to rein in before it built up any momentum. Panic never helped. Stay calm.

Slowly it came back to him . . . the gas, his muscles turning to overcooked linguine, falling into darkness.

Now he lay on some kind of bed—a gurney, he presumed, since it had a side rail where his right wrist was cuffed. He licked his lips. Thirsty as all hell.

He had a good sense of time and figured he'd been awake for thirty-five minutes. He hadn't fully opened his eyes—he could be on camera, for all he knew—but had taken peeks through slit lids. The concrete ceiling and walls threw him for a moment until he remembered the tale Pickens had told about Osterhagen's bunker. The Lange-Tür bunker. Was that where he was—fifty feet under Lakehurst Naval Air Station?

A while ago a door had opened to his right. He'd

overheard a muttered discussion between a man and a woman. He gathered he was the subject of the conversation but couldn't quite make out the words.

And just a few minutes ago, the door had opened again. He'd moved for show, to see what they'd say, and heard, *He's getting light . . . I'll go order him a booster dose.*

Which meant he'd be having company soon.

Whoever they were, they'd twice looked in on him in person—a good indication that he wasn't under video surveillance. Still, he lay quiet and waited.

On the downside, he was a righty, and his right wrist was cuffed. Upside, with the door to his right, whoever came would approach from that side, which allowed him a cross-body blow with his left fist. He could put some power behind that.

The door opened a third time, followed by approaching footsteps. Rick slit his lids again and saw a beefy guy in a dark blue coverall holding a capped syringe—his "booster dose," no doubt.

The guy slowed as he closed. He removed the cap and swiveled the syringe to a dagger grip as he raised it over Rick's thigh. The booster needle was going to be jammed right through his pants leg.

Rick folded his left fingers into a Nanquan fist and jabbed the leading knuckles full force into the guy's Adam's apple.

Cartilage crunched and the syringe dropped to the floor as both his hands flew to his throat. His eyes went wide with panic as he tried to shout through his crushed larynx, but all he managed were faint, strangled sounds.

He tried to turn but Rick was already off the gurney. He grabbed the back of the guy's collar with his free hand and kicked his feet out from under him,

making sure he landed hard on his back. Then Rick
flipped him onto his belly and straddled him. The
guy struggled wildly, but not for long. His exertions
chewed up what oxygen he had in his bloodstream
and he wasn't replacing it. Rick picked up the fallen
syringe, then watched the guy's movements weaken
and diminish as his skin turned a dusky hue.

When he stopped moving, Rick flipped him over
and emptied the syringe deep into his quadriceps.
Then he grabbed the sides of the flattened laryn-
geal cartilage and squeezed. With a crunch the tube
partially opened, letting the trapped air out with a
whoosh and allowing fresh air to whistle in.

After a few wheezing breaths, the guy's color
slowly eased back toward normal and the glassy look
started to leave his eyes. Rick searched his pockets.
He found a key ring, a swipe card, a four-inch folding
knife, and a rubber-topped injection vial filled with
clear fluid. One of the keys looked like a good fit for
the cuff. He tried it and it worked.

The guy tried to roll onto his side but Rick easily pushed him back. No doubt weak from his near-
death experience, but the injection might be having
an effect too. He tried to shout again but achieved
only a hiss, like weak steam.

"Be quite a while before you get your voice back,"
Rick whispered. "Maybe never a hundred percent."

His eyes were starting to glaze. Whatever was in
that syringe worked fast.

"Where are we?" Rick said.

A hissed "Fuck you."

"I'm guessing the Lange-Tür bunker, right?"

The guy's eyes narrowed in puzzlement, showing
no sign of recognition.

"Lakehurst—Lakehurst, New Jersey?"

But the eyes were already closed.

Crap. Could he be somewhere other than the Lange-Tür bunker?

He looked around. A twin bed against the wall, a sink, a bathroom. Like a room at the Bates Motel. Definitely a bunker feel to the place.

He gave a mental shrug. Sooner or later he'd know. As for right now . . .

Rick started stripping him.

8

QUEENS

Stahlman put down his phone and said, "That was NYPD. They're finally giving me some info."

"And?" Laura said.

She'd grown increasingly worried about Rick's fate at the hands of his abductors.

"The van Marie identified—they found it in the long-term parking lot at Newark Airport. The plates were listed as stolen. They must have transferred the four from the first van to this one and headed straight to the airport."

Laura shook her head. "Newark Airport? That doesn't make sense. You can't just haul unconscious people through security and onto a plane."

"Not on a commercial flight. But private planes have much looser rules about cargo. Dump them into trunks and roll them aboard. And if, as you suspect, the whole nadaný project or whatever it is might be connected to the Department of Defense, then all rules are off. They'll be telling TSA what it can do, not the other way around."

She tried to imagine folding Rick into a trunk—ludicrous and upsetting.

A knock on the door, then Kevin stuck his head in. "I think I found what we're looking for."

"What's that?" Stahlman said.

Laura explained about searching online for a GPS recorder small enough for Ruthie to swallow.

"What?" Stahlman looked baffled. "Why?"

"For when she jumps back to wherever they were holding her," Kevin said. "All she's gotta do is stay long enough for the recorder to note the GPS coordinates—we're talking less than a minute—then hop back to her room upstairs."

Stahlman made a face. "And how many bowel movements before we're able to get the reading?"

Kevin frowned. "Oh, crap. Hadn't thought of that."

"Oh, 'crap' is right," Laura said. The intestinal mechanics hadn't occurred to her either. They were all new at this. "Maybe we could give her some ipecac to induce vomiting."

"Or wrap it in a condom and stick it up the other end."

Good luck with that, Laura thought.

Stahlman waved him off. "Where is this GPS thing?"

"In the Spy Shop on East Thirty-Fourth. I was going to hop over and—"

"Do it. Let's not worry about the other issues until we have the device on the premises. We'll deal with them then. And save the receipt for reimbursement."

"Will do," Kevin said and ducked out.

Stahlman was shaking his head. "Like so many plans, they sound great in theory but fall apart on execution."

"You don't think it's going to work?" Laura said.

He shrugged. "Depends on convincing Ruth. And then it depends on where they're being kept. If it's in a basement with a big building overhead—say, like the Pentagon, or in an old missile silo—that little recorder's not going to pick up a GPS signal. Not in a million years."

Yet another thing she hadn't considered. They'd have to play this Ruthie thing by ear. Until then . . .

"Speaking of buildings where they might be," she said, "why take Rick along at all? He wasn't what they were after. Why not just leave him in one of the vans to sleep it off?"

Stahlman spread his hands. "How can I answer that? The only reason I can think of is that the ones in the field doing the abductions aren't in on the reason for the abductions. They're just doing what they're told. They could be Special Forces guys recruited for the job, or some of the mercenaries the Pentagon likes to hire. They were targeting Marie, they found Rick and Marie together, they missed Marie but they netted Rick. Now they've got Rick and don't know whether or not he's someone of value, so they keep him and leave it to whoever's giving the orders to sort it out later."

"That's what I'm worried about," Laura said. "The sorting out."

Stahlman grimaced. "I know you and Rick are involved, but I've known him longer than you. I put you two together, don't forget."

"I'm not about to."

"I know he means a lot to you, but he means a lot to me too. He's not just an employee—maybe the best employee I've ever had—he's also a friend. I not only value and trust the guy, Laura, I *like* him. But I take comfort in the fact that we've no reason to believe these people are killers."

"But we've got good reason to believe that Defense is involved—I mean, everything I've heard from Rick and learned myself points that way—and that means we're dealing with a huge conspiracy here. Government-funded maternity clinics administered some secret chemical or biological agent to unsuspecting pregnant women that changed their children, turned them into X-Men or X-Kids or whatever they're called. I never watched those movies."

"Rick would know."

"But Rick's not here." She swallowed as her voice threatened to break. "He's in the hands of people who will probably do anything to keep all this secret. Can you imagine if it got out? Altering the brains of unborn children? Without parental consent? Even *with* parental consent, for god's sake! And have you noticed that virtually all the nadaný belong to minorities? I'm seeing headlines with words like 'racism' and 'genocide' and 'Nazis' and 'Mengele' and on and on. And I'm sure those responsible are seeing generals' heads rolling down the halls of the Pentagon."

Stahlman rubbed a shaky hand over his face. "Christ, you're right."

She hadn't realized how much she wanted him back. What an idiot. She'd pushed him away, but now that an unknown someone had taken him away and might not give him back . . .

She couldn't allow that, would not stand for that. The worries assaulted her.

"At least the nadaný they grabbed hold some value for whoever made them that way. They can be studied, just like we were doing. But what about Rick? He's got no nadaný value. In fact, he's a huge liability. He's ex-CIA and knows way too much."

"Yeah, I suppose he does," he said through a sigh. "But there's one thing we shouldn't forget: He's Rick. They don't know him. They'll check his wallet and think he's just some security grunt from Westchester. They will underestimate him. Which means they'll have their hands full."

"But we can't count on that," Laura said as an idea struck. She leaped from the chair and rushed for the door. "I need to catch Kevin for a ride-along."

"Why?"

"To find a surgical supply place."

9

LANGE-TÜR BUNKER

According to the syringe guy's badge, his name was H. Watts. His blue coverall was a snug fit over Rick's clothes—definitely too short in the legs—but would attract less attention than Rick's street clothes. No chance of passing even casual inspection, but if it allowed him to get close, that was all he needed.

Close to whom? Good question. He had no idea what he'd find beyond that door.

While undressing Mr. Watts, he'd noticed the same scar on his back as on the back of one of the guys on the abduction team. More like a brand, really.

So were these guys part of some cult? This past spring had involved him in enough cult trouble to last a lifetime. The crazies in 536 had been out for blood—his and Laura's. Were these jokers connected?

He saved that concern for later. Right now he needed recon. He had to operate on the assumption he was in the Lange-Tür bunker, that the people behind his abduction were after nadaný, and he was picked up by accident. Or was he? Had his inquiry into Osterhagen tripped an alarm somewhere? Or had Pickens sicced the dogs on him?

No . . . they'd definitely wanted Marie.

He capped the used syringe and stuck it in a pocket with the injection vial. He checked the door and found it unlocked. Easing it open, he peeked out at an empty hallway, lit by naked incandescent bulbs stuck in the ceiling. A dozen or so doors on each side, and what appeared to be heavy-duty security gates at each end. A couple of the doors stood open. The one at the far end to his left threw a shaft of light into the hall.

Rick had to assume that Watts wasn't alone down here. If he had a buddy or buddies, that seemed the likely place to find them. Rick might have Watts's keys but he wasn't going to be allowed to waltz out of here.

Okay. Assess the threat and decide how best to

deal with it. Then see if he was the only abductee. Had they grabbed the nadaný too, or—worst-case scenario—Laura as well?

He checked along the walls and ceiling for security bubbles or cameras and was surprised to find none. Folks were hiding cameras everywhere these days, even in lightbulbs—in floodlights, not these household incandescents here.

Rick eased through the door and found a metal key in the outside keyhole. Well, all right. He locked the door and pocketed the key, then slipped down the hall, staying close to the wall. He was tempted to peek inside each doorway he passed but kept moving. He'd have time for that after he neutralized security—if he could.

He stopped just outside the lighted doorway. Be so nice right now to have one of those angled dental mirrors for a look around the doorjamb. Instead he risked a quick, one-eyed peek: A guy in a similar coverall sat about a dozen feet away—back to him, hands behind his head as he leaned back in a chair, feet up on a desk, watching TV. Rick recognized *Jaws* playing. Disk or cable? Four flat screens were arrayed on the wall. Was the guy even awake? Rick couldn't tell from the rear.

Well, if he wasn't asleep, he would be soon.

Rick pulled out the injection vial and filled the syringe. Taking a breath he closed the door as he stepped into the room and quickly crossed the floor.

"Everything okay down there?" the guy asked without turning around.

Rick threw an arm around his throat as he emptied the syringe into his right trapezius, then put him in a choke hold. He kicked, he flailed, he thrashed, he grunted and tried to shout, he fell out of the chair, and the two of them dropped to the floor. The pounding of his feet against the concrete didn't make much noise and soon he lay still.

Rick left him snoring on his back and explored the room. A desk, chairs, a bunk. Just like his own room, except for the monitors. Rick studied each but couldn't make out much more than arrays of blinking lights and a desk where some longhair in a white lab coat was working a computer keyboard.

So they had some security cameras after all. But where were they?

After relieving the new guy of his swipe card, key ring, and badge—which said he was H. Woolley—Rick checked the desk drawers where he found a big-screen Samsung phone. Excellent.

He opened it and saw zero bars. He punched in 911 and got a *No Service*. Bummer. But at least it bolstered the underground bunker theory. He pocketed it—just in case—and checked the desk for a landline phone. No go. Just an intercom. Shit.

Stepping back into the hall, he found the outside keyhole empty. He selected a likely suspect from Woolley's key ring and it locked the door.

Okay, two guards down, how many more to go?

He stood at the end of the hallway a few feet away from the heavy steel security door covered in yellow and black warning chevrons around a red-lettered sign:

WARNING
RESTRICTED AREA
NO ADMITTANCE

The door sported a small window, maybe four by six inches, made of thick glass, set about five feet off the floor. He bent for a peek but all he could make out in the low-lit room beyond were rows of blinking lights. The same blinking lights as on the monitors? He risked a swipe of Watts's card. Nothing. Tried again with the same result. Woolley's was no better.

So. Security wasn't allowed beyond this door.

Why would that be? Well, if this was the Lange-Tür bunker, then the reason for its existence must be on the other side, and security folks couldn't be trusted with whatever it was.

Fine. As much as Rick wished to know what was in there, it could wait. Priority number one was establishing the presence of Laura or any nadaný and spiriting them out of here.

Another similar door, sans window, waited at the opposite end of the hallway. Locked too?

Only one way to find out.

He eased down the hallway, again suppressing the temptation to check behind each door.

Oh, hell. Had to check at least one. He picked at random, found it unlocked, and peeked in. Same Bates Motel motif with a gurney just like the one in his room—empty but for a blue sweat suit on the floor with some weird circular thing that looked like a dog collar.

Okay. Move on.

He reached the other end without seeing or hearing any signs of life. He tried Watts's card again, this time with success. He winced as the doors retracted with a low rumble. He didn't need the noise. He pressed back into a doorway and waited to see if anybody came to check.

Nope. Nobody.

Back at the door, the first thing he noticed were a couple of golf carts and, beyond them, a long straight corridor—*long* as in multiple football fields long. A couple more carts down that end as well, parked near a recessed set of doors that could belong to an elevator.

A ride to the surface?

He hesitated, then hopped into one of the carts and raced to the other end. He didn't see any cameras, and even if they had a couple, he was dressed in security overalls. From a distance he'd look like he belonged here.

The paired doors at the far end sported an Otis logo. Most definitely an elevator. Only one button on the call panel, which meant the car offered a one-way ride. No arrow on it but his money was on *up*.

His way out.

But not yet. If they'd also grabbed Laura or a couple of nadaný, he wasn't leaving without them.

He returned to his starting point and swiped the card again to close the doors. Still nobody came to check. Maybe opening and closing them was no big thing.

Okay, time to check out the rooms. The first room on his right was labeled *20*. Good a place as any to start. He tried the knob—unlocked—and eased it open. Dark inside. He reached in, found the wall switch, and flipped it. Hearing no reaction to the sudden light, he stepped inside to find some sort of office. Desk, computer, a row of filing cabinets, and a single bookshelf. A smaller room than the security office down the hall, and lots smaller than where he'd awakened earlier. Definitely a single-occupant setup. But who? Some sort of administrator?

Rick moved to the center and looked around. No photos, no degrees, no *World's Best Boss* or *World's Best Dad* mugs or statuettes. He rifled through the desk drawers but found nothing but pens, pencils, and legal pads.

Back to the hallway and on to the next room—nineteen. Empty. Okay, the next—

Someone lying on the bed in eighteen. A young woman. Familiar . . .

"Oh, shit! Annie?"

She jerked up to sitting and gaped at him.

"Rick?" she screeched.

He put a finger to his lips and eased the door closed behind him. "Keep it down!"

"But how—?"

"Same as you, I imagine. I—hey, what's that around your neck?"

"It shocks me!" Her face scrunched up. "If I try to disappear, it *shocks* me!" She broke down into sobs.

"Hey, easy, easy," he said. She had to get a grip. "Crying never helped anything."

"I c-can't h-help it! I'm scared."

"I get that. But put a sock in it, okay?"

"*What?*" The sobs morphed into an angry glare as she spoke through clenched teeth. "I'm in this shit because of *you*! If you'd just left me alone to do my thing, I'd be back in Queens right now. But *nooo,* you had to get into my life and make promises and now everything is *fucked*!"

He smiled at her. "Well, at least you're not crying anymore."

A confused look, then her shoulders slumped. "Okay, you got me. But we're still fucked. What do we do?"

"First thing, we get that collar off you. Lemme take a look."

The collar was a crude contraption—looked jury-rigged, in fact. A hinge at noon, a lock at six o'clock.

Rick guessed someone had thrown it together on the fly.

"So . . . when you try to disappear, it shocks you?"

"Big time. And it *hurts*."

He looked at her. Was she going to cry again? No, she was holding it together.

"The man said it got something to do with my brain waves."

This could be useful. "What man?"

"The one with the lady."

"Okay, how many people have you seen since you woke up?"

"Three. Counting you."

"Any idea where they are?"

"No. Just glad they ain't here. That guy . . . ooh, man, the way he looked at me."

Uh-oh. "Like he was undressing you?"

"No. Least I'd be human then. Fucker's got these dead-fish eyes lookin' at me like I was some kinda *thing*."

Rick figured whoever was behind the abductions wanted to find out what made the nadaný tick. Yeah, she was a thing to this guy—a Rolex he wanted to disassemble.

He concentrated on the collar. The obvious solution seemed to be to remove the batteries that fueled the shock, but they appeared to be arrayed on the inner surface. No way to get to them from here.

The lock, however . . . the lock was clumsily attached and looked like the weak link. The keyhole was too small to pick, even if he had a kit, but that meant it might be small enough to force. He pulled out Watts's folding knife and flicked it open.

Annie flinched away when she saw the blade. "What you gonna do with that?"

"Cut off your head, slip off the collar, then replace your head. Simple."

That glare again. "You think that's funny? You think you Chris fucking Rock or something?"

"I guess I'm an acquired taste. But all that aside, I'm gonna try to force the lock on this contraption, so hold still or you might be losing that head after all."

He inserted the point of the blade into the keyhole and worked it as deep inside as it would go, then gave the knife a sharp twist. The lock popped half-way open. He stuck the blade into the gap and gave another twist. The collar sprang open and fell away, dangling by the electrode wire.

With a cry, Annie tore it off, held it up for a quick look, then hurled it across the room.

She faded from view, then reappeared, hands raised in triumphant fists. "Yes! I could love you if I didn't hate you so much."

Made perfect sense to him—which was kind of scary.

"Now get me outta here!" she said.

"Whoa. Was anyone else grabbed along with you?"

"Oh, shit! Ruthie!"

The scene in that room he'd checked: the empty clothes, the empty collar . . . it all made sense now . . .

He laughed. "Ruthie's back home. She left her clothes and her collar behind."

"Then we can go?"

"*You* can go. I'm staying in case they grabbed others, but I need you to go get help. And here's how you're gonna do it . . ."

10

QUEENS

"Oh, shit, that burns!" Ruthie cried, clutching her upper thigh just above where Laura was injecting the lidocaine.

"Just like I warned you," Laura said. "But it doesn't last long. Just hang in there a little and you won't feel a thing."

It hadn't been easy, but Laura had organized the equivalent of a family intervention for Ruthie. But instead of an addiction, the problem was fear. Of death? No. Of appearing naked, exposing her body to strangers—*possibly* exposing it. And how did that possibility weigh against helping save her friends, especially Iggy?

She'd coached Stahlman, Cyrus, Tanisha, and Leo in what to say but, because she was such a newcomer, Laura had stayed on the periphery during the confrontation, willing Ruthie to see the light.

Finally convinced there was no other way and that she was the only one with a prayer of getting results, Ruthie had agreed to hold the GPS recorder—tucked inside the finger of a sterile latex surgical glove—in her mouth when she made the jumps to and from the mystery location. Unfortunately she had a hypersensitive gag reflex, and even though Kevin had picked up the smallest unit available, she retched every time it touched her tongue.

Knowing nothing was ever easy with Ruth, Laura had prepared for the possibility with a stop at a surgical supply store. You couldn't walk in off the street and buy the supplies she needed, but her medical examiner's ID had cleared the way.

After multiple retches, it took surprisingly little to convince her to allow Laura to implant the GPS just below the skin of her thigh.

She was doing this for Iggy, she said. And maybe Annie. But not for that asshole Ellis.

Fine-fine-fine, Ruthie. Just do it.

Now she sat on the sheet-covered pool table, dangling her legs and looking scared.

Laura gave the skin of the target area an extra coating from the betadine swab, then donned another pair of sterile gloves. She'd bought half a dozen pairs just to be safe. Marie had volunteered to act as surgical assistant. She'd had no medical training but was willing, and that was more than half the battle.

"Ready?" Laura said.

Marie nodded.

Laura looked at Ruthie. "Ready?"

"I guess." She sounded anything but sure.

"Lie back."

"I wanna watch," Ruthie said.

"No, you don't. Just lie back and look at the ceiling. You won't feel a thing and this will be over before you know it."

She lay back and Laura put out her hand.

"Scalpel."

Marie tore open the packet as Laura had instructed, allowing Laura to grab its handle without contaminating it. She preferred a number eleven blade—very sharp point with a straight blade, not the beveled number fifteen usually shown on TV. As she plunged the point through the skin of Ruthie's thigh, she heard a gasp.

Not Ruthie—Kevin's face had gone white. His back was against the wall and he was sliding down to a squat.

"You okay?"

"I think I'll be better off closer to the floor," he rasped.

Laura made a one-inch diagonal incision along the cleavage line of the anterolateral thigh—and hid her surprise as it started to bleed. Of course it would bleed, but all the skin she had been incising for years upon years was dead and never bled.

Not much blood now. She'd used a lidocaine-epi mixture to minimize the bleeding and extend the local anesthesia as long as possible.

She quickly slid the GPS recorder—wrapped in a fresh sterile glove finger—through the incision into the fatty layer beneath the skin, then closed the slit with three quick nylon sutures. Would the sutures go with her? Who knew? They were in *terra incognita*. She taped a lump of gauze over it to act as a make-shift pressure dressing. She had no doubt that would be left behind when Ruthie teleported but she felt compelled to cover the incision anyway.

"Done," she said, snapping off her gloves.

"Already?" Ruthie said, sitting up and staring at the bandage. "You fast!"

"But you've got to be even faster. Get back to wherever they had you, learn whatever you can about where it is, then jump back here and let us know."

"Okay."

Instead of jumping off, she sat there looking pensive, worried.

"Well?" Laura said.

"I'm thinking."

Laura knew what was going on in her mind. The

room she'd left could now be full of people and she'd be popping into their midst stark naked.

"While Iggy's scared and alone," Marie said.

"Iggy ain't scared a nothin'!" The heat behind her words died as she said, "Shit," and disappeared.

Her clothing collapsed onto the pool table as something hit the floor with a metallic *clink*: the bloody GPS tracker. The sutures, the tape, and the bloody gauze followed.

"Shit," Kevin said in the same tone.

11

LANGE-TÜR BUNKER

Ruthie always closed her eyes during that sick-dizzy instant when she jumped. She couldn't help it. And this time was no exception. She opened them immediately upon feeling the air on her bare skin, ready to jump straight back to her apartment if she saw anyone.

No one. She released the breath she'd been holding.

And yeah, same room—she'd pictured it before the jump. She saw her clothes in a pile under some weird sort of collar. She grabbed her underpants first and that was when she noticed the blood oozing down her leg.

"Fuck!"

She'd expected to leave the bandage, but what about the GPS thing?

She felt the area above the bleeding cut. Nothing under the skin there. She'd lost the GPS—left it behind. She tossed the underpants onto the rolling bed. No sense in getting dressed now. Might as well go back.

But Iggy was here. Maybe she could find out the location of this dump without the GPS.

The underpants got bloody as she pulled them on. She needed to stop that bleeding. She grabbed her bra and tied it around her thigh, right over the cut. It seemed to work. She'd just ruined a good bra, but she could always buy another. She pulled on the sweatpants and top.

Now what?

Find a window and see if anything looked familiar. Like what? The Washington Monument? The Brooklyn Bridge? But damn if she could find a single window. The walls were solid concrete. Like a prison. But hell, even Rikers had windows. Not that she'd ever been there, but she just assumed. So what was this place? It gave her a shiver. Made her want only one thing: out.

Okay, the fastest way out was to get to work. No windows, so what next?

Go find Iggy, she guessed. Or even better, find Rick. Laura had said he'd been snatched too, and he seemed like a tough mother. Yeah. Find Rick first if he was here. She could use a tough mother on her side right now.

She slipped into her sneakers and padded to the door.

Please don't be locked, please don't be locked, please don't be . . .

She tried the knob and the door pulled open.

Yes!

A peek revealed a quiet hallway with lots of doors just like this one. Steeling herself, she slipped out, eased her door closed behind her, and sidled to the next door to her right. The knob turned but the door wouldn't budge. Then she saw the big metal key sticking out. She gave it a quick turn, then tried the knob again. She pushed the door open enough to stick her head inside.

Iggy sat on the bed staring at her in shock.

"Ruthie! What—"

Ruthie shushed her as she slipped through and closed the door.

"Keep it down, girl!"

Iggy was up and running at her. They threw their arms around each other and hugged. Iggy sobbed against her shoulder and Ruthie felt herself tear up as well.

"How'd you get free?"

"I jumped back to the warehouse and then came back here."

Iggy pushed back and grinned, dimpling her wet cheeks. "You came back for *me*?"

"Believe it, girl."

"You bring help?"

"That's just it. Can't bring no help because nobody knows where the fuck we are. Do you?"

Iggy shook her head. "No clue."

Ruthie noticed the collar. "Hey, what's that around your neck?"

"I don't know." She tugged at it. "I had it on when I woke up. Maybe it's some kind of tracking thing, so they can find me if I run away."

Tracking . . . that reminded her.

"We've gotta find out where we are. I ain't seen one window yet. You?"

"I've been locked up in here. Had a couple of visitors but that's it."

"Yeah, so did I, but I ghosted soon as I woke up. Maybe we can—" Ruthie jumped at a knock on the door. "Shit!" she whispered. "Someone's here! What do I do?"

Iggy pointed under the bed. "Go!"

Ruthie dropped and crawled. A tight fit but she made it just as the door opened.

"Oh, good," said a woman's voice. "You're awake."

"Who can sleep?" Iggy said.

"Yeah, I understand. I'm really sorry about this. But let's try to make the best of it, okay?"

Make the best of it? Ruthie thought. Fuck that. Get her *outta* here.

"What do I call you?" Iggy said.

"My name's Maureen. I guess that'll do."

"Where are we, Maureen?"

Yes! Ruthie gave a tiny fist pump. Go, Iggy!

"We're . . ." She seemed to hesitate. "We're on the edge of the Pine Barrens."

"The edge of the Pine Barrens," Iggy said nice and loud, then started coughing.

I heard you, Ruthie thought. Don't know what that means but maybe somebody else will.

Then she realized the coughing was for a reason. People said she made a pop when she jumped, and Iggy was trying to hide it.

So Ruthie jumped.

12

Rick handed Annie the swipe card.

"This will open the big steel doors down the end of the hall. They make some noise but the two guards are out cold and nobody came looking when I opened it. Make sure you close it after you."

"What's out there?"

"A *long* corridor—good half mile, I'd say."

She groaned. "A half mile? Really?" She hated to walk.

"But they've got golf carts—"

"Golf cart? I can't use no golf cart! What if somebody sees it driving itself?"

"Nobody there to see you. And no cameras either."

"You been out there?"

"I did a quick reconnoiter. The elevator at the end takes you up to ground level and out."

"You know that?"

"Pretty sure."

"Well, if you been there, why didn't *you* go get help?"

He gave her a do-I-really-have-to-say-this look. "Unfortunately, I can't turn invisible, and odds are about a hundred percent that it's guarded up top."

"When those elevator doors open, they gonna know something's up."

"When they see the elevator's empty, they'll think it's some mechanical glitch." He grinned. "Knowing how smoothly you got in and out of that Starbucks yesterday, I don't think you'll have any problem slipping past whatever security they've got posted up there."

Well, he had that right. She'd had plenty of practice moving along crowded sidewalks unseen and untouched.

"Yeah, okay. Then what?"

He pulled a cell phone out of his coverall and handed it to her.

"You get a safe distance away and use this to call the state police."

"You got a *phone*? Why haven't you—?"

"No signal down here. When you're safe, call the state police and tell them you just escaped captivity but your captors still have some of your friends locked up."

Annie saw a problem. "Where do I say I am? I don't even know what state we're in. That dead-eyed fucker said we were in Fort Knox but—"

"Fort Knox? He told you that?"

"Yeah."

"Then you can bet that's where we're *not*. But anyway, tell the cops you don't know where you are. They'll lock in on your phone and locate you. I think we're in Jersey, by the way. But no matter, just get the cavalry riding our way and soon we'll all be out of here."

"'All'? If Ruthie's gone, who else is left?"

"That's what I plan to find out."

"You going out looking? What if you get caught?"

Rick shrugged. "I'm already caught. But any of your friends who're here may have collars that need removing."

This guy had fucked up her life by getting her involved in this mess, but she was finding him hard to hate. She kind of liked him, in fact.

"They could put one of those collars on you and start zapping you just for fun."

His eyes went flat. "Yeah. They could. But they won't."

She knew right then she wouldn't want to be the guy who tried to do that.

"Ready to go?" he said.

"Yeah. I guess."

He eased open the door. "I'll stay here and listen

for those big doors. When I hear them close, I'll start looking for others."

The first time she'd gone invisible was because she'd been scared out of her mind. Now she could vanish simply by thinking of that time. She didn't have to *feel* scared, just had to *remember* feeling scared. After triggering the invisibility, she held on to it like holding on to a thought.

The world shimmered and dimmed around her, which meant she'd vanished. The world got streaky as she stepped out into the hallway. Dr. Montero had told her that was from light bending and slipping around her as she moved.

Whatever.

He'd been totally amazed. To her it was like totally natural.

She was about halfway down the hall when she heard a door open. She froze. Why, she couldn't say. Not like she'd be spotted.

Turning, she saw an older woman—sixtyish, graying, a little chunky—step out of a room three doors down.

Hey. The bitch who woke her up with the nasty fucker who made the shock collar. Pretty clear to Annie she hadn't known about the collar beforehand. And the way she'd flinched every time it zapped showed she didn't like the idea at all.

Still, Annie had to restrain herself from braining her as she crossed the hall and passed within a foot of her.

The woman knocked on the door to room five. After waiting a second or two, she stepped inside and closed the door behind her. Annie had the hallway to herself again.

Who was in there? Annie was tempted to try for a peek but decided against it: Get out and get help. That was her mission. She'd have all the answers she wanted after the cops raided the place.

The world began to streak again as she moved on.

13

The edge of the Pine Barrens . . .

Maureen wondered why she'd phrased it that way. She'd meant to use the Fort Knox line, but then Lakewood Naval Air Station had leaped into her brain, yet that hadn't been completely accurate. Yes, they were on the NAS property but not truly part of the facility proper. The edge of the Pine Barrens had been the most truthful.

But since when did truth matter here?

She shrugged it off, just as she'd shrugged off the unlocked door. She thought Greve had locked it but maybe he hadn't. Not that any of the nadaný could leave anyway. Well, except for Ruth, of course.

"Need a drink of water?" she said as Iggy controlled her coughing.

She shook her head. "No, I'm fine now. But look, Doctor Maureen, if you're—"

"My friends call me Moe."

"Are we friends?"

"I hope we can be."

"Well, okay, *Moe,* if you're gonna ask me about what kind of gift I have again, don't waste your time. The answer's the same: I don't. Marie says I'm a nadaný, but if that's true, I'm a loser nadaný. I'm useless."

"Nobody's useless. Especially you."

For some reason she felt protective toward this

teen with the bleached pigtails. But that aside, what was the draw here? They couldn't have any common ground. Maureen was white middle class with an advanced science degree, Iggy was a Puerto Rican high school dropout from the ghetto.

And really, does anyone say "ghetto" anymore? That's how far out of it I am.

"No, you see I'm *especially* useless because that melis stuff you gave my mother before I was born didn't work on me like the others. I wound up with zero-zip-nada-nothing."

Melis? What the—?

"How do you know about—?"

"You told me, remember? You said you were 'intimately' involved in the Modern Motherhood Clinics that gave them the stuff."

Had she said that? Yes. She remembered now. Whatever had possessed her to do that?

"I was. I became Doctor Emily Jacobi and ran the places."

"'Became'?"

"Pretended to be."

What am I *saying*?

"I spoke out of turn—I'm *speaking* out of turn."

"You mean you weren't involved?"

"No—I mean, yes, I was, but—"

"Your pal there said it was a government thing. Really? Why's the government trying to create human freaks?"

"Freaks? That wasn't the intention at all. Anything but. Melis was supposed to increase intelligence."

"Did it?"

"It did in rats. When we mixed it with saline and injected into pregnant rats, their offspring ran mazes like nobody's business."

"So you decided to try it on humans. My moms wasn't the brightest bulb in the box but I just know she wouldn't say okay to that. Which meant you were experimenting on us without asking, right?"

Maureen shrugged. "How could we ask? Messing with the brains of unborn babies? Who was going to go for that?"

She couldn't believe she was telling her all this. An alarm bell rang about how this could backfire big-time. But then again, how could it? Her word against Iggy's—she said, she said. So why not? Maureen felt comfortable with Iggy, and it felt good to unburden herself.

"But how did you rope the moms in?"

Maureen smiled. "We used the magic word: *free*. We got the cities behind us. Look, don't go making us sound like monsters. We had the best intentions. Melis had proved harmless in limited trials so we decided to go wide. We set up free OB clinics to serve the lower end of the socioeconomic spectrum. Increasing the intelligence of those kids would allow them to pull themselves out of the economic slums."

Iggy's turn to shrug. "Didn't make me smart. The only reason I got as far as I did in high school is they didn't want to keep me."

"Yeah, well, none of the rest of your cohort turned out to be academic superstars either. We watched most of you through grammar school, but you were all average or worse. We closed down the clinics. We thought it was a bust. If we'd watched you all into puberty we might have seen the unintended results."

"So you dosed my moms with this melis. What is it? Some kinda super-vitamin?"

"That's what we told people. But the truth is, we have no idea what it is."

Iggy's eyes widened as she straightened up. "No idea? That's bullshit! You made it. You gotta know what it is."

"Truth is, we didn't make it and we have no idea what it is."

"Bull*shit!* You gotta. Where'd you get it?"

Maureen thought about how to respond to that, but couldn't come up with an answer that wouldn't sound completely insane.

I can't believe I'm doing this, she thought.

"It'll be easier to show you than tell you."

14

QUEENS

"The edge of the Pine Barrens!" Ruthie cried as she limped from the stairwell. She wore shorts and a T-shirt and was holding a paper towel against her thigh.

Laura wanted to cheer at the sight of her. "Back so soon? Good work! You found Iggy?"

"Yeah. What the fuck are Pine Barrens?"

"Fancy name for big pine woods. She told you that's where they were?"

She was dying to ask about Rick. But was that where he was? Could it be? The Long Island Pine Barrens preserve was just a few miles from her home. It seemed too good to be true.

"Not quite. I was hiding and she got the lady to say where they were."

"Lady? What lady?"

Ruthie shrugged. "Some lady. I didn't see her, just heard her. 'Edge of the Pine Barrens.' That's what she said."

"Did you see anybody else? You know, like Rick?" Hope-hope-hope.

"Didn't see nobody but Iggy, and she was good, except she had this weird collar around her neck."

Damn.

Okay, if Iggy was all right, could she assume the same for Rick? Yeah, she had to. And right now Ruthie's leg needed tending. Laura had been set up to remove the GPS recorder but that was moot now. The thigh incision was oozing slowly but steadily.

"Hop up on the table and let me see that leg."

"What about Ellis and Anulka?" Stahlman said. He'd come out of the office. "Any sign of them?"

They'd drawn a small crowd. Marie was there, of course, but so were Luis, Cyrus, Kevin, and Tanisha.

"Told you," she said as she scooched up onto the pool table. "Just saw Iggy. And this is starting to hurt."

Right. The lidocaine would be wearing off about now.

"It'll be sore for a while," Laura said. "I'm going to put a pressure dressing on it to stop the bleeding."

"What about pain?"

"Take some Tylenol."

"Tylenol? Shit, I need Vicodins at least."

"Sorry. Fresh out."

Her tone grew annoyed. "You know, you scientists think you so smart but you really kinda dumb."

"Oh?" Laura said as she tore off three strips of adhesive tape. She wasn't looking for an argument. "Got a for-instance?"

"Yeah. Like we coulda done a test run. You know, me jump to my place upstairs and see if the GPS thing came along."

Laura stopped and shook her head. "Now why didn't we think of that?"

She glanced at Stahlman who looked embarrassed as he gave a helpless shrug.

Ruthie said, "Yeah, why didn't you?"

"Because we all have dumb moments and that was one of mine. Sorry."

Ruthie seemed mollified, even a bit disarmed by Laura's admission. "Yeah, well, I didn't think of it either."

Laura finished taping the gauze down tight, then turned to the others.

"Ruthie heard someone there say they were on 'the edge of the Pine Barrens.' That's out on Long Island, right near the Moriches. We can ride out there—"

"Wait," said Marie. "Long Island? That's east of here."

"Right."

"Well, I'm sensing our nadaný to the south, remember? I don't know where or how far, but I do know they're not east."

"Jersey's got some pine barrens," Luis said, "and that's south."

"Yeah, but the Jersey barrens are huge," Stahlman said. "'On the edge' . . . does that mean northern edge, western edge, eastern edge?"

"Only one way to find out," Laura said. "Marie and I will start driving south. Marie will act as a divining rod and we'll adjust our course accordingly as we go."

"Just you two?" Stahlman said, shaking his head. "Two women driving though the Jersey Pine Barrens at night? Uh-uh. Bad idea. I'll go with you."

Laura did *not* want Stahlman along. He'd think he should do the driving and call the shots. No way. This was Laura's mission.

"Count me in too," Luis said.

Oh, great.

"It's not like we're leading a commando raid," she said. "Marie's going to help me locate them and then we'll call it in—you know, report it to the state police."

But Stahlman and Luis were adamant. Kevin wanted to ride along too but everyone put the kibosh on that. They needed him here to keep the computers up and coordinate communications.

"Okay, okay," Laura finally said. "The four of us will go. We'll meet at the car in five minutes. Okay?"

All three nodded. As Stahlman and Luis hurried off in their respective directions, Laura motioned to Marie.

"You come with me."

Marie fell into step beside her as they headed for Laura's car. "I thought you said five minutes."

"You and me—we're leaving right now."

"But what about—?"

"We don't want them. They'll only get in the way." Laura looked at her. "You okay with that? Because if you're not, we'll wait for them."

"No-no. I'm in but . . . you don't think this will be dangerous, do you?"

"If I did, I don't know if I'd be going. I don't like adrenaline and I have a daughter who needs her mommy. And those two—Luis and Stahlman? Think about it: If there was any danger—and we'll stay far away from any chance of that—*we'd* have to defend *them*."

They were laughing as they reached her SUV. As Laura opened the driver's door she heard, "Wait for us!"

Cyrus and Tanisha came running up.

"Whoa! Nobody said anything about—"

"We know y'all duckin' out," Cyrus said, his voice dripping New Orleans, "and we're going with you."

Laura was about to blow them off when Tanisha said, "They're our friends—at least two of them are."

"Which one isn't?" As if she needed to ask.

"Ellis is kind of a dick," Tanisha said.

Cyrus snorted. "'Kinda'?"

She shrugged. "But he's one of us, so . . . what do you say? Who knows? We might come in handy."

Maybe. She didn't know about Cyrus's magic disappearing grip, but Tanisha's telekinesis, weak as it was, might prove useful.

"Hop in the back."

Seconds later she was out on the streets of Long Island City.

Heading south . . .

15

LANGE-TÜR BUNKER

Annie watched the heavy steel doors squeeze closed behind her, then turned to the golf carts. She'd never played golf but every president seemed to be crazy for it. The carts they used always had tops on them. These didn't. She noticed the electrical wires attaching them to the wall. She unhooked one and slid behind the wheel.

A simple lever projected from a vertical slot in the dashboard labeled with *F—N—R*. Brake and gas pedal on the floor.

Simple enough. She turned the key, levered up to *F*, stepped on the gas pedal—electric pedal?—and the cart took off. Not exactly raceway speed but just fine. Hell of a lot better than walking. And quiet as could be.

Now she just prayed Rick was right about no security cameras, because this driverless cart was going to look pretty fucking weird to anyone watching.

But weird was the rule for her life, right? Pretty fucking weird for some time now. First finding out she could turn invisible. Then, before she could adjust to that, her mom discovering she had stage-four liver cancer and not lasting a year. Leaving her an orphan. Well, not exactly an orphan, because her father was probably still alive, but nobody knew where he was. Went back to Africa, some said. Anyway, she stayed with her mom's older sister, Aunt Zinne, but she turned out just plain mean so Annie ghosted and began living by her wits.

Yeah, she was homeless, but she'd never had to beg or live on the street. The invisibility trick let her crash all over town and jack food and cash whenever she was hungry or short. Kinda fun at first, but living like a leech got old real quick. She'd been thinking of trying the straight life, even if it meant continuing with the minimum-wage scut work, when Rick and Marie dropped from heaven with an offer she couldn't refuse.

Couldn't believe it: two grand a week plus an apartment just to let someone study her invisibility. Seemed too good to be true.

Well, she had that right. On her second fucking day she's kidnapped by the U.S. government and tucked away in Fort Knox or wherever this was.

Shit.

When she reached the far end, she parked the cart with the others and approached the elevator doors.

Okay. Hairball time. Her dear departed cat, Prince—named after the singer who she'd had the major hots for as a teen—had been a great mouser, but every time he got nervous he'd cough up a huge hairball. Looking at those doors made Annie's belly feel like it was full of hair. Maybe coughing up a hairball of her own would make her feel better.

She looked around for cameras. Rick had said there were none, but she checked anyway.

Okay. Here goes.

She pressed the only button and the doors slid open right away. Taking a deep breath she stepped inside and hit the *up* button. The cab jerked into motion—*slow* motion. The ascent seemed to take forever, but finally the cab stopped. Annie pressed her back against the rear wall as the doors slid open.

A middle-aged man stood a few feet away, staring straight at her. He wore an oil-stained mechanic's coverall, blue like Rick's, with an embroidered patch that read *Al*.

"What the hell?" he said. "Hey, Harv, it's empty."

"I can see that, Jon," said a voice from somewhere out of sight. "I saw it before you."

See? See how?

She glanced up and saw a silvery bubble embedded in the ceiling. That had to be the camera. So they could see who was on the way up.

"Then what—?" After a few heartbeats, Jon—she

guessed that was his name despite what his coverall said—stuck his head inside and looked around.

"Somebody's playing games downstairs," said Harv.

"Gotta be Woolley. Thinks he's a comedian."

Okay, Jonny Boy, Annie thought. You've had your look. Now move along. Nothing to see.

But he continued to stand there, blocking her way. Then the doors timed out and started to close. Impulsively, Annie reached out and jabbed the *up* button.

"Hey, now *that's* weird," Jon said as the doors reopened.

"Well, if you'd get outta the fucking way," Harv called, "maybe they could close."

"I wasn't *in* the way."

Jon backed up a step and Annie saw her chance. She slipped past and took a couple of slow, careful steps that put her behind him. She looked around to get her bearings.

The elevator opened into a big cabinet inside some sort of shed with a curved ceiling. She saw a heavyset black guy in coveralls who she assumed was Harv—despite the *Chet* on his coverall—standing at a console half a dozen feet away, staring at a bank of screens. Straight ahead, maybe twenty feet away, a pair of doors beckoned. Careful to make no sound, she began to take slow, measured steps in that direction.

"Holy shit!" Harv shouted. "We've got company!"

Jon whirled. "Out front?"

"No! Right here! Three feet in front of you!"

Panicked, Annie froze. They could see her? But how? The way the light shimmered around her, she knew she was still invisible. How—?

"Are you crazy?" Jon said.

"I shit you not!" Harv's head was swiveling back and forth between his console and right where Annie was standing. "Grab him!"

"Where, goddammit!"

"Right in front of you!"

Abandoning all caution, Annie turned to run, but a hand landed on her shoulder before her first step.

"Shit, there really is someone—!"

The fingers tightened on her shirt, yanking her back as an arm wrapped around her throat. The hand released her shirt as a second arm encircled her torso and she was tackled to the ground. They landed hard on the concrete floor.

"I don't believe this!" Jon was saying as he held her facedown. "I don't fucking believe this!"

"An invisible man!" Harv's voice said, rushing up.

Jon was patting her down, probably looking for a weapon when his hand closed on one of her breasts.

"Whoa!" He gave the breast a squeeze, then said, "Not a man! Invisible *woman*!"

"Wo—? Hold her. I'll get cuffs."

Cuffs? No!

She redoubled her efforts to squirm free but he was too big for her.

"Easy, easy," he said. "You're not going anywhere."

When she felt the cuffs snap closed around her wrists, a sob escaped her. She'd never make that call. She'd failed them all.

"Hey, don't cry, girl," said Jon. "We're not gonna hurt you. But we're not gonna let you go, either."

"An invisible woman," Harv said. "She must be one of the ones they brought in on stretchers. Y'know, you hear there's weirdness down there, but who'da thought . . . I mean, *invisible*?"

With her hands cuffed behind her back, Jon pulled her—not ungently—to her feet, but kept a firm grip on the links between the cuffs.

"What they do to you?" he said. "Are you stuck this way or can you turn visible?"

Annie didn't know what to say or do. When she didn't answer, Jon began to pat her down. He pulled the phone and the pass card from her back pockets.

"Hey, this is Watts's swipe. Where'd you get it?"

"And that's Woolley's phone," Harv said. "I recognize it."

What could she say? She didn't want to mention Rick.

"I-I stole them. I'm invisible, after all."

She guessed her voice coming out of thin air surprised them because they both jumped.

Harv said, "She talks! How about that?"

Jon added, "I'm taking you back below—the boss man's down there now so he'll decide what to do to you, but it'll make it easier all around if I can see you."

"But you already *can* see me," she said.

"We can see your heat signature on the screen over there," Harv said, jerking a finger over his shoulder. "Maybe you can trick our eyes, but your body still gives off heat, and the thermal imager picked you up."

Well, that was something to tell Dr. Montero—*if* she ever saw him again.

She dropped the invisible thought and everything around her zipped into brighter, sharper focus.

Jon blinked at her. "Damn, you're young."

"Please," she said, holding back the tears. "They kidnapped me and knocked me out and brought me here."

Harv was nodding. "We know that."

He said it so matter-of-factly.

"But that's against the law! They can't do that!"

Harv shrugged. "But they did. Rules are different where the project's concerned."

"What project?"

They glanced at each other, then Jon said, "*The* project. That's all we know." He tugged on her cuffs, toward the elevator. "Come on. Taking you back."

She tried to pull away but got nowhere. "Please! Let me go. Please?"

Jon shook his head. "Sorry. No can do."

She screamed "Help!" with everything she had, then screamed again.

Jon and Harv didn't move, didn't even try to shut her up. That was when she realized . . .

"No one can hear me, can they."

They both shook their heads, then Jon tugged again.

"Let's go."

16

EXIT 11 — NEW JERSEY TURNPIKE

"Okay," Laura said. "We're coming to a decision point: Switch to the parkway or stay on the turnpike?"

Laura's trip guide had taken her through the Midtown Tunnel, across Manhattan to the Lincoln Tunnel, and down the New Jersey Turnpike. But now they were approaching a major fork in the road.

"I don't know," Marie said. "What's the difference?"

"Well, check out the map," she said, pointing to

the dashboard display. "The turnpike takes us along a more southwest route while the Garden State Parkway is pretty much due south. Both flank the Pine Barrens—turnpike runs along the western edge while the GSP stays to the east. If we make the wrong choice it could mean slow going making the correction through the pines."

She glanced at Marie and saw her chewing her upper lip.

"I don't know these roads," she said. "I don't know New Jersey at all."

Cyrus chimed in from the backseat. "Nobody does. I hear people only come to Jersey when they have to and they get on out as quick as possible."

Marie leaned back in the seat and closed her eyes. After a moment she straightened again and pointed through the windshield.

"That way."

Her point was about thirty degrees left of their present direction—around ten o'clock or so. Pretty much due south.

"Parkway it is," Laura said.

She hit the blinker and eased right toward Exit 11 and the Jersey Shore Points.

17

LANGE-TÜR BUNKER

Rick waited until he heard the big doors grind open and then close again, then waited some more.

Okay. Annie was on her way toward the elevator and freedom. Time for some serious exploration. He pulled open the door but stayed in the doorway, re-orienting himself. All the doors looked pretty much the same. He'd have to remember the numbers.

So . . . he'd checked the little office at the end of the hall, then the empty room next to it, then this one—room eighteen. Annie's. He'd been chained up in seventeen, which meant he'd check sixteen next—might as well have a system.

He was just setting a foot into the hall when he heard a rattle and voices down to his right. He ducked back, eased the door closed, and pressed his ear against the wood. Wished to hell these doors had peepholes.

Listening, he heard two female voices, talking low. He couldn't make out the words. He eased the door back open enough to poke his head into the hall. Iggy, looking perfectly relaxed, like she didn't have a care in the world, was strolling along with an older woman—white-coated, gray-haired, old enough to be her grandmother. They were headed toward the heavy doors with the little window, the ones that had rejected his swipe card.

Did he dare?

He kicked off his shoes. The concrete floor felt cold through his socks as he slipped into the hallway and padded after them. If granny spotted him, he'd have to ad-lib. Maybe he could bluff his way through—he was wearing security coveralls, after all. If that failed, he'd have to resort to muscling his way in. One way or another, though, he was going to see what was go-ing down beyond those doors.

Granny pulled a card from her lab coat pocket, swiped it, and the red light turned green. With a soft buzz from the lock, the door popped loose. Granny pulled it open, let Iggy go first, then followed her through.

Sliding his feet to keep them from pounding, Rick raced forward and caught the edge of the door just before it closed. He froze there, waiting to see if he'd been spotted or, if not, to give Iggy and granny time to move away from the door. The question was, how long to wait?

The grinding of the double doors at the other end of the hallway starting to open decided for him.

Who the hell is that?

He ducked through and eased the door shut. The ceiling was higher here, fading into the dimness above. A jutting bank of dead electronics blocked his view of the right side of the room but what he did see was rack after rack of electronic equipment of all shapes and sizes and ages. Could have been a *History of Post-War Electronics* exhibit. Well, the place opened in 1947.

He peered back through the thick glass of the door's little window and suppressed a groan as he saw a security man guiding a very visible Annie down the hall. Her hands were behind her so he gathered she was cuffed.

Damn! How had they caught her? Obviously something had gone wrong, but what?

A squeal from Iggy somewhere around the corner to his right. Pain? Fright? Surprise? He turned and started toward it. He rounded the bank of dead electronics and saw Iggy standing with granny just a few feet ahead. They were staring at a ten-foot cubical chamber against the rear wall, with three sides of heavy-duty glass, easily three inches thick, set in a frame of thick, riveted steel.

And inside . . .

Rick slid to a stop as the breath clogged in his throat and his knees went rubbery.

No . . . couldn't be . . . not possible . . .

He'd seen this before, or something very much like it. Years ago. And it had haunted his dreams ever since . . .

18

"Sir?" The voice seemed to come from far away. *"Excuse me, sir?"*

Greve lifted his head and for a heartbeat or two wasn't sure where he was. Then he remembered: the conference room. He'd come in here with printouts of all the data they'd acquired on the nadaný they were hosting. He'd wanted space to spread out the papers, but apparently he'd dozed off before he'd got much done.

He blinked and saw one of the security men standing in the doorway.

"Yes, what is it?"

He pulled a frightened-looking Anulka M'Bala into the room. "We found her up top, trying to get away. And she was invisible!"

"'Up top'?"

"She took the elevator up, sir." He looked nervous.

Greve shot to his feet. "What? How did she even *reach* the elevator?"

"She used a swipe card, sir."

"Where'd she get *that*?"

"Um, it belongs to Watts, sir."

"Who the hell is Watts?"

"He has downstairs duty tonight, sir—along with Woolley."

Greve felt his teeth clenching. "All right then, *where* is this Watts? And this Woolley?"

"I don't know, sir. I just got down here and saw the light coming from the doorway, so I figured—"

Greve glared at the girl. "And where's your collar?"

She looked away and said nothing.

"She wasn't wearing a collar when we found her."

Wait a minute . . .

"How did you find her if she was invisible?"

"The thermal imager spotted her."

"Really." That was good to know. "Good work. What's your name?"

"Thank you, sir. It's Jon. By the way, she had a phone but didn't have time to use it."

That was a relief.

"Where'd she get a phone? Belonged to your friend Watts as well, I assume?"

"No. That was Woolley's."

Greve pounded on the table. "Where are these two, damn it?"

"I-I'll check the security office, sir."

"You do that. And meanwhile I'll return Ms. M'Bala to her room." He came around the table and gripped Anulka's arm as Jon released her. "Come with me," he said, guiding her into the hallway.

"Let go!" she cried, trying to pull away. But he held her firm.

"How did you get out of that collar? And how did you get out of your room after I locked you in?"

Her only response was a sullen expression.

He found the door to room eighteen unlocked—naturally—and pushed her in ahead of him. He spotted the open collar on the floor and inspected it. The lock had been forced open and looked broken.

Damn!

"Don't try to tell me you did this," he said. "Who forced this lock?"

More sullen silence.

"Sir!" Jon again, standing in the doorway.

"What now?"

"Woolley's out cold. I can't wake him up!"

Drunk or . . . ?

"What about his partner?"

"Watts isn't there!"

Suddenly all became clear.

"Check next door—room seventeen. I'll be there in a minute."

Greve removed Anulka's cuffs and hurried to the door, locking it behind him. She might be able to turn invisible but that didn't allow her to walk through walls.

Jon was unlocking the door to seventeen as Greve stepped up beside him. He preceded Greve into the room where a man in his underwear lay on the gurney formerly occupied by Rick Hayden.

"Watts!"

And, just as Greve had expected, no sign of Hayden.

Jon was shaking him, calling his name.

"He won't be much use for a while," Greve said as the man began to stir. "You wouldn't happen to be armed, would you?"

Jon hesitated, then reached inside his coverall and withdrew a semiautomatic. "Sorry, sir. In all the excitement I forgot to leave it up top."

Greve's longtime rule had been no weapons in the bunker.

"We'll make an exception this time. Start a room-to-room search. We're looking for a big, dark-haired fellow. Don't shoot unless you have to, but whatever you do, don't let him get away. I'll start at the other end and we'll meet in the middle."

"Do you want my weapon, sir?" Jon said.

"I have my own." Greve ignored the guard's surprised look. He kept a pistol in his desk. He'd made the rule, so he could break it whenever he wished. "And by 'search' I don't mean peek in and move on. I want a thorough search. That means in the closet, in the bathroom, even under the bed—*thorough*. Some of the rooms will be occupied. Do not let that deter you. Understand?"

Jon nodded. "Absolutely, sir."

"Then get started."

As Jon moved off, Greve headed for his office and his weapon. He didn't care if Garrick Somers—or his reincarnation, Rick Hayden—left here alive or dead, but should it be the latter, he wanted to talk to him first.

19

Leaning back against the bank of dead, decrepit electronics, Rick fought to keep his knees from giving out as he blinked at the apparition behind the glass. The sight of it had triggered a powerful visceral reaction, like a pile driver to the gut.

He watched its size fluctuate from six to ten feet across; sometimes it looked fusiform and sometimes like a disk and everything and anything between, never assuming quite the same shape twice. Its vaguely purple, shimmering outline writhed in constant motion, stretching, rippling, contorting into countless configurations—an animated Mandelbrot set—while its center remained black beyond any black imaginable . . . like a hole in the fabric of reality, revealing the nothingness that lay beyond perception.

Nothing could look like that, nothing *should* look like that. It radiated wrongness . . . wrong, wrong, wrong.

And yet it looked familiar . . . he'd seen something like it before . . . in Düsseldorf. The thing that had wandered through the inferno of the Düsseldorf farmhouse was here.

He released a shuddering breath. The older woman must have heard him because she turned and started at the sight of him.

"How did you get in here?"

His mouth felt dry. Keeping his eyes on the thing, he pushed off the electronics bank and forced a swallow.

"Sneaked in behind you."

Iggy turned then and smiled. "Hey, Rick. Come to rescue me?"

"Probably could use a little rescuing myself. Who else from the gang is here?"

"Ruthie came and went but I don't know about anyone else."

He turned to granny. "Did you grab Doctor Fanning?"

Granny shook her head. "No. We don't need her."

Relief banished the residual shock. Laura was safe back in Queens. Knowing that lifted a tremendous burden and freed up his options.

"Besides Iggy," granny continued, "we have Anulka and Ellis. As already mentioned, we had Ruth but . . ."

Iggy grinned. "But she went *poof!*"

"And we have you, of course," granny said to Rick.

"But I don't know if 'have' is quite accurate. You arrived unconscious and handcuffed. Now . . . who released you?"

"It's complicated." He pointed to the thing behind the glass. "What . . . how . . . ?"

A hint of a smile twisted granny's lips. "It's complicated."

Right then he decided he liked her. And maybe he should stop calling her "granny."

"I'm pretty sure you know my name. What's yours?"

"Maureen LaVelle."

"You can call her Moe," Iggy said. "She's also somebody called Emily Jacobi."

Rick hadn't been ready for that. "The doctor who ran the Modern Motherhood Clinics?"

She bowed. "One and the same. And you're Rick Hayden."

"Actually it's Garrick Somers but I go by Rick Hayden these days."

Now why the hell had he told her that? He never mentioned Garrick Somers—to anyone.

"A new name? Why?"

"It's complicated."

Just then a thin, cranky-faced old duffer with wild white hair shooting in all directions hustled into view from the right.

"Here now!" he cried, clutching the lapels of his wrinkled lab coat and looking authoritative. His voice carried a hint of a Texas drawl. "Neither of you is authorized to be in here!"

Rick couldn't help saying, "Doctor Brown. I'd recognize you anywhere."

That stopped him in his tracks. "What?"

"Looking for Marty McFly, I presume?"

The old man turned to Moe. "What on Earth is this man talking about?"

Her tone teetered on the edge of a laugh. "It's complicated, Doctor Stonington. But I think we can consider them invited guests."

"Who invited them?"

"Agent Greve."

"Oh, well, in that case . . ."

Agent Greve . . . since the bunker was a DoD operation . . .

"This Agent Greve is DIA, I assume?"

"Yes," Moe said. "You'll meet him soon enough . . . and probably wish you hadn't."

Rick craned his neck to where this Stonington guy had come from and saw a well-lit area hosting three desks laden with monitors. All in all, the rear section formed a wide, high-ceilinged rectangle with the glass-walled chamber and its occupant set against the back wall. His gaze was irresistibly drawn back to the thing in that chamber. It simultaneously fascinated, repulsed, and unsettled him.

"Can we go back to my original question?" he said, pointing again. "What *is* that, and how did it get here? And yes, I'm sure it's complicated, but I need to know."

"Not only complicated," she said, "but highly classified."

Time to show off what he knew—and maybe imply that he knew even more. "Look, I already know about Maximilian Osterhagen and I know this place was built to house the Lange-Tür Project, so you don't exactly have to start with the Book of Genesis for me."

Although he wished she would.

Her wide-eyed expression—Stonington's too—was evidence that the name-dropping had blindsided her.

"How . . . ?"

"Research," he said. "But my research never even hinted at *that*."

"That's because the Anomaly is even more classified than Lange-Tür itself."

"'The Anomaly' . . . and you call it that because . . . ?"

Stonington answered for her. "Because it breaks all the known rules of science and because even now, after more than sixty years of puzzling over it, we still haven't the slightest idea what the fuck it is. Oops." He bowed to Iggy. "My apologies, young lady."

"No worry," she said with a charming smile. "I think I've heard the word once or twice before."

"'More than sixty years' . . ." Rick said. "Since the fifties?"

Moe nodded. "The Anomaly appeared in 1957—not at all what the Lange-Tür researchers were looking for."

"What's Lange-Tür?" Iggy said.

Rick pricked up his ears while trying to look like this was old news. He desperately wanted to know.

"I'll give you the *Reader's Digest* version," Moe said.

Iggy frowned. "What's *Reader's Digest*?"

Moe laughed. "Oh, dear! It means the abridged—the shortened version. Here goes: After World War II, the U.S. government began gathering up as many German rocket scientists as they could find. They called it Operation Paperclip. Even though he wasn't working on rockets, a German physicist named Maximilian Osterhagen was hauled in with the rest."

Iggy laughed. "Some name! And I thought 'Igdalia' was bad."

"Well, anyway, Doctor Max—as he was known—was working on a project he called Lange-Tür, which translates to 'Long Door.' He had developed a theoretical basis for a way to move objects—inanimate and, hopefully, living things as well—instantaneously over long distances."

"Really?" Rick said. "Teleportation?"

"Not at all. Teleportation is where an object is broken down in one spot and reconstituted in another." She focused on Iggy. "If you've ever seen the 'beam-me-up' technology on *Star Trek,* that's teleportation. But that's not what Doctor Max was trying to do. He had a theoretical basis for creating a portal—sort of a door in the air—to compress distance between two points which would allow something or someone to step through the opening on one end and step out onto another locus anywhere on Earth."

"Okay, then," Rick said. "A wormhole?"

Pulled that one out of the air. He'd seen it mentioned in SF films like *Stargate* but never understood the concept.

"Again, not at all," Moe said. "Lange-Tür involves another branch of physics entirely, one that I don't pretend to understand. I do know it employs a high-energy modification of the Casimir effect to—"

"Doctor LaVelle!" Stonington said. "Whence the logorrhea? This is all classified! These two have no clearance to even hear the words *Lange-Tür,* let alone the details of the process!"

Moe looked troubled. "You're right, you're right. But it also seems right to tell them." She put her hand on Iggy's shoulder. "Especially this one. After all, she's . . . involved."

Stonington grunted and said, "Well, don't say I didn't warn you—or try to stop you."

"Noted." She glanced at Rick. "Where was I?"

"Not a wormhole."

"Right-right-right. The physics is esoteric and I'm a biologist, so I can't explain it anyway. And in the end the details aren't all that important. The main thing is that the Department of Defense wanted this technology very badly, and it's easy enough to see why. The potential military uses are obvious and enormous."

"Hell, yeah," Rick said. "Move personnel and matériel to the Middle East or Asia or anywhere else just by driving through a doorway? Total game changer."

"Right. Except they couldn't get it to work. Ten years of trying without a lick of success. After a decade of failures they were on the verge of shutting Lange-Tür down because funding was being siphoned off by projects like MKUltra. That was when—as I've been told—Osterhagen made some last-ditch modification. They did another run and . . ."—she pointed to the Anomaly—"this showed up."

Rick stared at the thing. "And then you what . . . built that big fish tank around it?"

"I didn't build anything. The Anomaly arrived on April 29, 1957—the same day I was born." She shook her head. "Kind of a strange coincidence, don't you think? We both arrived on Earth the same day."

He stared at her. Yeah, strange, but . . . "I don't believe in coincidences. So who decided to build the tank?"

"As I understand it, they had that chamber from the get-go: steel-reinforced ballistic glass three inches thick. They were flying blind. First off, they didn't know if it was even possible to open a portal, but if they ever did, they had no idea where it would be.

It could open at the bottom of the ocean or in the heart of a volcano. So they built the chamber as a precaution against a hostile environment. I'm sure they never expected anything like the Anomaly."

Keeping his gaze fixed on the shimmering miscreation, Rick sidled over to where Stonington stood on Iggy's far side. Close up he looked at least ten years older than Moe.

"I know you don't want to talk about any of this, but can I ask how long you've been here?"

He gave Rick a suspicious look. "A damn sight longer than anyone else alive."

"Stoney virtually lives here," Moe said. "The Anomaly has taken over his life."

"You said 'anyone else alive.' You referring to all the suicides of folks who used to work here?"

"No. Just stating a fact. But I'm well aware of them."

Rick wished he'd had time to study what was on the thumb drive Pickens had given him.

"I've been told a lot of their suicide notes mentioned a void in their lives. You've been here the longest. Any idea what they were talking about?"

He laughed. "Not *a* void—*the* void. The void beyond existence. If certain people stay around that thing and stare at that blackness long enough, they start to realize this is all we've got and all that awaits beyond is formless chaos. Some of them feel compelled to embrace that void."

Embracing the void . . . Rick tried to imagine that but failed.

"But not you?"

He shook his head. "I'm a different sort. I'm of the tribe that wants to avoid the void as long as possible." He chuckled. "'Avoid the void.' I kind of like that. Anyway, I've always been aware that life is a shit show from the git-go, so the Anomaly doesn't bother me one tiny bit. We're like old friends."

"Stoney," Moe said, looking at him with wonder, "I've never heard you talk like this."

"Neither have I. Don't know what's gotten into me."

She turned and stared at Iggy. "I think I do."

Iggy looked puzzled. "What?"

"I believe I've just had an epiphany."

"What's a piffanny?"

Rick was more interested in the Anomaly and what Stoney had to say.

"Mind introducing me to your friend?" he said, pointing to the chamber.

"Friend? Hardly." Stoney squinted at him. "I didn't know better I'd say you had a personal interest in this."

Rick was tempted to say that he and the Anomaly had met before but held back. No sense opening that can of worms.

Stoney led him to within a couple of feet of the front wall where Rick stared at the . . . thing hovering beyond the glass, expanding and contracting, flattening and bulging, its shimmering purple Mandelbrotish border writhing like a tentacle around the black void at its center. If it radiated simple wrongness from a distance, close up it became the essence of madness.

Hey. Remember me?

No reaction.

Up close like this, the blackness of that void called to him, invited him in . . .

He forced his gaze away and said, "After all this time nobody knows what it is?"

Stoney gave his head a quick, frustrated shake.

"Nope. The Lange-Tür worked for an eyeblink, and in that eyeblink something came through. The passage to wherever it came from closed after it arrived and we've been unable to reopen it. We're not sure if the Anomaly is aware or sentient or even alive in any sense we can imagine. Parts of it appear to be pure energy and parts seem to be pure entropy."

"What about that blackness in the middle?" he said without looking.

"We've got an elaborate system of airlocks over there on the side. We used those to shoot it with lasers, lightning bolts, and to toss objects at it. Any object that hit the black disappeared."

"Gone?"

"Yep. Passed into the black and kept going. Never seen again."

"Didn't show up in some Tibetan monastery or anything?"

"Now that would have been interesting as all get-out, but no. Gone. Swallowed. Somewhere Out There."

"So it's like a hole in reality."

"That's a colorful way of putting it, but yes, part of it could be called that. But what's around that hole seems different. More like a form of energy. But the bottom line is we can't communicate with it, we can't send it back, and we sure as hell can't set it free."

"So you're stuck with it," Rick said.

"Right. Lange-Tür was eventually shut down as an experimental project but they couldn't abandon the Anomaly—no telling what would happen. So a skeleton crew's been posted to keep watch. I volunteered to be a member of that crew and continue working on it. Come hell or high water, I'm gonna figure out what it is before I die."

Rick had a pretty good idea what it was—or at least where it came from.

"I'm amazed they've been able to keep it secret."

"Not like they have a choice," Stoney said. "First off, you've got to pass heavy screening before you're allowed back here. And as for keeping your lip zipped, I suppose all those suicides didn't hurt. Cuts down the number of folks in the know, if you get my drift. And as for the ones who don't off themselves, you hear about all those suicides and you wonder if they're really suicides or if that's what happens to people who decide to talk about Lange-Tür. So you keep quiet. Maybe some of them *were* homicides. I don't know. I do know the Pentagon sure as hell can't have the truth about Lange-Tür get out."

Rick felt a nausea welling up in him. Proximity to the Anomaly . . .

"I can see why," he said, backing toward Moe and Iggy. "They'd have to admit they let an unidentified and unknowable object or entity into our world—no, even worse: into our *country*. And then they'd have to admit that the government and its scientists and its military are impotent against it. Your all-powerful, all-knowing government, the font of solutions to everything, hasn't got a clue how to handle this thing."

"Well, all that's just fine," Iggy said to Moe as he stopped beside her. "But what's this got to do with those Motherhood clinics you ran? I thought you brought me in here to show me."

"That's right," Rick said, stepping up to Moe. "You were Emily Jacobi."

Iggy folded her arms across her chest. "And she injected our moms with melis."

"What's melis?"

Moe pointed to the Anomaly. "It comes from that."

"Eeeuw!" Iggy made a face. "Really?"

Moe nodded. "Really. I wasn't involved in any of this yet—I'm talking about when melis was discovered—but the story goes—"

"What Moe is about to tell you is hearsay," Stoney said. "I can give you an eyewitness account because I was here back in the eighties when it happened."

"Now who's got logorrhea?" Moe said.

"Touché," said the old guy. "But if he's going to hear the story, he might as well get it from a first-hand source." He turned to Rick. "Doctor Max was in his seventies back then and pretty much retired on a government pension, but he lived nearby and still visited the bunker regularly. On one of those visits he noticed some kind of residue on the floor of the Anomaly's chamber. He drove us crazy until we came up with a way to siphon off a bit. Using strict anti-contamination protocols, we succeeded. DoD took charge of it after that. They kept coming back for more, but never told us what they were doing with it."

"Okay, my turn," Moe said, picking up the story without lag. "I was working at Fort Detrick at the time. Agent Greve showed up with a sample of the weirdest substance I'd ever seen or heard of and charged me with finding out what it was. I named it 'melis,' experimented on it every which way imaginable, and eventually it found its way into the Modern Motherhood Clinics in an attempt to create brainier kids."

A blithe way to gloss over experimenting on the brains of unborn children. He didn't know if he liked her so much now.

"But I gather the 'brainier kids' part failed?"

"They turned out no smarter than their peers. We didn't know it at the time, but we wound up creating Iggy and her friends—what you call nadaný."

"In other words," he said, pointing at the Anomaly, "they come from *that*?"

A nod. "Yes."

Rick was having a hard time wrapping his brain around this. "Modern Motherhood was a DoD project? Why on Earth—?"

Cold steel pressed against his nape. He didn't need eyes in the back of his head to know it was a gun barrel.

"You're full of surprises, aren't you, Mister Hayden?" said a male voice he hadn't heard before.

How had he let him sneak up behind him? And then he knew: the Anomaly. It had a hold on him. And this had to be the guy Moe had mentioned before.

"Greve!" she said. "No guns in the bunker!"

"I know. My rule, remember. And I made an exception for myself."

"Is this really necessary?" she said.

"*Very* necessary. I know this man's capabilities."

Did he now? Time to say something.

"DIA Agent Greve, I assume?"

"Why, yes." He sounded just a bit taken aback. "How did you know?"

"Your reputation has preceded you."

"Running your mouth again, LaVelle?"

"I seem to have become an endless font of information," she said.

"Well, put a sock in it. The kaffeeklatsch is over. As for you . . ." The muzzle dug deeper into his neck as a hand extended over his shoulder. It held a set of long-chain shackles. "Put these on."

Rick gave them one look, then shook his head. "No."

A few heartbeats of what he imagined was shocked silence, then, "Put them on or I'll shoot."

Rick shook his head again. "Not gonna happen."

Moe's comment about Greve bringing him here for some unknown reason had led him to conclude—accurately, he hoped—that Greve had a personal interest in him. He wasn't going to pull that trigger. At least not yet.

Rick read frustration in Greve's grunt.

"Very well then," he said. "LaVelle, take the girl back to her room. I want a word alone with Mister Hayden"

"I don't wanna go," Iggy said.

Moe gave him a look. "Hear that? She doesn't want to go. She can stay here with me."

"She has no clearance to be here, LaVelle."

"She's a nadaný." Moe pointed to the Anomaly. "That gives her every clearance she'll ever need, Greve. She stays as long as she wants to."

Trouble in paradise? Rick wondered.

These two were definitely not a team. Or if they were, they weren't receiving the same signals. An exploitable situation, perhaps?

Greve tossed the shackles to her. "Well, at least make her wear these."

Moe caught them but said, "I don't think that's necessary . . ."

"No, hey, they're cool," Iggy said. "I like the chain."

She took them and snapped the cuffs around her wrists, then started twirling the chain like a jump rope between them.

"Now you," Greve said as the gun barrel was replaced by a hand tugging on the back of Rick's collar.

"We'll have to have our talk somewhere else. You're coming with me."

"What if I say no?"

"I shoot you in the ankles and you can crawl out of here."

Rick wished Greve had left the barrel against his neck. Always good to know the location of your enemy's weapon. But now it could be anywhere behind him. A good move on Greve's part. Showed he was well trained, and had taken his training to heart. To make a move on the pistol, Rick had to know its exact location. Even an instant of fumbling could result in a slug in his gut.

Wounded and ruined ankles would put a definite crimp in Rick's future plans, so he shrugged and said, "Let's go."

He allowed Greve to march him away from Iggy and the Anomaly.

20

EXIT 100B — GARDEN STATE PARKWAY

The sign read *Monmouth Service Area*.

"Anyone need a pit stop?" Laura said. "Speak up now if you think you might. I've no idea how far to the next one."

She checked her two passengers in the rear seats. Both had earbuds plugged in and were playing with their phones. Neither said anything.

"You okay?" she said to Marie in the passenger seat. She nodded. "Fine."

"Are we still on target?" Laura said as she sped past the exit ramp.

Another nod. "I think we made the right choice. They feel straight ahead, although I can't say how far."

Still straight ahead . . . a good indicator that the "edge of the pine barrens" Ruthie heard mentioned had meant the eastern edge. The trouble was, if Laura remembered correctly, the Jersey pines ran almost to Cape May.

"But I'm assuming if we pass them you'll feel them off to the side?"

"I hope so," she said. "I haven't been at this very long."

"And I'm also assuming that if you can sense them they're still alive?"

"I think that's safe. Although . . ." She touched Laura's shoulder. "I know that doesn't give you much comfort where Rick is concerned."

"I . . ." She felt her throat thicken. "Yeah, I guess not."

"I'm sorry."

"Don't be. You're doing all you can. He can take care of himself."

"Oh, no doubt," Marie said. "It's just . . ."

"What?"

"Nothing."

"You're thinking the same thing I've been thinking, right? Awake and on his feet, he can handle pretty much anything. But the last time you saw him he was out cold." Her voice broke. "God knows why they took him or what they're doing to him!" She slammed her hand against the steering wheel. "*Damn* it!"

They drove in silence for a while, then Marie said, "What *is* it between you two, anyway?"

Oh, hell . . . this was not a subject she wanted to discuss, especially now. Best to put the kibosh on it.

"Nothing."

Marie laughed softly and shook her head.

"What?" Laura said.

"If you don't want to talk about it, fine. Just say so. I'll respect your privacy. But don't hand me that 'nothing' line because anyone who's seen you two within a hundred feet of each other knows that's pure bullshit."

Laura's turn to shake her head. "It's that obvious?"

"Trust me. You two keep veering away from each other."

"We have issues."

"Issues? Don't tell me he has issues with you, because I'm not buying. He's crazy about you. Even a blind person could see that. He's Mister Tough Guy until you show up, then he's Mister Lapdog. So you must be the one with the issues."

"Well, okay. Yes, I do I have issues with him."

"So you say."

"What's that supposed to mean?"

"Look at you. You're so worried about him you're banging the steering wheel. And look at him: totally hot and totally crazy about you. What kind of issues can you have with that?"

"I can't get into it."

"Somebody do something bad?"

Laura could see Marie wasn't going to let this go.

"Nothing recent. Something in the past, before we met, and let's put the brakes on right here, because it's something he told me in confidence and I cannot-not-not get into it."

"Wait. It's something bad and he *told* you about it?"

Laura nodded. "Right."

"*He* told *you*. You didn't just happen to find out on

your own or hear it from someone else. He came out and *told* you?"

"Right."

"Are you in*sane*? That shows he's being straight with you. Isn't that what you want from a man? Honesty? I mean, how bad could it be?"

How about mass murder—twenty-six lives? Laura thought, saying nothing. That bad enough for you?

Marie said, "All right. You're not talking. I can respect that. But whatever it is—or rather, *was*—it's in the past. The Rick I know is a rock-solid guy. Not too many of those around."

"No argument there."

"So what else is it? Values? Beliefs? Does he belong to some weird cult that worships toads or something?"

Laura shook her head. She was pretty sure their core values were in line, although they might vary in the way they expressed them. And as for beliefs . . . in the past few months everything she'd believed about the world and the way it worked had been turned on its head.

"So why don't you be honest with yourself?" Marie said.

The question took Laura by surprise. "What do you mean?"

"This trip isn't to rescue the nadaný."

"Of course it is."

"Okay, maybe a little bit. But the big reason you're here and don't want anyone else calling the shots is you're worried about Rick—worried sick about him."

Laura had to admit she was right.

"Yes. I am. Whoever they are, they have him, and he's helpless, and God knows what they're doing to him. And thank you."

Marie looked confused. "For what?"

"For putting things in perspective and helping me realize something."

The huge gaps she'd imagined between them really weren't huge at all.

"Which is . . . ?"

"If we get out of this in one piece, and if he'll forgive me for making things so difficult—"

"Have no fear, Laura."

"Well, I'm never letting him go again."

She could see it now. They'd start over—go back to square one, the way things were between them after they returned from Orkney. She'd invite him over for dinner, he'd bring Champagne and hang out with Marissa while Laura cooked. They'd take it easy and see if everything developed the same as before. Just let things take their course, slow and natural.

"Damn!" Marie said.

"What?"

"The good ones are always taken."

21

LANGE-TÜR BUNKER

Agent Greve ushered/prodded Rick down the hallway and into the smaller, officelike room he'd briefly visited before. He closed the door behind them and pushed him toward the desk chair.

Rick turned and finally got a look at his captor. Thin, balding, older than he'd expected—older looking than Moe, anyway. Old enough to be retired. Why was he still on the job? And his pistol . . .

"You've got to be kidding. Is that a Luger?"

"A Stoeger copy."

"It's a beauty."

A sour smile from Greve. "If you're hoping for some adolescent-level bonding over weaponry, save your breath. I have no fetishes, least of all guns. I saw it for sale and made an impulse buy. That is *all* there is to it. It may look like a showpiece but the magazine is stacked with nine-millimeter hollow points. It has a hair trigger when the hammer is back—which it is—and I will not hesitate to squeeze that trigger should you make the slightest threatening move."

This guy was an overwound clock.

"Whoa-whoa-whoa." Rick raised his hands. "Just be cool, okay? I don't have any nadaný mojo. I'm just a normal human being."

"Normal? I don't think so. The last time I saw you, you were unconscious and shackled to a gurney. By the time I see you again, two security personnel have been drugged unconscious, a nadaný has been freed—and, fortunately, recaptured—and you have invaded a restricted area wearing stolen security clothing. These are not the accomplishments of 'just a normal human being.' And, familiar as I am with your record with the CIA, I know exactly what kind of human being you are, Mister Garrick Somers."

That gave Rick a bit of a jolt. His file was supposedly buried so deep that only the director and a few others had access.

"How—?"

"You'd be amazed at the level of interagency cooperation between the clandestine services. I looked into you after you intruded on my past—"

"Intruded? When?"

"We'll get to that. But imagine my surprise when I

discovered that you're now intruding on my present. Such a coincidence."

"I don't believe in—"

"Nor do I, Mister Somers. Nor do I."

"It's Hayden now."

"Very well, Mister Hayden. Have a seat."

"I'll stand, if you don't mind."

"Oh, but I do mind. Very much. The seat." He waggled the pistol. "I insist."

Rick rolled the chair out from under the desk and dropped into it. Being seated, especially in a wheeled chair, put him at more of a disadvantage. Something the DIA man obviously knew.

"Care to explain what this is all about?"

"'This'?" Greve leaned back against the door but the pistol remained steady. "Depends on what you mean by 'this.' From what I overheard of your conversation with Doctor LaVelle I gather you're already well versed on the Lange-Tür Project. No, 'this' concerns another matter entirely."

Greve stepped to the solitary bookcase and pulled a large-format volume from the top shelf. Something vaguely familiar about the glossy black cover . . .

Keeping his distance from Rick, he dropped it on the desk, saying, "I believe you are acquainted with this infamous tome?"

Rick looked closer. No cover illustration, not even a title on the cheap black binding. He'd seen this book before . . . or one just like it. His hands shook as he lifted it from the desk and opened it to a random page. German . . . the text was in German.

No . . . couldn't be the same book. He read a brief passage—he'd been raised in Switzerland so German was a second language for him—then slammed it shut.

Impossible. But here it was. That single paragraph had been enough. The same book used by the Düsseldorf sickos, the book that had started them down the road to mutilating children.

He tapped the cover. "This was burned to ash. Where the hell did you get it?"

"This is a copy," Greve said. "As was the one you saw in Düsseldorf."

"I saw Xeroxed sheets."

"Made from the copy I gave them, I'm sure. The original is extremely rare and in a safe place." He waved a hand at the bookshelf. "I have two more copies like this in reserve."

"Why . . . ?" Rick shook his head. "Why would you want even one copy?"

"I donate them to select groups and individuals to see how they'll react."

"You *what*?"

"I said I—"

"I heard what you said. I just can't believe—you mean that's where the Düsseldorf sickos got their copy? You?"

He nodded. "They seemed the perfect recipients, especially since they could read it in the original German."

"You're one sick fuck, you know that?"

Greve smiled. "A rather harsh assessment, don't you think? I prefer 'agent *provocateur*' myself. They weren't the first. Over the years I'd doled out a few to carefully screened recipients, but every single one of them went and burned their copies. Those lovely Düsseldorf nihilists were the first and only to act on it."

Act on it . . . yeah, they'd acted on it all right.

Visions of those mutilated children swam before him.

He resisted the impulse to hurl the book at Greve and leap across the room, trap his scrawny neck between his hands, and watch his face turn purple as Rick squeezed the life out of him. But the pistol was still pointed at his chest.

Later. Then and there he made a promise to kill Greve. When and how . . . to be determined. For now, he had to let the twisted bastard rattle on.

"We humans are a strange lot, don't you think? The practices recorded in that book, culled from primitive and not so primitive cults all over the world, sicken most people. But every so often one comes across others who are inspired to unthinkable levels of atrocity."

"Where'd it come from?" Rick said. "What sick mind would even think to compile those . . . those obscenities . . . those . . . ?" He ran out of words.

"Some crazy nineteenth-century German intellectual traveled the world and put it together. Oddly enough, a distant relative of Doctor Osterhagen owned a copy. The good doctor hid it away for decades but eventually the book passed into my hands. Unfortunately, I don't speak German and it turned out to be an absolute bitch to translate. What do you do when the translators keep quitting on you? Finally I photocopied it and ran it through some translating software. The resulting English was awkward but I was finally able to appreciate what the translators had found so off-putting."

"And you didn't?"

"Find it off-putting? Of course I did. Those ceremonies are unspeakably monstrous. But I saw a way in which they might serve a purpose."

Rick shook his head, thinking, What possible purpose . . . ?

"You're not going to tell me DoD wanted you to—?"

"Oh, no-no." He laughed. "That stodgy bunch? Not on your life."

"Then what?"

"Let's just say I have varied allegiances."

Things began to fall into place.

"Those scars on the guards' backs . . . on one of my abductor's too . . . the brand . . ."

"You saw it?"

He tugged at his security coverall. "I didn't arrive with this. Had a good look while I was stripping Watts. I'm guessing you have one too?"

"I am not the topic of our conversation."

Which meant he did. What was it with these secret-society guys? Why'd they feel they had to tag themselves with their cult logo? Didn't that undercut the "secret" part?

"Like hell you aren't." Rick tossed the book back on the desk. "You're the one distributing this cult porn." And then it hit him. "Oh, wait. When you said I 'intruded' on your past, you meant Düsseldorf, didn't you."

"Now you've got it."

"But what . . . ? Why would you want children harmed . . . mutilated?"

The son of a bitch pressed his free hand over his heart. "That's the last thing I wanted! Who knew they'd choose *that* cult to emulate?"

"Are there any cult practices in that book that *don't* involve painful death? What were you *thinking*?"

"As I said, I have varied allegiances with varied agendas."

"Who're we talking about?"

"Not germane to our discussion. As to what I was thinking, I wanted to see if they could create a breach. You see, sometimes, on rare occasions when enough chaos and misery are concentrated in a single locus, a breach occurs, allowing something to break through . . . to sup on the misery."

"No shortage of misery in that farmhouse."

"But it probably wasn't enough to achieve what they wanted."

Rick remembered their mantra: *Bringing the Dark Man*.

That was all those sickos had talked about . . . their lousy Dark Man who was going to . . . what? Rick could never pry out a clear idea of what they thought the Dark Man was going to do for them when they lured him/it/whatever across from wherever. They seemed to believe the Dark Man was going to act as some sort of WMD for them. Considering how they hated everything, why not?

"The mutilated children," Rick said. "They called them 'the Choir.'"

Greve nodded. "Yes. A recurrent concept: Singing to the Void."

"But they couldn't speak. Their tongues . . . their vocal cords . . ." Rick swallowed back a surge of bile.

"No sound necessary. Their misery is a melody that reverberates and resonates with the miseries around them and beyond. You may have heard their song without realizing it. But that would not prevent it from affecting you."

Was that why he'd felt as if he'd been moving through a black fog back then?

"I'd been watching the group intermittently," Greve said. "My time was not entirely my own, and I was often called away. And during one of my absences, you acted."

Rick hadn't been able to stomach it any longer. The

Company had ordered him to stay away because it had determined that the group was no longer a threat to the U.S. or its allies. No matter how Rick had begged and pleaded and threatened that they were a danger to any child they could find and abduct, no one was listening.

So he'd acted on his own . . . forced to play God, because if a God ever existed in this reality, it had been on a cigarette break.

He trapped them in their farmhouse and ignited the explosives and incendiaries they'd stockpiled there. They'd booby-trapped the barn where they kept the children—couldn't allow anyone to see what they'd done—and when the farmhouse went up, so did the barn.

Eleven adults gone—good riddance—along with fifteen irreparably damaged children—a mercy.

Greve said, "The fire and explosions you ignited added to the chaos the nihilists had created. All those young Germans burning alive pushed the level past the threshold that would allow something through. I wasn't there to see it, but you were."

"I wish I hadn't been."

"You were the only witness. What did you see?"

"You really want to know?"

"Of course I want to know. That is the only reason you're here!"

Rick briefly considered trying to use what he'd seen as a bargaining chip to get him to release the nadaný, but was pretty certain that wouldn't fly. Greve was too invested in the nadaný. Probably thought of them in some twisted way as his property.

"Okay. I saw a version of what you've got in that fishbowl back there."

Greve made a fist. "I knew it! I knew it! It briefly

disappeared around the time of the Düsseldorf explosion. That's where it went!"

What a pathetic clown.

"Don't tell me you really think you've caught an ICE."

"ICE? What's an ICE?"

"My pet acronym for Intrusive Cosmic Entity."

"Yes! That's exactly what it is!"

"Are you kidding? If that's in any way, shape, or form related to a real ICE, it's a toenail clipping."

"No, it's—"

"You don't see the big picture, do you?"

Greve looked insulted. "Of course I do. I'm privileged to be a part of that picture, to know where all this is headed."

Rick shook his head in disbelief. "Look, if you think you *caught* something, you're more clueless than I originally thought. That thing was *placed* here."

"Placed? Ridiculous. It's—"

"According to your pal Stonington, back in '57, after ten years without a lick of progress, DoD decided it had better places to spend its money and decided to shut down Lange-Tür. But then, on what was to be the last experimental run, miracle of miracles, something comes through . . . something not of Earth . . . something from Out There . . . something no one can explain. An Anomaly. And strangely and conveniently, Lange-Tür never works again after that. Doesn't that strike you as contrived? I mean, just a little bit?"

From Greve's frown, Rick guessed it did.

"But I'm told Doctor Osterhagen made some adjustments to the equipment before that last run."

Rick barked a harsh laugh. "Of course he did!

Because the previous run had been a failure, so it's only logical to change something before the next run. I'm willing to bet Osterhagen made adjustments before every new run. But if the last adjustment he made was the reason for the questionable success of bringing through the Anomaly, it stands to reason the Lange-Tür portal would keep on working, doesn't it. But it didn't."

"That doesn't mean the Anomaly was *placed* there. For what possible purpose?"

"To probe. To see how best to mess with our collective heads, for starters."

"Don't be absurd."

"What about the suicides, Greve? It gets inside people's heads, makes them come to believe there's no point in going on. And what if that's just the beginning, the exploratory run, the test probe to see what works best against us? What next? Multiple Anomalies popping up all over the world?"

"There's only one and a Lange-Tür portal is required to bring it in. We have it contained—"

"You only *think* you have it contained. It can leave any time it wants. It's been sitting there waiting for a signal or a trigger."

"Waiting? It's been well over half a century!"

"An eye blink where these things are concerned. Less. The initial twitch that leads to an eye blink. It's a pattern, Greve. We're an anthill and they're toying with us. I've seen it before."

"You've seen *nothing*. You *know* nothing. It's more than that . . . much more."

The way he said it . . . Greve knew. Rick had never run into anyone else who knew. Did it have something to do with that brand he and the others wore . . . the one he wouldn't admit he had? Did his group or cult or organization know more of the secret history than Rick did? Most likely they did, because Rick had been tackling it singlehandedly and knew he'd only scratched the surface.

"Listen, Greve: As an undercover CIA field agent, I blundered into your game with the Düsseldorf sickos. Now, years later, I'm back, blundering into your game with the nadaný. Coincidence? Neither of us believes in coincidences, so that means we're both involved in another game. You play games, the ICE play games, it's all connected, Greve. *All* connected. ICE-ICE, baby."

Greve was giving him a calculating stare. "You're far more entertaining than I had anticipated."

"'Entertaining'? I'm *entertaining*?"

"An expression I picked up during my apprentice days. But I think you'd be a good fit for my organization."

He had to be kidding.

"And what sort of organization might that be?"

"A fraternal order, you might say."

"Like the Masons?"

He made a sound that might have been half burp and half laugh. "Hardly. Septimus is to the Masons what NSA is to a backwoods country sheriff's office. They measure their age in centuries, we measure in millennia."

Septimus, huh? Rick wanted to say, *Ooh, do I get a funny-looking brand like the other guys?* but held back.

"I'll give it some serious thought."

And he just might. He never joined anything, not even the Book of the Month Club. He'd never heard of Septimus and normally would run from any organization that would accept Greve as a member. But if they'd been around half as long as Greve said, maybe they had a cache of arcane info on ICE and the secret history. If so, he wanted a gander.

But that would come later, if ever. Right now . . . enough of this.

"I'm going to stand."

Greve thrust the pistol forward. "Sit!"

"Nope. Gonna stand." Slowly he rose from the chair. "And now I'm going to walk out of here."

"I will shoot you dead, Hayden."

"No, you won't."

Greve blinked in shock. "If you think—"

"No, I don't think you're afraid to shoot or not man enough to shoot or any of that stuff." Didn't want to threaten the guy's masculinity. "I just think you suspect you might have use for me down the road, and I'm of no use dead."

Risking a lot here, but without Laura to worry about, and with Greve seeing him as a potential recruit for his cult or whatever, he felt he could take a few chances. But to minimize any impulsive move on Greve's part—like a trigger twitch—Rick planned to broadcast every move he made.

"I'm going to approach the door and step into the hallway."

"Don't—"

"Let's talk options. I don't have the option of leaving this bunker, so you've no worry there. You, on the other hand, have three options: You can back out the door, you can step aside and let me by, or you can shoot me. But no matter what, I'm headed for the door."

After hesitating a few heartbeats, Greve pulled the door open behind him and backed out, always keeping enough distance between the two of them to prevent Rick from grabbing the pistol.

Once in the hallway, Rick began a measured walk toward the door to the restricted area. He heard Greve following about six feet behind.

"Moe told me you abducted Ellis as well."

"That's 'Doctor LaVelle' to you."

"No problem. I was thinking, should we gather him and Anulka along the way?"

"Anulka is in lockdown and Mister Reise is far too dangerous to release from his quarters."

"What did he do to you?"

"*Tried* to do. He is neutralized and will stay that way for the time being."

Well, damn. Rick had been hoping Greve hadn't learned about Ellis's tricks yet.

So the question now was: What was Rick going to do when he reached the far end? He had no idea. But three other people would be there, and he figured they could serve only to expand his options on getting everybody who mattered out of here.

And killing Greve, of course.

22

EXIT 83 — GARDEN STATE PARKWAY

"They're not straight ahead anymore," Marie said.

Laura let up on the gas. "Where'd they go?"

"I don't think they went anywhere, but they're off to the right now. I've had a feeling they've been edging that way for a little while, but now I'm sure. Definitely to the west now."

Laura had been expecting this eventually. The parkway didn't run due south all the way. It angled south-southwest for a while, then south-southeast, but always stayed to the east of the Pine Barrens. So if the nadaný were on the edge of the pines, as Ruth had said, they'd inevitably shift from dead ahead to somewhere rightward.

"Good. That means we're getting close."

They'd just passed an exit ramp so they'd have to settle for the next one, which turned out to be Route 37 in Toms River. They took that west. Despite the traffic lights and congestion, they made decent time along the six-lane blacktop.

"I think we're getting close," Marie said as they passed a sign informing them they were entering the Borough of Lakehurst.

"Hey, Lakehurst!" Cyrus said, popping up from the back and thrusting his head into the space between the front seats. "I've heard of that."

"Well, yeah," Laura said. "The *Hindenburg* blew up at the air station there."

And right on cue, they passed a sign pointing straight ahead for *Naval Station*.

"I know," Cyrus said. "Crashed and burned back in the thirties. I saw it on *Ghost Hunters*."

"What's that?"

"TV show about paranormal stuff—you know, ghosts and that crap."

"Hey, I saw that one too," Tanisha said. "They went through that haunted hangar."

"Yeah. Hangar One. That's where they collected all the bodies from the *Hindenburg* to identify them. Supposed to be haunted."

Laura said, "You're both into the paranormal stuff?"

"Well, duh," Cyrus said. "Darlin', when you can make something disappear just by squeezing it, yeah, you're into paranormal stuff."

"Okay. Dumb question. Sorry."

"No problem. I follow a lot of that stuff but I've never found a show or a book that investigated or even *mentioned* anybody who can do what I do."

Tanisha said, "I've heard telekinesis talked about a lot but they never investigated anybody real."

"No spoon benders?" Laura said.

Tanisha laughed. "Yeah, but spoon benders aren't real. They're a joke. It's got to be a certain kind of spoon and they've got to hold it a certain way under certain conditions. Total bullshit."

"Can you bend a spoon?"

"Not one that's metal or silver. I can break a plastic spoon but I don't have to be holding on to it. I can break it while it's lying on a table. I'm not strong enough for a metal spoon, though. Not yet, anyway. I can move one across a table and make it float a little, but I can't bend it."

Following the *Naval Station* arrows they wound up on a two-lane county road designated 547 and followed that till they came to the main gate.

Welcome to
Joint Base
McGuire—Dix—Lakehurst

On impulse, Laura pulled in and stopped in the visitor parking area.

"This isn't it," Marie said. "We're close, but—"

"Just want to take a breather and get our bearings," she said. "And think."

Seeing *Joint Base* on the sign had triggered something. The mail drop for the supposed multivitamin injections at the Modern Motherhood Clinics had been positioned cheek-by-jowl with Joint Base Anacostia-Bolling.

Joint bases kept popping up . . . Rick's mention of Pentagon black funding for Operation Synapse . . . a synapse on the logo for the multivite injections . . .

Military bases, joint or otherwise, were run by the Pentagon . . .

She turned to Marie. "You say they're close?"

A confident nod. "Very."

"Then they're here . . . on this base."

"Yes!" Cyrus said, punching the back of the seat and jolting Laura and Marie. "Let's go find them!"

Laura pointed to a sign that said tours were Wednesday and Saturday and the base was presently closed to visitors.

"So much for the possibility of walking around and triangulating their location," she said.

"We can sneak in," Cyrus said.

"Getting ourselves arrested won't help anybody. Let's try driving around the perimeter first." To Marie: "Which way are they from here?"

She pointed to the access road that ran straight back behind the security kiosk. "Right down there."

Laura checked her dashboard map and saw where another county road—571—intersected this one a mile or so away, and would take them along the base's northern flank.

The new road turned out to be another two-lane blacktop. They traveled for about four miles or so through thick pine woods broken by scattered ranch houses to the left and right before Marie raised a hand and pointed past Laura through the driver's window.

"Okay. If there's such a direction as due left, that's where they are from here."

Another azimuth—something she'd learned from Rick on their panacea hunt. You can locate something by crossing two azimuths that point to it from different angles.

Just up ahead on the left, Laura spotted a light through the trees and slowed. Looking like a half-buried barrel, a battered Quonset sat at the end of a short, sandy driveway. The flat end faced the street; a light over the single door illuminated a sign proclaiming that they bought all kinds of scrap metal.

She slowed, then pulled in.

"This can't be it," Cyrus said.

"Somewhere behind it," Marie said.

Laura couldn't see any light or signs of life. "The place looks closed. Let's check the back for a road."

Her Audi had all-wheel drive so she figured it could handle a sandy road should they find one. She drove around past the Quonset and came upon a pile of rusting old cars, some intact, some in pieces. But the trees formed a solid barrier along the back end of the property, offering no break for a road.

"Are they straight ahead?" Laura said.

Marie nodded.

That meant they weren't in the Quonset hut, they were somewhere in the woods.

She brought up the satellite view on her dashboard and saw nothing but trees. And yet if Marie's sense was right, the azimuths would intersect dead ahead, putting the nadaný somewhere out there. Could the satellite image have been altered, erasing the building? Or was it camouflaged?

Or underground?

All four of them jumped and Tanisha gave a little yelp as someone knocked on the rear window. Laura's side mirror showed a heavyset black fellow in greasy mechanic's blue overalls.

"You be lost or sumpin'?" he said as Laura lowered her window.

"I'm afraid we are. We're looking for a road into the woods."

"Well, you inna wrong place, lady. Way wrong."

"I see that now," Laura said.

She was trying to get a handle on this guy. His name patch said *Chet*. He was clean-shaven with an intelligent look that didn't fit with his bad grammar. And he looked jumpy.

"If'n yer wantin' a road, you gots Hangar Road that way," he said, pointing back the way they'd come, "and you gots Oakwood Road the other way. But you ain't gonna find no road back here."

"Where do those other roads go?"

"Don't go nowheres. They goes into the trees and one just stops and the other comes back out agin."

"That won't help," she said. "Let me back this up to the front again. I need to ask you something."

Limping like a bad Walter Brennan impersonation, Chet followed her as she reversed to the front of the Quonset hut.

"No need to get out of the car," he said as she opened her door.

Now that seemed an odd thing to say, so she did just that.

"Lady, I said—"

"I know what you said but I've been driving a long time and I need to stretch a little." Which was entirely true.

Tanisha, Marie, and Cyrus did the same, ambling around to Laura's side of the car. Cyrus picked up a short steel bolt from the ground and was casually tossing it back and forth between his hands as he leaned against the SUV. Chet look jumpier than ever as he stopped by the front fender.

Laura was about to speak when a light passed by overhead. Even though it had been at treetop level, she ducked.

"What the hell was that?"

"They's called pine lights," Chet said. "Mostly y'see 'em on summer nights but we gots a lotta them hangin' 'round here."

Another one followed, maybe the size of a beach-ball, but it wasn't a glowing object. It had no discernible substance . . . just light. A globule of pale yellow light.

"What are they?"

"Dunno. Some say they's ball lightnin' or some kinda St. Elmo's fire. Some say it's swamp gas, and some say it's the souls of dead Pineys coming back for a visit."

"'Pineys'?" Marie said.

"Yeah. Folks like me what was raised here in the Pines."

Another light flew overhead. Laura noticed they all seemed headed for the woods behind the scrap yard.

Chet cleared his throat. "So I'm asking again: You folks lookin' for sumpin'?"

"As a matter of fact, yes," Laura said. "We want to know if there's any kind of building back there in the trees."

And now he looked ready to jump out of his skin.

"What you talkin' 'bout? Ain't nothin' back there but trees. That's Navy property, owned by the base."

"No military installation of any type?"

He squinted at Laura. "Where you get this crazy-ass idea? You been drinkin' or sumpin'? Nothin' back there. Never was. Check your Google maps. They tell ya."

Methinks he doth protest too much.

Laura turned to the others. "I think we've found the place we're looking for. Agree? Disagree?"

"Most definitely," Cyrus said as the others nodded.

"And what place would that be?" Chet said. "'Cause whatever you lookin' for, unless it's scrap metal, this ain't it."

What would Rick do here? Laura thought. He'd push some buttons and see if any lights came on. Okay. Let's mash down on a big one.

"Some friends of ours disappeared earlier today. No, wait. 'Disappeared' isn't right. They were *abducted*. And we're pretty sure they were brought here."

His eyes widened, then he gave a nervous laugh. "Whaaaat? That just could be the craziest talk I ever heard of!"

"Can we look inside?" Cyrus said.

"No," the man blurted, then seemed to reconsider. He shrugged. "Okay. Can't see no harm in lettin' you look. Go ahead. But on one condition: You don't find your friends, you get back in your car and you haul your crazy asses outta here."

"Deal," Laura said.

She was sure Chet was somehow involved in all this. He may not have participated in the abductions himself, but his junkyard backed up to military property, and everything pointed to military involvement.

She was also sure she'd find no nadaný tied up in the hut, but maybe something would point her in the right direction.

"Holy–!" Cyrus cried.

Laura saw him looking at his empty hands in wonder. "Something wrong?"

"I don't know." His voice was tinged with awe.

"Come on then," Chet said.

Shaking his head and muttering something about
how in all his days he'd never heard nothin' as crazy
as all this, he limped to the door and held it for them
as they filed in.

The inside was dimly lit, with car junk strewn everywhere. Windshields, fenders, bumpers, engines—an
automotive abattoir. A huge cabinet labeled *PARTS*
dominated the space.

The door closed and then Laura heard a distinctive
ratcheting sound. She turned to find Chet pointing a
pistol at them.

"Now look what you've gone and made me do,"
he said in an exasperated tone. "I offered you one
opportunity after another to move on, but you kept
pushing. So now . . ."

His diction had changed and his grammar was perfect.

Cyrus glanced at Laura. "And you told me no
guns," he said in a disgruntled tone.

Laura shook her head and said nothing. Another
gun right now might well turn this bad situation
tragic.

"All four of you," Chet said, waving the pistol, "lie
flat on the floor."

"It's filthy!" Tanisha said.

Chet—or whatever his name was—walked up to
her and pointed the pistol in her face. "This is not a
game, girl. Yes, it's filthy, but if you look you'll see
there's no blood on it. Let's keep it that way, shall
we?"

Laura noticed his limp was gone.

Cyrus stood beside Tanisha. In a calm voice he said, "See that little lever on the left side of the pistol? Can you flip it up for me?"

She frowned, looking puzzled. "What? Yeah, I guess so."

Laura wasn't sure what was happening until Cyrus's hand reached out and grabbed the barrel of Chet's pistol. He squeezed, then released, and most of the barrel was gone. The muzzle hit the floor with a metallic *clink*.

"Holy crap!" Cy said, staring at his hand. "Hey, y'all! Look at me!"

While Cy stared in surprise, Chet gaped in shocked disbelief at the back half of the pistol that remained in his hand.

"What? *What?*"

Laura was having a similar reaction. Cyrus hadn't been able to disappear metal before. Now . . .

But Cyrus wasn't through. He grabbed Chet's wrist and spoke in a mocking tone. "Now look what y'all gone and made me do." As Chet tried to wrench free Cyrus added, "Hold very still or I'll do the same to your arm, and then your hand will be hitting the floor."

She didn't know if Cyrus would do that, and she didn't want him forced into something he might long regret. But it was important for Chet to believe he would lose his hand if he didn't cooperate.

"Not that again!" Laura cried. "You made such a mess last time!"

For an instant Cyrus looked at her as if she were crazy, then he got it.

"Why not? This creep pulled a gun on us. I should make sure he never pulls a gun on anyone again!"

"No!" Chet said, close to a wail. He dropped the remnant of the pistol. "Don't!"

"You do what you have to, Cy," Marie said, jumping on board. "But I'm not cleaning up this time. All that blood . . ."

"Who cares about cleaning up?" Cyrus said. "It's not our place."

Laura nodded. Good one.

"Wait-wait-wait!" Chet said. "Don't do it! Whatever it is you do, please don't do it!"

Cyrus looked at Laura and affected a whine. "But I'm going to get tired of holding on to him. It'll be easier if I just—"

"We have zip ties!" Chet cried.

Every muscle in Laura's body tightened at those words.

She spoke through stiff lips. "Zip ties? Where did you get them?"

"Someone brought them in and . . . and left them."

Laura decided to leave it at that until he was secured.

Chet directed her to a console on the far side of the parts cabinet where she found an array of monitors. She wanted to study them, but allowed herself only a quick look. Some showed the outside perimeter of the Quonset, another showed what looked like the inside of an elevator.

An elevator . . . Rick and the others were underground.

She found the zip ties—the exact same type Rick always carried—in a gallon plastic baggie filled with all sorts of odds and ends and pocket paraphernalia—keys, gum, coins, a thumb drive. Next to the baggie she noticed a coffee cup emblazoned with *HARV*, and a revolver of some sort lying on the console. Was someone else on duty here?

"Where's Harv?" she said, returning to his side.

"Harv is me. Harvey."

"Your patch says 'Chet.'"

He shrugged. "We wear whatever fits."

Maybe, maybe not.

"Okay, Harv—if that's really your name—hands behind your back."

With Cyrus's help, she secured Harv's hands with one of the ties, using the figure-eight technique Rick had shown her.

"Who—who *are* you people?"

Laura ignored the question and shook the sheaf of zip ties in his face.

"Where did you get these?"

"I told you: Someone left them."

She looked at the other three. "They're Rick's. He's never without them."

Cyrus picked up the revolver, holding it by the grip. "Okay, tell the lady what she wants to know. And just so you don't convince yourself that what happened to your gun before was just a parlor trick . . ."

He squeezed the revolver's grip and the rest of the gun fell onto the console—minus the grip.

A sharp intake of breath from Harv. "Okay, okay! A bunch of people were brought in on stretchers earlier."

Yes!

"Conscious? Unconscious? IVs running? What?"

"No IVs, but all out cold. We were handed that baggy and told to stow it. I'm guessing their pockets were emptied along the way from wherever they came from. We were told nothing about them."

"Where are they now?"

"I can't tell you. Really I can't."

Harv cried out as Cyrus gripped the back of his neck. "No-no-no-no-no! Please!"

"Never done *this* before," Cyrus said. "Could be *real* messy."

Cyrus was turning in a convincing performance as a psycho tough guy—at least she hoped it was a performance. But Laura was pretty sure he needed to have his fingers closed around something to make it "go away." Harv didn't know that, however.

"They're below!" he blurted.

"Below?" Laura said.

"In the bunker."

An underground bunker. Who'd have thought?

"Why a bunker?" Marie said. "In case of World War Three?"

Harv shook his head. "I don't know."

"Or won't tell us?" Cyrus said, giving Harv's neck a little squeeze.

Flinching he said, "All we've been told is that 'the project' is down there. Some government-run thing tucked way, way in the back where we're not allowed to go. I can't tell you more than they told me, which is nothing. Our job up here is to make sure only authorized people get in."

The project, Laura thought. Did it have anything to with the nadaný or had they been brought here simply because it was secure and convenient?

"You'll take us down there?" she said.

A series of quick nods. "Yeah-yeah. Just make him take his hand off my neck."

"I can't make him do anything, but I can ask. Cy?"

He released Harv's nape. "Sure. But I'm sticking close, got it?"

Harv swallowed hard and nodded again. "Got it."

It occurred to Laura that Harv was a pretty poor excuse for a government agent. Granted, Cyrus's demonstrations were pretty unnerving, especially if you feared you were about to be on the receiving end. But she hadn't expected him to cave so quickly.

"Are you DIA?"

He shook his head. "Only Agent Greve."

Whoever that was.

"Who are you with, then?"

"Private contractor. Septimus Security."

That explained it, she guessed. Hired gun with no particular loyalty.

"Who owns the bunker then?"

He looked at her as if she were daft. "The Department of Defense. They hired us but it's a government facility. You're messing with the Pentagon here, sister."

Pretty much what she'd suspected, but she couldn't show a hint of intimidation. She gave him a fierce look.

"No, my man, the Pentagon's dealing with *me*. It's broken dozens of laws by abducting and imprisoning U.S. citizens without due process, and you're an accomplice." That seemed to cow him, but she wasn't through. She hardened her tone to let him know she wasn't asking. "You're going to take us down to this bunker."

"Okay. Yeah."

Maybe my hard-ass act isn't so bad either.

"Where's the elevator?"

He pointed to the huge *PARTS* cabinet. "In there."

"How many security people down there?" Laura said.

"My partner Jon, and maybe two more."

"'Maybe'?"

"When we caught the invisible girl she had things that belonged to the other two guys and—"

"Wait," said Tanisha. "Invisible girl?" She glanced at Laura. "Annie?"

"Yeah, invisible," Harv said. "As in perfectly transparent. Normally I wouldn't expect anyone to believe me, but after seeing what you can do, I figure you know all about it."

"And you caught her?"

"Yeah. We saw her heat signature on the thermal imager. Jon brought her back down."

Heat signature . . . Luis hadn't got into checking Annie's infrared yet.

No question Rick and the nadaný were here.

"How much firepower down below?" Cyrus said.

Harv shook his head. "No guns allowed."

Cyrus grinned. "Excellent! What are we waiting for?"

Despite his previous agreement, Harv held back. "I'll be in a shitload of trouble."

Even though he'd pulled a gun on them, Laura felt a little sorry for Harv. He was only doing his job.

Cyrus said, "You're already in a shitload of trouble—with me. You just tell them we threatened your life." He placed his hand on Harv's neck again. "Which I'm doing right—"

A loud buzzer sounded as a red light on the console began to flash.

"What's that?" Marie cried.

"The alarm!" Harv said, pulling away from Cyrus and rushing to the console.

"What did you do?" Laura said, following close behind.

"Nothing! You saw me. I was standing right next to you." He looked frantic, freaked. "I've been here for years and we've never had an alarm. I—oh, shit! The bunker's in lockdown!"

"Locked down how?"

"No one in or out."

"Well, isn't that convenient for you," she said.

Cyrus approached, his expression fierce. "You did something. What did you—?"

Harv cringed away and nodded to one of the screens. "Look! There's been a breach!"

Sure enough, the word *BREACH* was blinking on the center screen.

"Breach?" Laura said. "What's that mean?"

His expression showed genuine panic. "I don't know, but it can't be good!"

23

LANGE-TÜR BUNKER

What was that noise?

"What the—?"

Someone was banging on the restricted door. Maureen hurried over and peeked through the thick glass of the window to see a distorted version of Rick Hayden's grim face. Greve stood a half dozen feet behind him and still had that gun in his hand.

Greve nodded to her, which she took to mean she was clear to open the door.

"Welcome back," she said as Hayden stepped inside. "Wasn't sure I'd see you again."

"Maybe I'm an asset," he said with a sardonic grin.

She didn't know what to make of Hayden. He was smart and glib and big and good-looking and seemed utterly fearless—except when he'd got his first look inside the tank. The sight of the Anomaly had rocked him back on his heels. He'd recovered quickly, but didn't seem able to take his eyes off it. As if he didn't trust it.

She recalled her own reaction when she'd stepped through the restricted door for the first time. God, when had that been? Could it have been 1986? That long ago? It seemed like yesterday when she'd stood outside listening to Greve tell her that whatever her expectations about what waited behind the door, they were wrong. She remembered the foreboding, her crawling gut, and how she hadn't been reassured one bit when he'd told her that the source of melis wasn't horrible, simply . . . *different*.

Different, hell. Greve's warnings or reassurances or whatever he thought they were had not prepared her the slightest for the fucking off-the-wall apparition that waited within.

What she'd seen floating in the glass chamber had struck her as so *other,* so completely *wrong,* she'd screamed. Just once, but loud and long. Then she'd turned and hammered on the door to be released from this place. But Greve was having none of it. When she finally calmed down, he'd led her—dragged was more like it—over to the chamber and "introduced" her to the twitching, pulsing, vacillating thing they called the Anomaly.

She'd never accepted the Anomaly. The techs who worked with Stoney didn't seem to mind its presence—at least not on the surface. After years of working here they'd quit or transfer out and eventually kill themselves. Not all, of course, but an uncomfortably high percentage.

Ever since that first day, Maureen couldn't wait to escape its presence. She'd never become inured to its alienness, its otherness, and the black despair that beckoned from its core. Greve didn't mind, Stoney seemed almost drawn to it, but it made her want to run.

She wanted to run now but was hanging on for Iggy's sake.

Over the years her melis research had required occasional on-site visits. She didn't mind the enclosed, buried feeling of the bunker, just so long as she didn't have to spend too much time back here in the restricted area.

She imagined Hayden felt the same. After all, he'd exhibited such a visceral reaction to the Anomaly. Almost as if he recognized it.

Greve followed Hayden with his pistol aimed at his back.

"And what, Doctor LaVelle, have you accomplished during my absence?"

"I've been attempting to discover Iggy's gift."

"You're assuming she has one? Have you succeeded?"

"I believe so."

"What is it?"

"Come over and I'll show you."

Actually, she'd thought she had it sussed out before Greve had marched Hayden away, but in his absence she'd pretty much confirmed it to her satisfaction.

Hayden was standing beside Iggy, staring at the Anomaly. Stoney stood on her other side, talking to her.

When she and Greve arrived behind the trio, she turned to him and said, "Tell me a lie."

"What?"

"Just try to fabricate something untrue and tell it to me."

Greve made a face. "This is ridiculous."

"You won't do it?"

"I'm not at all in the mood for games, LaVelle."

Okay, if he was going to play it like that, she'd just repeat the *Ghost Story* question.

"So tell me, Agent Greve, what was the worst thing you've ever done?"

Without hesitation he said, "I fucked my younger sister half a dozen times when she was fourteen and threatened the life of her cat if she ever told anyone."

Maureen felt her mouth fall open. The Iggy-Stoney conversation stopped dead and the two of them did a slow turn along with Hayden to stare at Greve.

And Greve . . . Greve had gone dead white with his eyes bugging and his dropped jaw working spasmodically.

"I . . . I . . ." His voice was a raspy whisper. "I . . . didn't mean to say that. It just came out!"

"You mean it's true?" Hayden said, looking almost as shocked as when he'd first laid eyes on the Anomaly.

Greve nodded. "Yes . . . yes, but—" His voice rose to a scream. "*Why am I saying this?*"

"But-but-but," Maureen said, "that wasn't how you answered before!" She ran out of words and saliva.

It must have all come together for Greve right then because the gun slipped from nerveless fingers and clattered to the floor as his gaze snapped to Iggy.

"You!" he shouted, pointing a trembling finger at her. "It's you!"

He backed away and kept backing away until he was around the corner. Maureen heard the security door slam.

The others stared after him.

"Well, I'll be goddamned," Stoney said.

Hayden rubbed a hand over his mouth. "Double for me." He looked at Maureen. "What just happened here?"

She noticed Hayden's gaze drifting toward the pistol so she quickly stooped and picked it up and slipped it into the pocket of her lab coat.

"I think it best if this stays with me."

"You're sure about that?" he said, his gaze boring into her.

"Pretty much."

She knew he could overpower her and take it anytime he wished, but she'd feel better with it out of sight.

He gave her a curt nod. "Okay, then."

Relief. She couldn't help liking this man. She wondered what Greve had wanted with him.

He added, "But I reserve the right to change my mind should the need arise."

"Understood."

She sensed they both hoped it wouldn't.

I fucked my younger sister half a dozen times . . . She couldn't get the words out of her head.

"Okay now, Moe. What just happened?"

She snapped alert. What had just happened? She'd been monumentally stupid.

I fucked my younger sister half a dozen times . . . God!

"It's Iggy."

"Me?" Iggy said. The chain between the shackles gave a faint rattle as she pointed to herself. "How—?"

"No one can lie around you."

"What?"

Maureen nodded. "That's your gift, your power."

"It is?" Iggy looked dubious.

"What the hell are you two talking about?" Stoney said.

Obviously Greve hadn't explained the nadaný to him. But then, why would he? Maureen didn't want to get into all of that now, so she made it as plain and simple as she could.

"You can't tell a lie in front of Iggy."

He chuckled. "Aw, that's crazy."

"Agent Greve doesn't think so."

Stoney's grin did a slow fade. "Holy shit. You're not kidding, are you."

Right now I wish I were, she thought.

"Go ahead. Try to tell me a lie. I'll ask you your name and you try to give me someone else's. What's your name?"

His lips worked as if he were trying to move them against their will, and then he said, "Gerald Kevin Stonington, Junior." He slapped a hand against his forehead. "I was trying to say 'Richard Nixon.' Holy shit!"

She turned to Rick who was looking a little sick.

"Don't ask me that 'worst thing' question or I'll punch you in the mouth before you get it out." He had a stricken look as he shook his head. "I didn't mean for that to come out."

God, would he really punch her to stop her? Yes, he would. He'd spoken the truth because Iggy stood just a few feet away.

"Okay, okay." Maureen took a step back. "I won't."

"Can't be worse than Greve's," Stoney said.

"I've got blood on my hands." His expression told her he hadn't wanted to say that, either.

Why am I not surprised? Maureen thought.

"The thing is," she said, "you don't *have* to answer. If you'd rather not, you can simply say so. As long as that's how you really feel, then you've spoken the truth."

"And you know this how?"

"I was experimenting on Stoney while you and Greve were gone."

Stoney looked scandalized. "Like hell you were!"

"Remember all those classified questions I was asking you?"

The light dawned in his eyes. "You were *testing* me?"

She pointed to Iggy. "No, I was testing her. Sometimes you'd answer truthfully, and sometimes you'd say you weren't allowed to comment on this or that—also the truth."

"Well, I'll be damned." He frowned. "But then why didn't Agent Greve just hold his tongue?"

"I wish he had. I asked him the same question yesterday and he gave me a different answer. If he'd just made up some stupid lie like I asked him, this never would have happened. I figured he'd give the same answer as yesterday." She shook her head as revulsion welled in her. "I never dreamed . . ."

"But why didn't he just not say anything?"

"With Iggy here, maybe the real answer—the truth—got dredged up from his subconscious and popped out before he could stop it."

Hayden grinned at Iggy. "Oh, how I'd love to sneak you into the front row of a congressional hearing . . . or a White House press conference."

"Wouldn't that be a kick?" Stoney said.

Maureen found Hayden staring at her. "You seem like a good person, Moe. As you said, you don't have to answer, but what's the worst thing *you've* ever done?"

The answer leaped into her mind. She could have held it back but she let it out. "It's a tie between directing the Modern Motherhood Clinics or participating in this abduction scheme. They're both wrong on so many levels."

"Yeah," he said. "They are. But you've just been handed an opportunity here to undo one of them. With Greve out of commission, how about helping me get the nadaný out of here?"

A chance of redemption?

I fucked my younger sister half a dozen times ... How was she ever going to work with Greve again, or even sit in the same room with him?

Maybe she should grab a handful of redemption while she could.

"Ruth is already gone," she said.

"I figured after I came across an empty set of woman's clothing. I found Annie earlier. She tried to sneak out and go for help but they caught her and she's back. I have no idea where Ellis is."

"I do."

Hayden pointed to her pocket with the gun. "I don't need that now, but I may have use for it if someone or a number of someones tries to block our way out."

"Let's hope not. No guns allowed down here, but up top is different."

"So I really have a gift?" Iggy said. She seemed lost in her own world. "I'm really a nadaný?"

"The most powerful and frightening of all nadaný," Hayden said.

She gave him a puzzled look. "What?"

"*Truth!* You make people speak the truth! You have any idea how freaking dangerous you are?"

Her lower lip trembled. "You're scaring me, Rick."

"Hey, lighten up," Maureen said, putting an arm over her shoulders. "She's only eighteen."

With a chagrined look, Rick backed off, raising his hands. "Sorry. Didn't mean to. It's just that it's the most amazing ability. It touches everyone around you. Can you turn it off?"

She was getting a deer-in-the-headlights look. "Turn it *off*? I didn't even know I'd turned it *on*!" A soft moan. "People are going to be afraid of me, aren't they? I won't have any friends."

Poor kid. Maureen's heart went out to her.

"You will, Iggy," she said. "And the friends you do have will be true blue. When they tell you they're your friend, they'll really mean it."

"But sometimes lies are good, aren't they?" She was rubbing her hands together as if they were cold. "You know, like white lies?"

Maureen said, "You mean when you don't necessarily want the truth? Like when you ask 'Does this make me look fat?'"

A hint of a smile. "Maybe not."

"Well, in your case you're going to hear an honest opinion—maybe not the opinion you want to hear, but honest."

Iggy's smile faded as she pointed at the Anomaly. "All because of . . ."

"Yeah. Afraid so."

Her expression turned to disgust. "I still can't believe I'm related to *that*."

She approached the chamber and raised a shackled hand to the glass.

"Maybe you shouldn't get too close," Rick said.

"Not to worry," Stoney said. "We've banged on the glass, projected film at it, played music and every imaginable sound for it, bathed it in every available wavelength of the electromagnetic spectrum, run electric current through it, and never a hint of reaction. So that little girl's not going to—Holy shit!"

As soon as Iggy touched the glass, the Anomaly reacted. It changed shape, expanding in a flash from a shapeshifting ten-foot glob to entirely filling the chamber, pressing against the glass on every side, and then abruptly shrinking to a compact sphere the size of a soccer ball—still with that purplish outer glow around a black core of empty chaos. It reminded her of a total solar eclipse, except it looked the same from every angle, and its corona was purple.

"Wh-wh-what did you do?" Stoney cried, running up behind her. "What did you—?"

"It's responding to her," Maureen said, following him.

"But in the past it's responded to nothing and no one! I've never—*no one's* ever seen it do anything like this. No one!"

He did an abrupt about-face and brushed past Maureen on the way to his console.

"Where are you going?"

"The cameras! Got to make sure we're recording this!"

"Aren't they always on?"

"Yeah. Supposed to be. But wouldn't it be just my luck to have them go off now!"

Maureen came up behind Iggy. She sensed Hayden beside her and glanced his way. She was sure her own expression was awestruck; his was merely curious. But in a way that figured. He'd had no previous exposure to the Anomaly, so he'd find nothing unusual in this sudden bizarre behavior.

"What's going on?" he said.

The Anomaly was maintaining its globular soccer-ball configuration. Maureen had never seen it hold the same shape for longer than a heartbeat, but there it floated, just inches inside the glass, hovering before Iggy's face.

"I'm not sure," she told him. "This is unprecedented. It—"

Iggy said something in a hushed tone that Maureen missed.

"What did you say?"

"It knows me."

It knows me . . . The implications of those three words were mind-numbingly vast.

They meant the Anomaly was not only aware but communicating.

If Iggy was right.

She could simply be voicing an emotional response. But if she was right . . .

It could mean the Anomaly had spent decade after decade playing possum. Or it could mean the Anomaly had just now become aware—Iggy's touch on the glass triggering something, awakening it. Or maybe it had been programmed for this.

Iggy's touch . . . a small army of researchers had touched the glass countless times across the decades with no response. But one touch from Iggy . . .

It knows me . . .

Of course it does, Maureen thought. Melis is from the Anomaly and you've got some of it in you.

Okay, not really in you. I put it in your mother and the melis changed you, affected you somehow. You carry its indefinable imprint on your genes.

In a way, you're its child.

"It knows you?" Hayden said. "You mean it spoke to you? Greeted you?"

Iggy's pigtails flew as she shook her head. "No. Yes. It—this thing here—that's not what knows me. Something *behind* it knows me. Something bigger. Much, much bigger."

Was she linked to whatever . . . whatever *what*? Maureen didn't have a word for it. Didn't even have a concept for it.

"Is that where the Anomaly came from?" Maureen said. "From behind it?"

"It didn't come from anywhere. It just is."

"Why is it here?"

She turned and pointed at Hayden. "It came for Rick."

Confusion flashed across his face. "Me? That's impossible! Stoney told me it appeared in 1957. I wasn't even born yet!"

"Because you saw it when you helped bring it."

"But I saw it—or something like it—just a few years ago! This doesn't make any goddamn sense!"

"Time is different for them."

Rick stepped closer to her. "What does that even mean, Iggy?"

She shook her head, her expression baffled. "I don't know. It's just in my head."

"Okay, Iggy," Maureen said. "You said 'them.' Who is 'them'?"

"I don't know!" Her voice rose to a wail and she looked ready to cry. "Why do you keep asking things I don't know? I just know what I know but I don't know how I know it!"

Maureen wrapped her in a hug and tried to soothe her. "It's okay, Iggy, it's okay."

Look at me . . . getting all maternal. What's going on here?

"It's so crazy," she said against Maureen's shoulder.

"I know stuff I shouldn't know and don't know how I know it."

Hayden muttered something about "ice" and approached the chamber to stare at the Anomaly's new compact form with his nose almost touching the glass.

And then Maureen felt a tug at her lab coat pocket, turned to find Greve pulling the pistol free, grabbing Iggy by the pigtails, pressing the muzzle against the back of her skull and firing two shots into her brain.

Maureen watched blood splatter the glass of the chamber as the shockingly loud retorts faded away.

"She's too dangerous!" Greve screamed, his eyes wild. "Too dangerous to live!"

Maureen shook herself into motion and caught Iggy as she fell. Greve was already aiming past her and firing—at Hayden? Before she could look, Greve was in her face, grabbing her by the throat and jamming the muzzle against her cheek.

"And now you! You! How could you ask me—?"

She had an idea what he was going to say before he shot her in the face but he was interrupted by a wave of bone-freezing cold enveloping both of them as the Anomaly darted past, just inches away.

With a hoarse cry Greve lurched away, allowing Maureen to lower Iggy to the floor. Blood was spurting from the back of her head and from a hole where her left eye had been. So much blood.

She saw Hayden picking himself up from the floor. Without hesitation he rushed over and dropped to his knees beside Iggy, saying "What the fuck?" over and over. He rolled her onto her back and pressed the heel of his palm against her eye socket.

He looked up at Moe. "She's just a kid . . . just a kid!"

Pressure on the eye socket seemed to stanch that flow but blood continued to gush from the back of her skull, creating a crimson pool around her head. Her remaining eye blinked and her jaw worked but she made no sound.

Iggy . . . Greve . . . the shots . . . the Anomaly . . . too much to process . . .

The Anomaly! The Anomaly was out!

And then above it all she heard Stoney shouting, "Breach! Breach! We've got a breach!"

What?

Maureen tore her gaze from Iggy and looked up at the chamber—the empty chamber. The Anomaly was gone. The three-inch glass displayed a perfectly round hole the size of a soccer ball where the Anomaly had been floating.

Movement caught her eye. The Anomaly was sailing through the air toward the far wall. Without slowing it penetrated the ferroconcrete like a hot poker through a block of cheese, leaving behind a smooth-walled tunnel.

Stoney must have hit the emergency lockdown button because red lights began to flash as a deafeningly loud klaxon sounded again and again.

24

. . . BREACH . . . BREACH . . . BREACH . . .

Laura stared at the word blinking on the monitor and willed it to stop. She willed the red flasher and the buzzer to shut down as well.

No success on any front.

She turned to Harv. "How can you work here and not know what that means?"

"They keep us on a need-to-know basis and apparently no one thought we needed to know."

"That's insane!" Cyrus said.

"No argument here. When we replaced the government guys who'd been here before us, they told us about the breach signal and the automatic lockdown. But they also told us this place had been here since the 1940s and there'd never been a single alarm in all that time."

"But one happens as soon as we get here," Laura said. "I repeat: Isn't that convenient for you?"

"Maybe it's got something to do with those people on the stretchers."

Breach . . . What could that mean? It couldn't mean anything good. It meant a breakout, it meant something that was supposed to be contained had broken free. And if it triggered a lockdown, that could only mean that Rick and the others were in some sort of danger. Unless, of course, they *were* the breakout. And with Rick aboard, that might well be it.

Still she couldn't help worrying about something like a radiation leak. She imagined ionizing rays—gamma, X, whatever—piercing their tissues, mutating their genes to start cancers growing.

"Okay," she said to Harv. "The buzzer's going, the lights are flashing . . . what are you supposed to do when that happens? Is there special gear you're supposed to get into?"

Please don't say radiation suits. *Please!*

Harv shook his head. "No, nothing like that. We were told just to sit tight and wait for help to arrive."

"Help?" Not good. Help meant reinforcements— for the bad guys. "Where's this help going to come from?"

"Fort Dix."

Never heard of it.

"Where's that?"

"Browns Mills."

Laura suppressed a scream. Was he playing games?

"Where is *that*? Distance, Harv—I want to know *distance*!"

"About fifteen miles as the crow flies, longer by road."

Damn! That gave them almost no time.

Laura pointed to the *PARTS* cabinet. "You say the elevator is in there, right?" Receiving a nod, she said, "Let's go check it—just to be sure this lockdown story isn't BS."

She let him lead the way. With his hands behind him, he couldn't part the sliding doors on the cabinet, so Cy did it. At the rear an elevator cab stood open and dark.

"Never seen this before," he said.

"Never seen what?"

"The doors open and the lights off. Usually you've got to press the button to make them open. Must be part of the lockdown thing."

Cyrus stepped inside and started jabbing at buttons.

"Dead," he said.

Made sense. The protocol probably sent the elevator up to the top and locked it there so no one could leave the bunker.

"So you're telling me the U.S. government built this place with only one way in and one way out."

"Well, I heard talk of an emergency escape hatch when we took over from the government guys."

"Hallelujah! Where is it?"

He jerked his head toward the rear of the hut. "Back there somewhere."

"'*Somewhere*'?" she said. "Somewhere in the back of this building or somewhere back in the woods?"

"In the woods."

"*Where* in the woods, Harv? It's dark and there's a lot of trees back there."

A frightened look settled on Harv's features—as if he knew he was about to catch hell. "I don't know!"

"How can y'all not fucking know?" Cy shouted, his hands opening and closing. "Y'all don't know anything about *anything*!"

"Only what they told us, and they didn't tell us much of anything! They didn't think they had to. Their whole attitude was that a breach or a lockdown was never going to happen!"

Cy stepped toward him, his tone menacing. "Then you're not much use to us, are you?"

"Easy, Cy," she said. "The escape hatch is no doubt part of the lockdown, so we won't be able to use that either."

"But if we could find it, maybe we could override it."

"We'd be better off trying to override the elevator, but I know nothing about electronics. You?"

He shook his head. "They've cut the power to it, most likely from below. No way to override that from up here. But an escape hatch . . . we might be able to force that."

A long shot but, as far as Laura could see, the only shot they had. But in the dark . . . in a thick pine forest?

Something clicked. Her last conversation with Rick, talking about Pentagon black funding.

I'm talking a mysterious German scientist and an underground bunker and major weirdness. It's all on a thumb drive . . .

Hadn't she seen a thumb drive in that bag full of paraphernalia?

She rushed out of the tool cabinet and back to the console where she immediately spotted the drive among the junk. She pulled it out and sat down before the computer on the console, found a USB port, and poked the drive at it. Of course it didn't go in—somehow they never did on the first try. With only two orientations, the probability of getting it right on the first try was fifty percent, but Laura's wrong rate ran somewhere in the nineties. How was that possible?

The computer auto-ran the drive, opening it to reveal a half dozen folders, one of which read "Lange-Tür bunker."

She didn't know what Lange-Tür meant but it said "bunker" so she opened it. And array of .jpg, .pdf, and .doc files filled the screen. Cyrus, Marie, and Tanisha gathered behind her as she started scanning through the files. Harv stood on the far side of the console looking miserable.

A photo viewer toured her through an array of black-and-white photos dated 1946. They showed a lot of concrete being poured into a big hole in the ground in the middle of the woods. Whatever they built was covered over.

"Gotta be the bunker back in the day," Cyrus said. "The pines filled right back in, covered the bare spot like it never was."

"Nature abhors a vacuum," Laura said.

She tried the .pdfs next and found schematics of an underground building—obviously the bunker.

"Now we're talking," Tanisha said. "I took an architecture and mechanical drawing class in high school." She leaned closer and squinted at the screen. "But look at the date on these things—1946. Wow. Ancient. Where are the controls? Let's rotate this thing and see—"

"It's a pdf, Tanisha," Laura said. "It doesn't rotate."

"You mean these were done by hand? No CAD? Oh, wow. Okay, let's see what we can find."

Laura scanned through the .pdfs until she came to an overhead diagram. It showed the elevator, then a long tunnel leading to the main building with its central corridor leading to a blocked-off area labeled *RESEARCH*.

But no escape hatch.

She was about to switch to another drawing when Tanisha grabbed her shoulder.

"Wait!" she said, pointing to the last room on the left before the research area. "See that circle there? That's not in any other room. In fact, it's pretty much the only circle in the whole drawing. See if you can find another angle—a lateral view."

Three .pdfs later, Laura found one that showed a shaft of some sort leading up from the last room on the left.

"That's it!" Tanisha said. "Got to be! See? It's got

what looks like a steel ladder embedded in the wall. But, Jesus . . . that shaft's gotta be fifty feet straight up. That's a mean climb."

Laura rose and patted the chair. "Here. You take over. I'm putting you in charge of figuring out how far back from the elevator we have to travel before we find the hatch." She turned to the others. "I'm going to get the flashlight from my car, then . . . who's up for a walk in the woods?"

25

"She's gone," Rick said, hovering over Iggy's still form as the room blinked red and the Klaxon howled.

He'd felt the final, unmistakable loss of tension and turgor as the life went out of her tissues. On the far side of her corpse, Moe sobbed.

"Jesus God, *why?*"

Yeah. Why? Why any of this?

Why Iggy, of all people? Just a kid, and a sweet kid, at that. Never hurt anyone.

Although that power of hers . . . *truth*. So dangerous to so many.

For years now Rick had been lying about pretty much everything in his past, including his name. "Rick Hayden" had become an automatic response whenever asked his name, yet when Moe had asked Stoney his name, Rick had had to battle an urge to blurt "Garrick Somers."

He would have advised Iggy to keep it under wraps because it threatened powerful people in so many walks of life. If someone like Luis could find a way to spread that talent, that gift around, it could change the whole damn world. And the people who held the reins would not let them go without a fight.

But now the threat had been eliminated.

"What the hell happened?"

Moe wiped at her tears with her lab coat sleeve. "Didn't you *see*?"

"I assume it was Greve, but I was having a staring contest with that thing in the tank when I heard the shots. Before I could react the thing rushed the glass and melted through it like it wasn't there. Came straight at me. Might've melted through me if I hadn't ducked and covered."

Moe was nodding. "Greve, right. He came out of nowhere and just . . . just . . . executed her. That's what he did, he just fucking *executed* her!"

Her voice slipped its gears, double-clutching, finally stalling as she sobbed again. Rick gave her a moment and used the time to scan the area for a sign of Greve.

"Where'd he go?"

She pulled herself together. "I don't know. I was next on his list. He had his gun in my face and I'd be gone too if the Anomaly hadn't taken us by surprise. The near miss must have spooked him and he took off."

Greve was nowhere in sight. Rick didn't buy him being genuinely "spooked" by the Anomaly, but he probably assumed that direct contact with it would be unpleasant at the very least, and most likely fatal.

Stonington rushed up then and skidded to a halt when he saw Iggy.

"Oh, my God! Did the Anomaly—?"

"No," Rick said, rising to face him. "Greve."

"Greve? What assholery is he up to now?" He

looked around. "Look, I didn't know her and she seemed like a nice girl and I'm sorry and all for your loss, but we've got a major problem here."

"The Anomaly?" Rick said.

"Goddamn right, the Anomaly. It's on the loose."

"Any idea where it is?"

"Not a clue. And since it appears to treat walls like they don't exist, it could be anywhere."

"No way to track it?"

"Something has to have identifiable properties— let's make that at least *one* identifiable property— before you can track it."

"I get it. Any reason to believe it's still here?"

"'Here' as in the rear section? No." He jerked a thumb over his shoulder. "It carved a tunnel through the wall over there. If you mean somewhere in the bunker? Maybe."

"Any idea where?"

Stoney shook his head. "None whatsoever. But I think we should look for it."

"Why?"

"Because we should know where it is." He pointed to the tunnel through the wall behind the console. "If it can do that to ferroconcrete, imagine what it can do to a person."

Rick didn't want to imagine it—unless that person was Greve. He'd decided to kill Greve before the sick fuck had murdered Iggy. Now he wished for a way to kill him twice.

He was feeling a little crazy, and the Klaxon was only exacerbating it. He felt like he was in a giant submarine that had been hit by a depth charge.

"Any way to shut off that racket?"

Stoney nodded. "Not while we're in lockdown

mode. Got to enter the override code in the computer."

"Well, do it. Please. Wait, did you say 'lockdown'? Does that mean what I think it does?"

"Yep. No one in and no one out of the bunker."

"The elevator?"

"Its power gets cut. Won't budge till the override code is entered."

"Well, enter it."

"The only one who has it down here is Greve."

"Only Greve? What if he's not here?"

"The response team from Dix will have it. They can enter it upstairs when they arrive. If they come."

"*If?*"

Stoney shrugged. "Maintenance here hasn't exactly been a priority for DoD. The system dates from 1947. I've been here thirty-plus years and I don't ever remember it being tested. Never a drill—not once. So Fort Dix may have no idea we've got ourselves a breach emergency."

Okay. Greve just got a brief reprieve from his kill-on-sight sentence. Very brief. Just long enough to enter that code.

Rick walked away, searching for the Klaxon. He found a cylinder with a flared end mounted on the wall above the entry door. He pulled a chair over, located the wires leading to the cylinder, and yanked them free.

It shut off, leaving the rear compartment in blessed relative silence—relative because another Klaxon was honking away out in the hall, but the heavy door muffled it.

The red light continued to flash, but that didn't bother him. Now he could think.

"This override code," he said, returning to Stoney. "It can be entered only upstairs and into this console?"

"You got it."

Well, good. That meant Greve would have to return here sooner or later. All they had to do was wait for him. But one thing bothered him . . .

"I know DoD doesn't have to follow local building codes, but I can't believe they built this place with only one way in or out."

"They didn't. There's an emergency exit—or at least I'm told there is."

Rick didn't like the latter half of that. "*Told* there is? You mean you don't *know*?"

"Well, I was told it existed, so I'm sure it does. Supposedly there's a shaft to a surface hatch, and if I remember correctly—it's been a while now—the entrance is in the conference room. But I can't say I recall ever seeing it."

"Never seen it? You've been here, what, decades, and you've never seen it?"

Stoney shook his head. "Not that I recall. But then again, I was never looking for it. And if I did see it, I just plain don't remember. My memory isn't what it used to be."

"Wouldn't it have some signage directing you there in case of emergency?"

"You'd think so, wouldn't you. But as I said, I've never seen it. The bunker's interior's been repainted and remodeled a few times over the years, so maybe it got covered over."

"I don't believe this . . ." He shook his head. "We've got to find it."

"What for? Won't matter if we do. The emergency exit would be included in a breach lockdown. I mean, the whole idea of the lockdown is to seal the place off so that nothing inside can get outside."

"I appreciate that, but we need to find it anyway. Maybe the system here is so old it's forgotten about the emergency exit and didn't lock it."

"Maybe, maybe not. But either way, we can't let the Anomaly out."

"Why not?"

Stoney pointed to the hole in the wall. "Do you see what it did over there? We've got to find that thing before it gets out in the world."

"I do see what it did over there and what I see tells me that we can't stop it from getting out into the world if it wants to. It tells me that thing can go pretty much anywhere it damn well pleases."

"Be that as it may," Stoney said, giving him an appraising look. "You gonna help me?"

"Help you what?"

"Find the Anomaly."

"And what do we do when we find it?"

That gave Stoney pause. "I . . . I don't rightly know . . ."

"Damn right, you don't. So let's find that emergency exit."

"We can hunt for both at once."

Rick could only shake his head. Stoney was hopeless.

"The exit . . . if you don't remember seeing it in the conference room"—he gestured abound the research area—"could it possibly be in here?"

Stoney shook his head. "No way. I know every inch. It's the one area that's never been renovated—couldn't let any workers see the Anomaly. Don't waste your time here—no exit and no Anomaly. They're both elsewhere."

The Anomaly . . . Rick looked again at the hole in the wall behind the console. It sat maybe seven feet off the floor.

Just out of curiosity . . . "Maybe we should start with that wall."

Grabbing the chair he'd used before, he dragged it over, stepped up, and peeked through the hole. The Anomaly had bored-drilled-melted-whatever a soccer-ball-width tunnel with sides as smooth as glass through the six inches of the wall into the adjoining room.

Rick recognized the room—he'd surprised the security guy named Woolley there and shot him up with some of the stuff that had been meant for him. But Woolley was nowhere in sight. Must have come out of it.

"That's room eleven," Stoney said. "The monitoring room. They can keep watch on pretty much everything that goes on in here—except the Anomaly. Those guys don't have clearance to know about it."

"Empty now," Rick said.

He looked across the monitoring room at the far wall where he saw another mini-tunnel.

"Went straight through eleven and into twelve," he told Stoney. "Wonder where it stopped."

"I'm wondering *if* it stopped. We need to go look. It might bore through the Earth and keep on going."

Fine with me, Rick thought as he hopped off the chair.

"Tell you the truth, I'm just as happy not knowing where it is."

Stoney jutted his chin toward where Moe still knelt by Iggy. "Unless Greve's plans changed, I'm guessing that a few more like that poor girl might be locked away down here. They could be in trouble."

The nadaný—Annie and Ellis! With everything that had happened, they'd slipped off his radar.

"Yeah. They damn well could."

He hurried over to Moe and gently pulled her to her feet. She seemed to have composed herself some.

"You okay?"

She shook her head. "Not really. I don't know why this has hit me so hard. I mean, I just met her today."

Rick didn't know the answer for sure, but maybe it went something like: *Maybe if you hadn't fucked with her brain she'd be alive and safe back in Brooklyn right now instead of lying stone dead in a puddle of her own blood, and so you're feeling guilty as all hell,* but he toned it down. He wanted her help.

"You feel responsible in some way."

"I do, I do."

"Then help Stoney and me find Annie and Ellis before something happens to them too."

"You mean . . . leave Iggy?"

"She's not going to miss you." Moe flinched and Rick reminded himself to go easy here. "And sooner or later Greve is gonna come back. You say he tried to kill you once. I'm not leaving you alone so he can finish the job."

"Okay, okay, I get it, but can we at least . . . cover her?"

Stoney hurried over to his console and returned with a lab coat. He arranged it to cover Iggy's head and most of her torso.

Rick turned Moe away from Iggy so that she was looking straight at him.

"Listen: Stoney says this place was built with an emergency exit. Know anything about that?"

She shook her head. "This is the first I've heard of

it. I've only been in and out as a visitor. Never had a proper orientation. I'll bet Greve knows but—"

"Yeah, well, we'll be doing our best to avoid Greve." He turned to Stoney. "Let's start looking for the others. We'll go room by room and—"

"I know where they are," Moe said. "Or at least where they were."

"Great. That'll help." He knew where Annie used to be, but Greve might have stashed her in another room. "Stoney wants to find the Anomaly as well."

"Can't help you there," she said. "Not even sure I want to."

Amen, sister.

"Greve's out there," she added.

"I know."

"With a gun."

Tell me something I don't know, Rick thought. He appreciated how she was scared and still in shock after witnessing Iggy's cold-blooded murder, and how she didn't want to go through that door, but he wasn't leaving her here alone.

"I know that too. But we've still got to round up Annie and Ellis and get them out of here. So let's get started."

26

Greve stood in the middle of the flashing, honking hallway and tried to control his shaking.

He'd never killed someone before. Sure, his actions had led to people dying, but he'd never directly snuffed out a life until today—until just a moment ago.

He lifted his free hand and watched the tremor. Not fear. Adrenaline.

He'd intended to kill the four of them—everyone who had heard what he'd said. He could still see their shocked expressions, the revulsion in their eyes when he'd blurted out the truth.

He still didn't understand how it had happened. He hadn't thought of Cheryl in decades. They never spoke, let alone saw each other. She could be dead for all he knew.

And yet when that rotten, sneaky, stinking bitch LaVelle had asked her question, Cheryl had popped into his mind from out of nowhere, traveling nonstop from deep in his subconscious to the tip of his tongue and, before he was aware of what was happening, out into the world.

I fucked my younger sister half a dozen times ...

If words were physical objects he would have snatched them out of the air and crammed them back into his mouth. But the damage was done. They'd all heard.

Which meant they couldn't be allowed to live. They all had to die. Every one of them.

That had been his intention in returning. He'd worked it all out. The girl first, because she was the most dangerous, the most unpredictable, and no one knew the extent of her powers. He'd rehearsed every move he intended to make in there.

With the girl out of the way, he'd immediately remove Hayden, the second most dangerous person in the room, shoot him down like the dog he was. After that he could dispose of LaVelle and Stonington in no particular order, virtually at his leisure. They'd have no way to resist.

But the Anomaly had ruined his plans. First off, it had changed its shape. In all his years in and out of the bunker, Greve had never seen it shrink into such a compact sphere. That had thrown him off balance. Just a little. Not enough to alter his plans.

Just before he grabbed the girl, he'd marked where Hayden was standing—directly in front of the Anomaly, staring at it. As soon as he'd put the two slugs through the girl's brain, he took aim at Hayden and fired.

But Hayden had moved. He was ducking the Anomaly as it flew through the hole it had made in the chamber's glass. The gunfire seemed to have an effect on it. Or was it the death of the girl? Whichever, it swerved in midair and streaked straight toward him and LaVelle.

At that moment he was convinced it was after him, so he turned and ran.

But of course, it wasn't. A glance over his shoulder as he reached the door showed it swerving again and heading back the other way. But for how long? Greve wasn't taking any chances. He kept going and didn't stop until he was halfway down the hall.

The Anomaly was free. He found the idea terrifying. The only reason this bunker remained operational was because the Pentagon didn't know what to do with the Anomaly, and so they'd kept it locked away.

He remembered Hayden's contemptuous smirk.

You only think you have it contained. It can leave any time it wants. It's been sitting there waiting for a signal or a trigger . . .

Greve had brushed him off. What did Hayden know? What *could* he know? And yet . . .

. . . waiting for a signal or a trigger . . .

Had Greve provided that trigger?

Too late to worry about that now, whatever the

truth. He had to worry about his next step. Did he dare go back?

He had to go back. He couldn't bear the thought of anyone knowing the truth. If—

Voices down the hall grabbed his attention. He guessed who they were so he moved toward them.

He found the guard who'd brought the invisible girl back to him—Jon—and two others who looked somewhat worse for wear after their doses of the sedative. They were pacing the room in an attempt to walk it off. One wore a security coverall while the other wore street clothes.

"Keep moving," Jon was saying. He snapped to attention when he saw Greve. "Yessir!"

The other two stopped and faced him.

"There's trouble in the research section."

Jon looked worried. "Is that the reason for the lockdown? Is there danger?"

"Not to worry about anything toxic. The problem is perfectly human: The one who injected these two is running amok there and cannot be allowed to leave that area."

Jon waved at the others. "They're not a hundred percent yet."

"With three against one, that should not matter."

"*Three* against one?" Jon said. "You won't be with us?"

The impertinence of the man. "I have an urgent matter pertaining to the lockdown that cannot wait. And let's not forget that you're armed and he isn't."

Greve waited for Jon to mention hearing gunfire, but he didn't. The research area was supposedly soundproofed, but you never knew.

"Yessir. What do you want us to do?"

"Very simple: You set up guard outside the research area and do not let him or anyone else leave. That includes Doctor LaVelle and Doctor Stonington. All three must be confined to the research area until help arrives from Fort Dix. Think you can handle that?"

"Yessir." He looked relieved that he'd be required only to contain people, not physically subdue them.

"Get to it then."

As Jon mustered his troops, Greve slipped out and headed for the emergency exit. He needed to know if he could escape the bunker. The direction of his future actions down here would be determined by the answer. Now that he'd had time to think about it, he wasn't about to commit mass murder before assuring himself of some means of escape afterward.

27

They had Harv safely zip-tied to one of the Quonset hut's side supports where he couldn't reach anything.

"Can one of you get us a GPS reading?" Laura said to her companions as she pulled out her phone and found Stahlman's number. He answered on the second ring.

"We found them," she said.

"Where the hell are you? What's the idea of running off alone without telling anybody where you went?"

She wasn't going to argue with him because he was one hundred percent right.

"Didn't you hear me? We found them."

She nodded her thanks as Marie handed her a slip of paper with the coordinates.

"Yes. And I'm delighted to hear that. Is everyone okay? Rick included?"

Thanks for asking about Rick, she thought. She was glad to know she wasn't the only one who cared.

"I haven't seen them yet."

"I thought you said you found them."

"I mean I know where they are. I'm practically on top of them."

"Where are you?"

She read him Marie's coordinates.

"Where the hell is that?"

"The back end of Lakehurst Naval Air Station."

"What? The *Hindenburg* place?"

"That's it. I'm sure there's a very long and very interesting story behind all this, but I don't know it yet."

"None of that matters right now. Call the state cops and let them take it from here."

"Supposedly a contingent of soldiers is on its way from Fort Dix as we speak."

"If the abductions are military, they may not be on your side."

She hadn't thought of that. This was a Pentagon operation, after all.

"Maybe not, but what are they going to do—shoot us?"

"Okay, never mind. After your disappearing act tonight, I don't know if I can trust you."

"Hey!" That hurt.

"You're acting reckless so I'm going to do it for you." His voice became muffled as he said, "Luis, call the Jersey State Police and the Lakehurst Police and the Ocean County sheriff's office and tell them there's a major emergency—abducted people—at these coordinates."

Maybe all those chefs stirring this pot could work to her advantage. Imagine the jurisdictional disputes.

"Okay, Laura. You just stay put and wait for help to arrive."

"Aye-aye, sir!" she said and ended the call.

She wasn't waiting for anyone.

"Find any flashlights?" she said.

"Got three that work," Tanisha said.

"All right. Let's go. Cyrus, you want to lead?"

"Y'all mean clear the way?" he said.

"I confess I was thinking along those lines, yes."

He grinned. "Deeelighted."

"Great." Laura stepped toward Harv. "Just let me check on our friend here before we go."

They'd released Harv's hands from behind his back and used a couple of zip ties to secure his left wrist to one of the hut's support struts. Marie had rolled one of the desk chairs over so he wouldn't have to sit on the floor.

"Comfortable?" she said.

He gave her a sour look and lifted his left wrist as far as the zip ties would allow, which wasn't very far at all. "Really? You're really going to ask me that?"

His ingratitude irked her. "You know, it would have been a lot easier for us to simply secure you there and leave you standing with your hands behind you."

"I'm still a prisoner."

"I wouldn't look at it that way. Just consider yourself restrained from causing any mischief at the console and making any unauthorized phone calls."

He looked away. "Whatever."

"As you said, the cavalry is on its way. So are the staties and the locals. Just a question of who gets here first."

He rolled his eyes. "I'm gonna be in such deep shit."

"Don't blame us. Your bosses started all this when they kidnapped our friends."

She left him stewing. He looked so miserable she almost felt sorry for him. Almost. Too bad his job would wind up as collateral damage but, after all, he *had* pulled a gun on them.

She and the others exited the hut and filed along its flank, then past the junkers behind. Cy led the way, followed by Tanisha and Marie, with Laura bringing up the rear. She let the others go ahead as she searched among the wrecks and scrap metal until she found a length of steel reinforcing rod.

"A weapon?" Marie said when Laura caught up.

"A poker."

Marie gave her an odd look but said no more.

When Cyrus reached the pines he plunged in among them without hesitation.

"How far?" he called over his shoulder.

"The tunnel from the elevator to the occupied area was a good quarter mile," Tanisha said. "The hatch should be a couple of hundred feet beyond that—a straight line from here."

Cyrus and Tanisha trained their flash beams ahead. When vines strung across their path, Cyrus would hand Tanisha his flash and grab handfuls; the vines fell away. Same thing when a fallen sapling or low branch blocked their way: He'd grab it with both hands, arms spread wide, and the wood between would fall to the ground.

"I finally found a use for this gift," he said. "Pathfinder."

"More like path*maker,*" Laura said.

He laughed. "Even better!"

After what seemed like a two-mile walk but obviously wasn't, Marie stopped and pointed down. "We're directly over them."

"And directly under *them,*" Tanisha said, pointing up.

Laura looked up and reflexively recoiled at the sight of a half dozen pine lights, ranging in size from Ping-Pong to beach ball, gliding in random patterns overhead. They made her uneasy. What would make light coalesce into a ball like that? Apparently she wasn't the only one affected. The surrounding woods had gone dead silent.

She shook it off. Couldn't worry about swamp gas or whatever now. She'd reached the last leg of this journey—but the most difficult and dangerous. Harv had been undertrained and barely motivated. She doubted the next line of defense would fall so easily.

"Okay, everyone," she said, "I've got a feeling the hatch will be massively overgrown. The diagram made it appear to rise a couple of feet above ground level, so look for a mound of vegetation between the trees."

Marie turned on her flashlight and began to search. Laura followed close behind. She had a feeling about Marie. She was the finder, after all . . .

Sure enough, her beam found a mound of twisted vines about three feet high, surrounded by mature trees.

"I think we've got it," Laura said.

Cyrus and Tanisha hurried over as she started poking her steel rod through the living weave.

"Now I get it," Marie said. "Very clever."

On the third poke she was rewarded with the clank of metal on metal.

"Has to be it!" she said. "Now let's get to work clearing the—"

She jumped at the sound of more metallic clanks, this time coming from the underside of the hatch. Someone had started banging on the inner surface.

28

Rick peeked through the door's tiny window, hoping to see an empty hallway.

No such luck.

Watts—sans his coverall—and Woolley were marching his way, looking a little bleary-eyed in the red flashing light—a dozen feet away and closing like the Earp brothers headed for the O.K. Corral. They flanked a new guy wearing a security coverall and carrying a semiautomatic. No sign of Greve anywhere.

He glanced at Stoney and Moe. "We've got company."

"Greve?" Moe said, her voice quavering.

"No. The hired help. You two stay out of the doorway." He didn't mention the pistol, but he wanted them out of the line of fire should things go south. "I'll reason with them."

He opened the door and immediately the blare of the hallway Klaxon washed over him. When the new guy saw Rick he raised the semiautomatic to waist level.

Stoney must have been peeking because he burst out behind Rick and raised his hands in a *stop* gesture.

"Hey, wait, guys, just wait! You know me. And Jon, you know the rule about guns down here!"

"This isn't for you, Stoney," Jon said as he waggled his pistol. "It's—"

Although Rick had wanted Stoney out of sight, his presence was causing a convenient distraction, allowing Rick to plow ahead with his original plan. A guy with a gun expected people to pause or hesitate when they saw it. But instead of slowing or stopping, Rick increased his pace without breaking stride, knocking Jon's weapon aside as he barreled into him and head-butted him in the nose.

The pistol discharged, the bullet ricocheting off the floor. As Jon reeled back, spurting blood, Rick ripped the pistol from his hand and smashed the grip against the side of Woolley's head, then aimed a chop at Watts's throat.

But Watts was ahead of him, covering his already injured throat with both hands as he stumbled away with a hoarse cry of "No! Don't!"

Quick survey: Jon on his knees with his hands over his face, blood seeping through his fingers. From the looks of Woolley, he hadn't fully recovered from his dose of sedation, and the blow to his head seemed to have banished what little fight he'd had left in him. He leaned against the wall, looking sick as he pressed a palm against his bleeding scalp. Watts continued his wobbly retreat down the hall.

"'Reason with them,' huh?" Stoney said. "What school of philosophy is that?"

"Hard knocks?"

"I guess so. Plenty of times I've heard people say, 'Didn't know what hit them,' but I've never seen it. Now I have. Damn, you're a ballsy son of a bitch."

Rick shrugged it off. "It's all training and attitude. These guys may think they're hard guys but they're in the same class as rent-a-cops. And they aren't killers."

I, on the other hand . . .

"But Jon there had a gun."

Rick checked the pistol. An HK VP9. Nice piece. He eased back the slide to check the chamber and found it loaded.

"And Jon thought just having it was enough—his

first mistake. His second was expecting me to act a certain way. When I did something else, he wasn't prepared. He flinched. He who flinches loses."

He realized Watts had now wandered about thirty feet down the hall. "Hey, Watts! Get back here!"

Without looking back, Watts increased his pace. Rick aimed and fired. The bullet kicked up a puff of concrete an inch from his left foot.

"The next one goes in your ass."

Watts turned and began walking back.

All right, what to do with these clowns to keep them out of the way? He wished to hell he had his zip ties but they were gone. Somebody had cleaned out his pockets after he was gassed.

He pulled Jon to his feet and waved the HK under his nose.

"Empty your pockets onto the floor. You too," he told Watts as he approached.

He indicated to Stoney to make Woolley do the same.

The sight of Jon's pistol in the wrong hands seemed to have a demoralizing effect. No one argued.

When he was satisfied all their pockets were empty, he checked room one, labeled *Storage,* and found it full of junk. Room two proved empty so he herded them in there, but not until Stoney had checked for signs of the Anomaly. Once he gave the all-clear, Rick locked them in.

"Anulka was in eighteen," Moe said.

"You two get her," Stoney said. "I'm going to check the other side of the hall. We know the Anomaly went through two of those walls. I want to see if it stopped anywhere."

"Watch out for Greve."

"He's got no beef with me."

"Yeah, but does *he* know that? Just be careful, okay?"

Stoney seemed all right, but Greve was totally out of control. Who knew what he was capable of right now?

Pistol ready, Rick motioned Moe behind him and pressed himself against the wall as he unlocked the door to room eighteen and eased it open a few inches. Greve had to know Rick would come eventually for the nadaný. What better place to lie in wait than one of their rooms?

"Annie?"

"Rick? Oh, Rick, thank God!" She rushed up to the door and pulled it wide open. "I heard shots and—" She froze when she saw Moe. "What's *she* doing here?"

"She's okay–"

"She's one of them!"

"Greve is off the deep end, so she's changed sides."

"Who's Greve?"

"You've already met my former boss," Moe said. "The kidnappings, the shock collars, they were all his ideas."

"You trust her?" Annie said.

Rick couldn't say exactly why, but he knew Moe had been crushed by Iggy's death—couldn't fake that. And sometimes you had to go with your gut, so . . .

"Yeah, I do. And you can too." He kept checking up and down the hall. Still no sign of Greve. Where was he hiding? Or had he found a way out? "Damn shame they caught you, though. They rough you up any?"

She shook her head. "The two guys up top seemed so proud and amazed they'd caught an invisible girl that I don't think it ever occurred to them. And what's his name—Greve? He wasn't exactly gentle when he shoved me back in the room here, but nothing serious. He was more anxious to find whoever let me go—and he seemed to have a pretty good idea it was you."

"He found me. But what matters now is getting you out of here. And that means finding the emergency exit." He turned to Moe. "Stoney said an exit shaft runs up from the conference room. Where's that?"

Moe's expression turned dubious. "From the conference room? No way."

Rick needed to see for himself. "Show us."

Rick checked the hall for Greve and, finding no sign of him, let Moe lead them to a larger space with a big conference table. The food-wrapper-filled wastebaskets, refrigerator, and microwave said it doubled as a break room.

Folders littered the table. He stopped by its corner and scanned the room.

Moe said, "I spent many an hour in here bored out of my skull. I've stared at these walls from every angle and I can tell you there's no emergency exit here."

"Then why did Stoney say there was?"

"Want to know what I think?" she asked, but didn't wait for a reply. "I think Doc Stoney has spent too much time back there with the Anomaly. I think it's scrambled his brain."

Just to be sure, Rick quick-walked the perimeter of the room, kicking the walls and banging them with the heel of his fist.

"Solid," he said, returning to the two women. "All solid as rock."

"Then we're trapped?" Annie said.

"*Has* to be an emergency exit," he said. "I refuse to believe they built this place without one. I'll do my damnedest to get you out of here, but first we have to locate Ellis."

"Hey, don't forget Iggy," Annie said.

Shit. No way to soft-pedal this . . .

"Iggy's dead."

Annie's hand shot to her mouth as she staggered back. "No! Ohmigod, no! Who'd do . . . ? *No!*"

"She died in my arms," Moe said, puddling up again.

"But why? Who on this fucking Earth would want to kill Iggy?"

Rick and Moe spoke in unison. "Greve."

"But *why?*"

"Long story," Rick said. "I'll explain when we get out of here. Right now—"

"Hey!" Stoney's voice echoed from down the hall. "Hey, you gotta see this!"

29

Greve stood inside the bunker's storeroom with his ear pressed against its locked door. He'd heard a couple of shots in the hallway and had got the impression that Jon and his fellow security men had failed to contain Hayden and the rest.

Well, no surprise there. A security job here at the bunker had always been considered a sinecure, a position given to trainees and those nearing retirement, because nothing ever happened here. Until today.

He'd hidden when someone looked in the room. Now that the voices had died away, he got busy clearing a path through the piles of junk.

Shortly after the discovery of melis and the Pentagon's decision to invest in researching its potential, the bunker had undergone an internal facelift. Greve remembered the old and faded signage directing to the emergency exit . . . signage that had never been restored after the paint job. Same with the signage on the entrance to the escape shaft. It had receded to a flush, unadorned, rarely noticed panel in a rear corner of the conference room.

And then they moved the conference room to a larger space. The original room became a storage area for anything that didn't fit or couldn't find use elsewhere. People moved on from the bunker—many to prematurely terminate their own existence—and their replacements had never seen the old conference room, and never knew the space had ever been used for anything other than storage.

After squeezing and sliding past desks, chairs, cabinets, and even old mattresses, he finally reached the rear corner where he found a tall, four-drawer filing cabinet backed up against the wooden panel that acted as the door to the escape route. Pocketing his pistol, he pulled on a drawer handle and found it full of stuffed manila folders. The bunker had gone digital years and years ago, yet some people couldn't part with their paper files. Damn them.

The cabinet was too heavy to lift, so he began removing the drawers and laying them wherever he could find a reasonably flat surface. He'd just pulled out the last when he sensed movement behind him. He turned in time to see the Anomaly emerge from a wall at perhaps three feet off the floor and dissolve everything in its path as it raced across the room to disappear through the opposite wall.

Greve stared in disbelief as desks and tables and

chairs collapsed with the sudden loss of a leg or other support. The Anomaly had put holes right through them—all without a sound.

The thing was running amok. If it kept up this pace of destruction, it would make Swiss cheese of the bunker, destabilizing the walls. With uncountable tons of packed earth above it, the whole structure would collapse in a rush. He couldn't see anyone surviving that.

Which prompted an abrupt change in plans. He couldn't stay here. He didn't have to worry about anyone knowing his secret—they'd all be dead soon. So escape became the prime directive.

Grunting and groaning, he was able to tilt the empty cabinet this way and that, rocking and swiveling it back and forth on its corners until it resettled in a spot far enough from the panel to allow him to pry it open. It came loose with a deafening screech.

He pulled his Luger and waited to see if anyone responded from the hallway. He thought he heard voices shouting and a woman scream somewhere in the distance but it wasn't repeated. Nothing close by. He turned back to the panel and eased it open just enough to let him past.

The air inside the round concrete shaft felt at least ten degrees cooler and smelled damp and musty. He felt along the curved wall till he found a light switch. He flipped it but nothing happened. Wiggling the toggle up and down a half dozen more times didn't improve the situation: still no light.

Well, what did he expect? Without maintenance, the decades-old bulbs had either burned out or the switch contacts had corroded past the point where they could conduct a current.

And, with no idea he'd be in a situation like this, he hadn't brought a flashlight.

With only faint, indirect light from the storeroom seeping past the panel to guide him, he found the rungs of a wrought-iron ladder set into the wall and trailing fifty feet up into the darkness above.

A long climb, and he was hardly in peak condition. Back in the day, when he'd made a point of staying in shape, he wouldn't have given the climb a second thought. But as his years advanced, he'd become sedentary and deconditioned.

Not like I have a choice, he thought.

He started to climb. The ladder was narrow, the rungs dusty and probably a little rusty as well, all of which would make for a precarious climb in the light. Rising into an increasingly Stygian darkness, it became downright dangerous. Here and there the ladder shook, as if some of the inserts that fixed it to the wall were loose. The farther he climbed, the lower his chances of surviving a fall. But he pushed on.

Greve noticed the air in the shaft warming, which he took as a good sign. And sure enough, his ladder soon ran out of rungs. He'd reached the top—or so he hoped. He felt around in the dark and found what seemed like a platform.

Of course. That made sense: Climb to the platform where you could stand and open the hatch.

He levered himself onto the platform, gave himself a moment to catch his breath, then stood and felt around. Another short length of steel ladder rose to the upper lip of the concrete where a round, solid steel hatch capped the shaft. He had two major concerns now. One, was the hatch locked down along with everything else? Two, if not locked down, after more than half a century of neglect, would it be so overgrown that he'd be unable to open it?

His hands found the wheel that would retract the latches. He tugged on it, first clockwise, then counter. It wouldn't budge. He put all his strength and weight behind it with the same result.

He wanted to scream but didn't dare because the sound might echo down the shaft and give away his location.

Then he heard something on the other side— rustling and scraping, followed by a clank—metal on metal against the hatch.

Someone was up there—not only up there but trying to open the hatch.

Throwing caution to the wind, he began shouting and hammering on the inner surface.

Faintly he heard a woman's voice, barely audible through the hatch.

"Who's there?" she said. "Rick, is that you?"

Rick? Someone looking for Hayden? That wasn't good. Oh, that wasn't good at all.

Greve pulled his pistol and double-checked that it was ready to fire, then hid it away. He began voicing nonsense syllables as he fabricated a cover story.

30

Turning in a circle as he walked, Rick guided the two women down and across the hall to where Stoney's head protruded from a doorway.

"Take a gander," the older man said, gesturing through the door when they arrived. "I think I found one of the ones you're looking for."

The Anomaly hovered near the ceiling inside, directly over a cowering Ellis Reise. He sported a shock collar like Annie had worn and was manacled to a leg of the room's desk. The Anomaly had changed, expanding from the soccer ball form to the more discoid shape it had displayed back in the chamber, though not quite so large now.

"Ohmigod!" Annie said. "What is *that*?"

Before anyone could answer, Ellis shouted, "Hey, don't just stand there gawking! Get me out of here!"

But Rick couldn't resist a little more gawking as he took in the scene.

"You checked the rooms upstream from here?" he said to Stoney.

"Yep. It sailed through the walls, one after the other, straight as an arrow. Every single one."

"But it stopped here."

"Maybe because it's occupied? I don't know who that fellow is or why he's chained up, but the Anomaly seems to have taken a shine to him."

"Because he's nadaný?" Moe said.

"Get me outta here!" Ellis shouted. "Whatever it is, this thing is trying to freeze my ass off!"

He wasn't kidding. Frost rimed the desk that restrained him, and Ellis's breath fogged as he spoke. Rick pulled out Watts's key ring and found the one that had worked on his own shackle. Now . . . what?

The Anomaly looked as bizarre as ever but not particularly threatening. Still, anything with an ability to dissolve its way through walls demanded a high level of respect.

However . . . Ellis couldn't free himself, so someone had to do it for him.

How would the Anomaly react? Was it, as Moe had suggested, hovering over Ellis simply because he was nadaný? Was it protecting him or trying to freeze him? Whatever the reason, would it object if he moved away?

Did it even possess that level of awareness? Was it aware at all? Or was it being guided by another intelligence?

Yeah, well, whatever the case, someone was going to have to go in there, and Rick knew who that someone would be.

Lowering himself into a crouch, he kept an eye on the Anomaly as he eased across the room. Ellis hadn't been kidding about frostbite. The closer he moved to the Anomaly, the colder it got. Ellis was visibly shivering when Rick reached him.

"Never thought I'd be glad to see you," he said, teeth chattering. The bruise on his cheek wasn't as blue or as swollen as it had been.

"It's all relative, ain't it."

"What the fuck did you get me into?"

Typical Ellis. Rick wasn't about to delve into it here, or mention that Ellis had been a few minutes away from the loving arms of a car crusher when Rick first met him.

"Cut the whining or I'll go back to the hall—without you."

Ellis's lips straightened into a tight, angry line but he kept mum while Rick unlocked the manacle encircling his wrist.

"Okay now, let's move. Low and slow."

"Got a key for this?" he said, tugging on the collar as the manacle dropped away.

"No, but I can get it off you—just not here."

"I hear that." Ellis stared up at the Anomaly. "How dangerous is that thing?"

"Potentially . . . *very* dangerous. You saw how it got here?"

"Yeah. I mean, no. I looked up and spotted it floating across the room. But I saw the hole it left behind so I guessed it came right through the fucking wall."

"It did. Which means it can probably go right through you."

"Then I guess I should be glad it only stopped over me. Not that the end would be any different. I swear it's trying to freeze me to death."

Rick doubted that was the case—unless, of course, the Anomaly found Ellis as annoying as everyone else did.

Keeping his eye on the Anomaly, Rick grabbed a fistful of Ellis's shirt and tugged him back toward the doorway in a slow crouch. The Anomaly held its position until they were almost to the door, then it began to move.

"Oh, hell," Rick muttered.

With a panicked cry, Ellis pulled away and dove for the door.

But the Anomaly didn't seem interested. It compacted itself into its soccer-ball form again and headed for the opposite wall. Rick watched fascinated as it plowed straight through—no noise, no flashes, no steam or vapors, no dust or debris, just . . . a hole. And then it was gone, leaving its trademark tunnel.

Annie was gaping. "What the—?"

Reaching the doorway, Rick grabbed Stoney's arm. "Where does the concrete go—I mean the part that it eats away?"

"Probably the same place as all the stuff we threw at it over the years—nowhere. Or somewhere."

"Why's it so cold?"

Stoney raised a finger. "Now *that* I can answer. We've measured its surface temperature many times since it appeared and it's a consistent thirty-nine-point-two Celsius."

"I don't do Celsius."

"About one-oh-two Fahrenheit."

"So it's warm?"

He nodded. "What we determined is that it *absorbs* heat—sucks it right out of anything within a couple of meters—that's six feet to you."

"That's what it was doing to me?" Ellis said, rubbing warmth back into his arms. "Sucking off my heat?"

"Yep. And it would keep on sucking until you stopped generating heat."

"I'm taking that to mean until I was dead."

"It does, sonny. It does indeed."

Ellis turned to Rick and tugged at his shock collar. "You said you could get this off?"

"Right."

He hoped he wouldn't regret this. He didn't know how far he could trust Ellis, but a little telekinesis just might come in handy on their way out of here. He took out Watts's folding knife and used it to pop the lock as he'd done with Annie's.

Ellis yanked it off, bringing the scalp contacts with it, and stared at it.

"You're okay, Rick. A pain in the ass, but okay."

"I'll take that as a thanks." Rick noticed burns on his neck. Annie's neck hadn't been blistered like that. He leaned closer. "What happened here?"

Ellis nodded toward Moe. "Her pal upped the current."

"Greve," Stoney said.

Ellis's face darkened. "That's his name?"

"Yeah. Why'd he do that to you?"

"Thought he was teaching me a lesson." He twisted the collar out of shape and hurled it back into the room. "I've got a few lessons of my own to teach him when I catch up with him."

Rick wondered why he didn't seem to bear the same animus toward Moe, then noticed the ointment on the blisters.

"He burned you, then gave you ointment?"

Ellis's expression softened as he nodded toward Moe again. "That was her doing."

Rick wasn't surprised. "Yeah. Figured it wasn't Greve. Okay, we've got everybody, let's look for that emergency exit."

"Hey, wait," Ellis said. "They took Iggy too. We can't leave without her."

Kind of shocking to hear Ellis voice concern for someone else.

As with Annie, he simply laid it out. "Iggy's gone. Dead, I'm afraid."

Ellis's jaw dropped as he stood there blinking. "What? No. How?"

"Greve. He shot her dead."

"*WHAT?*"

Rick felt something hit him like a body slam from a giant swinging door. The blow sent him flying back into Ellis's room. He saw Moe and Annie tossed to the sides and Stoney flung into the center of the hall to land flat on his back.

Ellis looked as surprised as everybody else. "Whoa! I was never able to do *that* before!"

No, he hadn't. Not even close, as Rick knew from personal experience.

What was amping up his gift? Had it been the shocks? The bunker itself? Or the Anomaly?

Rick's best guess settled on the Anomaly. Melis
came from the Anomaly and the Anomaly was presently buzzing around and feeling its oats.

Moe and Annie were getting to their feet. Moe's
expression said she still hadn't accepted the reality of
the nadaný while Annie looked angry.

"Ellis Reise, don't you dare do that again!"

He was staring at his hands. "I don't know what I
did. It's never happened like that before. I could move
pool balls but never people!"

"What the fuck just happened?" Stoney said from
a supine position in the middle of the hall, propped
up on his elbows and staring at Ellis in disbelief.
"Pardon the language, ladies."

Rick hopped back to his feet and returned to the
doorway. "Maybe it was the shock of hearing about
Iggy."

"Yeah, Iggy," Ellis said, his face darkening.

"Easy-easy-easy," Rick said. "We don't need a repeat performance."

"I want that guy Greve. I want him soooo bad."

Rick was about to ask him if he and Iggy had had
something going when the Anomaly zipped past, not
two feet away.

"Dear God!" Moe cried. "That just missed me!"

Rick had felt the cold of its passing—and it had to
have been traveling at eighty or ninety miles an hour.

"What got into *that*?" Stoney said, still on the floor.

Rick watched it pierce the door into the research
section and disappear.

Something had energized the Anomaly. Its move-
ments had been measured, almost languid until now.
Had Ellis's use of his amped-up power juiced the
Anomaly, or vice versa?

Down the hall to his left Rick could see a hole

through the barrier that opened into the tunnel. The Anomaly must have bored through all the rooms and then looped back through the hallway.

Stoney was slowly regaining his feet, wincing with the effort. Rick bet he was riddled with arthritis.

Movement to the right. The Anomaly had made another hole in the research barrier and was streaking down the hall again, still only three feet off the floor.

"Hey, Stoney!" Rick called. "It's back!"

As Stoney turned to see, Rick realized the Anomaly was heading straight for him.

"Hit the floor!" he shouted. "Hit—!"

Instead Stoney dodged to the side and wound up against the far wall, eyes wide as he watched the Anomaly race by.

He waved and said, "Thanks for the heads-up. That was too close!"

The Anomaly veered to its right and entered another wall.

"It's gone crazy," Moe said. "When's it going to stop?"

Rick shook his head, baffled. "Can't tell if its movements are random or following some sort of crazy pattern."

"It seems to me like it's looking for something," Annie said. "You think that could be it?"

Moe said, "That would mean it has a purpose, and a purpose would mean intelligence. It's never exhibited intelligence or even awareness before."

"The intelligence may belong to something that's controlling it," Rick said.

That thing had ICE written all over it. He was sure of it and he wasn't letting go.

Looking both ways like a wary pedestrian crossing

a highway, Stoney started back toward them. He'd made it halfway when the Anomaly emerged from the floor about a dozen feet to his left and zoomed his way.

"Oh, no!" Annie cried.

Stoney froze, then turned to see where it was.

The Anomaly caught him square in the chest, passing straight through him without the slightest hesitation. And Stoney . . . Stoney showed no sign of impact or resistance, didn't even wince. His eyes showed no pain, but were filled instead with dazed wonder. His mouth worked spasmodically as he pivoted to show the perfectly round, soccer-ball-size hole through his abdomen.

"What . . . ?" he said in a shocked tone as his knees began to fold. "Did you see . . . ?"

For a single heartbeat the opposite wall was clearly visible through the hole before it filled with ruined, collapsing organs and spewing blood.

Around Rick, Moe screamed and Annie gagged and Ellis made incomprehensible shocked sounds as Stoney, spraying red in all directions, sagged to his knees. With no spine to stop it, the top half of his torso folded backward as he accordion-crumpled to the floor.

Rick started for him but the Anomaly, after passing through the tunnel barrier on its way out, was back through and into the hallway again, racing their way.

He pulled the two women into Ellis's room. Ellis followed.

"Did you see that?" he said in a hushed, shocked tone. "It came out of the floor and went through him like, like, like Pac-Man!"

"We've got to get outta here!" Annie wailed.

"No shit," Ellis said. "And how do we do that?"

Rick explained about the escape hatch and its attendant problems.

Ellis threw up his hands. "You mean, there's a way out but nobody fucking knows where it is?"

"Right. Which means we've got to go look for it."

"Look for it? As in wander around while Pac-Man's on the prowl? If that thing can pop out of the floor, it can show up anywhere, any time! We are *so* fucked!"

Rick wanted to clock him a good one on the jaw and shut him up. Here he was trying to keep morale from going down the toilet and Ellis kept hitting the flush handle.

The Anomaly zoomed past again.

Annie sobbed. "We're *never* getting out of here!"

31

"You hear that?" Cy said. "Someone's down there!"

Laura turned to Marie. "Nadaný?"

She shook her head.

Could it be . . . ?

Laura leaned closer and heard a faint male voice on the other side. He seemed to be shouting something about the hatch but she could barely make it out.

"Who's there? Rick, is that you?"

The voice stopped for a few seconds, then started up again, but she couldn't understand a word.

It had to be Rick. If she knew nothing else about him, she knew he was driven by duty. If he was in lockdown with the rest of them, his duty would be to round up the nadaný and get them to safety; and with the elevator not working, the only way to safety was through the escape hatch.

Suddenly, with a rustling-ripping sound, the vines began parting and receding to the edges of the mound, revealing a dome of rusted metal.

"Wow!" Tanisha said. "I've never been able to do anything like that!"

"That was you?" Laura said.

"Yeah. Looks like my gift is in hyperdrive too. Back home I could only move little stuff. What is it about this place?"

Laura wanted the answer to that question as well. And not knowing it made her uneasy. Could the well-spring of their powers be here? Was this where it all began? And was that the reason the abductees had been brought here?

But more than anything right now she wanted to know who was under that hatch.

Cy had been giving it a close inspection with his flashlight.

"How do we get this thing open?" he said. "There's no wheel, no sign of a release."

Tanisha said, "I got a sense from the diagrams that it wasn't meant to be opened from the outside, only from inside. No way to sneak in—just escape."

"Then whoever's down there has to open it," Marie said.

Laura suppressed a groan of dismay. This was what she'd dreaded all along. "But if it's part of the lockdown . . ."

"Here, take this," Tanisha said, handing Laura her flashlight.

"Why?"

"I really have no idea, but I'm going to try something."

"Should we stand back?" Cyrus said.

Tanisha shrugged as she stared at the hatch. "Probably not a bad idea."

Everyone took a step or two back.

For a few seconds nothing happened. And then, with a strange groan, the lip of the hatch began to bend upward. One inch . . . two . . .

Tanisha released a harsh, ragged breath and stumbled back. Laura caught her.

"I'm okay," she said. "But that's the best I can do."

"That's plenty!" Cyrus said. "That's awesome!"

And now Laura could hear the voice from below. Her heart sank when she realized it wasn't Rick's—nothing like Rick's.

"Hello? Who's up there? Can you open the hatch?"

"We're trying. Who are you?"

"I'm Special Agent Benjamin Greve, Defense Intelligence Agency."

Laura peeked through the opening and saw an older, balding man in a wrinkled suit standing on a steel mesh platform eight feet below.

"Where's Rick—Rick Hayden?"

"Never heard of him. Was he one of the patients?"

"Patients? What are you talking about?"

"The scientists . . . they brought in some patients with a rare illness for treatment this afternoon."

"Those weren't patients!" Cyrus shouted. "And they weren't sick!"

"I only know what I'm told," Greve said. "They're very secretive about their work here—all highly classified, above my clearance."

Well, that sounded consistent with Harv. Maybe that was the modus operandi around here—keep everyone in the dark.

"Okay, where are these 'patients' now?" The long

pause that followed made Laura's gut clench with dread.

Finally: "I can't help but assume you had friends among the patients . . ."

She wanted to scream *Stop calling them patients!* but he could only know what he'd been told.

"Did something happen?"

"Yes. I fear they're all dead."

Wails from Tanisha and Marie, a shouted "No!" from Cy as the words slammed Laura like a blow.

She knew she had to hold it together, which proved easier than she would have imagined. Probably because she couldn't imagine Rick dead. Somehow he'd survive. She knew it, she just knew it.

Her forensic brain had already parsed his words.

"What do you mean, 'fear' they're all dead? You don't know?"

"There was an explosion in the rear section where all the research is done. The walls there are extra thick and the doors blast-proof—just in case the worst happened. And today the worse happened. The blast was contained but it triggered a lockdown."

Her mind raced. Could it get any worse? The concussive force of an explosion could kill, but even if it didn't, contaminants and chemicals could finish the job.

"What was back there that could explode?"

"I have no idea. The walls held but the doors are buckled and I was able to get a look inside. It's all a horrendous mess, but I thought I saw movement among the carnage. That's why I need to get out and call for emergency services. Someone might still be alive in there. But they won't be for long if they don't get help."

"Marie," Laura said, "call 911 for EMTs." She

turned back to Greve. "I'm a doctor . . . if I can get down there . . ."

She didn't mention that all her patients were dead by the time they reached her. She didn't care about Greve, but it wouldn't exactly inspire confidence in her nadaný crew.

"Then you need to widen this opening," Greve said.

"Let me try something," Cy said, gently elbowing her aside.

He gripped the upturned lip of the hatch cover with both hands. Laura saw his knuckles whiten as he squeezed. When he removed his hands, the areas he'd gripped were gone, the edges looking like something had taken bites out of the metal.

"I can do this!" he cried.

"D-do what?" Greve stuttered below. "Wh-wh-what just happened there?"

As Cyrus grabbed two more handfuls of lid, Tanisha pulled Laura aside.

"I don't trust this guy," she said in a lowered voice.

Laura nodded. "I don't either. I don't expect him to be on our side, but I have to get down there."

"That's not what I mean. He's lying about the reinforced wall in the back area. I went over those plans real careful-like when I was looking for this escape route and those back walls ain't no thicker than anywhere else in the bunker."

"Maybe he just thinks they are."

"Maybe. But how do we even know he is who he says he is?"

Good question, Laura thought. And now it occurred to her that all she had for proof about an explosion down there was the word of a man she'd never seen or heard of before.

She pulled Tanisha farther back. "Before the lockdown alarm went off, do you remember the ground shaking at all, even the slightest tremor?"

Tanisha frowned, then shook her head. "Nope. Not a thing."

"Neither did I. It might not mean anything. After all, the bunker was half a mile away and fifty feet down from where we were standing. But still . . . time for this guy to pony up with some ID."

A small thing. It didn't mean he was telling her everything, but she'd know he was telling the truth about at least one thing.

She stepped back to the hatch. Cy had made progress. Still not open enough for someone to slip through, but he was getting there. She motioned him to back away.

"Agent Greve," she said. "Could I see some ID please?"

"*Now?*"

"Yes. I'll feel better knowing you really are who you say you are."

"Your timing is questionable, but I suppose I can understand that."

His expression was irritated as he reached into the breast pocket of his jacket. His irritation turned to a concerned frown as he tried his other pockets.

"Damn! In all the confusion, I must have left it in my office below."

"Told you so," Tanisha said behind her.

"Then we've got a problem. How do we know if anything you've told us—?"

"Wait-wait. Here it is."

He pulled a small black folder from his pants pocket and handed it up through the opening. Laura flipped it open.

"This is a passport!" she said.

It looked like the real thing with a photo of a younger looking Benjamin Greve, yet unquestionably him. But she wanted something with the Department of Defense logo to confirm he was with DIA.

"Oh, hell," he said. "I guess you'll just have to trust me."

"I'm not so sure about that."

He was looking agitated now. "I don't see what the problem is. You want to get down here and I want to get up there. Both ends can be accomplished by widening that gap."

"The EMTs are on the way," Marie said. "Maybe we should wait."

Laura fumed. She didn't want to wait. She was burning to get down to Rick and the others, especially if they were hurt. But this Greve was hiding something, she was sure of it. She feared she might never reach Rick if she trusted him.

"Give me back my passport then," he snapped.

Still struggling for a decision, Laura extended it toward him. But instead of taking the passport, he grabbed her wrist and wrenched her down against the opening. A gleaming pistol had appeared in his other hand and he was pressing the muzzle against her cheek.

"Tell Cyrus there to get back to work on the cover," he gritted through clenched teeth, "or he'll find himself splattered with your brains."

Cyrus? She didn't remember anyone calling him by name. How did he—?

"You know his name?"

"I know a lot more than his name, Laura Fanning. I know everything you know about him. And everything about you. So get me out of here—now!"

32

"Look," Rick was saying. "I've been watching the Anomaly and it never seems to cruise below three feet above the floor."

"Except when it comes *out* of the floor," Ellis said.

"Thank you, Captain Obvious." Again that urge to punch. "If we stay on hands and knees and keep our heads down, we should be safe."

Ellis said, "Unless, of course—"

Rick jabbed a finger within an inch of his nose. "Zip it! And keep it zipped unless you've got something constructive to contribute."

"Just sayin'."

"And I'm just sayin' that it could come out of the floor right under your ass while you're sitting here, which means there's no safe place, which means moving around is no more dangerous than staying put so we might as well be looking for the way out instead of sitting here waiting for something to happen." He looked them each in the eyes, one after the other. "Got it?"

When all three nodded, he said, "All right. Let's go."

"Wait!" Moe said, grabbing his arm.

Now what? He felt he'd already waited too long.

"Wait for what? Godot?"

"No. The security guys. They're locked up!"

Oh, right. Crap. He had to give them a chance.

"I'll get them out. That's three extra sets of eyes looking for an exit."

"You think they'll help?" Moe said. "You were pretty rough on them."

"Oh, they'll help. I'm sure they've seen the Anomaly by now, which means they'll want to get the hell out of here as badly as we do. I'll head for their room. The three of you split up and—"

"You know what happens when they split up in horror movies," Ellis said.

Always helpful . . .

"This isn't a haunted house movie. And the Anomaly isn't Jason or Freddy, so we increase our odds of finding the emergency exit if we're not all looking in the same place at the same time. Make sense?"

They all nodded.

"Okay. Moe, you know the place. Point them in the most likely direction while I go free the Keystone Kops."

Behind him, as he started to crawl away, he heard Moe instructing the two nadaný.

When he reached room two, he noticed water leaking under the door. He knocked and said, "You guys all right in there?"

He was answered by a confused and frightened chorus of pleas to let them out. He unlocked the door and did just that. They tumbled out just in time to see the Anomaly race by in the hall.

"It's that thing again!" Watts rasped, pointing. He looked terrified. "It came right through the walls— twice. The second time it came through the bathroom and ate its way through one of the pipes."

That explained the water.

Rick motioned them into a crouch. "It's safer if you stay low."

The one called Jon regained his composure first and turned on Rick.

"You fucker! You locked us up with that thing!"

Rick kept his voice calm. "Believe me when I say you were safer in there. It's been spending most of the time out here in the hall. Doctor Stonington got in its way."

That apparently hit Jon hard. His expression slackened. "W-what happened?"

"Not pretty." Rick jerked a thumb at the body on the floor down the hall. "Made a big hole right through the middle of him."

"Is he dead?" Woolley said.

Hoo, boy.

Watts whacked his shoulder. "'Is he *dead*?'" His voice was harsh and faint, like it hurt to talk. "A big hole through his middle? You kidding me?"

Woolley clapped a hand against the side of his face. "Oh, yeah. Right. What was I—?" He broke off to gag but didn't hurl.

"What the fuck is it?" Jon said. "Where'd it come from?"

"The back section," Rick said. "They've been keeping it there since 1957."

"But what *is* it?"

"Nobody seems to know."

"And it just happened to get out today?" His eyes narrowed. "You?"

"A guy named Greve. You know him?"

They looked at each other. "Our boss," Jon said. "He let it out? Why'd he do that?"

"He murdered a teenage girl right in front of it and that made it bust out and start to travel."

From their shocked expressions Rick could tell these guys weren't true hard cases—just wannabes. He had no idea if Iggy's murder was the real cause for the Anomaly's behavior, but for now, it would do. Might even drive a bit of a wedge between these guys and Greve.

"You know we're in lockdown, right?" Rick said. He noticed Woolley's gaze wandering. "You with us, Woolley?"

"Yeah, sure."

Jon was nodding. "Lockdown means we can't use the eleva—"

"There it is!" Woolley cried, pointing.

A glance down the hall showed the Anomaly cutting across, emerging from one side wall and boring through the other.

Farther down, Annie was crawling across the hall on her hands and knees in the opposite direction.

Watts watched wide-eyed. "What the f—"

"Can we focus here?" Rick said.

"But what's she doing?" Woolley said, staring.

"I'm about to explain: There's supposed to be an emergency escape route. Does one of you happen to know where it is?"

The three of them shook their heads.

"News to me," Jon said.

"Before he died, Doctor Stonington confirmed that there is one, but it may have been covered over during a remodel. We need to find it, and if we all search we can find it sooner and get the hell out of here. You guys game? Woolley, you game?"

"Yeah, sure."

"Okay, we'll all split up." He pointed to Jon. "You can assign your guys different rooms. Look for signs that something has been papered over or boarded over. And stay low, like that gal you saw down the end of the hall. Got all that, Woolley?"

Woolley nodded. "Yeah, sure."

Jon looked annoyed. "Why do you keep asking Woolley?"

"He's sort of the canary in your coal mine here. I figure if I get through to him, the rest of you are good to go."

From Jon's expression, this apparently made perfect

sense, but Rick didn't wait for a reply. Intending to leave this end of the hall to Jon and his crew, he maintained his crouch and started back to join Moe and the two nadaný. He'd traveled maybe a dozen steps when he heard someone start shouting.

Watts was crouching outside a door. "Hey, I hear noise in here." Rick could barely hear him. "And it's locked!"

Rick made a U-turn.

"That's the storage room," Jon said when he arrived. "We go in and out all the time. It's never locked."

It hadn't been locked when Rick had looked in just a short while ago. Things started clicking into place.

"Gotta be Greve."

Jon didn't look like he was buying that. "Why Greve?"

"He's the only one missing and he's got the keys to everything. I'm betting that's where we find the escape route."

Now Jon looked downright dubious. "Based on what?"

"The only person here longer than Greve was Stoney, and he said the escape was off the conference room. But what if they changed the conference room when they remodeled? What if they turned the old conference room into a storeroom?"

It all fit. Stoney had been so sure they'd find it in the conference room, but they hadn't. Moe had said his memory was showing signs of slippage. Very possible that a switch in location of the conference room had been one of the things that had slipped.

"The excape is in there?" Watts said, hope lighting his features. He rose to his knees and started banging on the door and shouting in a wrecked voice. "Agent Greve! Agent Greve!"

Jon pulled him back. "Knock off that crap! He might already be gone." He felt around his pockets. "Damn! You took my key ring!"

Rick handed him the one he'd taken from Watts. "Try this."

Jon found the key he wanted but it wouldn't go in the keyhole.

"Fuck! He left the key in the lock!"

Watts was suddenly back on his knees and banging. "Agent Greve! It's Watts from security. I'm with Jon and Woolley. Let us in! We need to get outta—"

The Anomaly came through the door and made a direct hit on his face. It passed through his head, leaving only a strip of skin that contained his left ear. As the ear flopped down, twin geysers began to pulse-pump straight up from the stump of his neck. The pumping continued as he slowly fell back to sprawl on the hallway floor, legs and arms akimbo, while the Anomaly veered rearward toward the research area.

Woolley let out a high-pitched scream and Jon dropped forward onto his hands and knees, retching. Rick was up and moving. If he was going to get through that door, now was the perfect time.

He risked getting his head blown off by sneaking a quick peek through the hole left by the Anomaly. No sign of Greve. Another peek and he spotted a section of wallboard pulled back from the wall, revealing a dark space.

If that didn't lead to the escape route, he'd offer to have Greve's baby.

Rick turned and shouted down the hall. "Moe! Annie! We've found it!" He realized he'd forgotten to call Ellis, but hell, he'd hear.

He snaked his arm through the hole and felt around until he found the key. A sharp twist and the latch snapped back. He pulled the HK from his pocket and checked the breech. He knew it was loaded but checking was a habit he didn't want to break.

"Hey, that's mine!" Jon said.

"Yeah, but I'm keeping it for a while. Any objections?"

"Well . . . it's pretty dangerous out here."

"You think a nine-millimeter slug is going to stop the Anomaly?"

"What's the Anomaly? Oh, you mean—"

"Yeah. The thing that made your buddy's head disappear."

"Okay, I guess not."

"Better believe. And if Greve's in there with his Luger, I'll need this. You guys wait here and don't let anyone pass—either way."

If Greve had found an escape route, Rick had no doubt he'd taken it and was long gone. But if the lockdown sealed it . . .

Cautiously, he eased his way in. He stood still a moment, scanning the crowded jumble of junk as he listened. He heard something moving in the dark space behind the angled wallboard.

33

"You've gotta be kidding!" Cyrus said from the blackness above.

He had his flashlight trained on Laura Fanning's head. Greve couldn't see him so he pressed the Luger's muzzle a little deeper into her cheek for emphasis.

"I assure you I'm quite serious. So don't try anything cute."

"I could just walk away," Cyrus said. "Then what'll you do?"

"Let's not find out, okay?" Fanning said.

"Yes, listen to the good doctor."

Cyrus said, "No, seriously. What are you going to do if I walk away? Kill her? What for? You're still stuck there until the cops come. And then you go up for murder. Lose-lose, Agent Greve."

Greve knew damn well that killing Fanning would rob him of all his leverage, but he had an answer for that.

"Who said anything about killing her? Imagine what a nine-millimeter Parabellum into the shoulder joint feels like. First one, then the other. Then—"

"All right, all right!" Cyrus said. A pause, then, "I'll have to have Tanisha hold the light if I'm going to work with both hands."

Tanisha—the other telekinetic. Of all the possible nadaný. Damn! Montero's files described her power as pretty damn weak, but still . . . anyone who could move things with her mind had to be considered dangerous.

"I know all about Tanisha too. Just remember that this pistol has a hair trigger. I'm well aware that Tanisha is telekinetic, and if I feel the slightest pressure on my throat or anywhere on my body, the gun will fire."

Cyrus looked off to his right. "Hear that, Tanisha? A hair trigger. So come over here where you can see and help me take care of this."

Something about the way he phrased that set off an alarm in Greve but he couldn't say why. He was in a supremely awkward position: pitch black below except for a tiny sliver of light at the bottom through the opening into the storeroom; equally black above save for Cyrus's flashlight beam. Reflected light from the beam gleamed off the Luger's nickel plating, lending it a menacing look. Were they planning something? Whatever, he still held the aces: Fanning and the Luger. All he could do was keep a tight grip on both, and his finger ready on the trigger.

"Remember . . . try anything and your friend here suffers."

A young woman with a strained face came into view and took the flashlight. She trained the beam on the rim of the cover as Cyrus bent to his task, but her eyes were fixed on the Luger.

Pretty, isn't it?

Then he sensed a vibration in the weapon. What—?

He chanced a look and it took him a second to realize the safety lever had moved up. Before he could thumb it down again a hand had gripped the short barrel and angled it away from Fanning—Cyrus's hand. When he released it, the Luger's entire barrel as well as the front part of its receiver were gone.

What? How—? Montero's records flashed through his mind—Cyrus had never been able to disappear metal. And yet now . . .

Greve had levered the safety down again by then, so he pulled the trigger. He heard the firing pin click but nothing happened.

And then something was pushing him backward, like a hundred angry invisible hands shoving him. The small of his back struck the platform's guardrail. Panicked, he dropped the Luger and grabbed for support but his hands found only empty air.

With a cry of pure terror he toppled over the rail and tumbled into the midnight darkness of the shaft.

Falling headfirst, he rolled in the air and his flailing left arm banged against a ladder rung. His fingers grabbed and missed but found the next one. He clutched at it, felt it slip through his fingers, but then they caught the third one. He grabbed tight and cried out as his shoulder joint separated with a loud, agonizing *pop*.

The pain spasmed in his fingers, numbed them. He couldn't maintain his grip and they slipped free. But at least he'd broken the acceleration of his fall enough for his right hand to grab another rung and hold on to it. His right shoulder wrenched but held together. His feet found a rung below, and he clung there, gasping with relief and repressing moans of pain—he would *not* moan.

He heard what was left of his pistol hit the floor with multiple metallic clatters and knew it had smashed to pieces. After a moment he was able to think about something other than the pain in his shoulder and listen to something other than his own breathing.

A glow from the flashlights at the top of the shaft, disembodied voices echoing down . . .

"Tanisha, what did you do?" he heard Fanning say.

"Saved our asses is what she did," Cyrus said. "He was gonna shoot you, and us as well, if he could."

"But you probably killed him."

Tanisha's voice: "Whoops."

Cold-blooded bitch.

He saw flashlight beams start to pierce the musty air of the shaft. Inevitably, one found him.

"Christ, there he is!" Cyrus cried.

"He doesn't look so hot," Tanisha said.

Fanning said, "We've got to go down. I need to find Rick and the others."

Greve looked down and saw the floor of the shaft, visible in the light from the storeroom. Only twenty feet or so below but looking like a mile or two.

"Why's he just hanging there?" Tanisha said.

"He's gonna try and block the way," Cyrus said. "Can you knock him off?"

Fanning: "No! We may need him."

Tanisha: "He's too far. But when we get closer . . ."

That was the convincer. Cyrus still had work to do on enlarging the opening in the hatch, which meant Greve had a little time before they could enter the shaft and follow him. He started down.

Progress was agonizingly slow. His left arm was useless—less than useless, since every twist or jolt of his body sent shots of pain down his arm and into his chest—so he had to rely on his right and his feet.

As he neared the bottom, he heard the clatter of feet on metal above, which could only mean that Fanning and the nadaný had entered the shaft and were on the platform. And now the scrape of feet on the ladder, the vibrations on the rungs tingling through his good hand. All he wanted to do was to stop and baby that left arm, but he had to keep moving.

When he reached the floor, he leaned his back against the curved wall of the shaft and tried to maneuver his upper arm back into the shoulder socket. He'd seen it done but couldn't remember which way to rotate it. He tried outward and inward but all he succeeded in doing was increasing his pain.

God, the pain—it had his breath hissing in and out between his teeth.

The flashlights continued to descend from above. And then someone began banging on the storage room door . . . banging and calling his name.

Watts? Who the hell was Watts?

And then a loud, horrified scream—a man's voice but at a woman's pitch. What had happened out there? And loud. Had someone opened the door?

With a sick, crawling sensation in his gut, he realized he was trapped. He couldn't go up, and someone was at the door to the hallway—maybe more than one someone.

He resisted an impulse to surrender—to slide down the wall and sit on the floor to await his fate. He might have a chance, and he had to take it, no matter how slim.

He peeked into the storeroom to check on the door. Still closed. Good. But it had a hole through it—a hole that hadn't been present earlier. Which meant the Anomaly must have passed through.

God, what a horrendous mess this had turned out to be. He wished he'd never heard of the Anomaly or melis or the nadaný. He especially wished he hadn't thought bringing them here was a good idea. His life had turned to shit since their arrival.

He undid the two lower buttons on his shirt, the ones just above his belt. Gritting his teeth and doing his own version of Lamaze breathing against the pain, he worked the hand, wrist, and lower part of his left forearm inside the shirt so it could function as something of a sling.

When the spike in pain from the movement quieted, he could say that it didn't hurt quite so bad now. That was something, at least.

He left the shaft and slipped into the storeroom. He wished the lights were off. He felt so exposed out here. He was sure he could find a place to hide amid all the clutter . . .

34

Rick reached the angled wallboard and stopped to listen again. Echoed voices and clatter from the darkness beyond, seemingly without the slightest attempt at stealth. And one of those voices . . .

Laura?

He aimed his flash beam inside and saw her stepping off the ladder to join Cyrus and Tanisha on the floor. Marie was descending behind her.

"Laura! What are you—?"

Without a word she pushed past the others and slammed into his arms.

"He told me you were dead!" she said through a sob against his chest.

Rick had a pretty good idea who "he" was but didn't want to ruin the moment by asking. Instead he wrapped his arms around her and crushed her against him. If he had his way, he'd never let go, but they had the small matter of the rampant Anomaly to deal with.

"That, as they say, was an exaggeration. But what are you doing here?"

"I came to get you."

"We thank you for that, but—"

She leaned back and looked at him with teary eyes. "No. You don't get it." She poked her own chest, and then his. "*I* came to get *you*."

Did that mean what he thought it meant—what he wanted it to mean?

"You always had me. You know that."

"But I didn't know what I had."

"This is all very sweet," Cy said, "but where are the others? And where's Agent Greve?"

Rick tensed. "Greve? You saw him?"

"A lot more than saw him. Pulled a gun on the doc here, but Tanisha sent him back down the shaft—the express route."

"When?"

"Just a couple of minutes ago. You didn't pass him?"

"No. And I've been right outside the door."

"That means he's still in there," Laura said, pointing past Rick to the storeroom. "He must be hiding."

Just then Jon and Woolley, who'd been crouching by the door, were pushed into the storeroom, propelled by the arrival of Moe, Annie, and Ellis.

"There's a guy out there with no head!" Annie said, looking sick.

"Hey, the invisible girl!" Jon said.

"No head?" Laura gave Rick a please-don't-tell-me-you're-responsible look. "What—?"

Just then the Anomaly emerged from the wall of the shaft, dissolved a section of the steel ladder, and just missed Marie and Cyrus. As it sailed toward Tanisha she reflexively put out her hand to fend it off. It passed through her hand, leaving behind a spurting stump.

"Oh, my God!" Laura cried, leaping forward as Tanisha screamed. "Oh, my God!"

As she grabbed Tanisha's truncated wrist, the Anomaly entered the opposite wall, then emerged into the storeroom to chew a hole through whatever stood in its way before exiting through the far wall.

Rick rushed to help Laura as she squeezed Tanisha's arm.

"What in God's name was *that*?" she said as the spurting slowed. "Rick, what is going on here?"

"I'll explain up top. Right now, what do we do about Tanisha?"

"You take over here. Press right there over the radial artery—that's the main spurter." She called over her shoulder, "Anyone have a shoelace? *Please* somebody have a shoelace!"

Tanisha's face had gone sallow and her knees were buckling. Rick got his free arm around her waist to keep her from falling.

Annie pushed forward with a sneaker in one hand as she pulled the lace free with the other.

"Got one here!"

Laura snatched it from her and tied it around Tanisha's wrist.

"Okay, let it go and see if this worked."

Rick loosened his grip on the wrist. Blood started to dribble but nothing more.

Laura inspected it and nodded. "That'll do for now. She needs a hospital ASAP."

"I'll take her up," Cy said.

With Rick's help, he slung the semiconscious young woman over his shoulder.

"Good thing she's skinny," he said and started to climb.

"Watch out for that missing rung," Rick said, then turned to the rest. "All right, everybody. We've got to get out of here. Immediately. As in *now*. That thing is honeycombing the place. It could all start coming down on us."

Woolley started for the ladder. "Don't have to tell me twice."

Rick shoved him back. "Women first." He pointed Laura toward the ladder.

"Uh-uh," she said with a quick shake of her head. "I busted my butt to find you. I'm not leaving till you leave."

"But—"

Laura pushed Annie toward the ladder. "You're next." As Annie started to climb, she pointed to Marie. "Keep your flash on Cyrus and Tanisha until they reach the top. Then start up. We don't want too many on the ladder at once. If that goes, we're all stuck." She peered out into the storeroom. "We're missing Iggy."

Rick sighed. "Yeah, about Iggy . . ."

Her hand flew to her mouth. "Oh, no! That thing that just—?"

He shook his head. "Greve. Killed her. Murdered her."

Laura closed her eyes and leaned against him. "Oh, no. That sweet, innocent girl. Where is she? We have to bring her with us."

"Uh-uh," Rick said. "We're not going back there. The only place we're going is up and out. Iggy can't be hurt anymore, but I can't say that for the rest of us."

"Did anyone else not make it?"

"Two people you didn't know, neither of whom deserved to die."

"And what about her?" Laura said, looking past him into the storeroom. "Who's she?"

She meant Moe.

"Name's Maureen LaVelle. You might know her as Doctor Emily Jacobi."

Her eyes widened. "Really?"

"That's what Iggy said, and she didn't deny it." He signaled to her. "Come on, Moe. You follow Marie, then the men will start."

"Don't worry about me," Ellis said. "I'm not leaving till I find Greve. Got a bone to pick with that sonovabitch. A whole *lotta* bones. Anybody have an idea where I can find him?"

"He's got to be hiding right here," Laura said, waving

toward the storeroom. "Tanisha knocked him off the ladder and Rick didn't see him leave, so . . ."

"In this mess?" Ellis said, taking in the jumble.

"Could be," Rick said. "But it might take half the night to find him, and the whole place could be flattened by then."

"Maybe," Ellis said. "Then again, maybe not."

As he stepped to the left side of the doorway, a chair began to move. It dragged along the floor for a foot or two, then rose and flew through the door to clatter on the hallway floor outside.

"Holy shit!" Woolley said, backing against the wall. "You see that, Jon? You see that?"

"Yeah, I saw it." He looked at Rick with a befuddled expression. "First an invisible girl, now this? What the fuck?"

Rick shook his head. "You want an explanation, don't look at me."

Cy and Tanisha had made it to the top, so Marie started up. She had her foot on the first rung when Annie called down from halfway up.

"Hey, this ladder's pretty shaky. Maybe we should stick to one at a time. I'll move as fast as I can."

Rick didn't like the delay but better to play it careful. If the ladder came loose from the wall, they were sunk. One of the women was already topside and another on her way. That left Marie and Laura. He wouldn't breathe easy until she was up there with the rest.

His shoe kicked something metallic as he turned toward her.

"Could you shine your light on the floor?"

The beam of Laura's flash picked up parts of a pistol. Rick recognized the nickel plating as belonging to Greve's Luger. At least he wasn't armed.

And out in the storeroom, the contents continued to sail through the door—some smoothly, some banging against the jambs on their way.

As a mattress rose and sailed through the air, Ellis shouted, "There you are, you mother—"

"I'm hurt! I'm hurt!" Greve cried as he crouch-cowered against the far wall. That mattress had probably seemed like an excellent hiding place when he'd crawled under it.

Rick could see how his left arm was tucked inside his shirt and how his upper arm hung limply from the shoulder. Dislocated for sure.

The soles of Greve's shoes were scraping along the floor as he pressed back against the wall, pressed like he thought he could push through it.

"Listen!" he cried. "I'm sorry about the shocks!"

"Shocks?" Ellis said. "You think I give a shit about you giving me a lousy bunch of shocks?" His voice rose to a scream. *"YOU KILLED IGGY!"*

With those words Greve rose into the air with a cry of terror and slammed against the wall.

"They're lying!" he said through a groan when he'd caught his breath. "I didn't kill her! Why would I kill her? I brought her here to study her!"

"And you studied her and found out she had no power so you disposed of her!"

"No-no! She had an amazing power! The most dangerous power of all!"

Ellis looked at Rick. "What's he talking about?"

Well, why not? Rick thought. "No one could lie in front of Iggy. And Greve here admitted to something he couldn't allow anyone to know. So he murdered her in cold blood."

"Is that true?" Laura said, her expression horrified.

Rick nodded. "Right in front of Moe and me in the rear section."

Ellis was shaking with barely controlled fury. "You murdered my girl?"

"His girl?" Marie whispered from the ladder. "But she wasn't—"

Rick raised a hand and lowered his own voice. "He's rolling. Don't rain on his parade."

He'd felt the impact of Ellis's enhanced power and wanted to spare Marie and Laura the experience.

Legs kicking and good arm flailing, Greve rose into the air. He rotated to a horizontal position, supine, and gave up struggling as he began to float feet first toward the doorway.

For no good reason, an errant line from T. S. Elliot popped into his head: *"Like a patient etherized upon a table."*

Ellis was saying, "You and I are going for a little walk, you sonovabitch. I'm gonna see what you did to my girl. And then . . . and then I don't know what I'm gonna do."

"Hey, that's the boss," Woolley said. "Shouldn't we—?"

Jon waved him to silence. "You do what you want. I'm staying right here until it's my time to go up the ladder. I didn't sign on for this kind of crazy shit." He looked at Rick. "How am I going to tell anybody about this?"

"I'm pretty sure if the government has its way, you won't be allowed to say a word."

Rick couldn't dredge up any sympathy for Greve as he disappeared through the doorway. He'd been lord of the manor down here, doing anything he damned well pleased. But killing Iggy like that . . . Rick didn't know what Ellis would do to him, but he didn't see how it could be worse than the guy who instigated the Düsseldorf atrocity deserved.

"Made it!" Annie called from above.

Marie started up.

Damn, this was taking too long. The Anomaly could be back any minute.

He put his arm around Laura and drew her down into a crouch.

"You're up next."

"Uh-uh." She pointed to Jon and Woolley. "They're next. I found you and I'm not leaving you. The only way I go ahead of you is *just* ahead of you."

Rick found himself dismayed at her stubbornness but delighted with the sentiment.

35

Helpless . . . Greve had never imagined being so completely helpless. He floated a few feet off the floor, trailing on an invisible leash behind this freak of nature, able to grab hold of nothing that might impede his progress. Nothing but empty air.

And all around him, flashing red lights and wailing Klaxons, piles of broken furniture hurled from the storeroom, and a headless body sprawled in a huge pool of blood.

The bunker—he'd come to think of it as *his* bunker—had devolved into chaos and anarchy.

He saw his chance as Ellis led him toward the door to the rear section. When they reached it he managed to plant his feet against the jambs. The freak turned and gave him a pitying look. Greve's ankles suddenly

slammed together and he was on the move again. He
tried to grab a jamb with his right hand but his fingers couldn't hold.

A moan of fear escaped him as he floated toward
the still form on the floor near the containment chamber. Thankfully someone had covered her with a lab
coat, but she wouldn't remain hidden for long.

And then what? He didn't want to go there but
knew he was well on his way and would find out
soon enough.

Suddenly he was falling. The jolt of hitting the floor
flat on his back triggered a blast of pain from his
shoulder. Groaning, he rolled onto his good side and
saw Ellis standing over Iggy's covered form. Watched
him kneel and slowly remove the lab coat. Heard his
wail of anguish, and then felt the air slam against him
like the shockwave from an explosion.

He flew through the air, his flight ending in another
burst of agony when he slammed against the wall by
the door. Things around the room were breaking—
anything breakable was shattering, even the bullet-
proof glass on the containment chamber was webbing
with cracks.

The door . . . if he could get out the door—

No. He was moving again, an invisible hand drag-
ging him feet first back toward Ellis and the dead girl.
When Greve reached them, Ellis grabbed him by his
collar and twisted him around until he was face-to-
face with Iggy.

"Look what you did to her! Look what you did!"

Staring into her glazed right eye and her empty
left socket, lined with clotted blood, Greve inanely
thought how this catastrophic exit wound shouldn't
have happened with the hollow-point rounds he'd

loaded, but maybe because the back of the eye socket was made of such thin bone . . .

"How could you do this?" Ellis screamed.

What could he say, what could he do?

"I'm sorry! I didn't mean—"

"Didn't mean to shoot her in the back of her head? You're going to tell me that was an accident? Look at her! She's in shackles! How could she be any kind of threat to you?"

If you only knew, Greve thought. You have no idea . . .

"What am I going to do to you?" Ellis said. He seemed to be talking to himself. "It needs to be vile and nasty but . . . *appropriate*."

He yanked Greve around onto his back, igniting another blast of pain, and crouched over him.

"Please . . ."

"I know!" His face lit. "Your eye! You ruined Iggy's, so it's only fair that I start by ruining—"

The Anomaly zoomed into the room—where from, Greve had no idea—but instead of passing through, the sphere of flaring blackness began to circle them.

"What's that thing up to?"

"I-I don't know."

But Greve had a suspicion the Anomaly was attracted to human agony—why else would it or something very much like it have appeared at the Düsseldorf atrocity? And it might well be hovering here in anticipation of impending agony—Greve's.

The very real possibility sent a shudder through him. He didn't want to die—the thought of that was terrifying enough. But dying in agony . . .

"Get outta here!" Ellis shouted.

Greve could swear he saw the edge of the Anomaly's sphere flatten for a second as it backed away.

"Yeah, that's right," Ellis said, rising and moving toward it. "Get outta here!"

Kill him! Greve urged. Tear a hole through his heart and let me watch him bleed!

Again the brief flattening and a backward jump, this time to the doorway.

Ellis was laughing now, sounding like he'd suffered some sort of psychotic break. "Finally met your match, eh? How does it feel?" His voice rose to a shout. "*OUT!*"

The Anomaly was shoved out of the rear section and into the hallway. Ellis followed.

How . . . how could this be happening? Greve forced himself to his knees. Ellis overpowering the Anomaly?

He struggled to his knees, then his feet, and staggered toward the doorway.

The Anomaly had stopped perhaps twenty feet down the hall. Ellis was shouting something at it but Greve couldn't make out the words over the honking Klaxons. It appeared they'd reached a standoff.

Greve realized then that the Anomaly had increased its size, moving beyond soccer ball to beach ball. And now Ellis was backing away.

The broken furniture in the hallway started to move, sliding toward the Anomaly, then lifting into the air to fly at it. Why was Ellis throwing things at it? What purpose—?

Instead of disappearing into the Anomaly's black center, the furniture began to circle it, as if going into orbit. That had never happened before. Whatever they'd thrown at it had always disappeared into the void at its center. But then, it had never been a sphere before.

The furniture revolved faster and faster, breaking up and splintering into progressively smaller pieces. And Ellis, still backing away from it, kept tossing more and more furniture its way. The first few pieces had been reduced to sawdust by now.

What was he thinking?

A broken desk slid along the floor and struck him in the back of his legs, almost knocking him off his feet. He stumbled away from it and let it rise and join what was left of the other orbiting furniture now forming a glowing ring.

And then Greve knew: Ellis wasn't hurling the pieces of furniture at the Anomaly, the thing was drawing them to itself.

Ellis stumbled to the side and gripped a doorframe to one of the rooms as the headless corpse started to slide. He pushed against the closed door but it wouldn't budge. Greve didn't remember locking that one. The suction from the Anomaly, maybe? Greve himself was feeling a tug toward the thing. But not suction. Leaning in the doorway, he felt no breeze of air in motion from behind him. Yet the Anomaly was drawing him toward it.

Hayden appeared at the doorway to the storeroom—the place Greve wanted to be—and seemed transfixed by the sight of the Anomaly. Well, why not? The thing was putting on quite a show.

Greve watched the headless security man's body rise toward the Anomaly and go into orbit. It seemed to stretch like an elastic mannequin before being torn into tiny pieces that were further reduced to a red soup that became part of the glowing, spinning ring—now a disk.

Disk . . . like an accretion disk . . .

No . . . this wasn't possible. And yet . . . that

pull didn't feel like suction. No wind at his back as it pulled at the air. This felt more like gravity . . . steadily increasing gravity. Unless Greve was going as crazy as Ellis, the Anomaly seemed to have turned into a miniature black hole.

36

Damn near killed Rick to allow Woolley and Jon on the ladder before Laura, but she was so stubbornly adamant about not leaving him, she left him no choice. The process was taking so *long*. Made excellent sense to restrict the ladder load to one person at a time, but no one was moving fast enough to suit him. Marie had reached the top and now Woolley was on his way. He hadn't said so, but Woolley appeared scared of heights. At least he climbed like he was. One step up, bring the trailing foot up beside it, another step up, bring the trailing foot up—

"Move it, Woolley!" Jon yelled. Apparently he was becoming as impatient as Rick. "You climb like a fucking girl!"

"Hey!" Laura said. "I resent that!"

"Sorry," Jon said. "But look at him. You could climb a lot faster than that, I bet."

"Damn right I could."

Rick knew she was right. He'd seen her climb. She had no fear of heights.

Gazing up at Woolley's slow progress, Jon shook his head. "What a pussy."

"Do you *mind*?"

Rick pulled off his coverall and tossed it on the floor, only to see it drag itself out of the shaft and into the storeroom—and what were those scraping sounds coming from out there? He backed up a step and saw the reason: The furniture had started moving again.

Ellis?

Rick had assumed he'd taken Greve to the rear section where Iggy lay. Was he back already? And if so, what was he doing with the furniture?

The mattress Greve had hidden behind started sliding then flew toward the doorway, slapped flat against frame, then bent and disappeared through. A bent desk chair wheeled out after it.

From his vantage point, Rick could see only a sliver of the hallway, but it looked different. Something about the light. The red emergency lights still flashed, but a strange glow, steadier, brighter, was blotting them out.

"Rick?" Laura said behind him. "What—"

"Stay back, okay? Something weird going on."

"'Weird'? You mean *weirder*, don't you? And weirder is a good reason to get back here with me."

He started edging toward the door. "I'll just be a minute."

"Dammit, Rick, you should know by now that you move *away* from weird, not toward it."

Good advice, but he wanted—needed—just a peek. It might be important to know.

"Half a minute, Laura."

The new light was originating down the hall, from near the midpoint. Rick felt a definite tug toward the hallway, almost as if the floor had tilted that way. Nearing the door, he saw Watts's headless corpse begin to move, leaving a large red smear as it slid away from its pool of blood. Then it lifted off the floor and glided out of sight.

At the door, Rick steadied himself against the jamb, peeked around, and froze.

"What on—?"

He'd been about to ask what on Earth, but clearly this was not of Earth. It resembled the Anomaly but was big and ringed with a glowing disk of fire—or, rather, superheated matter.

Watts's corpse seemed to stretch to an impossible length as it neared the Anomaly, then it came apart and melted into the glowing, whirling disk. Rick searched for Stoney's corpse beyond the apparition but couldn't find it. Already sucked into the disk, probably.

Movement two doors down caught his attention and he spotted Ellis clinging to a doorframe, trying to keep from following Watts. Rick shouted his name a number of times but Ellis didn't seem to hear. Being that close to the Anomaly had either mesmerized him or affected his hearing.

The Anomaly . . . what had changed it? He stared at the deep, empty blackness of its core, and couldn't help remembering Düsseldorf and how he'd been living in the best of all possible lives in the best of all possible worlds until he was assigned to Düsseldorf, and how this thing had appeared and wandered through the killing ground, and that slammed home the memory of how he'd been powerless to help those mutilated children, how he'd come to the devastating realization that the best—the *only* succor he could offer was the oblivion of death.

And that same oblivion was now being offered by the Void at the core of the Anomaly. Why not? Why not accept the offer? Embrace the Void. No memories of Düsseldorf in there, no nightmares of eyeless faces and tongueless mouths screaming in silent terror, no—

Whoa-whoa-whoa!

What was going on here? The Anomaly was not only devouring everything in sight, it was sucking off the will to live, making death and the Void look endlessly attractive. More than attractive—the next logical step.

Groaning, he pushed away from the doorway and staggered back toward Laura and the escape shaft. Perhaps the Void ruled, perhaps it was inevitable and unavoidable and all that. But not yet. Not quite yet.

And not without a fight.

37

Ellis clung to the doorjamb. He'd tried to force his way into the room but the draw from the Anomaly proved too strong; the door wouldn't budge. And as for making his way back to the rear section—no way was that in the cards. So he stayed where he was and watched the flying headless dead guy dissolve into the disk around the new and improved Anomaly.

New and improved . . . did I do that? Had his gift done that?

He'd used it against the Anomaly, to shove—slug it, actually. Seeing Iggy like that, he'd been pissed beyond thinking, beyond sanity. He'd needed to break something, hit something, and the Anomaly had shown up at just the wrong time. He'd felt so great when he whacked it and dented it and made it back up—top of the world. He forgot now how many times he'd bashed it, but then it had stopped retreating and turned into this . . . whatever this was.

And now it would kill him.

Yeah, no way could he survive this, not with the pull of the Anomaly steadily growing in strength.

He'd long sensed death waiting for him, anxious for him. Always knew he'd never reach a ripe old age, but he'd hoped to hit forty, at least. Hit forty and he could consider himself a bona fide Old Fart. He'd flip the Universe the bird and dare it to do whatever it pleased with what was left of his future. He'd already won.

His future . . . a future with Iggy hadn't been totally impossible but, when he got down to it, he'd never believed they had a chance. The deck had been stacked against the two of them getting together and staying that way. And now Greve had taken that future completely off the table.

Ellis forced his gaze from the Anomaly's empty center and looked back at Greve, cowering in the doorway of the rear section. Their eyes met and Greve smiled. Fucking flashed his death's-head grin at him

You think you're getting out of this, Greve? Fuhgeddaboudit. See that blackness at your pal's center? That's where you're headed—where we're all headed. It's had our names since the day we were born, and now it's come calling. Time to go, Greve. Your time's up.

And so is mine.

He turned back toward the Anomaly.

You want me, mofo? We both knew sooner or later you was gonna get me, so why don't I make this easy on both of us? I ain't gonna fight. You don't gotta strong-arm me. As a matter of fact, I'll tell ya what I'm gonna do: *I'll* come to *you.*

He was almost looking forward to this now.

He flipped Greve the bird, then stepped away from the doorway and spread his arms.

This is how it's done.

His feet dragged as he was pulled toward the disk.

He lifted into the air and pain like he'd never known ripped through him as his cells began to tear one from the other. But he wouldn't scream.

This is how you die, mofo.

38

Clinging to his doorway down the hall, Greve looked at Ellis, his expression fierce and yet questioning.

Wondering if you caused this, freak? Well, who else are you going to blame? You did it, asshole. No one else. Greve forced a grin. Yes, you did it. And now you pay the price.

But why had it happened? And how had he done it? Using his power against the Anomaly? Had that triggered the change—sending it into defensive mode? Or was this aggressor mode?

Either way, it seemed intent on gobbling up everything in sight.

Greve saw a change come over Ellis's face. The anger and puzzlement morphing to . . . what? Acceptance?

Nodding to himself, Ellis raised his middle finger to Greve, then stepped out of the doorway. He spread his arms as if welcoming what was about to happen, and then he began to move, sliding at first and then rising and flying headfirst toward the Anomaly. His body seemed to stretch like taffy as it approached the accretion disk, and then it dissolved and joined the glowing swirl.

Ellis Reise was gone.

Suddenly particle beams—narrow shafts of light, intolerably white and intolerably bright—shot upward and downward from the Anomaly's poles, piercing the ceiling and the floor. The light struck him almost a physical blow. With his good arm he began to swing the door shut to block it out, but it was pulled from his grasp to slam into the jambs with a force that shook the wall.

Greve lowered himself to sitting with his back against the wall beside the door. How was he going to get out of this? He knew the answer: He wasn't.

He couldn't bear that thought. He'd always arranged his life so that he'd be in charge, he'd call the shots. But this . . . he had to accept that he was helpless against the Anomaly and what it had become. Its imperturbability and incomprehensibility left him weak and numb.

His fate was out of his hands. He had no hope of defeating or escaping it. His only chance at survival was the Anomaly's seeming capriciousness. It had turned into a black hole for no discernible reason—maybe Ellis had triggered it, maybe not. Through that same capriciousness it might return to one of its former states. Maybe the passive form that had spent decades sealed in the containment chamber. Even the randomly destructive floating sphere would be preferable to what it had now become.

The only thing he could do was huddle here and do nothing . . . wait and see what would happen. Maybe he'd be lucky. Maybe—

With an awful screech the metal door twisted and folded before ripping from its hinges and disappearing through the frame.

"Hurry up, Laura!" Cy shouted from above.

Laura was three-quarters of the way up the shaky ladder and moving as fast as she dared. The darkness of the shaft seemed to clutch at her. The hatch was off—Cy must have disappeared the latches earlier, before they'd descended. She could see his anxious face in the backwash of the flashlight he had trained on her.

"I am! Why are you still here? You should be getting Tanisha to the EMTs."

"She won't leave until she knows you're safe. Annie and that other lady are tending to her, but that's not why you should hurry."

"You mean the ladder? Yeah, I know it's—"

"No, it's this beam of light that's shooting out of the ground."

What?

"Out of the ground? Where?"

"About fifty feet away. I don't know where it's coming from. Some kinda laser, maybe? All I know is it's white-hot and you can hardly look at it, it's so bright. And it's shooting way, way up—shit, it looks like it's shooting up to the stars."

What on Earth? It had to be related to that Anomaly thing or whatever experiments they'd been conducting down there. Would she ever know? Maybe that woman Maureen—

A horrible racket welled up from the bottom of the shaft. Laura stopped her climb and looked down to see Rick bathed in white light as he braced himself against the doorway leading to the storeroom.

"Rick? You okay?"

His shout echoed off the concrete walls. "The storeroom door just tore off and flew away."

Oh, God.

"What's happening down there?"

"I don't know. The Anomaly's changed. Last I looked, it was sucking everything into it. But this light—I can barely see."

"Time for you to start up, Rick. And don't even *think* about going out there to see what's going on."

She knew him enough to know how curiosity and a need to know often overruled his common sense.

"Hey, look," he called, "I know I've pulled some dumb stunts in my time, but I can live on very happily without knowing what's happening out there right now." He waved up at her with one hand and banged on the ladder with the other. "Get moving! I don't trust this thing to hold both of us."

Laura resumed her climb at full speed, but after only two steps, she heard a crack above her and felt the ladder tremble.

And then she was falling backward through the darkness—her hands and feet were still on the rungs, but she was falling just the same—but slowly. She couldn't help the scream of terror that escaped her.

Cyrus's beam lit the shaft enough to flash images to her brain: The ladder had broken a half dozen feet above her and was pulling free of the shaft wall one set of supports at a time . . .

. . . until the broken end struck the opposite wall with a jolt that shook Laura's feet free of their rung and left her dangling forty feet in the air.

Alarmed shouts from above and below echoed around her as she hung there, kicking in the darkness. She hooked an elbow over a side rail of the ladder and managed to swing her leg up to the top side.

With a lot of grunting and groaning and huffing and puffing, Laura hauled herself up and around and over until she was clinging to the top of the span of ladder instead of dangling below.

"I'm all right!" she called into the darkness.

She caught her breath and swore that if she made it through this she'd never neglect her gym workouts again.

But now what? With Cy's beam flicking around, she could see the upper part of the ladder still attached to the wall on the far side of the shaft—way too far for her ever to reach.

She was stuck.

"I'll see if I can find some rope!" Cy shouted.

Yes, rope would be a big help.

Cy left and returned almost immediately. "Wait . . ."

Wait . . . Did he think she had a choice?

"Tanisha thinks she can help."

And just then she felt her body begin to lift. Her instinct was to grab the sides of the ladder and hold on, but she realized what was happening, so she let go.

Then Cy's words struck her: Tanisha *thinks* she can help?

"Tanisha!" Laura called. "Can you do this?"

"I *am* doing it!" came her reply, her voice weak but tinged with annoyance.

"Oh, yeah, well, right. Of course. Just . . ."

"Just what?"

"Nothing."

Laura had been about to say, *Just don't drop me,* but decided against it. Don't derail the girl's confidence.

And she *was* doing it—floating Laura through the air. The oddest feeling ever. She'd maintained her sitting position from when she'd been on the ladder, but now something else was pressing up against her butt, lifting and moving her.

"I'm going to move you over to the ladder so you can climb the rest of the way up."

"Great!" *I hope.*

Not all that far to go. Six feet to the other side of the shaft and then another half dozen up to the rest of the ladder . . . what was the hypotenuse of that right angle? Somewhere between eight and nine feet, she figured. That was it? The total distance of her trip was less than nine measly feet, but from midair it looked like miles.

"Laura!" Rick called from below. "What's happening up there? You look like you're—"

"Yes! I'm flying! Tanisha's doing it!"

And she prayed that Tanisha kept on doing it. To help her along, she thought of Christmas, thought of snow, thought of sleigh bells . . .

Finally the rungs were in reach. She grabbed hold and started climbing.

"Thank you, Tanisha! Thank you, thank you, thank you!"

She scrambled the rest of the way up to the platform, then found her own flash and turned it on.

"Rick!" she called. "Start up! Climb as far as you can and Tanisha will take you the rest of the way."

She watched him climb from the bright light of the floor and disappear into the darkness above it.

"Not a moment too soon!" he shouted. "The whole place is coming apart."

Laura felt the shaft vibrate for a few seconds, then stop, then vibrate again. She hoped the platform held.

Her flash beam found Rick and followed him to the highest point at which the ladder still remained attached to the wall. With the broken tip wedged against the opposite side, it looked fairly stable.

Now it was Tanisha's turn.

"Okay, Tanisha—do your thing!"

From the top of the hatch Cy said, "Tanisha passed out. I can't wake her."

40

With the door gone, the searing light from the Anomaly's particle beams lit the research area. Greve pressed his back harder against the wall as debris started sliding/flying through the opening. The lab coat that had covered Iggy was pulled off her and fluttered away.

What now? Had the Anomaly grown? Would it ever stop?

He had to see.

Lowering himself to a prone position, he belly-crawled to the doorway—not easy using only one arm—and peeked around the edge to squint against the searing light. The Anomaly itself hadn't enlarged but he couldn't say the same for its accretion disk. Furniture, debris, anything that wasn't attached— and even some things that were, like doors—had fallen victim to the Anomaly's relentlessly strengthening gravitational field and were tumbling toward it. He could see bits of the concrete walls, floor, and ceiling chipping off and forming a fine gray mist flowing into the disk.

No doubt about it . . . he was doomed. The only recourse he could imagine was to find a remote corner here in the research area—maybe in the containment chamber itself—and wait out the storm. That assumed that the Anomaly's black-hole stage would run its course or peter out before it sucked him into the void.

Then again, what if it didn't change? What if it remained a black hole and kept devouring everything—literally *everything*? That could mean the end of everything. And would that be so bad? If he had to die, why shouldn't everyone and everything else come along with him? Seemed only fair.

Pushing back from the door to look for his corner, he glanced behind and saw Iggy sliding his way. The gravity pull had flipped her prone and caught her manacles and their connecting links in its grip, seeming to drag her along by the chain. With her arms out straight before her she had stretched into a flying Supergirl configuration.

She gathered speed so quickly that Greve was not able to move out of her way in time. She slammed into him from behind and slithered atop his back with her outstretched arms framing his head. The chain between her manacles was suspended just beyond his nose.

They both began to slide through the doorway.

"No!"

He grabbed the nearer jamb with his good hand but the tug of the Anomaly's gravity, along with Iggy's extra weight, proved too much. His fingers slipped free, so he pressed his palm and dug the toes of his shoes hard against the concrete to slow him down, but he kept sliding.

Iggy . . . the girl's weight was doing him in. He tried to shake her off, twisting this way and that, but she hung on as if she were alive, as if she were haunting him.

Had to get *free,* goddammit!

He gave a particularly violent twist and felt her slide to the side and slip off.

"Yes!"

Her sliding body tumbled onto its back, flipping her wrists and wrapping the manacle chain around Greve's neck. He made a strangled noise as he tugged at it, but he couldn't do much with one hand.

He dug his toes in harder to slow his progress, but Iggy's slide was now unencumbered, so she began to move ahead of him and, in the process, rolled prone again. Which further twisted the chain around his throat.

"Help! Please!"

He didn't know why he said it. No one could hear him. It simply came out.

Iggy was now sliding feet first toward the Anomaly, her tangled chain trapping her hands against each side of Greve's face as she stared at him with her remaining eye. He closed his own eyes, not just to shut out the sight of her, but because the glare from the particle beams literally hurt them. Not that it helped much—the light pierced his lids.

He dug in his toes even harder, but the more he resisted his slide, the tighter the chain became. Had to get it off—*off!*

Then Iggy's feet began to lift toward the accretion disk, followed by her legs and torso, accelerating their combined slide.

"No-no! Please no!"

And then her whole body was airborne, with her manacle chain lifting him as well. He watched her legs begin to attenuate and stretch to impossible lengths as she was pulled into the accretion disk. Greve followed helplessly. The agony was brief as his body dissolved to its cellular components and his

cells released their molecules and those molecules released their atoms . . .

. . . but somehow his consciousness persisted into
the Void . . . the waiting Void . . . the Void that was
not a Void at all, but full, and waiting, and hungry . . .

Had he possessed a mouth he would have screamed.

41

"Tanisha passed out. I can't wake her."

"I heard that," Rick shouted.

He clung to the ladder just below its last intact
wall anchor. Above him the unanchored portion bent
away from the wall to rest its broken end against the
other side of the shaft.

"Oh, Rick," Laura said, "I'm so sorry!"

"Not your fault. We'll figure something out."

I hope.

What else could go wrong?

The shaft trembled like a malaria patient with the
chills. He couldn't see worth a damn so he examined the ladder's nearest wall fittings by touch. Loose
powder around where they entered the concrete. That
couldn't be good.

Another shudder, worse than the last.

By the time he'd stepped on the first rung down
there, the storeroom had been emptied and it looked
like the doorframe to the hall was beginning to pull
loose. The whole damn place was coming apart,
and right now his biggest fear was the pull from the
Anomaly latching onto the lower end of the ladder,
ripping the rest of it off the wall, and sucking it and
Rick out through the storeroom and into the hall to
who knew where.

He called up again. "Somebody mentioned a rope before."

Cy's voice echoed down. "Yeah, that was me."

"Let's try that."

"Well, I, um, I didn't go get it because, you know, Tanisha . . ."

Should've known.

"Okay, I get it. But how about checking to see if you can find some now?"

"I'm on it!"

And yet another tremor.

Rick didn't know if he had time to wait for a rope that might not come at all, so he crawled atop the diagonal section and began climbing across the shaft.

"Rick?" Laura called from above, training her flash on him. "What are you doing?"

"Keeping busy while we wait for Cyrus."

"Do you think that's such a good idea?" Her tone said she wasn't a member of the good-idea group, and perhaps she was right, but . . .

"At the moment I think it's the *only* idea."

Yet another tremor. Below, near the brightly lit floor of the shaft, Rick thought he saw the bottom of the ladder move.

Not good. Not good at all.

He reached the opposite side where the broken end was wedged against the concrete—the exact spot Laura had occupied before Tanisha levitated her to the higher remnant.

He stared up at that remnant. If only he had some way to bend the lower part back toward the upper. The shaft was only six feet across . . . its concrete surface had been left unfinished, Berlin Wall style . . . and his shoes had rubber soles . . .

Worth a try.

He put his feet against the wall and pushed the end of the ladder free. Then he angled his body around, squeezing himself between the wall and the end of the ladder.

Laura's voice from on high: "My God, Rick, what are you *doing*?"

"Not sure yet, babe."

"Did you just call me 'babe'?"

"Uh-huh."

"You've never called me 'babe.' Ever."

No, he hadn't. And he didn't know why he'd done it now. He never called anyone "babe."

"It just slipped out. Do you mind?"

"I don't know," she said in a musing tone. "I guess what matters is the spirit in which—"

"No, I mean do you mind not talking while I attempt whatever it is I'm gonna attempt."

"Oh, please, don't do anything reckless. Cyrus will be here—"

"Or he may not. A little quiet. Please?"

She couldn't feel the tremors rattling through the ladder from below, and he didn't want to worry her. But if he didn't get off this thing soon . . .

He had two choices of how to do this. The first was to do a standing broad jump off the top of the ladder here; but if he fell short he'd slam against the wall and tumble all the way down unless he could grab the ladder again, and even if he could he'd probably damage himself. The second was to take the ladder with him. Much harder, but at least he could count on multiple tries. He hoped.

Planting his soles against the wall, he gripped the top rung, flexed his knees to the max, took a few deep breaths, and shoved off with everything he had. He and the top end of the ladder sailed across the shaft.

Only six feet across—*six feet!*

He angled his body over the top and stretched an arm toward the bottom rung of that last length of ladder on the wall . . .

. . . and didn't make it.

Above him, as he and the ladder fell back, he heard Laura muffle a scream. His feet hit the wall again and he had a very bad moment when his rubber soles slipped, but then they caught.

Damn.

"Rick, please-please-please, I beg you—"

The whole shaft shook. Even Laura had to feel it.

"What was that?"

"The whole bunker's coming apart."

"Cyrus!" she cried. Rick looked up and saw that she'd climbed the short ladder to the hatch and was peering into the dark. She cupped her hands around her mouth and screamed, "Cyrus, where are you?"

After a few heartbeats, Rick said, "Any sign of him?"

"No," she wailed as she scrambled down.

"Okay then . . ."

He gave himself another shove. He'd thought he'd put everything into the last jump but he found a little more with this one and this time his questing fingers found that bottom rung and wrapped around it. He twisted his body to let the ladder fall back, and then chinned himself up, grabbed a higher rung, got a knee up, and he was home free.

When he reached the platform, he allowed himself a brief hug from Laura, then he was scooting her up through the hatch and following close behind.

Up top he found a surreal scene. Tanisha lay on her back on a tangled pile of vines; her eyes were open but she looked dazed. Marie, Annie, and Moe knelt around her, hovering. Moe was keeping Tanisha's wrist stump elevated.

Jon and Woolley were nowhere in sight.

And just like Cy had said, a beam of white-hot light—he'd called it a laser and maybe it was and maybe it wasn't but it was goddamn impressive—was shooting up through the trees to the stars, casting wild shadows all around. Way, way back beyond that, faintly visible, the red and white and blue lights of cops and emergency vehicles flashed deliriously.

Someone was rushing their way through the trees.

"I couldn't get the rope," Cy was saying. "The whole area is crawling with—" He skidded to a halt. "Oh, hey, you made it."

"Yeah. But thanks for trying."

"Look, there's a whole bunch of cops and soldiers and firemen and EMTs heading this way."

Rick felt a steady tremor through his soles. He lifted Tanisha and placed her in Cy's arms.

"Get her to those EMTs, then tell everyone to stay the hell away." He turned to Annie, Moe, and Marie. "You three go with them—get away and stay away. There's gonna be a cave-in or something worse."

"Gotcha," Cy said. "But what do we tell them back there?"

"Tell them the truth. Annie, tell them you were kidnapped and brought here, and the rest of you came looking for her."

Moe shook her head. "That's not going to fly—at least not very far."

"Yeah, it's a short-term story. Let's hope Stahlman's connections can straighten out the rest for them and the Pentagon can go to bat for you."

"What about you two?" Marie said.

Rick did not want to deal with officialdom. He never knew when his Hayden identity might collapse. But Laura . . .

"Take Laura with you and—"

"Oh, no," she said. "I came this far. Where you go, I go. Team, remember?"

Yeah, he remembered. And he knew that tone.

He waved Cyrus and the others off. "Get going, and tell everyone to stay away."

He turned to Laura and found her gazing up at the treetops. "Where'd they go?"

"What?"

"The pine lights."

"The what?"

"Never mind. Tell you later."

He pointed toward the faint glow pinking the sky. "Could that be dawn?"

"Seems about right."

"Gee, how time flies . . ."

"When you're having fun? You think this was fun?"

"Not a bit. But dawn means east is that way and it looks like east will take us away from the bunker and away from the po-po. So let's go."

Rick led the way, plowing through the bushes and the brush. They hadn't gone very far when a helicopter zoomed overhead.

"Probably on its way to check out the light," he said. "I hope the pilots are smart enough to keep clear."

"You think it's dangerous?"

"It burned through steel-reinforced concrete and fifty feet of packed earth so, yeah, I think it's—"

Then the ground shook hard enough to knock both of them to their knees.

"It's happening," he said.

"What?"

"The bunker's gonna collapse. Or worse. Maybe it's gonna implode. Or get sucked into the Anomaly." He started walking back. "Wait here."

"What? Why?"

"I need to see."

"Are you crazy?"

Yeah, probably.

He kept walking. He had no rational reason for this, but after what he'd been put through in the last twelve hours—and all the years leading up to it—he needed to see this end. Call it closure, call it whatever, but Greve's copies of the Black Book were down there, and so was whatever remained of the man responsible for the Düsseldorf atrocity that had haunted his life for years, as well as the thing that had appeared at the Düsseldorf conflagration to sup on the human pain and misery there. Maybe he could lay all this to rest at last.

The silhouettes of the pines around the beam began to tilt toward it. That could only mean the bunker's ceiling and supports had given way and were collapsing. The beam itself began to wobble, swinging in wide arcs. Rick saw the lights of the chopper hovering nearby and sent a mental message to the pilot to get the hell away from here.

The chopper began to turn, but too late. One of those swinging arcs brought the beam in contact with its blades, neatly slicing off the ends as they rotated through it, and that was all she wrote.

The chopper lost altitude and dropped into the pines on the far side of the depression, the remnants of its blades shearing off treetops and branches as it crashed among the trunks. It never hit ground, but ended suspended in the trees. Rick saw the pilot and copilot scramble down to safety.

Rick stopped thirty feet from the escape hatch and crouched to watch the crazy gyrations of the beam, making flaming kindling of the surrounding trees leaning over it. He started as someone crouched beside him. Laura. Should have known.

"It's dangerous here."

"Didn't stop you," she said, the light show reflecting in her eyes.

"It's personal for me."

"Well, then, that makes it personal for me too."

No sooner had he slipped an arm around her shoulders and hugged her against him than the beam disappeared like someone had flipped a switch. One instant wreaking havoc with its surroundings, the next—gone, leaving burning pine trees as the only evidence of its existence.

Movement to his right in the flickering light caught his eye: Moe, standing and staring at the sunken earth. And Marie next to her. Rick thought he understood Moe's presence.

"Couldn't stay away?"

She shook her head. "Tried, but no."

Marie gave a wan smile. "Same here. Cyrus and Annie took off in the ambulance with Tanisha. There wasn't room for me, so . . ."

Maureen said, "Down there was where it all started—the stuff that took control of my life." She cleared her throat. "Let me rephrase that: The stuff that I *allowed* to take over my life." A single sob escaped her. "God, I've got a lot to answer for."

Yeah, she did, but he couldn't see her as evil. She

seemed to care for the nadaný—genuinely care.
Greve, on the other hand . . .

"Iggy," Marie said, "she's still down there. And Ellis."

"Stoney too," Moe said.

Rick noted that Greve's name was conspicuous by
its absence.

"And then again, maybe not," he said. "If the
Anomaly got them first, they could be anywhere in
the universe . . . or in another universe . . . or nowhere at all."

Laura stared up at him. "You really believe that?"

"It looked like it had become some sort of black
hole, with lasers shooting out each pole."

"More likely particle beams," Moe said. "That's
why the chopper went down."

"There'll be a crowd here any minute," Rick said.
"We'd better move on. Laura and I are gonna cut
through the woods and—"

"I just remembered my car's back by the scrap
yard," Laura said. "Someone's going to trace it and
come looking for me eventually. Why not deal with it
now? We can say we were driving by, saw the light,
and went to investigate. Who can say otherwise? My
E-ZPass records will confirm I was on the parkway
not too long ago."

Not Rick's first choice, but Laura was still registered as an assistant medical examiner with the state
of New York—a truly solid citizen. Yeah, it might
work.

"Okay. Let's do it." He turned to Marie. "You said
Cy and Annie are with Tanisha?"

She frowned. "I think so."

She sounded strange. "'Think'?"

"I'm not sensing them."

Oh, crap. "Could something have happened to them?"

"I don't know." She looked truly baffled. "I don't sense them or any nadaný—*anywhere*."

That wasn't good—not good at all.

42

"Well, so much for taking it slow and easy," Laura said, snuggling against Rick in the motel bed.

A sliver of sunlight slipped between the edges of the closed curtains. Dimly visible were the scattered clothing on the floor and the uninspired seascapes on the walls.

"I held off as long as I could," he said.

She laughed. "Not that. Us. My grand plan."

"Which was . . . ?"

"Returning to square one. You know how we were kind of awkward with each other after Orkney. I figured we'd be back to awkward after the way I made things so difficult for us."

"You didn't—"

"I certainly did. So I thought we could go back to those first dinners and become comfortable with each other again before . . ."

"Before what?"

"Before *this*!"

"You mean sex?"

"Yes! We're basking in afterglow in a no-tell motel in Toms River in the middle of a Saturday afternoon. How decadent is that?"

"Decadent?"

"I don't know about in your life, but in my prosaic, Little League–mom world, that's decadent."

He grinned. "I guess we got comfortable with each other again ahead of schedule."

"I guess we did."

And Laura couldn't be happier.

They'd returned to the Quonset hut to find first-responder chaos—state cops, town cops, sheriff's deputies, multiple volunteer fire companies, and a security contingent from the Naval Air Station—all strobe-lit in blue, white, and red. Laura, Rick, Marie, and Maureen made it to her car but were blocked from driving away. Stahlman—bless him—arrived with a couple of fast-talking suits who Laura later learned were lawyers. After everyone was identified to the sundry authorities' satisfaction, and names and contact information were recorded, they were allowed to leave.

Stahlman and company continued on to Community Medical Center to check on Tanisha. Marie went along with them because she asked to, Maureen because Stahlman wanted to talk to her.

Which left Laura and Rick on their own. Both admitted they were exhausted and that some shut-eye would be wise before traveling back to New York. They stopped at the first motel they found on Route 37 with the intention of getting two rooms. At the registration desk they'd looked at each other and Laura said, "Who are we kidding?"

They got one.

And they still hadn't slept.

Rick rose onto one elbow and looked at her. "Are we back on track?"

"We are. We most certainly are. I've decided I love you."

His eyebrows rose. "'Decided'?"

"Let me rephrase." She seemed to be doing a lot

of rephrasing lately. "I've decided it's okay for me to admit that—even without Iggy around."

A troubled look passed over Rick's face. She thought she knew why.

"Yeah," she said, remembering Iggy's childlike glee when Ruthie teleported and left her blush floating in the air. "Poor Iggy. Such a sweet kid. Of all people . . ."

"Yeah. The truth. No one can know the truth."

His face remained troubled.

"What?"

"Nothing."

"Iggy aside, you feel happy and you still don't think you deserve that. Am I right?"

He had to get over this.

"It's not that cut-and-dried."

"It will never be." She kissed him on the cheek. "I can't make the past disappear, but I've figured out a way to deal with it: You're a soldier home from a war. You had to do things over there—"

"Like play God?"

"We don't need to get into specifics here. Let's just say things you'll never be called on to do here. So, the past is over there, and the present and future are right here. That past hasn't gone away. It's just in perspective." She poked his bare chest. "But you've got to do something about it too. It's been a cloud over you."

He pursed his lips a moment, then said, "Dealing with Greve allowed me to put a human face on Düsseldorf. And somehow—not sure why—that's allowed me to stuff the whole thing into a mental box. And I'm locking that box in a room. So like you said, it's not gone, but it's no longer on display either."

"Then why this troubled look that seems stuck on your face?"

"It's just . . . just that our little piece of the future is starting to look pretty good."

"And that's bad?"

He gave her a wry smile. "Have you ever known me to trust the future?"

"I think you have to start making exceptions. Start with the near future . . . the very near future."

"Like what?"

"Like we have this room until tomorrow."

"Well, okay. Can I trust we'll find a way to not waste it?"

"There you go."

Laura slipped her arms around him and felt a sudden lightness of being, like an enormous weight had been lifted from her. This was going to work. This time things were going to work out.

TUESDAY

1

QUEENS

Laura's heart went out to the surviving nadaný as she watched them take their seats in a circle. Even Tanisha, fresh from the hospital with her bandaged stump, had shown up for the impromptu memorial service for Iggy and Ellis. Those who wanted to speak had said their piece, offering what memories they had and their wishes that things had turned out differently. Ruthie broke down about Iggy too many times to finish.

Then it came time for Luis to confirm what Laura had feared when Marie could detect no nadaný anywhere, and what all the nadaný already knew. Laura, Rick, and Stahlman stood to the side while he moved to the center, his ever-present iPad clutched against his chest, and turned in a slow circle as he spoke.

"I've checked and double-checked all of you and there's no doubt: Your zeta waves are gone."

Annie sobbed openly. She was taking it the hardest. Iggy had been her first friend among the nadaný, and now this: Invisibility had been part of her everyday life for years—a *way* of life for her.

"How'd this happen?" Leo said. Normally he'd be floating a few inches above his chair, just because he could. Now his butt was parked like everyone else's. "You go to bed special and you wake up ordinary."

"Yeah," Ruthie said. "Freaks one day, dweebs the next."

Laura was struck by the two contrasting self-images. Leo had been working hard to develop his talent, while Ruthie, in many ways, had wanted to hide from it.

"I think I can help there," Rick said from outside the circle. "But it's a long story."

The nadaný were unanimous about wanting to hear it, so Rick stepped into the middle and pulled a sheet of paper from his back pocket.

"Need my notes," he said. "I'm starting at Genesis."

Laura, Rick, Stahlman, and Maureen had spent hours last night piecing Maureen's recollections together with the information from the CIA thumb drive to collate a coherent timeline.

So Rick started not with Genesis but with World War II, the Kohnstein, and the Lange-Tür theories, moved through the construction of the bunker in 1947, the arrival of the Anomaly in 1957, the discovery of melis in 1984, and the opening of the Modern Motherhood Clinics in the 1990s.

"Okay, that's how we became nadaný," Cyrus said. "But now we're not. What happened?"

"That's where the guesswork comes in," Rick said. "We've talked to all of you and not one of you remembers being able to use their gift after dawn yesterday. The Anomaly disappeared just before dawn yesterday. Coincidence? We don't think so. We think the Anomaly's presence on Earth or in this dimension or whatever the case may be—we'll probably never know where it came from or where it went—

somehow fueled your gifts. When some of you were brought into proximity with it, your gifts were amplified. And when it left, your gifts powered down."

"'Powered down'?" Cyrus said, balling a piece of paper in his fist, then opening to show how it remained in his palm. "It's gone!"

"Now, we don't know that," Luis said. He'd backed away but now moved again to the center, which Rick seemed all too happy to yield. "It might just be dormant."

"Bullshit!" Leo said.

Luis shrugged. "Maybe, maybe not. You can get mad and walk away, but that won't get you an answer."

"What will get us answers?"

"Stay and work with Luis," Stahlman said, moving into the circle. "I'm offering the same terms and accommodations as before. Who knows? Doctor Montero might be able to discover something. And if he can't, if it should turn out to be a total waste of time, at least you'll be well compensated for that time."

When everyone started talking at once, Rick took Laura's arm and led her back to Stahlman's office, where Maureen waited. Not knowing how the others would react, she'd elected to audit the meeting out of sight.

"That went pretty well," she said.

Laura didn't know how to feel about Maureen. So many conflicts. Although nothing like Laura's mother, Maureen was the same age. Her graying, maternal look made it hard for Laura to believe what she'd done. And she couldn't help but hate what she'd done—experimenting with unborn children would remain forever unforgiveable in Laura's book.

But then, one on one, she'd found the woman smart, sincere, and . . . likable. Not without a moral compass, either. How had she gone wrong?

Laura faced her. "You're the biologist. You think there's any chance they can get their gifts back?"

"Truth?" Maureen hesitated, then shook her head. "No. Or at least I doubt it very much. Melis had a definite impact on their genes—changes we might be able to identify. But identifying them won't be enough, I'm afraid. The Anomaly's presence or influence seemed to be necessary to activate them."

"Maybe that influence can be duplicated or mimicked," Rick said.

She smiled. "That's just what I'm hoping to do."

"You?" Laura said.

"Mister Stahlman has asked me to help, not just with the nadaný but with other potential manifestations of melis."

That jolted Laura. "'Potential'? You don't mean . . . ?"

"Who, me? No way. I did what I did and you know what I did, and that was it. I wish I hadn't, but it's done and I can't go back. I can be useful going forward, though."

"I've wanted to ask you that," Laura said. "How did you come to do what you did?"

Maureen leaned back against Stahlman's desk. "I wish I knew. All I can say is I got lost in the project. I started out doing pure research—learning its properties and such. I was never supposed to get involved in testing it on animals except for toxicity."

"But you went beyond that." *Way* beyond.

"Not because I wanted to."

"They forced you?" Rick said.

"Yes. At first. Then I got into it. Melis was my

baby—I named it, after all. And then, after the Pentagon allowed me to see where it came from, I . . . I don't know. It was like I'd been admitted to a cult—a select group who knew this strange and wonderful and terrible secret. I never thought it could happen to me, but you can become so immersed in something, in a subculture—and as much as I didn't like Greve, he and I and the others at Lange-Tür formed our own private echo chamber where melis ruled. After a while, all that mattered was finding out what it could do—or what we could make it do." She shook her head. "Total loss of perspective."

Rick said, "So if you only did the clinics, what other 'manifestations' could be out there?"

A shrug. "Who knows? I wasn't the only researcher handed a supply of melis. It went to other places."

Laura felt her stomach turn. "Really? Like where?"

"I don't know. I asked Greve many times but he never gave me a straight answer. He used to love to tell me how far it was above my clearance. But he'd drop hints, you know, like you can be sure some melis has been doled out to places like Plum Island and the animal research center in Nebraska. Things like that."

Bad enough about animals, but . . . "What about people?"

"I don't doubt it."

"That's awful!"

Maureen seemed to take offense. "I'm sure the researchers don't think so. I thought I might be increasing kids' intelligence. I'm not justifying the means, but the end was noble. Back in the day I overheard talk at the bunker about using melis to make stem-cell therapies more effective. Who knows where that could lead?"

Rick had a sour expression. "Knowing where it came from, I'm saying it can't lead anywhere good."

Maureen sighed. "After the other night, I tend to agree with you. But Mister Stahlman wants to see if I can come up with a marker to identify people who've been exposed to melis."

"And then what?" Rick said.

"And then see what's different about them."

"Without a finder like Marie," Laura said, "that sounds like a tall order—like looking for the proverbial needle in a haystack."

"Maybe not. According to Greve, DoD has spread a lot of melis around."

Rick didn't look too happy about that. "Really? How much we talking about?"

Maureen gave another shrug. "He said stem-cell applications look very promising. But even big pharma companies like Merck and Schelling and Pfizer have been given supplies to experiment with for new drug development. Never told the origin, of course. DoD has a whole vat of it. Plenty to go around."

Laura stared at Rick. "Oh, my."

2

SHIRLEY

Did it get any better than this?

Rick slouched on the couch next to Marissa and pretended to be engrossed in the Mets game against the Braves, their rival for a playoff spot, while Laura puttered around in the kitchen. They'd feasted on filet mignon—marinated by Laura, grilled by Rick—and Champagne.

Hanging out with the two best people in the world. He'd never dreamed he'd know this kind of bliss, and he was still pretty sure he didn't deserve it.

And then the Braves' left fielder hit a single that drove in the man on second, giving them the lead.

Marissa shook both fists at the screen. "I *hate* the Braves!"

"Don't hate, honey," Laura said from the kitchen.

In a low voice, Rick said, "Say you have great antipathy for the Braves."

"What's 'antifathy'?"

"Antipathy. Means strong dislike." Or something like that. "Tell your mother."

"Hey, Mom. I have great antipathy for the Braves."

"That's nice. Wait—what?"

Marissa chortled. Did nine-year-olds chortle? This was the only little girl he knew so—

And then Marissa grabbed his hand—well, mostly his thumb—and squeezed.

"I'm glad you're back, Rick. You make me smile inside."

He didn't respond. Couldn't. His throat had locked.

It came to him then that if the two best people in the world thought he was okay, how bad could he be?

When Marissa wasn't looking he ran the cuff of his shirt across his damp eyes.

Damn allergies.

THE SECRET HISTORY OF THE WORLD

The preponderance of my work deals with a history of the world that remains undiscovered, unexplored, and unknown to most of humanity. Some of this secret history has been revealed in the Adversary Cycle, some in the Repairman Jack novels, and bits and pieces in other, seemingly unconnected works. Taken together, even these millions of words barely scratch the surface of what has been going on behind the scenes, hidden from the workaday world. I've listed them below in chronological order. (NB: "Year Zero" is the end of civilization as we know it; "Year Zero Minus One" is the year preceding it, etc.)

THE PAST

"Demonsong" (prehistory)
"The Compendium of Srem" (1498)
"Aryans and Absinthe"** (1923–1924)
Black Wind (1926–1945)
The Keep (1941)
Reborn (February–March 1968)
"Dat-tay-vao"*** (March 1968)
Jack: Secret Histories (1983)
Jack: Secret Circles (1983)
Jack: Secret Vengeance (1983)
"Faces"* (1988)
Cold City (1990)
Dark City (1991)
Fear City (1993)

YEAR ZERO MINUS THREE

Sibs (February)
The Tomb (summer)
"The Barrens"* (ends in September)
"A Day in the Life"* (October)
"The Long Way Home"+
Legacies (December)

YEAR ZERO MINUS TWO

"Interlude at Duane's"** (April)
Conspiracies (April) (includes "Home Repairs"+)
All the Rage (May) (includes "The Last Rakosh"+)
Hosts (June)
The Haunted Air (August)
Gateways (September)
Crisscross (November)
Infernal (December)

YEAR ZERO MINUS ONE

Harbingers (January)
"Infernal Night"++ (with Heather Graham)
Bloodline (April)
The Fifth Harmonic (April)
Panacea (April)
The God Gene (May)
By the Sword (May)
Ground Zero (July)
The Touch (ends in August)
*The Peabody-Ozymandias Traveling Circus & Oddity
Emporium* (ends in September)
The Void Protocol (September)
"Tenants"*

YEAR ZERO

"Pelts"*
Reprisal (ends in February)
Fatal Error (February) (includes "The Wringer"+)
The Dark at the End (March)
Nightworld (May)

* available in *The Barrens and Others*
** available in *Aftershock & Others*
*** available in the 2009 reissue of *The Touch*
+ available in *Quick Fixes—Tales of Repairman Jack*
++ available in *FaceOff*